The
45th NAIL

by

Michael Lahey & Ian Lahey

S & H Publishing, Inc.
Purcellville, Virginia

Ian Lahey/S & H Publishing, Inc.
P O Box 456
Purcellville, VA 20134
www.sandhpublishing.com

Publisher's Note: This is a work of fiction. The places are real. The history is real. The names, characters, and their actions are a product of the individual author's imagination. Any resemblance to actual people, living or dead, or to businesses, companies, or events is completely coincidental.

Ordering Information:
Quantity sales. Special discounts are available on quantity purchases by corporations, associations, and others. For details, contact the "Special Sales Department" at the address above.

The 45th Nail/Michael Lahey and Ian Lahey – 1st ed.
ISBN 978-1-63320-032-6
Ebook ISBN 978-1-63320-033-3

TO PAT,
who came back home.

Chapter I

*At the end of World War II, more than 79,000
soldiers were still missing and presumed dead.*

My uncle, Sgt. James Savorski of the 36th engineers, was listed as missing in action on May 25, 1944 at Anzio. Some time after the war he was declared dead, killed in the line of duty. There's a picture of him visiting us on leave. Tall and thin and 23 in his uniform, balancing me on his right shoulder. I am fat, bald and ten months old, and my name is Robert Svenson. My mother, his sister Agnes, 24 and very pretty, is smiling with her arm around his waist.

I wish that hairstyle would come back.

I learned from my father that Jim had been a real hell-raiser as a boy. I suppose there's an uncle like this in a lot of families, but what makes Jim unusual is that in August 1987, two months after my mother died, I got a Christmas card from him.

It was a bright Italian card with a chubby Gesu Bambino in his mother's arms on the front. Inside, across from the big BUON NATALE greeting, were these words:

> *Dear Bob,*
>
> *Very sorry about Agnes, your mother and my sister. I thought the world of her. I think she liked me and that wasn't easy. I ought to be dying shortly, so I guess you'll be getting my stuff. The cash anyway. Hope you like the picture on the front. That's how I*

remember you.

Your Uncle Jim Savorski.

The envelope was postmarked Anzio. My wife Beth and my 12-year-old son Bret hadn't seen it, and I didn't show it to them. Instead I showed it to my father.

"Let it be, Bob. He's a deserter at best, maybe worse. Let Beth and Bret go on thinking he was a hero."

"But at least to know what he's been doing all these years..."

"Nothing very edifying, you can bet. And after all these years, he's like a total stranger — who really cares? He was a rotten apple, Bob. The only thing I'd like to know is how on earth he found your address."

"Well, the obituary in the *Tribune* might explain it. I suppose you can buy the *Trib* someplace over there. Or maybe he has a contact here, someone who keeps him in touch. It's one of the things that make him interesting."

My father smiled for the first time in a long time. "Well, if you're that curious, why don't you go over there and look for him?"

This was heavy humor for my father, about like saying "why don't you get yourself a crystal ball?"

"Yeah, sure."

My father even managed a laugh. "Beth would love the trip. Hah!"

This was really heavy humor. My wife's world was bordered by the Lake to the east, the Wisconsin line to the north, the Golf Mill shopping mall to the west and Soldier's Field downtown. Her breathing would get more and more labored the farther she got beyond those limits. And she always had Bret for an excuse.

But I had a little something of my mother's wanderlust in me. As I drove home I was nagged by the feeling that this was my last chance to do something

2

exciting in my life. But once at home, my sense of responsibility, etc., etc., made short work of that feeling, and I was able to come to an easy compromise. I would respect my father's desire to avoid "fuss and talk" while quietly and discreetly leaving a trail of breadcrumbs to let my uncle know I'd gotten his message.

There was no return address on my uncle's card, but I sent him a letter care of the post office in Anzio. I wrote that, if he couldn't come home, I was willing to make the trip to see him. I also ran a notice in the Personals column of the *Trib* for four days, asking Jim to get in touch. Then I ran the same notice in the *International Herald Tribune*. Nothing came of any of this.

Then four months later, at Christmas time, I got a small package from Jim — sent to me at St. Michael's, where I teach French literature, not at home. Almost as if Jim had decided to help me keep his existence a secret from my family.

Still no return address, but this time the postmark was Salerno. Between the brown wrapper and the little white box there was a piece of notebook paper which said:

"Well, May 25th will make 44, and from then on it's sudden-death overtime. When the game's over you'll be notified for the money. Meantime, this thing here might bring you luck."

Inside the box there was a sort of medallion about three inches in diameter with a little tube segment running along the edge at the top, so that you could run a cord through it and hang the medallion around your neck. It was embossed with strange, elaborate figures on both sides, and it was pure gold. I stared at it on and off for the next two weeks, and concluded that:

1) it was very old, and

2) Uncle Jim was crazy. You don't drop something like that in a box and send it off with no insurance, no return address, nothing.

I didn't show it to Beth. She loves to talk. I believe I am the most informed husband in town, but that comes at a price. Beth's PA system works both ways. So I didn't tell her about the medallion, hoping to keep the medallion or whatever it was from becoming the talk of the town, at least until I could find out more about it and decide whether I wanted my name associated with it. I also wanted to respect my father's desire to keep Jim in his family niche as a dead hero.

Instead, after the holidays I showed it to Father Tom Perini, S.J. who had studied in Rome and now taught Ancient History at St. Michael's. I knew he spent lots of time in the Field Museum, and I considered him a friend. I was the only non-Catholic on the staff, and Tom had always done his best to make me feel welcome.

When I walked into his office he got up and came around his desk to greet me. I put the medallion in his hands. He looked at it for a moment, then he looked at me very hard, and finally he went to the window for help from the pale January sun. He let his index finger run lightly over the figures.

"Beautiful. The best one I've ever seen."

"The best what?"

"It's called a *bulla*."

"Is it Roman?"

"No. It's Etruscan. I'd say about 5th century BC. Young males of the noble class wore them around the neck. For divine assistance. Some were hollow, with herbs and spices inside to ward off disease."

"What do you think it's worth?"

"Well, it's a wonderful piece." He gazed at it again.

4

"The central figure on this side is Tinia, father of the gods. And I think the central figure on this other side is the great mother goddess, Uni. Whoever wore this was well protected. And this goldsmith was a true artist. Wonderful. In a certain sense it's priceless. Bob, how did you come by this?"

"You're good at keeping secrets, aren't you?"

"I've got some real beauties. We start with the Seal of Confession, then we just get into the habit of keeping things to ourselves."

"I should have married a Jesuit. Anyway, my new secret for you is that I seem to have a long-lost uncle in Italy."

"An uncle in Italy? Named Svenson?"

"No, on my mother's side. Named Savorski."

"Oh."

"It's a long story. Anyway, he mailed that thing to me. Sort of a Christmas present."

"He mailed it to you. So much for Customs. You're lucky it wasn't opened. And your uncle didn't say where he got it?"

"No. All he said was it might bring me luck."

"Well, that shows he knows something about these things. But he also ought to know better. Something like this loses a lot of its archaeological value when we don't know exactly where it was found. It was almost certainly stolen out of an Etruscan tomb. But whose? Where? It's important..."

"Stolen?"

"Not necessarily by your uncle, but by buying things like this he keeps the *tombaroli,* the Italian grave robbers, going. Almost as efficient as their Egyptian counterparts."

I sighed. "I suppose you're saying I shouldn't sell it."

"Not at all. The damage is done. It would be worse

5

for you to hide it away. Unless maybe you want to wear it."

"I'm tempted. These gods sound pretty powerful. As a liberal Protestant, I don't discriminate. But I'll take the money."

"Take it from a museum, not from some collector. I'll help you. Something like this should be put back into the right hands, the hands of scholars."

"I agree. Absolutely."

"And another thing you can do..."

"Name it."

"See what you can find out from your uncle about where this came from."

He put the *bulla* back in my hands. I pressed it against my chest and smiled.

Chapter II

Fellini's 1960 film "La Dolce Vita" helped Italy shed its rural past and fuelled a wave of American tourism, and English language, to the Italian capital.

I decided to go look for my uncle that summer, as soon as school let out. Ostensibly I would be going to France, a "refresher" trip for the language that was in fact long overdue. A semester at the University of Caen in Normandy as a graduate exchange student was the full extent of my European experience.

Father Tom sold the *bulla* for me. He didn't drive a hard bargain, and after making a suitable donation to the Jesuit missions I barely had enough to cover my trip, D.C.R. Tourist (Discount for Confirmed Return).

I told my father that I just might hop down to Rome to see if Jim could be looked up but that anything I discovered I would keep quiet, at least until I could talk to him. In return for swearing discretion at all costs, he let me have the old photo of Jim in uniform with my mother and me. The picture would probably be of no use. A man changed a lot in 45 years, whether you started with a baby or with a young soldier.

But Jim was right. I did look a lot like the Bambino on his Christmas card.

Beth and Bret were no problem. Bret preferred a computer camp in the mornings and a baseball clinic in the afternoons. Beth wanted nothing to do with Europe and its unsanitary ways. With great effort and commiseration she had agreed to the utility of a trip to France for a French teacher, but the idea of a wild-uncle-chase to Italy would have left Beth aghast.

"Why can't you go to Montreal?" she kept suggesting. "They speak French, and it's not so far, and Canadians are a lot like Americans..."

"I don't just teach the language, Beth. I teach French Civilization — that means customs, institutions, clothes, food..."

"You'll get dysentery."

"I'll be careful."

"Stay in the center of the city, and eat at Wimpy's. That's what Gwen did in Paris."

"Didn't she go to Rome, too?"

"Somebody felt her derriere in the Colosseum the second day she was there, so she spent the rest of the time in the hotel. I'm glad you don't teach Italian."

"My derriere is in no danger, Beth."

"Europeans aren't that particular."

"I'll be very careful."

During the flight over I reviewed my plans, which was easy enough because I had very few. At Charles De Gaulle Airport I would have three hours to mail a bunch of Paris postcards before catching the first possible plane to Rome.

I figured on spending some time in France after my Italian adventure to buy the books and souvenirs I would need for my return. I would phone Beth a couple of times from Italy by dialing direct, and she'd have no way of knowing the calls weren't from France.

How was I going to look for my uncle Jim? Maybe he lived in Anzio, maybe in Salerno — he might be well-known to the people who deal in Etruscan art. And I had learned from the Italian consulate in Chicago that records were kept both on the national and local levels of all foreigners residing in Italy.

The trick was to convince the authorities that I had "just cause" for seeking access to those records, a trick that was much easier on the local level than on the national level in Rome.

How much could I say about Jim without getting him into trouble, for instance tax trouble? And of course, it remained to be seen whether he had acquired formal residency. Or maybe he had become an Italian citizen.

I would start making discreet inquiries in Anzio, which was close to Rome. Then Salerno.

What language would I make these inquiries in? That was another aspect of the adventure. I knew no Italian. I hoped that with English and French I could get through to most people.

Everything went smoothly right through Paris and all the way to Rome, and even there I landed on the right foot. I sailed through Customs, and strode to the "hotel assistance" desk.

The line looked long and slow, so I was almost grateful when a man came up to me and said: "You need a nice hotel, mister? And not so expensive?"

"And clean," I answered.

I knew I was taking a chance, but I felt adventuresome and lucky.

The man himself was clean and decently dressed, with friendly eyes and thick brown hair. He looked about thirty.

"You go here," he said, handing me a card with an address hand-written on it. "I call now, tell them you coming. You take terminal bus into city, then a taxi. Is good hotel. Okay?"

9

"Okay," I answered, reaching for my wallet.

"No money. The hotel give me something. Come on, I help you for the bus." And he picked up my two suitcases, led me out to the correct bus stop and started to walk away.

"Don't you need my name for the reservation?" I called after him.

"Uhh, yes, is better."

"Svenson. Robert Svenson."

"Okay, I remember."

"And you're sure there's a vacancy?"

"Excuse me please, there's a what?"

"A vacancy. A room I can have."

"Oh, yes, is no problem. How many nights you stay?"

"Two. Maybe three."

"Okay, goodbye, I have to call now."

"Goodbye. And what's your name?"

"Renato. I am Renato."

By 7 pm, I was standing in front of my hotel, which looked like it would be fine for the short time I would spend in Rome getting my bearings before proceeding down to Anzio.

A big stone staircase led up to the front door of the hotel, and I was about to start the climb when another young fellow, but this time a black-haired one in a threadbare blue suit and a red porter's cap, came out from behind the staircase with a big, friendly smile.

"You are Robert Svenson from the airport? Yes? I take the bags, mister. I have lift in back. Bags are heavy, too much stairs. I see you up desk. *Benvenuto*! You are good here, very nice!"

"Thank you," I said, "I'll see you upstairs."

Still smiling profusely, my bell-hop picked up my bags and disappeared behind the staircase as I headed briskly up towards the lobby. Behind the reception desk there was a portly but powerful-looking man of about fifty who smiled less than the bell-hop but spoke better English as he checked me in, until I asked him where the porter with my bags was.

He stared at me, then slowly closed his eyes, gritted his teeth and said:

"*Grandissimo figlio d'una mignotta!*" Then he re-opened his eyes, sighed and said. "We have no porter, sir. I'm afraid your bags are..." He slowly drew his left hand, palm down, in towards his chest while fanning his fingers.

That's how Italians say "stolen."

They can say a great many things with signs, I was to learn. I had had my first lesson. I ran outside and downstairs, but of course my "bell-hop" and my bags were long gone.

I instinctively slapped my back pocket where my wallet was and made sure it was buttoned. Well, I had planned on buying some clothes anyway.

The hotel man came outside and put his hand on my shoulder.

"Bad luck, bad luck. You have been played. A man called me with your reservation..."

"Renato. From the airport." I mumbled, still looking up and down the street. "He's your man, isn't he?"

"I have no man at the airport. There is a 'hotel assistance' desk, you know. Anyway, the man said you gave him money to make the call for the reservation, because you don't speak Italian. He said you were standing there with him."

"I wasn't."

"I am so sorry. After me he called his friend; together they played you. First time at my hotel, first time. Other

11

hotels, yes, these things happen, but first time here. And last time, I tell you. You lose your money?"

"No, thank God," I said, and slapped my wallet pocket again.

"Good, that's good. Listen, I give you first night *gratis* in my hotel, free of charge, sir, because I feel very bad, very bad. I am very sorry, okay?"

"Thank you. Very kind of you."

"I like Americans. I remember when many, many Americans tourists came all the time to Rome, for *La Dolce Vita*. Now not so many. I went to America once. I have a sister in Buffalo. Nice people, nice people."

"No chance to get my bags back?"

"No chance, no chance. But you can report it, maybe something can turn up, maybe they discard some things. Go down this street to the piazza, a big piazza with a fountain in the middle, a beautiful fountain by Guerrieri, and you will see a *carabinieri* station. You tell them. They will call me, and I will confirm okay?"

"Okay. See you later. Thanks for your help."

"It is nothing, sir. *Arrivederci!*" He waved.

I started off at a brisk pace. It was more of a residential than a business area, and there weren't many people on the sidewalk.

But I never made it to the piazza.

About a hundred yards down the street, at the second intersection, a gypsy woman stepped around the corner and right into me. I didn't run into her that hard, but down she went.

She had a big bundle wrapped in a dirty sheet hanging from her neck, and from this bundle now came a child's cries of distress. I tried to help the woman up but instead she slipped the load from around her neck and motioned to me to lift it off of her.

12

I picked up the child whom I had not yet seen, but who had the weight and lungs of a three-year-old, and stood waiting while the woman, who was young enough but rather heavy, began struggling to her feet.

That was when I felt the hands on my butt.

The pickpocket had easy pickings, because he didn't care about what I felt as he tore open my back pocket and grabbed my wallet.

I spun around with my bundle and looked at him eye to eye. His eye was young and taunting, mine was old and helpless.

"Thank you, *Papà*! Careful with baby!" The boy laughed and bolted away.

I turned back to the woman, who had made it to one knee. She put out her arms for the bundle and motioned with her head that I should chase the thief. As soon as I was free I took off after him.

When you're 45 and out of shape, what happens is that you can sprint pretty well for about 60 yards, then all hell breaks loose.

As I was leaning on a lamp post gasping, it dawned on me that the pickpocket and the woman with the kid formed a team. I looked back the 60 yards and she too had disappeared.

I started walking back to the hotel. All I had now was the clothes on my back and my passport, which the hotel man had taken when he checked me in. I still had to report all this to the *carabinieri*, but I wanted to do some thinking first.

I trudged back up the stone stairs into the hotel lobby and told my story. When I got to the part about picking up the gypsy's baby the man joined his hands as if in prayer and silently pointed them up and down, up and down for the rest of the story.

13

That's how Italians say "How dumb can you get?" and it was my second lesson.

"Nice country you've got here," I said in conclusion.

"I am very sorry for the suitcase. Not so much for the money. You were very foolish. That is a very old trick, only good for fools and foreigners. They must have watched you talking to me in front of the hotel. And they saw you slap your back pocket."

Again he joined his hands in prayer.

"My friend Renato saw me go for my wallet, at the airport. Do you think it's possible they're all together on this?"

"Mm. Did the porter look like a gypsy? Did your Renato look like a gypsy?"

"Not really. Not my idea of a gypsy, anyway."

"Then it would be very difficult. The gypsies don't like to work with those who aren't, with the *gadje,* as they call us."

"Nice work. Nice way to treat people."

"In New York they hit you on the head or put the knife in your stomach to take things. Here it is done with civility. And you have the chance, if you are clever. In New York, no chance. Which is better?"

"Listen, I've got to get that money back."

"No chance, no chance. No traveler's checks?"

"No traveler's checks, no credit cards, just money." I had cleverly brought only cash for this "adventure" because cash leaves no traces.

"You lose plane ticket?"

"It was with the luggage."

"No problem, they give you new one."

"But it's from Paris. Chicago-Paris-Chicago. And I came here from Paris with a one-way ticket."

That was because I didn't know where my search for

14

was a melancholy thing to have to put my dirty clothes back on, I felt more like slipping in between clean sheets. I also wanted to do a little thinking about Renato and how I had been ripped off.

There was something strange about it. But I had to go down and hear what Egidio would propose. Also I was a little hungry.

The hotel dining room was quite small, and in fact only three or four guests were eating. Egidio and I sat down at a little table near the kitchen and behind a screen.

"Not many of our clients eat in our dining room." said Egidio.

"I understand. They want to see Rome, eat in tourist restaurants with mandolins."

"But our food here is very good. And our wine." With that he reached for the one-liter beaker of white wine already on the table and poured two full glasses, the first of many.

"Try this wine. *Vino dei Colli Albani* — from the Alban hills. You like it?"

I liked it.

"This is just normal wine, table wine, nothing special. But it is good wine, honest wine, like you find all over Italy. You know what you get in France at the table?"

"You get *vin ordinaire*, table wine like this."

"No, not like this!" he said, thumping his thick hand on the table. "This is honest wine. In France it is *vino tagliato*, cut wine."

"Cut wine?"

"Wine that has been mixed with other things to give it more alcohol, more flavor. And you know what they like to use?"

I couldn't imagine.

17

"*Mosto Siciliano*!" And he thumped again. "A concentrate of our wine from the south, to give strength to their... their fruit juice. France does not have enough sun to produce a lot of good wine, only some, the rest is water and must be strengthened by us. And they say French wine is better. Bah! What French wine? That is why I say they are worse than thieves. They are dishonest!"

"I drink California wine, sometimes. Usually I don't drink wine. But this is very good."

"California! Yes, you have Italians who make the wine for you. It will be all right, I'm sure, but the...the land, the ground, what do you say? The soil is too good in California, too good for good wine. *Terra avara, vite generosa* we say, the vines must grow in difficult soil, poor soil, with stones, to have character. Like men! Now we eat."

A red-haired girl brought out two big plates of spaghetti with meat sauce, and it was so good that I let myself forget my plight and get into Egidio's free-swinging conversation-diatribe.

"Your waitress here has red hair," I said, "and I saw some blondes on the bus — our Italians in Chicago are all dark-haired."

"Maybe in Chicago you have pureblood Italians. Here in Rome are no pureblood Italians. Rome is a great *mignotta*, the greatest of the world. How do you say *mignotta*, *puttana*? A girl who..."

"Yes, *putain* in French. We say whore. Or prostitute. Or hooker. Lots of ways to say it."

"And lots of ways to do it. Rome knows them all, does them all. She sells herself to everybody, you can have a piece of her at any price, even at no price. You can take her by force. Everybody has done it, all the armies

18

have taken Rome, but she is a smart hooker, very smart. She always takes more than she gives. Everyone comes to Rome, she is raped, she is ravished by everyone, but she gets richer, and fatter, and older, and smarter, and she absorbs you all, all of your seed, and she grows, she becomes Spanish, and French, and English, and German, and American! And now Japanese, and all these at once, but always Roman, an enormous, soft, warm Roman hooker. Hah! I remember you. I was a boy when you all invaded Rome with the General Mark Clark. 'I have taken Rome!' he said. 'The first general in fifteen centuries to take Rome from the south!' he said. Hah! Like a good *mignotta*, a good hooker, you can take her from the south, north, east, west, is no problem. She is always open, she was declared an Open City, easy to enter, not so easy to leave! I remember the chocolate, and the hard candy you threw from the jeeps and trucks; that was just the start. Millions of you have come to...to see, to study, to spend your money, to fall in love, to stay — Rome is full of Americans. Rome is American for you, she does whatever you want because she is a good hooker, and that is the best profession, the oldest profession, the first and last profession, and Rome is the Eternal City because of that. You want some more spaghetti?"

"Well, I..."

"Annamaria! *Ancora due piatti di pasta, per favore!*"

And we both started in on another bowl of spaghetti.

"So you remember when General Clark liberated Rome," I said.

"Yes. June 4th of 1944, I was very young, but I remember, we were very happy. The last year with the Germans was very, very hard. My father was a tailor, very good, he always had work, but there were aunts and cousins from the country with us, it was very hard. Mark

Clark was a *sciocco*, a fool, you know, he was not supposed to take Rome, he was supposed to cut off the retreat of Kesselring from Cassino, he was supposed to block the German Tenth Army. But he wanted glory for his Fifth Army, so he cut left, up through the Alban hills, the hills of this wine. That's why this wine has character. There is blood in the soil. Two thousand years of character, of blood. What is in the soil in California?"

"You were saying about the Fifth Army..."

"Yes, you let Kesselring escape to the north, and you came here instead. A big tactical error, but you know what? I think Clark was a fool, but sometimes fools do better things. In Rome we were losing our heart, we had waited so long, maybe to hell with Kesselring and it was better to liberate Rome, for the moral of the Italians."

"The morale. Not the moral."

"The morale, the morale. It was very low, you know. Anzio was such a delusion. 'The Allies have landed! Only sixty kilometers from Rome!' Everyone was so excited. Except the Fascists, but there were less and less of them. Everyone was becoming anti-Fascist. All but a few, like one crazy uncle of mine...the rest, we were happy when you landed so close. And we waited, and waited, and waited. *Niente. Niente di niente.* Nothing, for months and months. You stayed there on the beach. Maybe to make sand castles. I don't know. Then you finally broke out strongly. Hah! My crazy uncle died with the Germans, trying to stop you. Why you wait so long? You have a girlfriend in Anzio, you ask her about it. Maybe Anzio girls have special attraction for Americans, enough to keep them there."

"I will never get to Anzio without money."

"Now we talk about that, with our *braciole di maiale*."

"With our what?"

20

He simply pointed to Annamaria, who was arriving with a trayful of food — breaded pork chops and red lettuce.

"But the spaghetti..."

"The spaghetti was the *primo piatto*, the first plate. This is the second plate, the principal plate. You are in Italy. Always like this. Relax, eat slowly, we have time. In New York, Tokyo, no time. They come here looking for time because we have it all. Hah!"

"But really I'm full. The spaghetti was so good..."

"You need more weight. A man should be...an imposing figure. Women like that. Your girl in Anzio will like you more. You know, a small man pleases a woman only once each time, but a big man pleases her twice, both when he gets on, and when he gets off! Heh hah!" And he poured more wine.

"Hah hah," I echoed, and started working on the chop.

"Hah hah hah!" he insisted, and called to have the wine beaker refilled. "Now for your job," he said with red lettuce in his mouth. "I have a friend who is like a brother, in fact we are related, because my nephew's daughter married his wife's cousin — no. I think he was the son of this cousin, a good fellow, he sells tickets at the train station." He stopped for a long sip of wine.

"And so?" I asked.

"So what?"

"I can't very well sell tickets at the train station."

"Of course not. As a foreign tourist you can do nothing legally. You must be careful. We will have to think of something else."

"But what about your friend who is like a brother?"

"You mean Remo?"

"Yes, I think so."

"He's a good friend, but he can't keep a job for himself, so how can Remo help you?" He leaned over the table as far as his belly would allow: "Remo has a problem with the drink, you know."

"Then it's not Remo...I mean your friend who is like a brother because in fact you are related?"

"Related?" He was puzzled, and sipped some wine. "Perhaps you mean Saverio, but he isn't really related, only his wife's cousin married Roberta..."

"That's the one! What does Saverio do?"

"Oh, Saverio does very well, he has a *trattoria*, and...and..." Bang! His hammy left hand came down hard on the table, bouncing wine onto my pork chop.

"Saverio can help us! He is redecorating. He wants to bring in the tourists, he wants to raise the prices. He needs help with the menus and the languages, he is looking for somebody not Italian to give the international touch, you know? American speaking French. I see you perfect. I call him now, okay?"

"Okay, thank you very much, if you think—"

"I think, yes. Wait here, drink some more wine." He emptied his glass, poured another for me, and lurched up and away from the table. I took my wine glass and sat way back in my chair. I discovered that I could see around the screen into the rest of the dining room. All the clients had left but one, an old gentleman with his back to me. He was close enough to have heard everything we'd been saying, or at least everything Egidio had said since the wine started getting to him. A little free entertainment. I didn't care.

I finished my food as best I could. Annamaria came back with more pork chops, but I was able to fight them off. In about fifteen minutes Egidio returned and sat down heavily. He smiled and poured more wine, to keep

22

He looked at me for a while, then puckered up and said, "Doo yoo spik Ingliss?"

"I sure do," I answered with relief, "and it'll be a lot easier if you do. My Italian isn't very—"

"Okay! okay! Doo yoo spik Ingliss! Doo yoo spik Ingliss!" Then he put both hands on my chest, meaning "wait here," and went and got two of his menus.

"*Italiano*," he said, and handed me one. Sure enough, it was printed in Italian.

"Ingliss," he then said, and handed me the other, which was hand-written in English. "Eez okay Ingliss?" he asked.

I looked closely. The first entry was for "noodles with the long holes after the manner of whores."

"Eez not okay theez Ingliss," I quickly said. I wasn't yet speaking Italian, but I was getting as close as I could.

"No okay?" He was unhappy again. He touched my chest, went away, and came back with a large Italian-English dictionary.

He pointed at it and said "Ingliss!" — this time with a certain belligerence.

"Ingliss, *sì sì*," I said, "but no okay. *Non perfecto*."

Saverio smiled for the first time.

"*Allora tu me lo farai diventare perfetto*," he said, handing me the dictionary.

"Huh?" I said.

"*Perfetto! Perfetto*! You-menu-Ingliss-*perfetto*, okay?"

"Okay, no problem, Saverio."

"Okay, no problem, Roberto," and he stuck out his hand. I juggled my menus and book, freed my right hand, and we shook on it.

And so began my short life as the "international" in Saverio's international *ristorante*. I found it was not always easy to improve upon Saverio's by-the-book translations of Italian specialties. In fact I ended up leaving *Bucatini alla Puttanesca* as "Noodles with Long Holes after the manner of Whores," and it turned out to be a big favorite. A few other of Saverio's that were too good to change were "Little Squid, Humid with Peas" for *Seppioline in Umido con Piselli,* and "Greedy Swordfish from Messina" for *L'agghiotta di Pescespada alla Messinese.* I put the rest of the menu into prosaic but clear English — only after insisting on trying most of the items at lunch and dinner for a few days, to keep my translations precise: *"Per la precision,"* as I said to Saverio.

His dictionary and his food started doing wonders for my Italian.

So much so that after three days Saverio let me start strolling knowingly from table to table asking: "Is everything all right? *Ça va bien? Tutto bene?*" I really think he would have let me begin the first night, but it took him three days to find me a dark blue suit that fit.

It belonged to the brother of the baker that brought Saverio his daily bread at noon. The brother had grown out of it by ten kilograms, but only after it had done three years' heavy duty. He was the *portaborse,* the gopher, for a parliamentary deputy. The suit was a little shiny here and there, but well-made and a decent fit, except maybe that the sleeves were a bit short. But if Saverio was content, so was I.

Saverio wasn't content, but it wasn't because of my suit.

He was making more money, but he had lost a lot of his regular clientele. The foreigners I was supposed to assist were sitting in chairs that had always been occupied by Roman families that had come once a week or once a month to have a meal and chew the fat with Saverio, families that couldn't afford the new prices.

Saverio was doing his best to please the foreigners — I was an example of that — but he was happiest when he could speak his Roman dialect, good rich *Romanaccio*, with the few locals who still managed to come.

Well, I did my best, and it wasn't my fault if I represented the unpleasant aspect of Saverio's change in style, the fly in his new ointment.

My menus were fine, and on my rounds of the tables I turned on the old North Shore charm in three languages — or at least two and a half. I would answer questions about the different kinds of mineral water, the ingredients of *besciamella* and the uses of Parmesan cheese, all with great aplomb, I was well coached by Saverio and his dictionary, both of whom I often recurred to simply by saying: "I want to be quite sure about this for you — I'll be right back."

The toughest people to help were the Japanese, most of whom spoke only a smattering of English. It took all my imagination to sort the sounds they made into words I knew. But on the other hand they put me under no real pressure, because they generally kept smiling and were grateful for anything edible I managed to procure for them.

Another source of trouble was the Americans who refused to believe that not only was there no salad bar, but the only "dressing" available was oil and vinegar, which you had to pour on one at a time.

"Whaddya mean, no French?"

"I agree with you, sir, it is hard to believe, but—"

"Well then, I'll settle for garlic dressing. They've gotta have garlic dressing, they put garlic in everything, don't they?"

"Just about, but not in their salads. This olive oil is really good, and..."

"I don't like greasy lettuce!"

"Why not skip the lettuce and have eggplant...?"

But my tensest moments came when I "winged it" as a wine expert. As I told Egidio the morning after my first night's work, Saverio had gone far beyond his two basic wines — white Frascati and red Chianti. He still had demijohns of these wines which he served as house wines — the cheapest and best choices a client could make. But now he had a fair selection of corked wines — even a few French ones — and I was sometimes asked by foreigners to give my advice. My "wings" didn't span out to actually pretending I was a *sommelier*. Saverio discarded that thought when, with the help of his dictionary, I asked him which of his table wines were sweet: *"Quali vino da tavola* eez *dolce?"* I said.

He stood looking at me silently as he had once before, then said slowly: "Eez no *vino dolce da tavola*. Eez *vino dolce, ma per* dessert! Dessert! *Con la torta, non con la carne, il pesce, la pasta...*"

"Sì, sì. Okay," I said, "but maybe the ladies — *la signora* love — *aimer* — *amant* the things *que sont dolce!* In America..."

"Qua" — Saverio pointed peremptorily at the floor — "eez *Italia*." And he walked away. His concessions to foreign whims would only go so far. So I made myself useful in a way Saverio never knew. Americans — a few, not many — would motion me over to murmur the horrible truth:

"We can't drink this wine. It's too bitter. Too dry." And I would furtively glance around and then whip out little packets of sugar. "Act fast. I'll cover you," I would whisper, and then I would try to shield them from view as they sugared their wine.

Sometimes I fantasized about my Uncle Jim. He'd

30

been able to find out my address from across the ocean; maybe he was having me followed even now. I imagined myself as Sean Connery in a James Bond movie, tracked by spies with little round sunglasses and improbable accents. It helped pass the time.

About a week after I started working, the same old man I had seen eating alone in Egidio's dining room turned up for an evening meal at Saverio's. Although I hadn't seen his face I was sure it was him from the back — same short gray hair, same stiff posture, same safari jacket. And if it were him, so what? If it were him, I decided, he was part of Uncle Jim's organization. Maybe he was even...

"Is everything all right, sir?" I asked him. He looked up, surprised. For a moment his eyes looked deep into mine. Then he shrugged his shoulders.

"*Non parlo inglese*," he said calmly, with a voice like an idling engine.

"*Mi scusi*," I said, "*tutto bene?*"

"*Sì sì, tutto bene, grazie*," he answered and put his head back down.

His Italian sounded fine to me, and much to my disappointment he wasn't even wearing spy sunglasses. I kept an eye on him throughout his meal, but he didn't seem to be watching me.

Saverio served him his dessert. Saverio enjoyed wheeling the dessert cart around. He took special pride in his desserts, many of which he made himself. Afterwards, I asked Saverio about the man.

"*È un turista*," he shrugged. The next morning I described him to Egidio.

"Yes, it is Giacomo, he was here that first night, like you say. A quiet man. He comes maybe twice or three times a year, only to eat, sometimes we talk."

31

"How is his Italian?"

"Normal. Not Roman. Maybe the accent from Liguria, I think. Hard to know, because he says very little."

"He doesn't look Italian."

"In Liguria is even more bastards than in Rome. Sailors come to Genoa from whole world. In Liguria is Italians who look Chinese, Italians who look African. Giacomo is nothing new. Why you interested?"

"Oh, nothing. He came to Saverio's last night. Did you recommend it to him?"

"It is a long time that we don't talk. Not that night, I was busy with you. I don't know, maybe years ago I sent him there."

Well, it wasn't much to go on, but it kept my fantasy alive. I hoped "Giacomo" would return to Saverio's again, but he never did, and I never saw him at Egidio's except for that first night. Egidio also said that he had talked to Saverio, who was generally pleased with my efforts and hoped I would be staying for a while. In fact I was no longer in a great hurry to get down to Anzio, because I was really starting to believe that I would meet Uncle Jim, whoever or wherever he was, only if and when he decided on it. My reasons for believing this were still pretty meager, but I didn't need much of an excuse to stay put. It would take some time before I had enough money to get anywhere in any case, and besides, I had to admit I was enjoying myself at Saverio's. The food was great. "Winging it" was good for me too, because my wings needed stretching.

I had a hard time once with an Englishman who obviously knew a lot about wine and wanted to prove it to the moony brunette he was with.

"My good fellow, this *Est! Est!! Est!!!* you've brought us would not have inspired a single *'Est!'* from Bishop De

Fuk."

"Bishop who?"

"Never mind. This wine tastes of cork."

"I'll get you another bottle right away."

"No, thank you, I'd rather change. Listen, we're going to have Roman sheep cheese, *Pecorino Romano*, to end our meal. What wine would you recommend?"

"Red wine."

"Obviously, but which?" He was smiling at his placid girlfriend, who was clearly Italian and hopefully didn't understand what was going on.

"I think that with cheese you can follow your own preferences. Our *Pecorino* goes well with practically all red wines."

"Dry reds, of course."

"Of course."

"How aged is your cheese?"

"I want to be quite sure about this for you — I'll be right back."

"Never mind. We'll have some *Torgiano* wine."

"*Torgiano*? Is it on the list?"

"No, but if you serve *Pecorino*, you must have *Torgiano*. It's the most suitable wine — or so I seem to recall. Correct me if I'm wrong." The bastard kept smiling.

When I returned five minutes later, I was smiling too. "Our *Pecorino* is fourteen months old, and we have no *Torgiano*. But," — and at this point I displayed a dusty bottle — "we have this *Brunello di Montalcino* 1971, which as you know was a great year..."

"Yes, I know, but..." Now he looked uncomfortable. I lovingly held the bottle close to the girl for inspection but continued speaking to the man.

"And as you will probably recall, *Brunello* is even better than *Torgiano* with *Pecorino* that's fourteen months old. Of course it's a little expensive..." I said this slowly and clearly so that the girl would have every opportunity to understand.

"I can imagine," the man said hollowly. "Well, let's hope it hasn't been ruined by the cork." I turned and held up a finger. Saverio appeared with a corkscrew.

"This is such a fine wine that Saverio himself will open it for you," I said. After cleaning the bottle Saverio extracted the cork, examined it, sniffed it, and nodded, then he let me sniff it, and I nodded, then he let the Englishman sniff it, and he had to nod. I handed Saverio a clean glass, and he poured in an inch of the precious wine and held it up to the light. We all nodded in turn. Then he handed the glass to the Englishman who sniffed, sipped, sighed, and nodded. Saverio poured a full glass for the girl and another for the Englishman, set the bottle down and walked away.

"Your cheese will be coming soon. Enjoy your wine!" I said.

"Thank you so much for your help," my client said balefully. Sixty thousand *lires'* worth of help.

But things didn't always work out so well. A French couple didn't like Saverio's Bordeaux.

"*Ce Bardeaux n'est pas potable.*" The displeasure on his face was evident as he pushed the bottle away from him.

"*Desolé, Monsieur. Voulez-vous un bon Chianti?*"

"*Nous n'aimons pas les vins italiens. C'est pour ça que nous sommes venus ici, dans un* restaurant 'international.'"

Since they didn't want Italian wine, they were forced to return to Saverio's slim selection of French wines, which the man now scanned gloomily.

"*Donnez-nous ce Chateauneuf-du-Pape, alors.*"

But we were out of *Chateauneuf-du-Pape.*

"*Malheureusement il n'y en a plus,*" I said. "*Mais si vous voulez essayer notre Bandol...*" I proposed the Bandol because it was just about the only other French wine we had.

"*Pas de Bandol, pas de Bandol!*" the man said, vigorously shaking his head.

"*Avez-vous un bon Beaujolais, aux moins?*" asked the lady. They both looked very despondent, enough to walk out, so I decided to wing it.

"*Oui, oui, un bon Beaujolais! Je vous le porte tout de suite.*" The fact was that Saverio's *Beaujolais* must have been left out in the sun on the dock at Marseilles or shaken up too much on the train or something, because it had all gone bad. Saverio had ordered new cases, but they hadn't arrived.

I took a bottle of the awful stuff, opened it, dumped out the contents and filled it with Saverio's house Chianti. Then I put the cork back in halfway, reinserted the corkscrew and walked back to my clients' table, "struggling" to uncork the bottle and succeeding just as I arrived. Of course a real wine waiter never starts opening a bottle before he gets to the table — I suppose to prevent switches like mine.

But evidently my simple Swedish-American face discouraged suspicion, because the French couple seemed pleased at the sight of the French label on the bottle. I didn't let the man sniff the cork, which probably smelled awful. I just poured some of the wine into his glass and let him taste it, holding my breath. His eyes got wide and he asked for the bottle, which he examined carefully.

"*C'est un drole de Beaujolais, ca, mais il n'est pas mal. Pas mal de tout. Essais, Madeleine.*"

And he poured some *Chianti* for Madeleine, who also thought it was a strange *Beaujolais*, but not bad at all. I went away chuckling and kept chuckling until they had finished their meal, when they insisted on buying six bottles of the stuff to take out. Saverio heard me at a distance saying "*Non, non, non, ce n'est pas possible,*" and heard Madeleine in particular getting louder and louder with her "*Mais pourquoi pas?*" and so he came over.

When he saw the bottle he assumed I had served them that tainted wine against his orders, and that the couple was threatening to sue or something, so he got so mad he wouldn't let me speak. He took the check out of the man's hands, tore it up dramatically and escorted the couple to the door while repeating the only French word he knew: "*Pardon, pardon, pardon.*"

Afterwards, when I explained everything to Saverio — more with miming than with words — his feelings were obviously mixed. But most of them were still against me:

1) I shouldn't ever try stunts like that.

2) If I did, I should tell him first.

3) *Chianti* is nothing like *Beaujolais,* and we were lucky those people were crazy enough to fall for the switch.

4) He had torn up a seventy-thousand-*lire* tab!

5) But, in the end, he admitted that my intentions had probably been good.

He didn't even dock my wages. Mainly because there was hardly enough to dock, once I paid Egidio for the room. I wasn't a real table waiter, so I never got tips. And at first practically everything I saved had to go for new clothes. But I was given all I could eat.

So after two weeks I was putting on weight but only had about fifteen thousand *lire* in my pocket. That's why I listened when a white-haired but only middle-aged Italian called me over to his table one evening and asked:

"Do you free the mornings?"

"Yes I do. I am. Until noon. Why?"

"Do you want make the extra money?"

"Doing what?"

"Tour guide. I need American for morning bus tour. The one I have, he is okay but going. Do you come tomorrow? Eight o'clock?"

Was my uncle behind this man? Had Jim decided on the next move in his game? "All right, eight o'clock. I'll come and see."

CHAPTER IV

Guides say it takes one to four days to tour Rome, but
in truth, even its most elderly inhabitants haven't seen it all.

And that's how I got my morning job as a tour guide. It was a snap, actually. I had a speech all written out describing the sights along the bus route, with a "back-up" book giving in-depth information in case a tourist asked me questions that went beyond my speech material, which wasn't often — everybody was too busy snapping pictures. Besides, the boss preferred it if the tourists kept their questions for the guide book he wanted to sell them at the end of the tour. The only orders I had were to stay on schedule and not play with the women. I later learned that a number of guides had been lost — including the last — because of volatile love affairs with adventure-seeking tourists. But I had enough adventure on my hands, I thought.

The tours began at 8:30 in Piazza Venezia and ended back there at 11:30. They included ten-minute picture-taking stops at the Trevi Fountain, Trinità dei Monti, the Pincio, St. Peter's Square, the Pantheon, the Baths of Caracalla and the Colosseum, in that order. It was a crazy way for people to try to see Rome, but I suppose it was the best you could do in half a day.

Anyway we went careening around the city and I read as fast as I could: "And on your left...on your right...way back there...." After a few days I got good at it.

"It must be… interesting."

"If you like Yeats. I don't. Not keen on poetry in general, actually. Too explicit. Not like painting."

"What's more explicit than painting?"

"I think those Japanese people are trying to get your attention."

"Could be. I'll be back when I can."

The Japanese people wanted a side order of rice with their Chicken *Cacciatora*. Saverio didn't mind that so much; in fact I even caught him trying rice in his own *cacciatora* once, and he pronounced it very good. After ordering the rice I made the rounds, asking here and there if everything was all right. Most things were but a few things weren't, and when I finally got back to Ilene a man was sitting with her. An Italian. A well-built young fellow in a purple silk shirt that was open to his navel. The black hair on his head was straight and shiny and down to his shoulders, while on his chest it was in tight curls. He had fine teeth, some of them gold. He was smiling and talking smoothly but urgently. I understood very little.

"Everything all right at this table?" I asked.

"Hardly. This bloke won't take 'no' for an answer. Keep smiling, Bob, he can't understand us."

"You mean he just sat himself down? You don't know him?" I said smiling. The man had stopped talking and was smiling at us both.

"Of course not. He says he's seen me at the cinema. Convinced I'm a film star. A very corny line, actually. Is there any way you can get rid of him?"

I turned to him and said, "The young lady is not pleased with your presence here. I must ask you to take another table, or leave.

He just kept smiling. Ilene giggled. "That was

beautiful, but I told you he doesn't understand English."

I tried French: "*Monsieur, je vous an prie, ne derangez pas cette mademoiselle; elle veut que vous vous en alliez immediatement. Suivez-moi, s'il vous plait.*"

I started away, but the man made no move to follow me. Ilene giggled again. I would have to use my Italian. I remembered what Saverio always said to the stray cat that came pawing at the screen door in the kitchen. I knew it probably wasn't very elegant, but it was simple, and it was the only thing I could come up with:

"*Pussa via.*" I said with a smile. The smile didn't help.

"*Pussa via a me*?!" the man said, leaping to his feet.

"*Pussa via tu, stronzo!*" And with that he gave me a shove that sent me staggering backwards. I'm sure the blue-robed African would have wanted to be there to return my favor, but he wasn't. I hit Saverio's heavily-laden dessert cart. That afternoon he had made his wonderful chocolate eclairs. I sat down hard on a huge tray of them, squirting globs of chocolate cream in all directions.

Saverio hadn't seen me coming; he was turned away, talking to a lady he knew and admired. In fact all four of the people at this particular table were people he knew and admired. I got them all with my chocolate cream, including Saverio, who took a direct hit on the seat of his pants. The Italian language is richly endowed with suitable remarks for such moments. The guests began: "*Razza d'imbecille!*" said one of the two men.

"*Malnato deficiente, figlio d'una mignotta!*" added the other.

"*Imbranato! Impedito!*" said one of the ladies. I was waiting to see what Saverio would say. He was feeling the seat of his pants. His expression was pained. He looked around at his friends. The sight of each one sent his short fuse burning lower. When his gaze got to the lady he had been talking to and he saw her digging chocolate out of her ear, the fuse ran out.

"*Macchè, sei scemo*?!" he yelled. I understood this. He was asking me if I was a moron. Before I could answer, he continued:

"*Vattene, sciagurato! Pussa via!*"

Here I knew what to say, having just learned it from Ilene's acquaintance. "*Pussa via a me?*" I said proudly. "*Pussa via tu, stronzo!*" And I shoved him into the lap of the lady with the chocolate in her ear. Which meant that she now had chocolate on her dress. But nothing could match the chocolate mess I now showed to them all as I turned and strode out of the restaurant, stopping only to pick up Ilene on my way out. The gigolo had wisely vanished.

"But he stood in the door watching until the last moment," said Ilene. "He looked very pleased with himself. Maybe he's still around." And she began peering through the darkness in all directions.

"I would like to sit on his face, but he might not oblige. And my rear end can't wait." So once we were at a safe distance we ducked into the shadows and got most of the chocolate cream off the seat of my pants. Fortunately it had stopped raining.

"I think you're out of a job," said Ilene as she squatted and scraped behind me. "You know, this looks like very good chocolate cream."

"I've had enough, thank you."

"Would you like a new job? Just in the evenings?"

"I suppose I would. That's enough, Ilene. I'm going straight back to my hotel, anyway."

"By bus? With a brown behind?"

"I think I'll walk. It's a long way but it's a nice night.

45

Refreshing after the rain."

"Yes, it is. You sound Irish. We've learned to love the rain, we have so much, you know. It leaves everything sparkling. My digs are only about half an hour from here on foot. Let's go there and try to wash the brown color out of your trousers. Then I'll dry them with my hair-dryer. In the meantime we can have something to drink."

"In my underpants?"

"Oh, bosh. You can wear a blanket. Are you game?"

"I'm game. Very kind of you."

And so we headed for her place, which was back across the Tiber. We crossed over on the Palatine bridge, stopping for a moment for the view of Tiberina Island and St. Peter's in the distance.

"Do you like Rome, Bob?"

"Yes. Sure. How can you not like Rome?"

"But that's not why you're here."

"I told you. Everything was stolen the day I got here."

"But why did you come?"

"That's a long story."

"All right, I didn't mean to..."

"Basically I'm looking for a long-lost uncle."

"Why would you want to find him? I'd like to lose most of mine."

"Curiosity. And the fact that he seems to have struck it rich."

"In business? In real estate?"

"In Etruscan gold."

"Etruscan gold, is it?" she said with the same light giggle she had used in the restaurant. "I think you'd better come with me."

Not far from the bridge there was a square with two Roman temples. I didn't know anything about them because they weren't on my tour-bus route. There was also a medieval church with a square bell tower. That's where we headed. On the wall of the church there was a big round bas relief of a face with an open mouth.

"This is the Mouth of Truth," said Ilene with a serious air. "Put your hand in there and repeat after me: 'I'm from Chicago.'"

"I'm from Chicago. Well, the Chicago area. I suppose this guy will chomp my hand off if I'm not accurate."

"That's right. Keep it there, and keep repeating: 'I lost everything my first day here.'"

"Everything except my passport."

"'I'm in Italy to find a long-lost uncle.'"

"I'm in Italy to find a long-lost uncle." As I spoke Ilene was watching the Mouth very carefully.

"'This uncle has lots of Etruscan gold,'" she intoned.

"Well, he has enough to be giving it away." She waited a moment to give the Mouth time.

"Let's continue. Are you married?"

I looked at the Mouth, paused and said, "Yes I am. But she's back home."

"Last question. Are you going to be a perfect gentleman in my flat?"

I sighed. "Oh, I suppose so. Hadn't really thought it through, but I've been known to chicken out on similar occasions. Now it's my turn. Put your hand in there."

"All right. But one can always say 'no comment,' you know."

"Thanks for telling me. Anyway, first question: Do you want me to be a perfect gentleman in your flat?"

She sighed. "Oh, I suppose so. Hadn't really thought it through, but I've been known to chicken out on similar occasions."

"Are you married?"

"I'm only twenty-four. Irish girls wait longer than

that. That's why Ireland is underpopulated."

"Last question: Is this evening job you mentioned for me an honorable occupation, suited to a gentleman?"

"Hmm. No comment. You'll have to decide for yourself. It involves rape."

I stared at the Mouth, which didn't seem to quiver. "Well, is she pretty, at least?" I finally asked.

"Yes," she said, jerking her hand out of the Mouth of Truth. "No more questions now. Let's go get those trousers off. You're indecent."

Ilene's "digs" were two small rooms, a parlor with a kitchen nook and a bedroom, in a run-down building. Not really old, just run-down. I got out of my pants and into a light green blanket while she got out a bottle of Bailey's Irish cream liqueur. I told her about being a French teacher, and that I was supposed to be in Paris, and that I was saving up to get back there. She scolded me for deceiving my wife but then offered me the use of her phone to keep up the deception.

"I'm billed a minimum charge whether I use it or not, and I practically never do, so why don't you give it a good whack? What time is it back in Chicago?"

"It's..." I checked my watch and subtracted seven.

"...it's five in the afternoon. Beth's getting supper."

"Give her a buzz."

"Listen. I'll pay you for this..."

"You already have. Some of your tour members have been very generous up on the Pincio. Come on. I'm curious! Want me to make French sounds in the background?"

"Please don't make any sounds in the background."

She didn't. The call went very smoothly. Beth was in good spirits. She had just got back from T.J. Maxx, where she had got lucky with the clearance racks. She had even

48

found some beautiful summer wool pants for me, just my size for only $18.

"Wow. Wish I had them here." I said in all seriousness.

"I told you to pack more clothes," said Beth, so far away. "Well, go ahead and buy what you need, but you won't find anything as nice as these. Not for $18, you won't."

So Beth was fine and Bret was fine, and I told them that Paris was livable and I was healthy. I missed them and they missed me, and then Beth said I'd better not spend all my money on the phone if I needed to buy extra clothes, and that was that.

"Do you or don't you?" asked Ilene after I hung up,

"What? Wear dentures?"

"No. Miss your wife and child."

"Well, they're part of the world I must go back to. That I want to go back to. They're at the center of it. But there's no big hurry."

I ended up spending the night there, naturally. A little less naturally, I spent it alone on the parlor sofa. I didn't feel particularly timid, and I can't say it was because of my refreshed memory of Beth. It just didn't seem like a good idea at the time.

We didn't actually get much sleep that night, because we went on talking with the Irish cream for another two hours after the phone call. She came and sat on the sofa. She told me about herself and Ireland and her art. She both loved and hated her country. Ireland had stifled her creativity, had made her permanently provincial, had almost crippled her emotionally — but through it all she gave the impression that being flawed and Irish was better than being a perfect anything else.

I didn't mind a bit.

49

CHAPTER V

Spelled in reverse, Roma is Amor, or Love in Italian.

The next morning before going to work on the tour bus I called Egidio with Ilene's phone to tell him where I had spent the night, which he liked, and the reason why, which he didn't. He muttered some things in Italian, and then:

"Better for you not to go to Saverio today. I talk to him first. I see you here this afternoon."

"Okay. *Arrivederci*, Egidio."

"*Arrivederci*. I hope this girl was worth it."

On the Pincio that morning Ilene told me that she had called "Vittorio," and he was expecting me that night. She still refused to tell me about the job, except that we would have fun. For that matter, she was already having fun keeping me in suspense. What she didn't know was that suspense was a condition I was getting used to, waiting for my uncle to make his moves.

On a rational plane I continued to understand perfectly well that old Jim probably had nothing to do with Renato or anyone or anything else that had happened to me. And on that plane I knew the whole thing would end with a quick trip to Anzio and a long train ride to Paris, to take up my life where I should never have left off. But for a while it would do no harm to live on another plane, where I was participating in a strange game. I wondered what my uncle would think of Ilene.

Would he approve? Not that I'd let such considerations affect my relationship with her...or would I?

As soon as I got back to the hotel that afternoon, I asked Egidio what sort of mood Saverio was in.

"Oh, he is very mad. Mad at me for sending you to him. Mad at you for the mess, for the big bill for cleaning all the clothes. Mad, mad, mad."

"Did you explain exactly how it happened? About the guy who pushed me?"

"Saverio says the guy was handsome young Italian, not resistable for foreign girls. Says she probably liked him and you were crazy jealous."

"Hah! I told you, she wanted me to get rid of him!"

"Does this girl speak Italian?"

"Yes. Some, anyway."

"I think maybe if you wait a couple days, then go to Saverio with her to explain, I think maybe you get your job back, because I think he was content with you."

"Maybe I won't need the job back. I just want him to understand what happened. I'm sorry about the cleaning bill. He can keep the two days' pay he owes me. And I'll get the suit back to him. Clean."

"Maybe you can keep the suit. I talk to him again. For the job, now you will do more tours on buses?"

"No. I have an offer that sounds more interesting. Don't talk to Saverio yet. I'll tell you about it tomorrow."

"*Insomma, sai arrangiarti.* You are winging well."

My appointment that evening with Ilene was for eight o'clock in the Roman Forum. Luckily it was a warm evening, because Ilene had asked me to wear as little as possible, and I was in Bermudas and a t-shirt. I was to meet her right in the center of the Forum, behind the ruins of the Temple of the Vestal Virgins.

"Nice place for a rape," was the obvious thing I said

to her when I arrived.

"You're late," was the obvious reply. It was 8:20.

"In ten more minutes they wouldn't have let you in here. The show starts at nine. Come on, we have to find you a uniform that fits."

And we started walking towards another temple, the Temple of Antoninus and Faustina. On my right I noticed that people were already beginning to take their places on tiers of seats that went up the side of the Palatine hill.

"Why do I need a uniform? What kind of a show is this? Am I an usher?"

"No. You're a Roman legionnaire. You need a 'large'."

Behind a curtain alongside the temple about five men and five women were standing around dressed as Roman soldiers and, I took it, as Roman maidens in white tunics. They were all speaking English.

"Is this a remake of Quo Vadis?"

"You're close. That's where the costumes come from. This is 'Ghosts of the Forum,' don't you know? We re-enact the history of Ancient Rome, with our shadows and voices."

"In English?"

"In English at 9 pm, four times a week. It's also done in German, French and Japanese. And Italian of course. At 10:30. I think the Japanese do it best. They know more about using shadows. And I love the way their girls scream. So feminine. And the men are so guttural. So masculine. Put this on."

So I put on a Roman helmet complete with a red scrub brush on top, I buckled on a real leather breastplate, I got into a pleated skirt, I was issued a sword and a shield, and I was ready to win back the Empire. I felt like Victor Mature in his glory days. Except for my loafers.

"Ilene! Shouldn't I strap on some sandals?"

"No point. They don't improve your shadow any. Are you ready?"

"All set. Who do I slay?"

"Let's go ask Vittorio; he's our director. He directs everybody except the Italians; they've got their own." Ilene had slipped into her white tunic. She looked very nice. As she led the way, a phrase from God knows which old poem came into my mind: "The liquefaction of her clothes."

Vittorio spoke English, German, French, and he even smattered a little Japanese. Understandably, he didn't always keep them separate.

"Ah so, this is your new man you get for me? *Bon, bon.* very nice Ilene, nice and *grosse*, good for shadows."

"His name is Bob, Vittorio."

"Bob, Bob, good, Bob, now say this: 'Rome, Rome, widen your Via Sacra, prepare to receive my elephants!'"

"Rome, Rome, widen..."

"No no no no no, a *basso* voice, *plus fort*, slow and cruel, *puissant, verstehen Sie*? Try again please."

"ROME, ROME, WIDEN YOURSELF, PREPARE FOR THE ELEPHANTS!"

"*Besser*, better, now is okay, but you screwing the words, Ilene, write up the words so he don't screw them. Bob, Ilene will show you how to do. Tonight you are Hannibal. Be ready with the Hannibal helmet. *D'accord*?"

This sounded like some sort of final exam in the art of winging it. "*D'accord!*" I answered. "Thank you. I'll do my best." And we walked away to hunt up the Hannibal helmet.

"Hannibal the first night!" said Ilene. "You've hit it right off with Vittorio."

"Too bad," I said. "I kind of liked this helmet and being a Roman."

"Oh, you'll be a Roman too, and other things in the crowd scenes. We all have several roles. We've got a thousand years of history to get through, you know. Here's your Hannibal helmet, but you won't need it in the beginning."

"It isn't much of a helmet. And no elephants. A pretty sad Hannibal."

"It doesn't need to be much of a helmet. Remember, no one is supposed to see it or you, only the shadows on the buildings behind us. The whole stage is screened off. And of course you've got an elephant. Come along and meet Rosina." And behind the temple, munching happily on a bale of hay, was a baby elephant about waist-high.

"I'll be laughed out of the Forum."

"Not at all. Rosina is a fine actress, and one of the high points of the show. Her shadow will be cast on the front of the Senate building over there — and it will be enormous, you'll see. You have to get into the spirit of this thing. As Vittorio says, 'If we have the fun, the public has the fun.'"

Then she took me to meet the other actors. "Boys and girls, this is Bob. He's doing Hannibal tonight."

"We heard him," said a big heavy fellow with a false beard and a king's crown. "Something about Rome having to widen herself. A great line, let's keep it in!" And they all laughed, and I went around shaking their hands. The big fellow, Paul, was English, but there was a Scot, an Australian, even a girl from Mississippi, every accent imaginable, but all speaking English. I asked Ilene about it.

"The audience likes it that way. The Irish cheer when I speak, the Aussies cheer when Freddie speaks — you'll see. Now let's get ready for the first scene — The Rape of the Sabine Women. First we girls run screaming 'Help!

54

Help!' all the way across in front of the lights, then you men run lustfully after us."

"How do I run lustfully?"

"Watch Simon. He does it very well. Then you each throw one of us over your shoulder and lope gleefully back across in front of the lights..."

"And as to loping gleefully...?"

"Simon. Always watch Simon."

"And that's all there is to the Rape of the Sabine Women?"

"That's all there is to our version of it, luv. This is a family show, y'know."

"Okay, who am I supposed to rape tonight?"

"First come, first serve. Makes no difference, really. Be careful with Sue, she may be pregnant. And Rachel weighs about thirteen stone. Paul usually takes her, but I'm sure he'd be glad to let you try."

"No, I think I'll try for you, if you don't mind."

And so I did, and that first evening I gleefully loped away with Ilene over my shoulder. Other evenings I didn't get to Ilene fast enough, and my loping was less gleeful. It turned into staggering the time Paul was sick and I got Rachel — I almost didn't make it, much to the delight of the audience. I learned to do various one-line roles besides Hannibal: Romulus, Spartacus, even Julius Caesar. We all took turns, and Ilene was right, the important thing was to have fun.

One role I never took was Nero, which was Paul's because of his size, and also because of his voice. Like me, most of my fellow actors had other reasons for being in Italy, and Paul's was that he wanted to sing grand opera. So he was perfect for singing and fiddling while Rome burned. That was our most spectacular scene, with orange lights flashing throughout the Forum and all the men running around with torches while the girls screamed. You got the idea that women did a lot of screaming in Ancient Rome, because that's about all our girls had to do, except for a few words by Messalina:

"Kill them, kill them all, Claudius my dear, for they have dared to refuse my advances!"

Ilene said this fairly well, but not as well as Sue, who made your blood curdle. In fact not many dared to refuse her advances, and it turned out she was definitely pregnant.

The whole show was held together by the narrator, who was a pro that Vittorio had paid to make a tape in a studio. Alfio, our sound technician, used the pause button to make sure all our live action and speaking fit right in. After the show the cast, except for Rosina, always went out for a late pizza. Alfio never came because he couldn't speak English, and Vittorio never came because he didn't like pizza.

"Has he got an ulcer?" I asked Ilene in the pizzeria, the first evening after my Hannibal debut.

"No. I don't think Italians get ulcers. He really doesn't care for pizza. And he's got a wife."

"And when does he pay us?"

"Isn't it fun?"

"Well, yes, it's great fun, but..."

"And don't you think it's educational? I mean, think how well you'll know Roman history, shortly."

"That's nice too. But..."

"But you'd still like to be paid something, is that it?"

"I'm low on dough, dear, as I think I explained with my hand in the Jaws of Death, or whatever you called that thing..."

Ilene smiled and whispered, "You'll be paid. Thirty thousand a night. Tomorrow afternoon I'll show you

56

where we go to collect. But don't talk about it. We never do. The *Ufficio Stranieri* is rather suspicious of us. Tourists and students aren't supposed to have jobs, you know. The ones of us in the Common Market wouldn't have so much trouble, but the rest of you would, and Vittorio likes the global appeal. He also likes avoiding the unions, and certain taxes..."

"So what do you tell all these bad guys?"

"That it isn't a job. We do it for free, for the experience, because we love Rome, and love being together. Sort of a summer actors' camp. You know something? It's practically true. I think I would do it for free."

"So you could do without the thirty thousand? I didn't think the sidewalk-drawing business was that lucrative."

"I'm doing quite well, actually."

"I wouldn't have guessed it from looking at the pizza you ordered. Nothing but tomato paste, a little cheese, about three anchovies — looks like the Bargain Special."

"This is the classic *Pizza Napoletana*, I'll have you know, I happen to like classic things, traditional things."

"I wish you could taste a Chicago pizza. About two inches thick, with..."

"Spare me, please. And I suppose the Madonnas in your churches wear furs and jewelry?"

"Well no, but..."

"Not that you can't afford them. And I could afford fancy pizza, but I much prefer this. How's yours?"

"Oh, it's all right, I miss the sausage you get in Chicago. Anyway I'm glad to hear you're doing well. But as a sidewalk artist aren't you afraid of the *Ufficio Stranieri*?"

"Yes, I am. At least I was. But they never bother me.

Once the police did sweep over the Pincio picking up all kinds of peddlers and such, and I was certain my goose was cooked. But the policeman stopped, looked a while at my picture, dropped five hundred *lire* in my basket and walked away."

"What was the picture?"

"Oh, a Madonna. That's the tradition, you know. Can't recall which one I was doing that day. We always do Madonnas. We're called *Madonnari* in Italian, or so I'm told."

"Yes, and so to arrest you, the policeman would have had to step on the Madonna's face. Figuratively, anyway. What Italian would do that?"

"Lots of them, but perhaps not in the police."

"Police? Police?" It was Freddie, the Aussie, working on his pizza across from us. He had stopped talking to Sue long enough to overhear us. "Is that why you're here. Bob?" he continued. "Police, is it?"

"Logical enough," Ilene responded. "He's from Chicago, you know."

"Oh ho, now it's all clear!" said Freddie loudly. "Half the blokes in Chicago are cops, the other half are robbers. Which half are you with, mate?"

Ho ho, and ha ha, and on we went that evening and every evening, playing with each other's stereotypes, and only now and then talking about our real selves. Maybe it was better that way; the feeling was that we were all on a lark, a pleasure cruise in international waters. I felt fifteen years younger and was less and less in a hurry to head for Anzio, or Paris, or home. I was enjoying Rome and my crazy place in it, and I was enjoying my new friends — especially Ilene.

That's why my excitement was mixed with anger one evening in the pizzeria when Ilene told me that someone had asked her about me that morning after I had left the Pincio with my tour bus. I resented anybody's interference in my…delicate relationship with her.

"Was it the guy I described, the one I asked you to keep an eye out for?"

"No no, this was an old bloke, tall and hard-looking: wait a minute." And she got a sketch pad and pencil out of the burlap tote-bag she liked to carry around.

"Super!" exclaimed Simon when he noticed the move. "Ilene's going to do caricatures again! C'mon, do the one of Sue with enormous boobs!"

"But that wasn't a caricature, child," said Sue.

"And neither is this," said Ilene. "Just a sketch for Bob." The pencil was already dashing quickly around her pad, but she was sitting across from me. Simon was next to her and watching carefully.

"Bob's old, but not that old," he said.

"This isn't Bob, silly. It's just someone I'm trying to describe to him."

"Beats words, doesn't it?"

"Pictures usually do. Here you are, Bob; this is pretty close." Yes, it was. I took the pad and looked into the sunken eyes of Giacomo.

"So you know him, then?" Ilene said, interpreting the look on my face. "Is it the famous long-lost uncle?"

I studied the sketch in silence for a moment, and the jesters jumped in:

"That's nobody's uncle," said Freddie. "I'm betting he's an agent from Interpol."

"I say it's his wife's detective," said Paul.

"I suppose it could be my uncle," I finally said. "Lord knows what he looks like now. What did he say?"

"Well, he seemed a lot more interested in me than in you, actually. First he dropped ten thousand in my basket and started praising my work, but it was clear he didn't know a thing about art, poor man..."

"Doesn't sound poor to me," said Sue. "He's rich. A rich old lecher who's hot for you, Ilene! Reel him in slowly, but not too slowly..."

"Oh, there wasn't a bit of that," said Ilene, who seemed to enjoy holding everyone's attention, "...at least I don't think there was. He asked me where I was from, and what my plans were, and whether I was married..."

"Every rich old lecher I've ever known started with those exact same questions." said Sue.

"Nice girls should stick to poor young lechers," offered Simon.

"Anyway that's when he mentioned you, Bob," continued Ilene, much amused. "I said I wasn't married, and he said he thought I might be married to 'that feller with the tour bus that was talkin' to you so nice and friendly.' That's exactly how he said it!"

"When he talked to me he spoke Italian," I said. "He pretended he didn't know English."

"In fact he doesn't," laughed Ilene. "He only knows American!"

That was all the Brits needed; with Paul leading they broke into an incredibly twangy version of "The Red River Valley" that they had evidently done before, because they stayed together and did it well. The other people in the pizzeria started to applaud, so they kept right on singing while Ilene and I resumed talking:

"Come and sit by my side if you love me,..."

"So you said we weren't married and that was it?"

"Do not hasten to bid me adooo,..."

"Well, no. I said that actually you are quite nice and friendly... but nothing more, because you've got a family back in the States."

"But remember the Red River Valley,..."

"None of this is his business, you know, Ilene."

"And the cowboy who loves you so true."

"Oh, bosh. He's just a bit eccentric. So are you."

The singing went on for a while, and then Ilene did a few caricatures, which weren't all that good, I thought — technically they were fine, but they were too realistic. Not bold enough or imaginative enough, at least for my tastes.

But maybe I was too busy thinking about my Uncle Jim to appreciate Ilene's efforts. Despite what she had said, I was beginning to think that he was more than just "a bit" eccentric — if old Giacomo really was my uncle, and for fantasy's sake I decided he was. In any case he would have to let me choose my own friends. I said this to myself a few nights later when I was sure I saw Renato's face in the crowd at the Forum before our show. In fact I was especially lusty for his benefit when I "raped" Ilene that evening. I shouted loud and long so that he would recognize me by my voice, if by nothing else.

My swooping hungrily down on Ilene time and again to carry her off in that flimsy tunic was building up an attraction between us that was undermining our dikes. My dike was down to a vague puritan fear that I could never get away with it and a somewhat nobler fear that it might not be a very constructive experience for a nice young Irish girl. I've still got my teeth and hair, but Richard Gere I am not. That's why I was surprised it was her dike that sprung the first real leak, when I took longer than usual to set her down after the Rape.

"You make me wish I were really Sabine and not Irish," she sort of moaned.

"Why don't we try this scene tomorrow night?" I suggested. That was German night, and we were off.

"Mmmm," she said.

"We could start with dinner. It's not in the script, but..."

"None of the good things are in the script."

"Mmmm," I said. "Pick you up at your place? 'Bout eight?"

"Make it half seven, in Piazza Navona. I'm going to try drawing there tomorrow afternoon. As close to Bernini's fountain as I can get. You know? With the obelisk."

"You like obelisks, don't you?" This was a raunchy thing to say, but my dike was crumbling fast.

"I like to work near them," she said. "They attract people, not only girls. Now behave yourself and get ready. Aren't you Tarquinius?"

"Nope. I'm Scipio. Then I'm Constantine. Easy night."

"You've got to ham it up more as Constantine."

I did. Both for Ilene and for Renato, to show him, and through him my strange fantasy uncle, that they had a live wire in their hands. When the Cross of Light was flashed high in the sky I went down hard on my knees, took my sword by the blade and managed to project a good shadow-cross on what's left of the Emilian Basilica. Then I jumped up and battled "Massentius" on the "Milvian Bridge" with such vigor that he — Freddie — fell off and sprained his wrist. There was much applause because it all made for great shadows. Vittorio approved the whole thing including the fall, which would have to be perfected.

CHAPTER VI

*After WWII the art of the "Madonnari" was all but
extinguished. The few remaining artists organized an annual
meeting at Grazia di Curtatone.
Only 10 attended, in 1972.*

The next day I took a ride on our afternoon bus tour.
The afternoon tour was different from my morning
tour and went around Piazza Navona. I wanted to find
out where this piazza was, and perhaps pick up a few
clever things to say about it.

As the bus wended its way around the huge oblong, I
saw Ilene doing her thing about twenty feet from
Bernini's fountain, which my afternoon colleague was
going on and on about. Some things I caught and some I
did not, because I was noticing that another artist, a
fellow wearing a big floppy straw hat for protection from
the sun, was chalking something on the asphalt only
about ten feet from Ilene. They seemed to be talking
together, but it wasn't easy to tell because passers-by kept
stopping to admire their work, thus blocking my view. I
decided to quell my curiosity until 7:30. Besides, I had
some shopping to do.

I was tired of dressing like somebody who had had
all his clothes and money stolen. Italy was the leader in
men's fashions and I was going around like a gay bride,
in something old, something new, something borrowed,

and something blue. Ilene deserved something better. So once the tour ended I went to a department store — I had a little money, but not enough for the fashion shops — and got some decent shoes, a very breezy cream-colored suit, a pink shirt, and a grey polyester neck scarf. With everything on, I was a Swedish Tony Manero. I even mused a while about taking Ilene dancing after dinner.

When I got back to Piazza Navona that evening there was a big crowd of people standing tightly around Ilene and her work. It took some doing to get close enough to see. The fellow in the straw hat was still there, down on his knees next to Ilene. They were both putting the finishing touches on what had turned out to be a huge joint effort, about sixteen feet in height and ten feet in width.

"Hi, Ilene."

"Oh, hello Bob. Almost done. What do you think?"

"It's...impressive. Very impressive. Her neck's a bit long." The fellow with the hat couldn't suppress a laugh. He still hadn't turned to let me see his face. Ilene joined him in the laugh, then said,

"I was afraid you might say that, Bob. This is the 'Madonna of the Long Neck,' one of the most famous Madonnas. By Parmigianino. She's supposed to have a long neck, don't you see? He elongates everything here — he's looking for a 'grace' that goes beyond nature. Parmigianino was one of the first mannerists."

"He sounds like a type of cheese," I said. Ilene and her companion laughed again. I didn't mind the long neck half so much as the suspicion that this guy was the long arm of Uncle Jim again, like Renato. Now together with Ilene he finally stood up and faced me, and in fact the guy was exactly like Renato.

"Bob, this is Rap, a fellow *'Madonnaro.'* He says he can

explain everything."

"So it's 'Rap' now, is it?" I said, shaking his hand. "At the airport it was 'Renato.'"

"Renato is my official name, but it doesn't describe me. For all my friends, for the world I am Il Rapallese, or just 'Rap' for short."

"I get it," I said. "It means you're from Rapallo."

"As Parmigianino was from Parma. Think of Perugino, Correggio, Veronese… artists don't need their private names."

"But they do need money."

"Not yours. I have come to explain."

"Your English has improved dramatically since the airport."

"It was a slight deception. I thought you would be suspicious of a man with good English who could find no better job than to procure clients for a modest hotel."

"Rap has a degree in English," said Ilene.

"A degree only good for teaching," he said, "and I tried teaching but I am a poor teacher. Lousy. I am a lousy teacher. I wanted to talk with the pupils about so many things that I never finished the program."

"Well, I'm sure it pays more to roll tourists."

"Bob, he said he would explain," said Ilene.

"Why don't you start? You're in on it too, aren't you? A great little actress..." At this point only about half the crowd was still admiring the picture; the other half was edging close to us, to see if they knew enough English to make sense of what we were obviously getting excited about.

"In on it? An actress? Hardly!" exclaimed Ilene. "I do all my acting in the Forum!" she said with a smile. She seemed determined not to let things get ugly. "I met Rap for the first time this afternoon, Bob. And all he's told me is that he's got a happy ending in store for you. He's given me his word as a fellow artist — and he knows his art, Bob."

"Do you remember Joe?" asked the Italian.

"On my bus tour? Sure."

"The chap who sort of…introduced us?" asked Ilene.

"He's a friend of mine," said Rap. "I asked him — actually I paid him — to ride your bus, Bob, and tell me how you were doing, and when he told me that there was a very pretty 'Madonnaro' on the Pincio where you stopped, I asked him to get you together somehow. Just to see what would happen. I knew that I could always explain things to a colleague. And I knew she would he an interesting person to meet. For you, and now also for me."

"Just to see what would happen!" Ilene and I said this almost in unison.

"Bob, it has all been just to see what would happen. You arrived here, a closed box. Even what I knew about you, what I was told about you from America was the life of a closed man. What do you do to find out what's inside a closed box? You shake it a bit. I have been shaking you a bit, just to know you better. Well, and also to prepare you, to make you more…flexible."

"But…but…" I said.

"Rap, just what right did you have to…" began llene, but Rap cut her off by putting his finger on her lips.

"This is perhaps too public. My explanation will continue elsewhere. In a good restaurant. And now, Ilene, remember that first of all we are artists, who have made a beautiful picture come to life for these people. We must return to them for a moment, and answer their questions. Do you mind, Bob?"

There was so much to mind I didn't know where to

66

start, so I thought to hell with it, let's pretend to be very, very flexible. Sooner or later my chance would come to shake his box a bit. So I just said:

"Go right ahead. Why should I mind?" I smiled serenely, Ilene smiled uncertainly and Rap smiled winningly. The two of them turned to their public and began taking questions about their work.

It looked like they had done pretty well, financially. Ilene's little basket was about full, mainly coins, but some bills. Our animated conversation in English had probably been good for business. People like artists to be foreign and emotional.

"A land-office business today." I said smoothly to Ilene when things lulled a little.

"Yes, the Long Neck's a crowd-pleaser." she answered. "And ours is big, about twice the original. People like that. Actually it's easier. And Rap and I work well together."

"Amazing how you're able to — to blend your styles. I can't tell what you did and what he did."

"It used to be quite normal," said Rap, joining in. "A master painter would get a commission for a large mural, and his young apprentices might all work on it, following his directions and imitating his style. It's the best kind of schooling for artists."

"And how about con artists?" I said this with a grin, and I thought it was a pretty nifty way to get back to the point, or one of the points. "You need to work on your sting, you know? You messed up in the airport by not asking for my name! And what I really want to know is, am I going to get my things back?"

"I think my story will satisfy you. If the opinion I have formed of you is correct. Now, will you please let me take you both to dinner? There is a good place nearby

— 'Da Leccarsi i Baffi,' in the direction of the Pantheon. Good for everything, especially — pork hooves."

"Pig's feet!" Ilene and I said together.

"If you insist. But first..." He looked down at himself. "I would like to change my clothes a bit. You are so elegant, Bob — at least a jacket."

Besides his straw hat, Rap was dressed in tennis shoes, blue jeans, and a black T-shirt stretched over an athletic chest. He was lithe and intense, with a small Madonna tattooed on each arm. He looked better than he had at the airport in "decent" clothes. I wondered if he was mocking me. Then Ilene got in on it.

"Yes, me too," she said. "You look quite nice, you know, Bob? I shall have to get into something nicer. Listen, we'll just be a minute — Rap has a motorbike, and he says that my digs are on the way to his!"

"So should I just wait here? With your Madonna?"

"You know, she is still good for more donations," said Ilene wistfully, "as long as the light lasts, actually. Pity, isn't it? You don't suppose...?"

"For a lark, Bob?" challenged Rap. "You've done everything else, why not see what it's like to be a street painter?"

"Well, as long as I have to stand around anyway..."

"Bob, you're a super sport!" Ilene exclaimed. "Here, let me empty the basket, so we see how much you make — but you keep our chalk and things. People will assume it's yours. No harm in that. We'll be back very shortly — half an hour at most, right, Rap?"

"What was the guy's name again? I mean, in case they ask," I said with a resigned smile.

"Parmigianino!" said Rap. "*La Madonna dal Collo Lungo.*"

"*Collo Lungo,*" I repeated. "Long Neck."

"You'll be splendid." said Ilene. "We're off, then! Cheerio!"

"Okay, cheerio." And so I began my half-hour as a phony *Madonnaro*. I stood there without saying a word, examining Ilene's pieces of chalk one at a time. Each one seemed to represent a possible turn of events. I never touched the black chalk. I let the gray chalk stand for the dreariest scenario — Ilene and Rap never coming back. Still, I thought I knew Ilene well enough to put that chalk down. I toyed with the other colors, representing more or less implausible explanations for Rap's funny way of ripping people off. Then I especially caressed the bright green chalk that brought to mind Ilene, her eyes and Ireland. But I couldn't keep from gazing at the gold chalk, right in the center of the box, which represented an explanation for everything, the explanation dear to my fantasy. Uncle Jim. Rap hadn't mentioned him. And if he didn't, I wouldn't — I was already making a big enough fool of myself. But I would certainly mention Giacomo. He was the khaki-colored chalk. I put it right next to the gold.

That's how the first fifteen minutes passed, and as a Madonnaro I made about five thousand *lire*. Then along came the classic little old lady.

"*Complimenti, Maestro! Come si chiama questo quadro?*" She wanted the name. I was ready.

"*Collo Lungo — La Madonna*," I said carefully.

"*Ah! Lei è straniero.*" she said. I understood this too. She had somehow realized that I was a foreigner. "*E chi fu l'autore dell'originale?*" Now she wanted the artist's name. I was shooting my wad.

"Parmesanino," I said. I couldn't have been too far off. But she just stared at me for a while, then asked:

"*Di dov'è lei?*" I had learned that, too.

"*Da* Chicago. Illinois. America."

"Chicago! Chicago! *Mia sorella sta proprio a* Chicago! He *sposato uno di Bari che si chiama Masullo. Ezio Masullo. Lo conosce, per caso?*"

This was a lot harder, but the little old lady had a lot of time and patience. So we stood to one side in order not to block the best views of the Madonna, and in the end I was able to tell her that no, I didn't know her sister in Chicago, who was married to Ezio Masullo from Bari. I was pleased and proud. The little old lady walked away without dropping a single *lira* in the basket.

That's when I looked for the basket, which was no longer there.

But there were still seven or eight people standing around, looking at my Madonna.

"Where's my basket!" I shouted angrily. One boy about seventeen understood me.

"But the other artist taked it," he said. "He say is enough for today and thank you very much."

When Ilene and Rap came back — half an hour late — I gave them my handkerchief with about six thousand lire in it.

"Where's the basket?"

"The other artist taked it," I answered. "He say is enough for today and thank you very much."

"*Da Leccarsi i Baffi*" — moustache-licking good — no doubt about it, was the right place to eat. No fooling around with international menus — in fact no menus at all, just a happy-looking guy with a greasy moustache who rattled off the names of whatever the cook felt like doing that evening. Food names made up about two-thirds of my Italian vocabulary, thanks to Saverio, so I suavely asked for and got *tortellini in brodo* followed by *ossi buchi con gremolata*, good enough to make you wish

70

you had a moustache to lick.

That part of the evening was fine. The battle for Ilene's favors was less enjoyable. I was no match for *Il Rapallese*, who now had on a green snakeskin jacket, one of those things that you don't think anybody could wear without looking ridiculous until you meet a guy like Rap. The jacket seemed to complement the independence and readiness that he so casually projected. I decided to stop worrying about Uncle Jim and my suitcases. Rap would have to get around to them. That left me free to concentrate on being witty. For instance, Ilene had put on a bright green jump suit, which prompted me to break out with:

"St. Patrick's Day no more we'll keep,

His color can't be seen;

For there's a bloody law against

The wearing of the Green!"

"Not here, there isn't," she simply said. "I just wanted to match Rap's jacket."

"And I wear green because I am a Green," said Rap just as simply, "a *'Verde.'* Do you know what a *'Verde'* is in Italy?"

"I can imagine," I said. "It's that ecological movement that started in Germany."

"That's right," said Ilene. "In Germany with Petra Kelly. Nice Irish name."

"Another fugitive from Sligo?" I asked, glad to start up any sort of banter with Ilene.

"And just why did the Svensons leave Sweden?" she asked.

"Banished, for sexual profligacy," I said smoothly, but I couldn't keep it up. Rap got back in to tell us about his *Verdi*, among whom he was evidently some sort of a leader. He had been on their ticket for the regional parliament in the last elections.

"I accepted the nomination only because there was no danger of election. I am no politician," he said with a grin — and then proceeded to present his platform. He was a conservationist without being conservative, a respecter of traditions without being traditionalist. He was in love with the Italy everyone loves, the cradle of the arts and the garden of Europe. He was heavy, heavy wine for girl painters from Sligo. I recklessly tried a frontal attack, anything to get back into the thick of things.

"What I mean is, I suppose chalk copies of Madonnas are good practice, as Ilene told me, and you can pick up some nice change, maybe, but if that's where your art stops, if that's all you intend to do, you might as well hawk plastic copies of Michelangelo's *'Pietà'* in front of St. Peter's."

Complete silence.

"I see them every morning when my tour stops there."

Ice Nine.

"They cost nine thousand *lire*. They're not so bad."

Midnight in the cemetery.

"Well, what's the difference between a chalked Madonna and a plastic statue?"

I looked to Ilene for relief, but she was looking hard at Rap. My impression was that she was going to make a key judgment about him according to the way he handled this. Obviously she herself was unable to handle it. Obviously it was something that had been bothering her. I garnered all this information, whether false or true, during the fifteen seconds that Rap took to prepare his response.

"Do you like Shakespeare, Bob?"

"Yes I do. Very much."

"Do you prefer to read his plays, or to see them?"

"To see them, to see them. I've seen the whole BBC series. Wonderful, but even better in a playhouse. Plays are for seeing, not reading, especially Shakespeare. He never cared about publishing his plays, you know. Strictly a man of the playhouse. He wanted to please his audience, not readers." I went on like this because in spite of his degree in English, I felt sure that this was firmer ground for me than for Rap — I really happened to be a Shakespeare buff. Wouldn't hurt for Ilene to know it.

"I see, I see," said Rap. His look of pleasure meant that I was playing right into his hands. "But Shakespeare's audience, the one he wanted to please — it wasn't a well-educated audience, was it? It wasn't, what do you say, a high-brow audience?"

"Of course not. Elizabethan theater was entertainment for everyone. Okay, now that I'm set up, what's the punch line?"

"Think again of the Madonna of the Long Neck. Nice painting, don't you think?"

"I can't honestly say. I've only seen your copy."

Ilene was displeased. "We're not far off. You know, I wish you could see the original."

"Yes, well, at this point I'd like to. And of course I expect it's beautiful. More than your copy, surely."

"Naturally so," said Rap. He alone knew where he was going. "The original is in the Uffizi Gallery, in Florence. It is like a Shakespeare play. Dead, unless people see it. People, not just experts and high-brows. Ilene and I are like traveling street actors, like there used to be when theater was a thing for the people. We put on our performance, I mean we make a copy of a Madonna — we make it, Bob, we don't sell plastic. We make it, the way actors act, and the people can see the Madonna take her shape, can see how difficult it is but how easy it is to make a beautiful thing. The people see this, not the experts. They see our presentation, like a poor and simple performance of Shakespeare, and the art lives again. The art lives again."

Ilene reached across the table and squeezed his hand. I knew there had to be flaws in his argument, but the battle was over. I picked through the wreckage.

"Nicely done. I mean, I suppose I understand. But one thing I don't quite get yet — why do you always do Madonnas? Don't get me wrong, I like Madonnas, who doesn't like Madonnas, but..."

"There, you see why?" This time it was Ilene. "They...we do Madonnas because it's a theme everyone likes. In Italy anyway. A mother with her child. Nothing expresses more love. Nothing is closer to the people. The people Rap was talking about."

"Yes, it's partly that. It's originally that." Rap again. "But now it is more. It is a rich tradition. We *Madonnari* carry on a tradition that goes back at least to the fourteenth century, in Venice. We accept this strict limitation in order to join with six centuries of street artists, all exploring the same beautiful mystery, the joy and sorrow in a mother's face. All trying to spread the love for our great masters, for Caravaggio, Del Santo, Sansovino, Bellini, Tiepolo..."

I looked at Ilene. These names were like bells ringing in her soul.

"...but of course," Rap went on, "this does not prevent us from pursuing our own careers, if we wish, as original artists with canvas and oils. Some of us have done very well on our own. El Greco, for example. A *Madonnaro* who continued in his own work to explore the face of the Madonna, because he remained fascinated..."

"We have one in Chicago." This was kind of a dumb thing to throw in, I suppose, but what more could I lose?

"You have one...?"

"At the Art Institute. An El Greco Madonna."

"Ah yes, yes, 'The Assumption of the Virgin.' Beautiful. Strictly speaking not a Madonna. No child. But yes, a wonderful study. Someone did it at Grazia di Curtatone last year."

"Grazia di...?" asked Ilene.

"Curtatone. Curtatone. A town near Mantua where every summer there is a gathering of the best, the *Maestri Madonnari*. I think now there are seven of them. And other *Madonnari* come, who would like this title, this recognition, thousands of them. I am going again. It's next week." He looked at Ilene. He had won the prize. All he had to do was reach out and take it. He did.

"Would you like to come with me, Ilene?"

"Well, I don't know, perhaps I could manage for a few days..."

"For a week?"

"Perhaps for a week."

"I think the *Maestri* will be delighted to see you. You have true ability, Ilene. Everyone will love you. And you will love them."

"What will you say to Vittorio?" I asked her dolefully.

"Oh, he doesn't mind, as long as I find a decent substitute."

"One that's not too heavy, please."

"I know an American girl. Black. From Detroit, I believe. She's quite thin. You don't mind?"

"Her being thin?"

"Her being black. I know that Americans..."

"I only have to rape her, not marry her." I said this without smiling.

75

"You needn't get nasty."

"You wouldn't marry a black girl?" asked Rap.

"I'm already married. She's white. That makes me a hopeless racist. I suppose."

"No, of course not," said Ilene. "But you know, you read about race problems in Chicago, and riots, and..."

"Have you killed any Protestants lately?"

"What? I..."

"You know, you read about the I.R.A. and the religious strife in Ireland, and the riots and..."

"What's got into you, Bob?" An embarrassing moment of silence. I was a poor loser, feeling sorry for himself. I wanted to pick up my marbles and go home.

"Well, if you'll just tell me where I can find my wallet and bags. I'll leave you two to your vacation plans."

Rap checked his watch. "You can't go yet. We have a half-hour. He'll be here at ten."

"Who? The guy who has my things?"

"No. My father. Your Uncle Jim."

CHAPTER VII

The punishment for desertion during time of war is death or life sentence in prison.

Cousins! You're cousins!" exclaimed Ilene.

"Yes," said Rap, "millions of foreign soldiers have swept through Italy over the centuries. I am a trace of the last passage."

"But your father didn't pass." I said. "He's still here."

"Oh, very much so."

"And your name is Savorski. Renato Savorski, born in Rapallo."

"Savori, not Savorski. He Italianized his name."

"He did? What did he do with James?"

"James is Giacomo in Italian." Rap smiled slyly.

"James is Giacomo," I repeated dully.

"Why did your father call you Renato?" asked Ilene.

"He didn't. My mother wanted it."

"Your mother..." I began.

"Yes, your aunt, your uncle's wife. And I am their natural and legitimate son, Bob." He smiled still more slyly.

"I think we should celebrate!" said Ilene. "Two cousins meeting each other for the first time...Waiter! *Cameriere*!" And we ordered some *spumante*. Of course I was pleased at having found my uncle — it was why I had come to Italy, it was my fantasy come true. But my new cousin was still the man who had stolen my bags, my money, and my chance for an Irish Spring in Italy. And I couldn't deny the presence of that thought in the back of my mind: how much does a nephew inherit if there's also a son? So I was still a little wary when we clinked our glasses.

"All right," I said, "so what sort of a man is my uncle? I already know what Ilene thinks of him..."

"When did I ever meet him? Oh! The old bloke who asked about me and you..."

"Evidently that was my uncle."

"Seemed nice enough," said Ilene, placidly. "Wouldn't harm a flea."

"My...backside is much bigger than a flea." said Rap. "And it was often harmed by that 'nice bloke' when I was a boy. But what is the saying? Perhaps it hurt him more than it hurt me. Enough, now. He has told me not to speak about him. In fact, I myself do not really know him very well. He is a secretive man."

"You get that idea." I tried to say this very drily.

"Look, I will show you something," said Rap. "Few people have seen this." He reached inside his shirt. He had a strong gold chain around his neck. Lots of Italian men wear them, for crosses, lockets, dogtags, what have you. Rap used his for a *bulla*, a medallion like the one Jim had sent me.

"I don't wear it very often. It is too big. *Papà* tells me to wear it for luck, but I'm not sure I want his luck. He isn't a happy man. Tonight I put it on for him, and for you."

"He sent me one like it."

"I know, very foolish. *Papà* is wise in the ways of the world, but I don't know which world. You were lucky it arrived."

"So it is lucky!" said Ilene, who was enjoying the

spumante. "Is it Etruscan?"

"Yes," said Rap, "but this one is different from Bob's. This one can be opened, you see?" And he showed us an edge that ran all around its rim. "But I never open it. *Papà* gave it to me when I was a boy, and he made me swear not to open it until he dies. I am not particularly curious, and it is a good thing, because I think *Papà* would kill me if I opened it. It has great importance for him." Rap shook it. It made no noise. Shaking things to see what's inside evidently turned him on. "It is paper," he said, "things I will have to read."

"Well, it's beautiful," said Ilene. "Must be worth a great deal."

"Yes. I suppose so," said Rap. "So are my kidneys and corneas, on the black market. But I don't think about selling them." And he slipped the medallion back inside his shirt. Then he smiled and said, "Excuse me, Ilene. I was only making poor humor."

"Oh, I didn't..." began Ilene lightly, but I interrupted her.

"Cousin Rap, I'm the venal one, not Ilene; for example I can't help thinking about my bags and money..."

"Yes, that I can explain now. It is true, I organized everything. The false porter at the hotel was paid 600,000 *lire* to do his part."

"And Egidio? Was the hotel manager in on it?" This was important to me. It would hurt to think that even Egidio's friendship was contrived.

"No, no, I told him nothing. But we chose his hotel because *Papà* knows him and wanted to ask him about you. Casually. Without revealing the connection. But when he tried a few days ago, he discovered that you had preceded him, you had asked Egidio questions about him and had learned his name..."

"That's right. Giacomo. But I didn't know it meant James. Not that it would have helped me much..."

"But it did create problems for *Papà* with Egidio. He had to think fast. He said you had noticed him because in fact he had been keeping an eye on you — to offer you a job."

"Another job?"

"That's what he said, to throw Egidio off. As a salesman, to open up the American market."

"Open it up to what? He told Egidio once that he was in demolitions..."

"Fortunately they were at table together. By that time Egidio had drunk too much. It was not necessary to specify."

"But after this meeting, why didn't Egidio tell me...?"

"*Papà* told him he wanted to approach you in his own way, and if you learned about it from someone else, he would call the whole thing off. Egidio resisted the temptation to speak about it for your own good."

"Sounds like a nice bloke to me," said Ilene.

"He is," I said with some warmth. We were on our second bottle of *spumante*.

"But anyway," said Rap, "the time had come to meet and talk with you..."

"My question is," said Ilene, "how did you know I'd be in Piazza Navona this afternoon?"

"Ah, there were many ways I could have gotten us all together..."

"All right, but I'm curious about this one."

"You mentioned it in the pizzeria last night."

"Yes I did, but who...?"

"Sue is an old friend of mine."

"Rap!" said Ilene. She said it pretty loud.

"Sue has a great many friends, Ilene..." Rap somehow

thought this was a good defense. He continued: "...she is what we call a *nave scuola*."

"A...what?" asked Ilene. Maybe this was a good defense.

"A...a school ship. On which young sailors learn to navigate. And gain confidence. Very important for the entire fleet."

"Oh." Ilene sipped some wine, trying to think of a better response. I thought I'd help them both out by nobly changing the subject.

"Could we get back to my bags and money...?"

"As I said," said Rap, "the bags were no problem. It was much harder to convince old Nadia, the gypsy woman, to take your wallet. She's a proud lady. But before her boy grew up to rob for her I used to give her something every time she begged near me, and gypsies have long memories. For payment, she was content with half your money. How much did you have?"

"Oh, about five thousand dollars."

"And she was even honest! That's what she told me!"

"Be sure to thank her for me when you see her." I was getting good at saying things drily.

Ilene giggled into her *spumante* — it wasn't clear about what.

Rap reached into his pants pocket. "Here is the key to a locker at the airport. It contains your bags and your wallet with half your money. As for the other half...I'm sure *Papà* intends to make it up to you."

I accepted the key with a long sigh of relief. "Thank you. It seems like the end of a bad dream."

"Was it really so bad? I mean, living without security, by your own ingenuity?"

"'*Arrangiarsi*,' as Egidio taught me to say? But now I'm wondering how much I was really winging it, and how

81

much you were setting it up..."

"No, no. Very little. 'Strip him clean and see how he takes it,' those were *Papà's* only orders. Egidio could have thrown you out that first day — it might have been more interesting. Your restaurant job, your bus tours...they just happened. Other things might have happened instead."

"Except for Ilene here. She was your idea."

"Not such a bad idea, was she?"

"Not at all, but..."

"Nothing was forced. She might have told you to...to buzz off, as you say. Or you might have...have steered clear as you say."

"Very good." I said. "Your idioms are very good. But whatever words you use, I was being maneuvered."

"Well, Bob," said Ilene with her glass raised, "it seems to me that it was all in good fun."

"I only...posed a few problems," said Rap. "You did all the maneuvering. And you did...well enough. Joe told me I almost knocked an African into the Trevi Fountain, but you saved him instead of pursuing me. This is...humanity. But I especially liked the way you handled Tonino and Saverio that evening in the restaurant. "*Pussa via*!" Hah! Very goodl That was humanity, too!"

"Tonino? You mean that gigolo who tried to..."

"Yes, an acquaintance of mine. Another little challenge for you. He was impressed. And amused, of course."

"Rap, you're a beast!" said Ilene — but she seemed almost delighted.

"When do I come to bat?" I said. "When do I get to challenge you? When do we change places?"

"Oh, bosh!" said Ilene. "Be a good sport, Bob! Drink your *spumante*. It's quite good, you know."

I did take a long sip. When I put my glass down, I

said "I suppose I should save my...remarks for Uncle Jim."

"Yes," said Rap, "it will be interesting. For me, also. I really don't know why my father is doing this with you. I asked him. He said...to be exact, he said 'if a man comes nosing into my life, I want to know him, and you can't know a man till you see him under pressure.'"

"I think he wanted me to come."

"Yes, but I don't think he will admit it. I certainly wanted you to come." Rap laughed out loud. "You know, you said it very well a moment ago, when you asked to change places with me. I think that is what we will do! I am his...Italian son, I have no interest in his strange things, his war, his problems as an American. He also has wanted it this way, has not wanted me to be involved. But now I have noticed this need in him to speak finally, to talk to someone. Not to me. With me he does not want this relationship. For me he has only written things and put them in my medallion here, for me to read when he dies, but he does not need my reactions. He needs the reactions of an American. An American son, in order to pass things on. Or maybe to...to..."

"To come home again, in a sense," I said. "Before he dies. You know, he thinks he's going to die soon."

"I've gotten that impression. I'm sure you will discover why he thinks so. And I am very glad you are taking my place. I am not suited, not only because I am not American, but because I am not a good listener, a good learner. I am a talker, and *Papà* does not need that. Now, after watching you, he believes that you are these things he needs. I think he has always hoped for this. You have always had importance for him. He has always told me that I have relatives in America. My aunt Agnes, my cousin Bob. But for some reason he can't go back there, and he doesn't want me to go there. Then last year he told

83

me that my aunt, your mother, had died..."

"How do you suppose he found out about it?"

"Oh, he has a man in America. In Chicago. A professional detective. I think they were soldiers together here in Italy. He...has always kept Jim informed about you and your family. Your wife, who loves to talk. That is why *Papà* sent your *bulla* to your school, you know? As I said, he is bothered by talkers. I for one would enjoy meeting your wife..."

"And that's how Jim knew I was coming. This detective was tailing me."

"Yes. In fact, he was on the plane to Paris with you. From there he called about your flight to Rome..."

"And then he flew back to Chicago?"

"No. I think he stayed in Paris for a little vacation. Or perhaps for some other investigations. He does international work, *Papà* says. Looking for runaway husbands." Ilene smiled at me. I almost fit into that category.

"If it's the husbands that run away, it's because promising girls become disappointing wives." I said breezily. A little friendly banter. A little Chicago cool.

"If it's the husbands that run away," she countered, "it's because they can't keep up with their wives."

"Whoever runs away," said Rap, "it shows that marriage is a...a fiasco, an impossible institution. In fact, Saint Joseph is a mere accessory. The Madonna and Child don't need him; artistically and psychologically he is out of place..."

"Rap!" said Ilene. "Then how can you explain the beauty of Giorgione's 'Holy Family?' Saint Joseph is in perfect harmony..."

"Most of the Masters did not agree. In fact when they included Saint Joseph, they usually included the infant

John the Baptist to balance..." I let them go on with it. I sipped my *spumante* and started watching the door. It was almost ten o'clock, the time when Jim was due to make his appearance.

He was right on time. He wore the same safari jacket I had seen him in on both other occasions. He came to our table, shook our hands, and sat down stiffly without saying a word. After a few moments Rap broke the silence with a simple: "Hello, *Papà*."

"Hello," the old man grunted back.

Ilene and her *spumante* decided not to let things get too solemn. "Nice to see you again!" she suddenly said with considerable sparkle. "We need another glass! *Cameriere! Un bicchiere, per favore!*"

"No thanks, I don't drink. Little water, maybe. Tap water. Hot in here."

"The last time we met, you were speaking Italian," I said. I had to start somewhere. I think he was grateful.

"My Italian's a damn sight better than my English, nephew. Been here a lot longer than I was there."

"Mainly in Liguria," I said, remembering what Egidio had said about Jim's Italian. Rap reacted first:

"Bob, how did you know that?"

"I've got a deuce or two up my sleeve."

"Well," growled Jim, "Liguria more than other places, but I been pret' near always on the move."

"How come you never came home, Uncle Jim? At least to visit." The old man let himself bend back a bit into his chair. "Well, we might get around to that, and we might not. Not here and not now, that's for sure. Listen, your plane home from Paris ain't for a couple weeks yet. What I want is for you to come with me on a little trip in my van. You game?"

"In a...van?"

"No, no," said Rap, "it is more than a van..."

"A caravan?" offered Ilene.

"No, a house that you drive from inside..."

"A motor-home," I said.

"That's it!" said Rap. "A very nice one."

"Well," said Jim, "it ain't the North Shore..."

"That's no problem," I said. "I just think you owe a few explanations first."

Jim looked at Rap. "Didn't you explain to him about taking all his stuff?"

I answered. "He explained how it was taken, and he's given it back, I think. Some of it." I showed Jim the airport locker key. "What I'd like to know is, why you think you had the right to do this to me?"

He was shaken for a moment. There was a basic shyness to the man. But he had acquired many defenses.

"First off, let's talk about your right to come hunting for me."

"There's no law against that, but there's lots of laws against theft."

"Talk about theft. How was I to know you wasn't here for my gold?"

"You know damn well you sent me one of those things," I pointed at Rap's chest, "to tempt me into coming over here!"

"Now that ain't entirely true," said Jim quietly. "I just wanted you to know that I'm alive, and that I ain't been doing so bad. I think I had a right to do that. Then if you came over, well, that was your choice, and the Lord's choice. I just gave it a chance to happen. Just a chance."

"Well. I can assure you of one thing," I said. "I'm not here to take your gold or anything else. Of course I'm interested, but I wouldn't..."

"He most surely wouldn't!" exclaimed Ilene from

behind her glass. "Bob is a dear person, an honest person." She put her hand on Jim's arm. "Do you know what he said to me? He said 'I'd like my boy Bret to have a colorful relative to think about. To prove that life can be exciting.' That's what he said. Bob's interested in you most of all, not your gold. He's an honest man."

Jim gently drew back, away from Ilene's hand.

"That's the impression I get, Miss. That's what people been telling me. That's what I had to know. Well, you gonna come with me, nephew?"

"Hold it, hold it. Give me some idea of why you want to take this trip with me."

Jim put his head down a moment, then he drank a sip of water. "Rap tells me you're still out 2,500 dollars. I'll give you 5,000 and you can go back to Paris tomorrow. Either that or you come with me, and I ain't promising nothing except your 2,500 back at the end. And the fact that maybe you'll get to know me. Make your choice."

"First prove to me that you're Jim Savorski. That you're really my uncle."

It all could have been an elaborate set-up to blackmail me or something, but I didn't really believe that. What I wanted was to let the three of them know that my good faith was all used up.

"How am I s'posed to do that? Want me to tell you stories about your mother Agnes?"

"Not good enough. Your detective friend in Chicago could have found out lots of things about her. Show me a document. Something with 'James Savorski' on it."

"Bob, I told you," said Rap, "he doesn't use that name anymore. Not publicly. He's Giacomo Savori over here."

"I had to get rid of everything with that name on it, nephew."

"Listen, Bob, a little caution is a good thing," said Rap,

"but..."

"But you're being ridiculous!" said Ilene. "Why on earth would anyone cook up a story like this...?"

"*Fidarsi è bene, non fidarsi è meglio*," said Jim with a hint of a smile. "'Trusting is good, not trusting is better,' the Italians say, and it looks like you're learning fast. Listen, there's someone in Rapallo who knows my old name. That's where I wanted to head for first. Stick with me up to Rapallo, it's on the way to Paris anyway. If you ain't satisfied, or if you've had enough, I'll put you on a train or a plane in Genoa, whatever you want."

"Who knows your old name in Rapallo, *Papà*?" asked Rap.

My uncle looked hard at his son. "Off limits, boy. When you learn about Jim Savorski, he'll be dead, and that ain't changing. Your father's name is Giacomo Savori, and he's glad to be your father. But Bob here, he didn't come looking for Giacomo Savori. He come from home, from the States, from my American family, looking for Sgt. Jim Savorski. After forty-four years. And maybe he can be found again." The old man stared hard at his water glass. Anger came into his face; he had said more than he wanted to say.

"You coming with me, nephew?" he asked abruptly.

"Wouldn't miss it, uncle," I answered.

"Rap. I'm parked in my spot on the Aurelia. Get this man the right clothes and have him there by 8 am the day after tomorrow."

"Yes, sir."

"Nephew, that gives you a day to wind up your affairs here in Rome. That enough?"

"I hope so. I think so."

Jim stood up. He nodded towards Ilene and said, "Miss, it was my pleasure." Then he nodded towards Rap and me and walked out.

"Irish uncles aren't like that," said Ilene after a moment's silence. "They spend their time in pubs with their pints."

"Which is at least safer than doing what Bob's uncle does," said Rap.

"Really?" I said. "What's dangerous about looking for Etruscan gold?"

"How do you suppose he looks for it?"

"I...I can't imagine."

"With his minesweeper. In fact, he doesn't really look for gold. He looks for mines and other explosives left behind by the war. But he comes across a lot of other things..."

"He's still looking for mines? After forty years?"

"And they're still there. And they still kill people. It's a good thing that *Papà* does. In fact I know he has done many good things, other things for people. I don't really know why."

"Maybe he's just a very good-hearted man," offered Ilene.

"No. I wouldn't call my father good-hearted. He seems driven to do things. Many things, but especially the mines."

"So that's why he told Egidio he's in the field of demolitions..."

"And now you're in it too, Bob. For a little while. You're going to learn a lot about mines. Surely you will prove to be a better pupil than me. I hate wars, I hate explosives. And I must say that *Papà* never insisted with me. While he swept the coastlines, he let me play on the beaches. And watch the *Madonnari* drawing for the tourists on the boardwalks and promenades. I learned from them, not from *Papà*."

"But was your mother with you then?" asked Ilene.

"I can't remember my mother. She died when our boat turned over in a storm, off Rapallo. One of the many things *Papà* never talks about. My impression is that in order to save me, he had to let my mother drown."

"Oh, how dreadful!" Ilene exclaimed. "That poor man!"

"I really don't know, I was too small. Maybe it's written in my medallion here. Anyway, don't ask him about it lightly. But perhaps he will tell you something, Bob, when you reach Rapallo. You have seen that you are a special person for him."

"And special for me, too," said Ilene. "Rap, I don't just want to break off from Bob tomorrow and perhaps never see him again. Does this trip your father wants to make with him end up back in Rome?"

"I really don't know, I..."

"It might end up in Rapallo," I said. "I've got an option there, remember."

"There, you see, Rap? Can't we manage to pass through Rapallo? I mean, on our way to Grazia-whatever-it's-called?"

"Maybe this can be arranged. I too will like to know how you are doing, Bob. Do you mind?"

"By no means; in fact I..."

"Then tomorrow I'll ask *Papà* just when he plans to be in Rapallo, and we can organize to meet you. I think not before Grazia but after. *Papà* will take his time, and there are things I wanted to show you on the way up, Ilene. For example the fresco cycle that Perugino did for the Banker's Guild in Perugia. I think I have understood exactly where he was helped by his pupil, Raphael."

Well, Rap's line sure beat inviting a girl to see your butterfly collection. At least with this girl. The *spumante* may have helped, but the fact was she almost swooned.

"Oh, how wonderful! And we can stop in Fiesole, to visit Fra Angelico's monastery and see his 'Madonna and Child'..."

They went on like this for a while. I didn't even have a butterfly collection to propose. It was clear that if any meeting of the bodies was going to follow this meeting of the minds, mine would not be involved. I didn't know to what extent I would ever really "take Rap's place" with Jim, but Rap was already taking mine with Ilene. I chuckled at the thought, and not all that bitterly, because after the talk with Jim, it bothered me less. There had been a moment when Ilene and I would have felt right with each other, but that moment had passed. Rap the artist and my mysterious Uncle Jim had jolted our priorities back into place. A one-night stand would have been enjoyable, but she wasn't the type...and neither was I. Presumably.

CHAPTER VIII

Not only the roads, but even some of the aqueducts
built by the Romans centuries ago are still in use.

The nice thing about the wetback sort of job is that you can quit, because you often must quit, on a moment's notice. It's no great problem for your employer, because the world is full of wetbacks. That next morning when I told my bus tour boss that I was leaving, he was actually glad about it. I wasn't that bad a guide, but he wanted to do a favor for a guy from New Zealand. This young fellow had come to Italy to learn how to design shoes, but he had fallen in love with a fast lady and spent all his money on her. Fortunately there seems to be a safety net of human solidarity under people in Italy; nobody is allowed to really hit bottom. Probably just an impression. Anyway this New Zealander, living on borrowed money, stepped right into my tour job to everyone's relief. At the end of my tour that morning the boss kissed me on both cheeks and gave me my back pay, along with one of his souvenir guide books: 'Italy in Your Pocket', it was called. I was touched.

"Thanks," I said. "Thanks very much. You've been very kind."

"And you are okay guide. I'm glad you find uncle. You know, when they need money, Italians say 'I go find uncle in America.' You know we all have people in

America. All rich, we say. You are first American come to find uncle in Italia. The uncles are poor here, but you want to find, so I'm glad you find. *Buona fortuna!*"

In the afternoon Rap went with me to buy "the right clothes." He was good company. I had to admit that my cousin was a likeable guy. He took me to the huge open flea market in Porta Portese.

"Is this where you buy your clothes, Rap?"

"Always. These are street people, like me. Listen to the music they make."

Three thousand vendors hawking their wares, and each one has to find a distinctive tone, or cadence, or refrain to get attention —

"Venite quà! 'Sta bancarella tiene solo roba bella!"

"Ao! Regalo tutto! Mi voglio rovinare!"

"Sono sbronzol Approfittate, approfittate!"

— and the result is a kind of music, a wild Hallelujah Chorus singing the praises of the goods of this world.

"But Rap, most of this stuff is junk, poor quality," I said as we walked among it.

"If you're careful, you can do well."

"I don't think I'd do my shopping here unless I had to." It's true, I was fishing for more information about the finances of this new Italian side of my family. And that's when Rap became an even more likeable guy, because he stopped and said, "Bob, don't worry about the money. Yes. I have to shop here, because I never take money from my father. He helped me get a good education. I want nothing else from him. I am my own man. I am sure one reason he is interested in you is that I told him I don't want his gold. I will bury it back in the ground if he leaves it to me. You are taking my place, remember? Now this morning I will buy your clothes for you with my money because I want my cousin to have a good memory

93

of me. And they will be good clothes, but at the right price. First the shoes, the most important thing. You know what Italians say? 'Health and good shoes, and away you go!'"

And off we went, towards the shoe stalls. Using a more critical eye as we made our way, I began to see that there was also some very fine merchandise for sale. Suitcases, watches, cameras that were not necessarily new, but of the best brands. When I remarked about it, Rap laughed and said,

"You know another thing that Italians say? 'If it is stolen from you in Rome, you can always buy it back at Porta Portese.'"

"I don't want someone else's shoes, Rap."

"No, no, your shoes must be new. There is the stall. Now remember two things: you don't really like them and you don't really need them."

We began picking over the shoes as if we'd much rather be doing practically anything else. I was helped by the fact that I didn't know what sort of shoes we were looking for. Rap seemed to be interested in the tennis shoes.

"Not Reeboks," I whispered, "I like good ol' Spaldings, since I was a kid..."

"You don't want tennis shoes," Rap whispered back. "You need strong outdoor shoes. Timberlands, to walk with your uncle. They are over on the right. I will get to them. One must not show desire. Your size?"

"Eleven and a half. I think that's a 45 here."

"Mm. You are well-founded. Let me do it." He moseyed over and started fingering the Timberlands. The vendor moseyed over and asked him if he needed any help.

"*Quanto?*" asked Rap with supreme nonchalance.

"One hundred eighty thousand," answered the vendor flatly. "*Prima qualità.*"

Rap raised his hand as if to salute, but instead struck himself repeatedly between the eyes. This means "Have you gone mad?"

I did some fast mental money-changing. "That's not so much for Timberlands," I said. Rap was dumbstruck, but the vendor was ecstatic.

"No much, no much. Is *prima qualità.* You see!" And he thrust one of the shoes into my hands. I had to think fast.

"Very nice, very good," I said; "even 200,000 is an honest price. But today..." — here I handed the shoe back — "...today I wish to spend only 150,000."

The vendor smiled and asked Rap to translate. Rap did so, referring to me as "*Il professore.*"

The vendor stopped smiling. "Maybe 170,000," he said.

"No, no, they're worth 200,000." I insisted. "But I wish to spend only 150.000. I will go somewhere else. Let's go, Rap."

Rap translated, shrugging his shoulders as if to say that professors are eccentric, especially foreign ones. The vendor called me back.

"*Professore di che?*" he asked me.

"Of French," I answered. "*Français. Parlez-vous Français, Monsieur?*"

Without a word he gave me the shoes, and Rap gave him 150,000.

"Thank you very much," I said. "*Merçi beaucoup.*"

"*De nada,*" answered the vendor with a thin smile, as though all foreign languages were the same.

"You have talent," said Rap as we walked away. "You could be a good Italian. You have a sense of the *bella figura*, which is very important."

"*Bella figura*...?"

"The fine figure. You cut a fine figure with that man. Perhaps I could have got the shoes for even less with my tactic, but not with such a fine figure. The vendor was at a loss. *Una gran bella figura*. But now, please, you let me use my tactic, okay?"

So from then on Rap used his tactics, which were time-consuming and emotionally draining, but in the end I had Levi's jeans, a safari jacket like Jim's, and a hat like Crocodile Dundee's. I understood Rap's satisfaction: he hadn't just bought these things, he had fought for them and won them. I decided I wanted to show my gratitude by getting something for him. With my tactics. A belt, a flashy belt. I stopped at a table full of them.

"I think the belt you are wearing is sufficient..." Rap began.

"This isn't for me. It's for my cousin Rap, to remember me by. Which one do you think he'd like the most?"

Rap was delighted. "The most? Ah, he is a very particular man, extravagant, I think a little crazy...this one. And you know? I will have three reasons for liking this belt. First because I simply like it, then because it is from you, and last...because it symbolizes our common bond, my father, your uncle."

"It does?" It was a wide belt covered with brass studs. But Rap had no time to explain; the vendor, a big-bellied young man, had begun extolling the belt's merits to us.

"How much?" I asked when he finished. "25,000," he answered in Italian. Then he got a pad and wrote the figure for me.

"Very nice, very good," I said, "but today I wish to spend only 20,000."

I put the belt back on the table and slowly started

sliding away. Rap translated as he had with the shoes, shrugging and talking about "*Il professore.*"

"Twenty-five thousand," I heard the man repeat coldly. More than once. Rap soon joined me.

"This time it doesn't work," he said as we slid away together. "But that's okay, there are other stalls..."

"No. I want that belt."

"We can't go back now!"

"Why not?"

"Ah, Bob, you will never be an Italian."

"The *bella figura* business? That doesn't involve me. You stay here." I went back and handed the big-bellied young man 25,000 *lire*. His expression showed I had made his day, and not because of the money. I picked up my belt and walked away. I heard chuckling behind me.

"That's called 'American pragmatism,'" I said as Rap and I quickly left the market.

"In Italian we call it *figura di merda*," he replied. Then he laughed. "But yes. I will remember you better for it. Thank you very much, Bob; it is a fine present."

The jibe sounded unintentional, or friendly at most. So I just went on to what interested me.

"Okay, so how does this belt symbolize your father?"

"I really don't know. But sometime when you are alone with him, say that you gave me a belt covered with the heads of nails. Forty-four nails."

"Are there forty-four studs on the belt?"

"I don't know, it makes no difference. You say it, to see how he reacts, to get him to speak. With me he does not speak of these things, but sometimes he lets words fall, so I know that for many years he looked for certain nails, and that he found forty-four, and that they mean a lot to him."

"All right, I'll mention the belt. But not the way I

bought it," I added with a smile.

Rap laughed his easy laugh. "But I think it would make little difference to *Papà*. The figures that one cuts do not interest him. Remember, Bob," he added seriously, "your uncle knows many people, but essentially he has lived alone since the war. Even I was never close to him, never with him for long periods. He left me in schools, he left me with friends, he left me on my own. But I have no resentment. He did his best for me, he put me through the university, but he could not live with me. I think he was afraid to hurt me in some way. This is a kind of love, don't you think?"

"Yes, I suppose it is."

"He is not comfortable with people. He is a...strange man. You will have to make allowances. And you will have to be a little careful."

That evening Ilene and I gave our last performance together as ancient Romans. For the occasion Vittorio let Ilene do Messalina, and I did my Constantine bit again. They put an old mattress on the ground for "Massentius" to hit when he fell off the bridge, and he loved it. After the show I got two more kisses from Vittorio.

"*Adieu, mon ami*. You going back to America?"

"Yes. Not right away, but yes I am."

"I think you take back more than most Americans take back, *n'est-ce pas*?"

"You're right. Vittorio."

"You have been a part of Rome. Old Rome and today's Rome. *Non è vero*?"

"*Sì*. Yes. You're right. Thanks to you."

"*Sayonara*, Bob."

"*Addio*, Vittorio."

And early the next morning I had to say good-bye to Egidio. Two kisses and a bear hug. Rap had asked me to go along with Uncle Jim's story that he was only interested in hiring me as a salesman. No problem: I simply told Egidio that I had talked to "Giacomo" the night before, but his offer didn't interest me.

"I'm a French teacher, Egidio. I like teaching French. I'd be a terrible salesman."

"What was it that you would sell? I can't remember exactly what Giacomo said, he said so little..."

"Uh...a new explosive of some kind. For demolitions. And I have absolutely no experience..."

"But it was a lot of money, I'm sure. An important position to be so careful about finding the right man..."

"Well, yes...a lot of money. Much more than I am making. But...but I would have to travel, be away from my family — it's not the life for me, Egidio."

"I see. Well, it is still a little strange that the morning after you talk to him, you decide to leave..."

"I'll tell you the truth. I suspected that man might be my uncle! That's why I asked you about him! I was waiting for him to act!"

"No!"

"But now that this little fantasy is gone. I have no reason to stay in Rome. I have put together just enough money to have a look around Anzio and then catch a train to Paris."

"Old Giacomo would have been an ugly uncle for you. I'm glad it's not true. You go to Anzio, maybe you find a much prettier uncle, eh?" In the air he designed the shape he hoped my "uncle" in Anzio would have.

"I promise I'll look hard, Egidio, my friend."

"Bob, *mio* Bob, you have seen, eh? Rome is a good hooker. She took all your money, but she gave you a good time."

"Yes, she did. No complaints. All Americans should

get stripped clean the day they get here. I'm going to recommend it."

"Maybe not all. You are special, a good learner, you are good to...wing it."

"*Mi arrangio.*"

"*Bravo!*"

"But if I had been stolen blind in front of some other hotel...?"

"Only here. Recommend the Americans to come here. Perhaps I provide the service. I hire the criminals."

That gave me a big laugh. "In Rome, even this would be possible, I'm sure," I said. "But then, the first night here is always free."

"Also the first meal. Is important, the first lesson"

"*Ciao*, Egidio...*e mille grazie.*"

"*Ciao*, Bob, my friend. *In bocca al lupo.*"

"*In* what?"

"*In bocca al lupo.* Into the wolf's mouth. The best way to wish you good luck. Bob. It confuses the bad spirits. I hope you finish in the wolf's mouth."

I took a bus to Ilene's flat, where Rap was already waiting to take me to Jim on his motorcycle, a big, beautiful Gilera. He wasn't wearing the studded belt I had given him. He evidently didn't want Jim to see it and ask about it. Otherwise his clothes were the same as the day before. For all I knew he had spent the night there with Ilene, but that was no longer my business. They would be leaving together for Grazia di Curtatone that afternoon. A long haul on a motorcycle. An adventure for young people, a massive backache if I were to try it.

"Take it slow with her, Rap. Irish girls are fragile."

"Not a bit of it," said Ilene. "We're actually quite stout. Comes from drinking it."

"Drinking it?" Rap was perplexed.

100

"Sure, and you'll have to be teachin' the lad about Guinness, won't you now?" I said in my phoniest Irish accent.

"We'll all have some together in Rapallo," she answered. "If they have it. Won't we now?"

"RAPALLO, RAPALLO, WIDEN YOURSELF. PREPARE TO RECEIVE YOUR FAVORITE SON RAP AND HIS WILD IRISH ROSE!" I intoned.

"Kill him, Rap my dear, for he has dared to refuse my advances!" answered Ilene.

"Messalina, your perfidy knows no bounds," I ad-libbed. Rap was having trouble following all this.

"It's time to go, Bob," he said. "*Papà* is a punctual man."

I kissed Ilene on both cheeks. She kissed me on the mouth. Well, if I had refused her advances, it was because they hadn't been very convincing. Until too late. Games people play. Games need losers.

The Via Aurelia is the old Roman road along the Tyrrhenian coast to France. We picked it up just beyond the Janiculum hill. Five minutes later we came to where Jim was parked, under a Mediterranean pine, still within sight of St. Peter's.

His motor home was a big white whale. What really caused me to think of Moby Dick was the dark gray rubber boat strapped onto the roof. I could almost see Gregory Peck sitting there with a harpoon. I thought that might be a witty thing to say, if I discovered a sense of humor in Uncle Jim. Which didn't seem likely.

"Where you been?"

"Sorry, *Papà*, there is traffic this morning."

"When's the last time there wasn't? Well, come on, nephew. Let's get going."

I turned to my cousin and smiled. "So long. Rap. See

you in Rapallo."

"See you where?" said Jim sharply.

"In Rapallo, *Papà*. If you don't mind. Ilene and I are going on a little trip, and it will be easy for us to come to Rapallo if you tell us the day. We would like to see Bob again. You know, *Papà*, he is a good fellow, this cousin of mine! I think you will like him."

Jim looked extremely dour, seemingly at the suggestion that he might like me or anything else. But then he said, "Okay. Be at Rosaria's restaurant at 1 pm on the 15th. Can you make it?" As it turned out, Jim always looked dour when he thought, and he did a lot of thinking.

"We can make it easily, *Papà*. And we will have many things to recount to each other!"

"Well, have a good trip, Rap," I said, shaking his hand to avoid the kisses. "*In bocca al lupo.*"

"*Crepi il lupo!*" he answered with glee. The ritual answer, I later learned. Meaning something like "and may the wolf split open!"

CHAPTER IX

Tuscany gets its name from the Latin word
"Tusci" or "Etrusci"

Jim's motor home was called "*Crociato*," and on the inside it was plushy and roomy. It couldn't have been more than a year old.

"This isn't cramped at all!" I said.

"Over seven feet of headroom. That's why I got her. Have to stoop and hunch around in the other ones. Interior's pretty much custom-made. No sense in outfitting for six people. Two beds is plenty. Big ones."

"Doesn't *crociato* mean 'crucified'...?"

"Hell, no. Means 'crossed' in the sense of them soldiers that had crosses on their uniforms and went charging off to fight for God somewheres."

"The crusaders."

"That's it. This here van's a crusader."

"And it's your home."

"Ain't got no other."

"That makes you tough to get in touch with. I sent letters to the post offices in Anzio and Salerno."

"I never go there. If I have to give an address, I give Rap's in Rome. Hell, I know it's better to be settled down. I used to hate driving these things. Now I guess I'm used to it."

"Well, this is quite a bomb," I said, as we started off.

"Ain't no bombs on board right now, just a few mines."

"Mines? Rolling around in here?"

"They're defused and secured, Nephew. I'm dumb about a lotta things, but you can trust me on land mines. Been long dead if I didn't know what I was doing."

"All right, but why do you keep them around?"

Jim gave his attention to the traffic for a full minute before answering.

"I empty them, shine them up and sell them, or give them away. People like them for souvenirs, door-stops, what-not. Some people. Now listen, you might not be back to Rome. You might decide to leave from Genoa, so we better stop at the airport and pick up your old stuff. You got that locker key?"

"Right here someplace." Funny that I hadn't thought about my luggage. Maybe it really was "old stuff" to me. So we turned off the Aurelia onto the G.R.A., the Great Ring Road that circles Rome, and went to the Da Vinci airport where I got my things without any trouble. This didn't take us that far out of our way, because the airport is practically on the sea, so it was no trick to drive up to a little town called Palo and pick up the Aurelia just where it hits the coast. I settled into the big, comfortable swivel chair next to the driver with a map in one hand and my copy of "Italy in Your Pocket" in the other, and prepared to do some serious sight-seeing.

"What you got there?"

"A little guide book. To read up on what we see. It's called 'Italy in Your Pocket.'"

"That's where you should leave it."

"Listen, this is a one-shot deal for me, I'll probably never see these places again..."

"Guess I should've expected it. They said you were

104

hot stuff on that tour bus."

"You sure kept tabs on me, didn't you, Jim?"

"Yep. But now it's your turn. You're gonna find out a helluva lot more about me than I know about you. This ain't no tourist trip you're on. I'm gonna show you what Jim Savorski has been doin' over here since 1944."

"Shouldn't we start at the beginning? Shouldn't we start in Anzio?"

"Nope. That's where we'll finish. If...if you're still interested. If you stick with me."

"1944," I said slowly. "That's forty-four years ago. You know, I bought a belt for Rap at Porta Portese yesterday."

"That damn flea market. Is that where he took you to buy clothes?"

"We did fine. Anyway I let him pick out his belt, and he picked a big studded one, like movie cowboys used to have."

"Rap don't never do what you'd expect."

"He called the studs 'nail heads.' And he counted forty-four of them. That's why he liked it. He said it would remind him both of me and of you. I suppose it's because of 1944 being forty-four years ago, but why nails? He didn't say what nails have to do with you."

Jim's knuckles on the wheel were white. His face was turned away, I think deliberately. The man was fighting for control.

"Rap don't know nothing about the nails. One reason I ain't told him is that he's got a big mouth. Nephew, this is my story, you let me tell it, and we just might get around to the forty-four nails. But don't push me, boy."

"I'm sorry, Jim. I had no idea it was a sore point."

"I got lots of sore points."

"All right. I'll watch it. Thanks for calling me 'boy,' anyway. I haven't heard that in a while. I'm forty-five." I

105

was glad I wasn't forty-four.

"I know how old you are. I was there." He turned to look at me and cracked a smile. "You weren't so bad-looking as a baby."

"And you didn't look so bad in a uniform. I've got a picture to show you." So I went back to my new-found luggage and dug out the old photo of me as a baby with my mother and Jim. When I showed it to him he pulled over and stopped the *Crociato* to look at it. I made comments but he just kept looking. After about three minutes all he said was "Wish women would wear their hair that way again."

"So do I."

"How about if we stick her up here? I mean, just while you're along." Jim meant on a little clip just above the rear-view mirror.

"Fine by me. Add a little class."

So the tension had subsided. It never really disappeared in all the time I spent with Jim — it was too much a part of him. There was something taut in him that never relaxed, something he constantly returned to within himself. With me he made an effort to be outgoing, but his natural state was silence. In fact we proceeded in a silence that was broken only sporadically by small talk, mostly mine. I was going to wait, as he had asked, for him to tell his story. I waited past Civitavecchia and up to Tarquinia.

"This was an important Etruscan town, wasn't it?" I admit I was sneaking looks at my guide book.

"Yep."

"But we're not going to stop for a look."

"Nope. It's overrun by tourists in August." Silence again, then he went on. "I was in the Leopards' Tomb here once in August. It's got some of the nicest paintings.

I caught a kid, maybe sixteen, he was all set to draw a moustache on one of the dancers. I grabbed his hand just in time."

"What did you do, break it?" I said this lightly.

"I never found out. He sure screamed a lot. Anyway. I can't stand to see those things, so I don't go to places like that when there's so many people they can't keep an eye on them all. Ain't right to treat the dead like that, and especially not the Raséna."

"The who?"

"Oh, I call 'em that sometimes. It's their real name, it's what they called themselves. 'Etruscan' is a Roman word. Nothing wrong with it, but it ain't right to forget their real one. They feared that would happen. I don't know where they are now, but they might appreciate my using it."

"I suppose maybe they might. I suppose nobody wants his name forgotten. His real name."

Jim stopped talking. I kept looking out the window on my side, up at Tarquinia on its hill. "It looks like a medieval town," I said after a moment.

"What you're gawking at *is* a medieval town. The Etruscan town was about two miles northeast. There's just about enough left of it for a dog to take a leak on. Thousands of tombs. They got more tombs around here than Carter has pills, but you can hardly tell where the city was. It became Roman anyway. 'Tarquinia' is the Roman word. The Etruscans called their town 'Tarchna.'"

"Must not have been much, if there aren't any monuments left." This turned out to be another sore spot.

"Nephew, Tarchna had 100,000 people when Rome only had sheep! This here was the first city of the League of Twelve! Two kings of Rome were named Tarquinius! Does that tell you anything?"

107

It should have. I had even played a Tarquinius once as a Ghost of the Forum, but I hadn't made the connection. I moved things along: "Okay, then why is there only enough left for a dog...?"

"Hell, I ain't no expert. I only know a few things people have told me, and I know what I seen, and what I been able to dig up. I know what drivin' and sweepin' up and down this country have taught me. And I know for a fact that the Romans got real good at two things: building roads and wiping out Etruscans. This here's a Roman road..."

"I know that."

"I use the Roman roads whenever I can. That's most of the time, most all of them are still in use. Don't like those damn *autostrade*, whaddya call 'em..."

"Toll roads."

"They don't hardly get 'em built, and they start tearing them up for repairs; then you gotta pay for the privilege of creeping along single file."

"And I'll bet you can't see much. Boring, like the toll roads back home."

"Oh, they're boring all right. Course I wouldn't know about the ones back...Stateside. Didn't have them then. Hey, you getting hungry?"

"No, I can hang on."

"Ain't no need to hang on. Just go on back there and dig into the icebox or the cupboards or whatever, there's all kinds of stuff. Otherwise I thought we'd get out and have a bite at Cosa, about 30 miles up."

"No point in going to a restaurant, Jim, if you've got the makings for sandwiches..."

"Ain't no restaurants in Cosa. Just ruins."

"Etruscan ruins?"

"Nope. Cosa was a Roman colony. They used the

108

Etruscans as laborers to build it. Got a nice view though."

That turned out to be true. Cosa is up on a promontory called Ancedonia, overlooking the sea and the island of Monte Argentario, three miles out. To have our lunch we sat on a stone that Jim said was dedicated to Juno, the wife of Jupiter.

"The great mother-goddess," I commented lightly, "sort of like Rap's Madonnas — but a lot less virgin."

But there isn't too much you can say lightly with Jim. He took a big bite out of his cheese-and-tomato sandwich, to give himself time to think. I ate a sardine.

"Most people in America don't believe in much of anything anymore. I guess," he finally said.

"I wouldn't say that. In fact..."

"That's okay by me, nephew. I mean I respect your position, but I'm gonna expect you to respect mine. I think a man's convictions about the Next World always deserve respect."

"So do I, but..."

"And that includes respect for what the Raséna thought, and what the Romans thought, and what Rap thinks. Though to tell you the truth, I ain't never understood what Rap really believes."

"Maybe he just believes in art."

"I don't see how you can do that. Maybe he just believes in himself."

"Whatever it is, it seems to work for him. He's a...a rich person, full of life."

"I guess that ain't hay."

"You did a good job with him."

"By staying away from him. I ain't so full of life, nephew. But I taught him respect. And I sent him to good schools."

"Why did he do English at the University?"

109

"His idea. He loves to talk to strangers, to everybody, and I guess English is good for that. But the English he learnt from me was so bad people laughed at him. Now it's a damn sight better'n mine. But I don't need to talk much to do what I do."

"And what you do is sweep for mines. But you also come across other things, like Etruscan gold. Have I got the picture?"

Jim bit into a peach. "What do you think of that picture, nephew?"

I bit into an apple. "Well. I'd like to see you in action."

"You'll see me in action, if you stick with me. Not along the coast here. Years ago when I started you could still find mines and shells, especially all along from Pisa to La Spezia, but hell, it's all been developed for tourists, they've sifted and dug everything by now. Sometimes I swing through in October and do some beachcombing along with my visiting, but in August there's too damn many people. I don't usually come through here in August. Nobody will be expecting me. We'll leave it up to the Lord to decide who we should find. Just like when I sweep. He decides what I should find."

"I'd be curious to know how you got started..."

"How I got started! It was the U.S. Army's idea. They made me into a combat engineer. They taught me how to lay minefields. Then they give me a broom, an SCR 625, and taught me how to sweep them up."

"And after the war, you just kept on sweeping..."

"Nephew, hunnerds of Italians have died since the war from traps and mines and bombs and shells of all kinds left around. Mainly kids, that's what gets me. Kid sees one, calls his friends, they start pickin' at it...and there's still a lot of dangerous stuff that keeps turning up. Not like it was though, thank the Lord."

110

"So that's it? That's why you...disappeared? In order to stay on and try to save kids and people?"

"That sure sounds great, but it ain't quite the truth. And you ain't getting that today, nephew. If you're done, let's get going. Follonica's another fifty miles up the coast."

"Follonica?"

"I hope to find some people there. People you ought to get to know. It's a nice place."

I looked out at the big island with its resorts and restaurants, at all the pleasure boats, at the crowded beaches on the mainland, at the seafront parking lots packed with cars and buses. The ruins of Cosa seemed like an oasis above it all, of interest only to the reflective few. "It can't be as nice as it is up here," I said.

I was right. Follonica was nothing special. A seaside tourist town, like so many others. We got there at about six in the evening, but the sun was still hot and bright. The beach was a pretty thin strip. I got the impression that erosion was a problem there, the way it is at certain beaches in Chicago. The sea was a wide gulf, with the town of Piombino on one extremity, Punta Ala on the other, and Follonica set back in the middle. About fifteen miles straight out we could see an island: Elba, Jim told me.

"Where Napoleon did some time." I commented.

"Who?"

"Napoleon Bonaparte. The French general — you know."

"Guess I heard the name. Back in history, you mean."

"About two hundred years. Little less."

"I do better at two thousand years. Little more. I told you I'm dumb about a lotta things, nephew. Come on, let's go buy some fruit."

"Some fruit? There's still some peaches..."

"Yeah, but I can get a good deal here. I know the fruit-seller."

We got to an open fruit stand, four tables in a square, where the round and rosy lady in the middle was so busy she didn't see us until we were right behind her watermelons.

"*Ciao*, Agnese." said Jim softly. The big woman whirled around so hard she bumped the watermelon pile, but I averted a tragedy by throwing myself across them before they could rumble off the table top. "*Papà! Papà!*" she began to shout.

"*Papà?*" I shouted, and straightened back up. Immediately two watermelons rolled off the table and cracked open, one on my side and one on the woman's side.

"*Ferma i meloni*, Agnese! Stop the melons!" Jim shouted. So this time both Agnese and I threw ourselves over the watermelons and almost cracked our heads together at the summit of the pile.

"Bob, this here's Agnese, another cousin of yours."

"Pleased to meet you, Agnese." I said to the fat and happy face only four inches from mine.

"Agnese, *questo è* Bob, *tuo cugino americano*." said Jim, completing the introduction.

"*Mio cugino americano?*" Now she stood up, definitively abandoning the watermelons, and made for a corner space between two tables, picking up steam all the while, obviously trying to get to me, shouting "*Cugino! Cugino mio!*"

"*I meloni*, Agnese!" shouted Jim again.

"*All'inferno i meloni!*" she answered just as she reached me, still bravely trying to save my side of the pile. All for naught. She pulled me up and around and gave me a mighty hug. We embraced for the longest time, listening to the watermelons roll off the table. Jim half-heartedly saved a few, grumbling under his breath.

We cleaned up, loaded her fruit and tables into her little van and drove to her home. On the way we stopped at the fish market and bought the ingredients for *caciucco*, a kind of fish soup, a local specialty that Agnese was very proud of. Her home was a new fourth-floor apartment on the inland side of town, but up high enough to have a view of the sea. Agnese spoke no English; she had never lived or traveled with Jim as Rap had, and Jim had made no effort to teach her. Her mother was not the same as Rap's, but Agnese knew Rap, and she knew I existed, and she knew she was named after her American aunt, my mother Agnes. We got along fine, no thanks to Jim, who was a terrible interpreter. He would only translate what he considered important in whatever Agnese or I said, and that meant that rarely more than a few words ever got through. The fact was, even if I do say so myself, that my Italian had got to the point where I could understand most things, but when I spoke it was still rough going.

Agnese went to a bedroom and brought back a big Italian-English dictionary, the same kind I had used at Saverio's, so with that I was almost independent of Jim. The dictionary belonged to Teresa, Agnese's fourteen-year-old daughter, who was on vacation in the mountains. She studied English at school. Jim was unhappy about not seeing her and about not seeing Agnese's husband, a merchant sailor who was on his way to Buenos Aires.

"Course he's a hard man to find at home," said Jim, "but I was hoping you'd at least meet Teresa, she's a cute little devil. Looks like her grandmother." Agnese got out some pictures of her mother, taken in 1952, the year Jim met her. "Very pretty," I said sincerely. "*Molto bella*. And now, where...?"

"She died eight years ago," Jim said. "Listen, you two seem to do all right, and that fish soup needs to be stirred a lot. I'm gonna go keep an eye on it."

Jim wanted us to talk, he wanted me to learn whatever I could from Agnese, and he didn't want to interfere. He was leaving things up to the Lord again. Either that, or it was too hard for him to tell his own story. I found out that in 1952 Agnese's mother was already thirty years old, and a widow — her husband had died at Anzio. At the news of his death she had gone to pieces, to the point of letting herself get involved with a German officer — or perhaps with more than one. I'm not too sure about Italian plurals. And after the war she was no longer considered respectable.

She had a fruit stand, the same fruit stand, and one day, to be biblical about this, she gave her fruit to young Jim. No hard feelings afterwards. He had told her right off that he was a *vagabondo* who would never settle down. When Agnese was born he started sending or bringing money regularly. And the year after her mother died, her *papà* did her a *grande favore, grande, grande* — but I couldn't get her to explain. He still came through every year or so and always brought something for her.

At this point in her story she sealed her lips with a finger to keep me quiet and went to her bedroom. She soon came back with a ring, a man's ring like a class ring. She handed it to me and softly said that it was finely wrought gold. The red stone in the center had a naked male figure engraved onto it, holding a weapon of some kind. "Etrusco," Agnese whispered. Then she held her right hand out, palm up, and kept making as if trying to snap her fingers without succeeding. I knew this gesture from shopping in Rome. It meant "lots of money." I agreed.

"Agnese, *vieni qua, per me la zuppa è pronta!*" shouted Jim from the kitchen. Agnese slipped the ring into her apron pocket and hustled into the kitchen. Jim was right, the fish soup was ready, and it was delicious. Jim had a big helping. I had two. Agnese had three. I liked this new cousin. This new threat to my inheritance. She took such pleasure in so many things — especially in having company. Even Jim almost relaxed.

But he wouldn't spend the night there. We had to go back and sleep in the motor home. Agnese didn't insist — she evidently knew it was no use. As she gave me her farewell hug, I thought about exchanging addresses and telephone numbers with her, and promising to keep in touch — but I let it go. I silently memorized her address as we left. I still didn't know how much of all this I would want people to know about in the States. Discretion, as my father had asked. I was getting my feet wet, but I could still towel them off.

"I'm sorry, but I don't never sleep in other people's homes," said Jim when we got back to the *Crociato*.

"Not even your own daughter's?"

"Especially not there. I don't feel right. I don't feel like I have a right. I mean, the Lord let her be born to be a help to her mother, not to me."

"That's a little crazy. She thinks the world of you. She talked about a big favor you did her once. The year after her mother died. Couldn't get her to say what it was."

"Course not. I told her not to tell anybody."

"So that means I'll never know?"

Five minutes later, when we were both in bed with the lights out, Jim gave his answer: "Maybe I'll show you tomorrow morning."

115

CHAPTER X

Over three million Riegel mines were produced between 1943 and 1945.

We were back on the Via Aurelia by eight o'clock the next morning.

Jim had become very Italian about one thing — breakfast. Hot black coffee that you had to swallow fast before it could dissolve your dental work.

And that was it.

I ate a plain piece of bread and told Jim I wanted to shop for jam and butter sometime during the day.

"You can buy food where we're going now. I told you I'd show you the favor I did for Agnese. But you gotta keep it to yourself. To protect her. You never know with those bastards."

"Which bastards?"

"The ones that had set up this little protection racket all along the coast here. They wanted a percentage from all the street stands — the candy sellers, toy sellers, souvenir sellers..."

"And fruit sellers."

"You got it. They came around to Agnese, and she said no, and they came back and slapped her around hard, and told her that next time they'd go looking for her little girl. Couple days later I happened along. One side of her face was all bruised and swollen. Still remember that."

116

"Well, what did you do?"

"You know, I'm telling you this 'cause I'm thinking that you know what it is when your blood calls out and tells you something. I mean, there are times when a man becomes a sword in the Lord's hand."

"I'm not so sure about that, Jim."

"Neither am I....Well, let's see what you think of this. I asked around and found out that these bastards had their headquarters in Piombino, in a body shop on the outskirts of town. I'm gonna turn left up here and take you to see where it was. Seems they were also in the stolen car business. It was one of those things — everybody knew about these guys, but they couldn't be touched. Not enough evidence, or something."

"Or plenty of payola."

"Well, whatever. Anyway, I had two Riegel mines in the van. Not this van, the old one. This one ain't even a year old..."

"Jim, what did you do with the mines? How much of the law did you take into your own hands?"

"Oh, I left it pretty much in the Lord's hands. All I did was reactivate the Riegels and put them in the body shop."

"How'd you manage that?"

"Just drove in. Told them I wanted to have the van repainted. Told them I didn't know what color. When the guy went looking for his color charts I just took out the mines and set them on the floor, close to the stairs that led to the offices over the shop. Then I just told the guy I didn't like his colors and drove away."

"Okay, so what's a Riegel mine?"

"An anti-tank mine with about nine pounds of TNT. But it doesn't look like any other mine. It's shaped like a plank of wood — and sometimes they colored them to look like wood. The ones I had were gray with a handle at the end, looked like they might be tool containers of some sort. To set them off you have to roll over them with 450 pounds of pressure. But I put an anti-removal detonator under them. All they had to do was pick one up."

"All they had to do was...?"

"That's all they had to do. Boom."

"You call that leaving things in the Lord's hands?"

"One of those guys might have been through the war. Somebody could have recognized those mines."

"But nobody did."

"Nope, nobody did. I was three miles away when I heard the blast."

"How many of them did you get?"

"No idea. Never wanted to know. There was a fire. But I do know there ain't no more 'protection' around here."

We soon got to where the body shop had been. Now there was a small supermarket. I went in, bought my jam and butter, and got out quick.

I decided to try to take things in stride. Too much shock on my part, and Jim would button right back up. I didn't want that. And not just for the inheritance.

"Well, in any case," I said as we headed back towards the Aurelia. "Agnese is a fine person and...I can certainly understand that you can't just let people rough her up like that."

"Hell, no. She's my daughter."

"Which...which raises a point, Jim. Have I got any other Italian cousins besides Rap and Agnese?"

"Don't know. You got any other uncles over here?"

"I doubt it."

"Then you probably ain't got any other cousins."

"I was starting to wonder. I got the impression that

Agnese wonders about it, too. She suspects she has half-brothers and half-sisters all over Italy."

"I guess I sort of let her think that. Saw she liked it."

"But it isn't true."

Jim looked over at me before answering. "Far as I know. But I've known a few women, though. Women that had it tough. You give a little consolation, and one thing leads to another."

So Agnese was presumably my only competition, if Rap really wanted nothing. But I decided to refrain from asking Jim unseemly questions about the inheritance, at least until I knew more about it. Maybe it was much ado about next to nothing.

"So where's our next stop?" I asked, settling back with the map and guide book. "Another girl you gave some consolation to?"

"Nephew, try to get me on the first bounce. I ain't no Don Giovanni. That clear?"

"Okay, okay, just a little humor there. So where are we heading?"

"Viareggio. A pretty good hike, about ninety miles."

"Hey, wait a minute. We'll be going right by Pisa!"

"Yep."

"Well, can't we stop and see it? I mean, the Leaning Tower..."

"That damn thing'll come down some day, and it'll be a day like today, when it's crawling with people."

"But I'd at least like to have a look at it! Without going inside — we're going to stop someplace for lunch, aren't we?"

"That ain't the best place, nephew, with a million people around." He put on the dour face again for a few minutes. "I s'pose we can give her a try," he finally said.

But the closer we got to Pisa, the less Jim liked the

idea of driving into the city in the heart of the tourist season. By the time we got there, we had reached a compromise: we would stop at Marina di Pisa, the beach where the Arno River, from Florence and Pisa, finally empties into the sea. After lunch I would take the shuttle bus eight miles inland to Pisa and back, while Jim "did some work" inside his motor home.

We found a very good place to park, off the road in a grove of trees — so good that Jim said we might as well spend the night there, and I could take my time in Pisa.

"You're sure this doesn't foul up your schedule?"

"No, we got some leeway. I always give myself and the Lord some leeway, case something comes up."

"Well, I appreciate it."

"But I wouldn't go up to the top of that thing if I was you."

I found that it was easy to agree with Jim when I actually saw how far that tower is leaning. No wonder it's the most photographed building in the world. People want pictures of it before it topples. But my book said it isn't due to drop for years yet, so I stood right under it. I felt no particular desire to trudge up to the top.

While I stood there I got included in at least a hundred pictures, not counting videos. A kind of immortality, better than scratching my name on the walls.

Then a little old man backed into me. His picture was being taken by a younger man about fifty yards away.

The younger man laughed. The old man turned and said: "*Pardon, Monsieur. Je vous n'avais pas vu.*"

"*Il n'y a pas de quoi, Monsieur,*" I answered. And we got to talking, while the younger man, his son, went up to take pictures from the top.

They were on their way down south, past Rome, to Gaeta, Sorrento, places like that, so that his son could do some scuba diving — and be shown where his father had fought the Second World War with the French Expeditionary Corps, under General Juin. This Juin ate Nazis for breakfast, according to the old man. But evidently the Nazis liked big breakfasts too, because he was also going to look through the military cemeteries for his fallen comrades. Ten thousand of them.

"Dix milles? Dix milles francaises?" I asked. I didn't think the Free French had put that many men in the field, let alone got them killed in one campaign.

"Oui. C'etait très dur, la-bas."

"Et combien des Américains?"

"Morts? Je ne sais pas. Beaucoup."

The old man's son came down safely from the tower and took his father away, leaving me to wonder how much of Jim's story was buried in military cemeteries. The old Frenchman said a lot of Americans had died down there, but he didn't know how many. Could the attraction that an old soldier feels for his dead companions ever be strong enough to keep him from going home?

I stood there wondering, right under the Leaning Tower, getting my picture taken again and again, when sure enough, somebody else backed into me. Another old guy.

"Sorry, friend — didn't see you." he said. His accent was southern American. The younger man taking his picture from fifty yards away started to laugh.

"That's my son." the man said.

"I know."

"You know?"

"Uh...you look alike. Going up to the top?"

"You bet! What's the point, otherwise?"

That came as a disappointment, but then the man's

son reached us, and I learned that he had no intention of going up, having done it before, so he ended up waiting with me while his father made the climb. A nice fellow, about my age, and what he had to say was just as interesting as the old Frenchman's story.

He was on his way south, but to show his father the sights, not to visit old battlegrounds and cemeteries. He lived in Italy. He had been sent over by Chase Manhattan to do a three-year stint in Milan, but in the end he had married an Italian and refused to leave. Luckily he had found a job in an Italian bank, but he was making a lot less.

"So you're staying here for love of a girl. That's very romantic," I said.

"Not exactly. I think I fell in love with the girl to have a good reason for staying here. I love this country. You know what the UN says?"

"No. What does the UN say?"

"They did this global study, years and years, to catalog all the monuments and works of art that must be considered of world importance, essential to man's heritage — and you know what? Forty-five percent of them are in Italy. I'm saying 45 percent!"

"And that's why you're staying here?"

"Do you know how much there is of world importance in North Carolina?"

And so, when the man's father got back down and they went away, I was again left to wonder. Not about the monuments in North Carolina, but about the importance of such things for Jim. I would no sooner stay in Italy for its monuments than I would pitch a tent in an art museum, but Jim was certainly into his Etruscan thing — maybe enough to keep him here. Maybe that was the heart of it.

122

That evening after an early supper — Jim barbequed a chicken — we went for a walk along the shore. The sun was still shining hard from the west, but most of the bathers had left.

"Pisa's a nice town, Jim."

"S'pose so."

"Italy's full of beautiful things."

"Oh, there's a good bit around, I'm sure."

"Enough to make a man forget to go home. I met one today. He..."

"That ain't it, nephew. That sure ain't why I'm here. I don't hardly see all that stuff. Know what I see? Take a look out there."

We were right at the mouth of the Arno. The blue sea was brown for a mile out.

"Pollution, Jim. No surprise."

"Nope. But it's just one more thing that shouldn't be there. Like the mines. And that's the sort of stuff I see."

"If that's all you see, it must make for a tough life."

"Yep. Ain't no way to be."

"But you see the Etruscans. I mean, you're interested in what they left behind."

"It ain't their stuff so much. Hell. I sell most of it, or give it away. It's them I'm trying to get at. They knew something I need to know."

"Something about what?"

Jim turned, and we started the long walk back towards the *Crociato*.

"So did you go up to the top of that tower in Pisa?" he asked.

"No. I stayed on the ground and talked to people. I took your advice."

"Worst thing you can do. Only thing I know about is mines, World War II explosives. Don't pay no attention to

123

me otherwise."

That meant Jim didn't want to talk about his Etruscans. I tried World War II. "Another guy I talked to was an old Frenchman, a soldier under General Juin. On his way down to visit war cemeteries."

"Did he tell you about the End Run?"

"End Run? No. Wouldn't sound right in French, anyway. End run around what?"

"Around the Gustav Line. Helluva move. The Germans didn't think you could swing an army through the Aurunci Mountains. Nobody did, for months. We just kept banging our heads at Cassino..."

"Was that before you went to Anzio?"

Jim walked on a minute. "I gave you the wrong idea, saying 'we.' I never fought at Cassino, just Anzio. They was two different fronts. Simultaneous. Coordinated. But everybody said 'we.' It was all of us against all of them, nephew. You gotta see it. I mean, if you want to go ahead with this, and find out something about me. About what we were up against, about the things we had to do."

"And a lot of you are still down there. Buried."

"Yep. The ones that didn't keep their heads down."

CHAPTER XI

The Gothic line consisted of 200 miles of fortified defense, from Carrara on the Ligurian sea to Pesaro on the Adriatic.

Viareggio has a nice big beach, and the water looked reasonably clean. I felt unreasonably dirty, so I told Jim I wanted to put on my suit and go for a swim before lunch.

"With all them people? Listen, if you just want to get clean, my little shower here in the *Crociato* does the trick just fine."

"I'll use that when we're inland. Here I'd rather take advantage of the Mediterranean. And I saw they've got public beach showers, for after my swim. I won't be long."

Another thing I had seen was that about half the women on the beach were topless. I wanted to test my cool. I decided to walk among the crowd until my hands stopped sweating. That took a while, but in the end I got pretty nonchalant. The next test would be to talk to one of them. I picked out a beauty, put together an Italian phrase and eased up beside her.

"*Oggi è una bella giornata,*" I said calmly with my slight accent, which I figured would add to my charm.

Well, it was a nice day, but I admit this was not a dazzling opener; still it didn't make any difference.

"You're American, aren't you?" she answered. "I hope what you just said was polite. I wouldn't do this back in

Wichita." And with that she strategically folded her arms.

"That is Wichita's great loss, my dear," I said, then bowed and strolled down into the sea, feeling smoother than Yves Montand.

Jim had prepared another frugal lunch, which we ate monastically in the shade of the *Crociato*, parked, as usual, far from the wading crowd. I had no complaints. I was getting rid of some of the weight I had put on at Saverio's. Then we walked to a children's park.

"Like it?" Jim asked.

"Nice. Small but nice. I like the train." A miniature train ran around the perimeter of the park, hauling about thirty little kids at a time.

"Yep. Come on over and meet the engineer."

Jim meant the little old man who was running the kiddie train, sitting astride the engine and blowing the whistle at the two pedestrian crossings. But when he saw us he blew it long and loud.

"*Ciao*, Giacomo!" he said as he pulled into his little "station."

"*Ciao*, Nando. How've you been?" Jim said this in Italian, but I'm translating. As I say, I could understand the simple stuff pretty well by now.

"Fine, fine. Good season for the train. I've got a bridge over the fish pond now, did you see?"

"Looks real good. This here's my sister's boy. From America. Name's Bob."

"A pleasure, Bob."

"The pleasure is mine, Mr....Mr...."

"Nando. Just Nando. All the kids, everybody calls me Nando."

"It must be nice."

"My job? It's all I want. It keeps me out of trouble." He said this with a smile, and with a look at Jim.

"Nando! Nando!" — little voices were starting to call out — "Let's go, Nando! All aboard!"

"All right, all right! Only a moment! Giacomo, can we have supper together this evening? At Giuseppe's?"

That sounded like a fine idea to me, but Jim said, "Sorry, Nando, we're on a schedule. Just passing through."

"Always just passing through, Giacomo. Bob, try to convince your uncle to settle down. He's getting old."

"Nando!" a child cried. "Blow your whistle!" And he did.

"*Ciao*, Bob. Bring your uncle back at eight this evening and we will have a good meal, and talk."

"That won't be easy. *Ciao*, Nando."

Then the two old men affectionately tugged each other by the left ear, in silence!

"All aboard!" the Italian abruptly shouted. "*In carrozza! Si parte!*" And the little train slowly started off. Jim led me over to sit down with him on a bench that circled a palm tree right in the middle of the park.

"Did you meet Nando during the war, Jim?"

"No. Hell, no, I tracked him down here forty years ago. He was real down-and-out then. But when he was young he was a *gerarca*. Know what that is? A big-shot Fascist."

The one-time *gerarca* blew his train whistle, and his smallest passengers clapped their hands.

"You tracked him down…?"

"He wasn't here during the war. He was in Ferrara. Gung-ho, very good at his job. He's never regretted that. What he regrets was personally recruiting an infantry company to send with the ARMIR, the Italian army on the Russian front. He really believed in his cause, in Mussolini. I don't see how he's all that much to blame.

127

Anyway only three of those boys he sent ever returned from Russia. And it didn't do them any good. They got sent to fight us on the Italian Front. One died in Anzio, the other two got theirs later, near Bologna. That hurt Nando pretty bad: he thought anybody who made it back from Russia shouldn't have had to fight any more. But the Germans was in charge by then."

The train was in the station, changing passengers. When it pulled out Nando had a two-year-old in his lap.

"'Course he got the hell out of Ferrara and never went back. Just kind of bummed around after the war. I found him here, and it happened they was building this park. The train was his idea. I just put up the money. I thought he'd go crazy with all those kids every day, but I was wrong. Means a lot to him."

"Why can't we stay and talk to him tonight at that restaurant he said?"

"Talk about what? All he talks about is his kids on that train. He don't talk about Ferrara hardly at all."

"Maybe you don't ask the right questions."

"I don't ask questions, period. Man wants to talk about things like that, he will in his own good time. But we ain't got forever. I just wanted you to meet him, and see the park."

"Jim, you tracked him down, and you found him here. What does that mean? Why were you looking for him?"

"I owed him something. I owed a lotta people. Just want you to meet a few, to get an idea."

"I don't understand..."

"You will."

"If I could talk to Nando..."

"Just look at him, you'll learn more."

We sat in silence for another few minutes before

128

leaving, watching the train go round. Nando's eyes sparkled with the same simple delight as the children riding around behind him in his kiddie-ride.

Our next stop was Marina di Carrara, only about fifteen miles up the Aurelia. "You want somebody to talk to," Jim said as we drove slowly along the busy stretch of road, "I got just the man for you here in Carrara. The Captain — a retired sea-captain. Cargo ships, hauling that marble all over the world. He'll talk your leg off. He's missing one, so he does it to even the score. Drives me nuts. I'll go for a walk with Romeo."

"Who's Romeo?"

"Someone that don't ask questions. One thing, though: don't talk about me owing him anything. The Captain don't know nothin' about that anyway."

We found the Captain where Jim thought we would, sitting on a stone ledge at the end of a long pier, watching the big freighters loading — and unloading giant blocks of stone. That gave me a handy question to ask, at the right time. The old man wore a white suit and a panama hat, and the big dog beside him was brownish red.

"Hello, Captain. Hello there. Romeo," said Jim.

"Giacomo! You old son of a bitch!" the Captain said in good round English. Romeo started to growl. I stopped in my tracks.

"Who's your friend, Giacomo?"

"This here's my sister's boy, name of Bob. From America. Just passing through."

"Take this, Bob, and give it old Romeo here." The old man reached into a plastic bag that just emerged from his jacket pocket and handed me a minnow, which I looked at for a moment and then offered to the dog. He gulped it down and licked my hand.

"There, now Romeo's your friend, Bob. Giacomo's

nephew! It's hard to think anyone could be related to this old boar. So Giacomo, how are you? I see you still haven't found a mine with your name on it."

"I see you still love to talk, Captain."

"In English, Giacomo, I love the chance to speak some English. Since I retired my English is going to hell."

"It sounds fine to me," I said. I was busy patting Romeo, and wondering whether minnows would work with some other dogs I knew. "Do you speak English to Romeo?" I asked.

"All the time. But he answers in German." I laughed, the Captain laughed, and Romeo barked. Jim cracked open a smile.

"Poor dog needs less talkin' and more walkin'," he said. "Let me take him around a bit, so's you can talk the ear off my nephew here, and it won't hurt nobody else. He's a pretty good yapper himself."

"Go on, go on, take my dog, find a nice tree for him. Here, take the bag of fish."

"Don't want your fish. Gonna get him some red meat, food that's fit for dogs."

"He gets enough. I let him bite a tourist every day. Go on, get lost for a while."

So Jim and Romeo left, and I sat down next to the Captain, who smelled of the fish in his pockets. For openers I used the question I had prepared:

"Why are they unloading marble here in Carrara? Isn't that like selling ice to the Eskimos?"

"First place, that isn't marble you're looking at here in front of us. That's onyx, from Mexico. But if you sit here long enough, you'll see every kind of stone come in here. Hate to admit it, but the stone carvers of Carrara are some of the best in the world, and they don't work just their own marble."

130

"Why do you hate to admit it?"

"Because they can be slower than hell. I have spent months waiting to be loaded in this port. That's how I got to know the town, and to like it. That's why I live here now: I got so used to it."

"Where are you from?"

"From Cremona. The town of Stradivarius."

"Where's Cremona?"

"In the Po Valley, my boy." There was a tone in his voice that I sometimes used in class. It meant "You're not too bright, are you?" He sighed and continued. "Some of the best farmland in the world."

"So how come you went to sea?"

Another tone came into his voice. This was a story he liked to tell. The story of a young foot soldier in World War II, drafted off his father's farm, fighting for his country. Doing his duty. Obeying orders. Serving his king, serving his Duce, but anxious to get home, back to a girl named Fulvia, back to plowing his fields.

Instead he plowed North African sand from El Alamein to Bengasi to Tripoli. And from there he went to Sicily, but so did Patton and the 7th Army. Then he was pulled back to Salerno to prepare a welcome for Mark Clark and the 5th Army.

"There I was, all ready for your invasion, but then came September eighth." He chuckled and shrugged. He waited for me to say something. Evidently at this point in the story the listener is supposed to intervene.

All I could say was "So what happened on September eighth?"

He looked at me for a moment, then said slowly, "September eighth. September 8, 1943." Then he smiled and waited for the dawn to break over me.

"That's the year I was born," I said.

"Not your fault," he said after a moment. "I mean, it's not your fault, why should it mean anything to you? But for all Italians, the ones who remember, it was the worst of all our days. The Armistice with you had been signed. But secretly. Five days before. No one knew. The Prime Minister recorded the message, then left Rome. 'Every hostile act against the Allies must cease. Attack from any other quarter must be opposed.' I was standing with three Germans! I handed my rifle to one, and walked away. The phone rang. I started to run. Sirens, shots. It was dark. I ran the wrong way. Right into the minefield we had prepared for Mark Clark."

Then he reached down and knocked hard on his right leg, or rather on what was taking its place. "Good luck for me. I was sent home, not to a German war plant to work, not to Anzio to die. But I couldn't work in the fields. I only had a wooden stick, a peg. The peg would sink into the soil. No good. I went to sea. The deck of a ship is hard. I was a good sailor, under many flags, with many crews. I learned my English, good everywhere. I became a captain." He stopped.

"What about the girl named Fulvia?" I asked.

"No. That part wasn't lucky. The mine did me damage. I couldn't have children. But we are still friends. One of her sons sailed with me. In Rotterdam once, he..."

"Uh, could you first tell me about my uncle? I mean, how did you get to be friends?"

"You know how your uncle spends his time, don't you?"

"Looking for mines and things in the ground."

"Yes, my boy, and this is the area where the Gothic Line reached the sea. There used to be lots of mines and things in the ground around here. Also in the water."

"The Gothic Line. A German defensive line."

"Yes. Hitler liked to draw lines on maps. He drew lots of them. But in Italy he only drew two important ones, to be held at all costs: the Gothic Line and..."

"And the Gustav Line."

"Very good! You've been talking to Giacomo; he knows a lot about that line. It was bad enough up here. But down there it was really terrible."

"And you met my uncle...?"

"Yes, I saw him sweeping north of here one day, maybe twenty years ago, the year before I became a captain. I was walking my dog, not this one, of course, and I started talking. I have a curious nature. Your uncle likes dogs. We became friends. We have talked a lot about the war, about Anzio. I wasn't there, thank God; my best friend, who was not lucky enough to get a leg blown off before, he got killed in Anzio. I have no brothers, only sisters, but that man was closer to me than a brother. And I lost him. My greatest loss, in a long life. And maybe Giacomo has suffered some terrible loss, but for all we have talked together, I don't know much about the man. Your uncle is strange."

"Do you think it's true what you said, that he's looking for a mine with his name on it?"

"I don't know what he's looking for. But he's never content with where he is. Never really happy, always has to go."

"Maybe he wants to go home. But he doesn't think he can." This thought of mine must have made an impression, because the old man fell unusually silent. But then he said, "Giacomo never talks about his home. Are you from the same place in America?"

"No, he's from a small town in downstate Illinois. I'm from Chicago, more or less."

"Ah! I took a shipment of Carrara marble to Chicago

133

once. Through the St. Lawrence and those enormous lakes, one hell of a trip, but I enjoyed it. Chicago is a good port, a good town, but my men said the girls were expensive."

"That's because they've got class."

"Yes, I suppose. How did that building finally look? I mean the one I brought the marble for, the...the Standard building. I think..."

"Big Stan. Looks fine. You sure were late with that marble, though."

"I told you, they are slower than hell here. I think if you make lots of statues, you start to move like a statue."

It was late when Jim finally brought Romeo back from their walk, but I didn't mind. I had enjoyed my conversation with the old captain. He had told me many stories, but not that much about Jim — probably that's why I'd been "allowed" to talk to him. But I wondered if I had missed anything. I decided to ask Jim straight out that evening as we were turning in.

"Jim, just why were you anxious for me to talk to this old guy? What was I supposed to find out?"

"Nothin' much. Thought you both like to talk, that's all. Didn't he tell you about his leg?"

"He sure did."

"And he didn't step on much, probably just a little S-150, else he wouldn't be tellin' anybody about it. Everything you can find out about mines is gonna help you with me, nephew."

"And that's it?"

Jim turned off the lights without answering. Two minutes later his voice came through the darkness. "Didn't he mention Anzio?"

"He said his best friend got killed there. Man, I didn't realize so many Italians were involved at Anzio. I thought it was the Allies against the Germans, but just about everybody I talk to has somebody that got killed..."

"Wasn't all that many Italians," said Jim.

"Well, Agnese's mother, what was her name?"

"Silvia."

"Her first husband was killed at Anzio. And that soldier from Ferrara you told me about, the one that Nando tried to protect, and now the Captain's friend..."

"Yep."

"I get it."

"'Bout time."

"You had something to do with the way those people died in Anzio."

"Yep."

"That's why you feel you owe something to their...their friends and relatives."

"Yep."

"What did you do for the Captain?"

"How do you think he got to be captain? Course he don't know about it. I learned pretty quick to keep these things quiet."

"How did you do it? Money?"

"Nope. Made him look real good, with a harbor mine I found right near here."

"Good Lord, Jim!"

"Nobody got hurt!"

I lay there a few minutes thinking things out.

"Jim, what about Egidio? Now that I think about it, he told me his brother got killed at Anzio."

"How do you think he got that hotel?"

CHAPTER XII

*In order to reach Corniglia, one of the Cinque Terre,
you must climb the Lardarina, a flight of stairs
with 33 ramps and 382 steps.*

The next day we got off to a particularly early start, and soon I was looking hard into the hills behind Carrara as we sped away north on the Aurelia again. Many of the slopes were scarred by hundreds of years of quarrying marble, and I was trying to imagine Michelangelo clambering up and down, looking for just the right block for his Moses, or his David, or whatever. Assuming that's what he did. Anyway it was nice to think about, and fun to be heading north on the Aurelia on a beautiful summer morning. I had decided to be very...flexible about Jim's unfolding story. That quality was much appreciated in me, according to Rap.

"Where are we heading today, Jim?"

"Little place called Vernazza. It's one of the Cinque Terre, the five fishing villages between La Spezia and Levanto. Hard place to get to."

"What's there?"

"Some people. An old guy. Old fisherman named Steno."

"Has he got a dog for you to walk while I talk to him?"

"Steno ain't no big talker, no sir." Jim made a noise that could have been a form of laughter.

"That's why you like him."

"Yep. One of the reasons. He's some fisherman."

"And you like to fish."

136

"Every so often. Steno taught me everything I know about it."

"And you use the boat strapped on our roof."

"Well it ain't for water-skiing."

"I thought you went out after floating mines now and then. Like the one you used to...help the captain."

"No, that ain't my line. The mine I found was a fluke, it had broke from its mooring in the Bay of La Spezia and washed ashore, and was hid real good, half-buried and covered with driftwood. Only found a couple like that. You can see the bay comin' up on the left here. The navy, they swept the whole thing real good soon as we took it, 'cause they needed it fast. Helluva job for them. Back in '44 there were so many mines floating out there an eel couldn't slip through. Biggest naval base in Italy. Germans thought we might land here 'stead of at Anzio."

"Pretty heavily defended, huh?"

"Well, there were two Italian divisions, and their own 42ⁿᵈ Jäger..."

"Wait, hang on. It's time for me to get clear on this. We're talking about '44, but on September 8, 1943, the Italians broke with the Germans, so how come all these Italians were still...?"

"September 8. Sounds like the captain did teach you a few things. It's real simple. Not all the Italians broke with the Germans. There was Italian units on their side right to the end."

"But sometimes they didn't have much of a choice."

"Maybe. That don't help the guys they killed."

"If you hold it against them, why are you helping?"

"Nephew, there'll be a time and a place for everything, if you just hang on. Talk is cheap. Rather show you." And Jim lapsed back into his usual silence until we were in downtown La Spezia, which is a pretty

137

good-sized place. Then I noticed that we were getting off the Aurelia and heading for the beachfront.

"Now you're gonna see another reason besides fishing why I carry this boat around," he finally said.

That meant we had to get it off the *Crociato* and into the water. Luckily Jim knew a spot where we were able to park only thirty feet from the beach.

"Hey, Jim, how on earth do you manage this alone?" I asked between grunts as we muscled the boat down.

"Oh, I got a way of raising and lowering it with ropes and a pulley. And I got a little dolly I can wheel it around on. But with two men it's quicker just to heft it."

Jim had a Johnson motor which he got out and fastened to the sternboard, and with a low putter we headed away from the shoreline.

"Good thing for me that rowing isn't quicker," I said.

"It's better for fishing, but we ain't fishing."

"Just what are we doing?"

"We're goin' to Vernazza. Like I told you, it's one helluva place to get to by road, 'specially with a big thing like I drive, but it's no trick at all with a boat. There's still lots of little places like that along here, pretty much cut off, and I like 'em. No crowds. No bazaars. They're real places like they was, with men who fish."

Jim picked up speed and it became hard to converse, which had to be another big plus for the boat in Jim's book. We slipped between the island of Palmaria and the tip of the promontory that closed the Bay of La Spezia and opened up the huge Gulf of Genoa, which gently curved out of sight, to France.

Soon the "Cinque Terre" began coming into view: Riomaggiore, spilling down to the sea together with its little river, Manarola, inching down its steep coast, but unable to touch the sea, so that its fishing boats have to be hoisted to and from the water. Corniglia, high on its cliff, seeming to scorn the sea, and to center its attention on the big white church in its middle, then Vernazza.

"I can't see the fifth village," I shouted over the motor.

"Monterosso," Jim shouted back. "Ain't more'n two miles down, and it's the biggest of the five, but it's got its own little inlet, so it ain't that easy to see from here."

I concentrated my attention on Vernazza. As we drew closer I got the impression of a happy place, where men have had a successful partnership with nature for a long, long time. All the houses were plastered and painted in bright colors, reds, greens and yellows. All except the two most important buildings, the great, gloomy castle on the left and the stern little church on the right. Under the severe gaze of these two parents the village scrambled down the slopes to a tiny port, a tiny piazza, and four tiny trees.

We pulled the boat up onto the pebble beach and headed straight for a red house with a portico that marked the farthest point of the piazza. In the shade of the portico, at a table with a bottle of mineral water, sat a man about sixty with warts on his big brown nose.

"That's Steno," said Jim.

"I think he sees us."

"Hell, he saw us a mile out."

"He doesn't seem too excited."

"Ain't his way."

When we stood before him, he still didn't seem too excited, he just kept looking back and forth between Jim and me. Then he stood up strongly, threw his muscular arms around me and gave me two bristly kisses.

"He must see some resemblance," said Jim. "He knows we're related."

"He what?"

"Steno, this is my sister's boy." Jim said slowly in Italian, mouthing the words very openly. Steno was obviously a deaf-mute. He smiled, nodded vigorously, and then gave Jim a double handshake. Jim was not an easy man to embrace.

"*Padrino*! Giacomo." This came from a girl about fifteen who was now standing in the entrance to the red house. With a child's freedom she bounded over and into Jim's arms. Jim wasn't displeased, just awkward as he returned her hug. *Padrino*. Godfather.

Steno pointed to his bottle of mineral water and made a quick sign. The girl ran back into the house.

"That's Velia," Jim said. "Steno's granddaughter."

The three of us sat down. Velia returned and placed a tray on the table. It held a big beaker full of golden wine and two more glasses. Then Steno and the girl moved their hands and mouths at each other for about thirty seconds. Jim translated.

"He's tellin' her to run out and buy this, that, and the other thing, to cook us up a big meal. I'll tone 'em down a bit."

"Not too much," I said.

From the way Steno and Velia reacted to Jim's attempts to "tone 'em down," I saw I had nothing to worry about. The girl ran off happily, and Steno started to pour the wine. For himself and me. Then he poured a glass of his water for Jim.

"He knows you don't drink," I said.

"I live alone too much. Dangerous for me to get into the habit of drinking. Steno understands that."

"But not even to celebrate? In company? Like your friend here, he was drinking water before, but now..."

But now he was drinking his wine, and urging me to

140

drink mine.

"That there is *sciacchetrà*," said Jim, ignoring my question. "Local wine, from those vineyards that go right up the side from the sea like they was stairs..."

"Terraced. Terrace farming."

"That sounds right. Anyway, try it. Everybody says it's real good."

It was strong and delicious and complicated, sometimes sweet and sometimes almost bread-like. A wine for quiet meditation, undisturbed by talking — perfect at this table, where one man couldn't and the other wouldn't.

I pointed to the wine and then kissed the tips of my bunched fingers, figuring this would not break the spell.

Steno frowned, and made a few quick hand signs. I looked at Jim.

"Better last year, better next year, he says."

He filled our glasses again, and the three of us contemplated the sea for a while. Then I put together the Italian words for "How's the fishing?" and mouthed them very slowly towards Steno. His eyes widened and he looked at Jim, who mouthed exactly the same words. Steno looked relieved, then frowned again and quickly signed his answer.

"Better last week, better next week, he says."

"Okay, but how come he didn't understand me?"

"You mouth with too much accent. Tongue's all wrong, lip's all wrong. Bet he thought you were speaking English."

"Oh, great. We'll have a grand time." I smiled at Steno and took another sip of his wine. Then the old fisherman got out his wallet and handed me a dog-eared snapshot, a picture of an attractive young woman with a baby in her arms. Another Madonna.

141

I nodded appreciatively and handed it back. Steno set it on the table, pointed to it, pointed to Jim and pointed to me. Jim shook his head.

"I think he wants you to tell me about them, Jim."

"I know that."

"Well he sure can't do it."

"Hell he can't. You just don't know how to listen."

Then Jim pointed to the snapshot, to Steno, to himself, and finally to me,

"I get it. You want him to tell me, with your help."

And that's what was done. Steno started by pressing the picture against his chest: they were his wife and daughter. He went on, not with the abstract signs of the deaf-mute but miming, using Italian hand language and a face that came alive with a hundred emotions. Jim was needed for names and dates, but not much else. Mainly he just nodded confirmation, as I gave voice to what was coming across to me.

Steno was twenty-eight when he got married. He had proved to be a good provider, an excellent fisherman, and he desired to have a family. But who would marry a deaf-mute? Only Mara, a girl who was pretty but who had lost her honor with a young fisherman named Dino.

There had been an abortion. So Mara and Steno got married, because neither could hope for anything better. But with time Steno grew to love Mara and they had a child, a girl named Pina.

"Where do you come in, Jim?" I asked at this point.

"I'm already in. I was staying here in Vernazza that summer when Pina was born. Steno was teaching me fishing. Hell, this was over thirty years ago."

"Is this one of the people you 'tracked down...'?"

"Shhh. He's talkin' to you."

Steno got grim, pointed at his wife Mara in the

picture, pointed at Jim and then turned away to make the rapid chopping motions, down and in with the right hand, that mean "I warn you!" in Italian.

So Jim had warned him about Mara; she still secretly loved young Dino.

"How'd you know, Jim?"

"Weren't no secret for anybody who wasn't deaf."

And one day Mara and Dino ran away, taking little Pina with them. By then Jim was no longer living in Vernazza, but when he came through again, Steno was slowly letting himself die. Jim swore to him that he would find his wife and child for him. The only thing this Dino knew how to do was fish, he had to be in some seaside village somewhere, and Jim touched them all. Steno didn't want Mara back, she could do as she pleased. But he wanted his little girl Pina brought back. And he wanted Dino dead.

I shook my head no. Steno shook his head yes — in fact he made it clear that he still felt the same way.

Jim just shrugged his shoulders. Steno poured some more *sciacchetrà* and continued. It took Jim fifteen years, but he found them. They were on the island of Ponza, and Jim very rarely visited the Italian islands — too much trouble with his "van."

Pina, Steno's daughter, had grown up to be like her mother, and at age 15, only a year before Jim arrived, she had had a baby girl — and had died in childbirth, without revealing the father's name. When Jim burst into Mara and Dino's house one day, the little child was sitting naked on the floor. Dino was away fishing, and Mara was still in bed. Her hair was dyed red, and there was a bottle by her side. Jim asked her if she wanted to return to Steno or to start running — She jumped up, took what money there was, told him about the baby girl who still had no name, and caught the first ferry boat to Naples. Jim took the girl away, but just inside the door of Dino's house he left a German booby trap.

"You left a what?"

"Well, they don't always go off."

"Oh, you left it up to the Lord again."

"Yep. But don't tell Steno that. He still needs to think Dino's dead."

Velia came back from her shopping; now I knew who she was. "That's the baby girl you brought back from Ponza," I said after she disappeared into the house. Steno saw me indicate her. He pointed to her, pretended to cradle a baby and hand it to Jim, and then to pour water on its head.

"I know. You're her Godfather."

"Yep. And I picked her name. Steno wouldn't have it no other way."

"But aren't you a Protestant? A Lutheran, like Mom?"

"Steno wouldn't have nobody else but me."

"I didn't think a Catholic priest would let you do it."

"My Italian still wasn't so good, then. Didn't try to explain, just kept saying 'si, si.' Hell, could you explain what a Lutheran is?"

"Maybe not, but..."

"'Sides, I ain't nothing in particular anymore."

"Well anyway. Velia's a nice name."

"Etruscan name."

I don't remember all that much about the rest of our day in Vernazza. The things I recall are all tinged with the golden hues of *sciacchetrà*. We ate this marvelous meal — I can still taste the *gattafin*, big fried ravioli stuffed with cheese and dandelion greens, which took lots of wine to wash down.

Afterwards all four of us went to an ice-cream parlor

144

called "*Malagamba*" or something, to have an *affogato*, which is supposed to help you digest a big meal. It turned out to be vanilla drowned in good ol' *sciacchetrà*. This ice-cream parlor was hundreds of years old, and had a statue of a Madonna that I remember very well. The Bambino in her arms had lost his nose and his left hand, and she seemed to be pleading for help. I kept staring at her. I think tears came to my eyes, and Velia was very impressed.

Steno and Jim got me back to the house and put me to bed for an afternoon nap, while the two of them went fishing, I was later told. I know we had fish that evening, but I ate little and spoke less, meaning that it was practically a wordless supper.

We didn't stay there to sleep; there was a flurry of hand signals over this, and I remember Velia saying she would be glad to sleep on the sofa, but in the end we putt-putted back to La Spezia under the stars. I stretched out on the middle seatboard, looking up at them, aiming at them with Steno's gift to me: a bottle of *sciacchetrà*.

"Jim," I said while firing away silently. "There was a photo of some guy at the foot of the bed where I slept this afternoon. Some guy in uniform. Looked maybe 35."

"Yep. Steno's father. He went to war when Steno was 13. Stayed on after September eighth to fight with the Germans."

"And died at Anzio."

"Yep. Steno was real ashamed of his father. Ashamed of his being on the wrong side. I told him I was there, I knew his father, and he died helping us, not the Germans. Together we got out that photo and nailed it on his bedroom wall. Man, that made him happy..."

"Was it true?"

"Oh, God, was it ever.

145

CHAPTER XIII

The castle of Rapallo is traditionally "burned down" in a
fireworks display every year, in July.

The next morning the *Crociato* climbed slowly out of La
Spezia and away from the coast. I saw on the map
that the Aurelia wouldn't return to the sea until well after
the Cinque Terre. Evidently not even the Romans could
engineer a road through there. So I took my last look for a
while at the blue waters of the Ligurian Sea.

"I would've liked to go fishing with the two of you," I
said. "With you and Steno."

"First rule of fishing is go alone. Second rule is don't
take a talker. Third rule is don't take a drinker."

"I'm no drinker. That *sciacchetrà* took me by surprise."

"That's the fourth rule. Fishermen gotta be able to
control themselves, be ready for anything."

"I'll bet you've fished with Rap."

"Nope. He don't like fishing."

"Maybe now he doesn't, but there's no little boy in the
world that wouldn't like to fish with his dad. Didn't you
take him when he was a kid?"

He gave that one some serious thought. We
negotiated three curves in silence. Then he said, "I guess I
never wanted to get that close to Rap. Didn't want him to
take after me in any way. Less he has to do with me, the
better."

146

"Oh, I think there's more to it than that."

"Okay, Professor, what else is there to it?"

"You don't get close to anybody. The pain might stop. You're punishing yourself."

"You got it all screwed up. It's bein' with people that's a punishment for me."

"You're convinced of that because you're all screwed up."

Two more curves in silence. I had overdone it. I was trying to think of the right words to smooth things out, when he said, "I took Velia fishing once. I think she liked it a lot. That's why I stopped. Steno's got to be number one for her, not me."

"Listen, how much does she know about her mother, and grandmother, and the whole business with you on Ponza?"

"Most of it. Maybe all of it. Not from me, but Vernazza's a small place. Steno told some people, the ones he wants respect from, and word got around. Meant a helluva lot to him, to settle that score. He even had me show him how I did it. Wasn't so easy."

"Jim, it's bad enough that you killed that man, without being proud of how you did it. I don't really care to know."

After only one curve he said, "What I meant was, it wasn't so easy to show him how I did it 'cause I hadn't done it."

"What? You didn't put a booby trap in Dino's house?"

"Hell, I figured fifteen years with a woman like Mara was punishment enough for what he done. Sometimes you pay by dyin' and sometimes you pay by livin'. That poor devil hadn't lived by the sword. I didn't see as how he should die by the sword. But I hadda tell Steno I'd killed him, and I hadda show him how. I used a little

147

DZ.35 detonator with some TNT from a dud butterfly mine, and I blew the door off his tool shed. He loved it."

"You have to hope Dino never goes back to Vernazza."

"No way. You don't know about Italians in villages. No way. What I always hoped was that someday Steno woulda been sorry about Dino. Then I could have told him the truth."

"He still might soften up. He's not that old."

"He ain't, but I'm at the end of my road."

"Jim, you look as tough as an old tree. Good for thirty more years."

"God willing, nephew. God willing. But He ain't. I'm out of nails."

"You're out of nails? The forty-four nails?"

"Yep. Listen, nephew, this ain't the place to talk about the nails. Gotta go where they were. Where the Raséna were."

"The Etruscans? Are we talking about Etruscan nails?"

"Yep, and this is the wrong place for it. The Etruscans never came here. Nephew, let me handle this. You don't know beans yet."

"And I never will, if you don't start somewhere. Why didn't the Etruscans come here?"

Jim sighed. "Because this is Liguria, and it was full of Ligurians."

Keep him talking, I thought. Something might come out. "And the Etruscans didn't like to invade. I mean, they weren't great fighters. Is that it?"

"Too smart for that. I mean, you think about it, fighting is shit most of the time. Course sometimes they had to. Way I understand it, first they'd try to scare the enemy off, with masks and noise. Worked pretty good. If it didn't, they used their secret weapon."

"Okay, so what was that?"

"Shoelaces. They was the first ones to tie their shoes. They could outrun anybody. Listen, you want some music? This thing's all wired up, you know, there's the radio, and there's a tape that Rap give me once. In the glove compartment."

I found the tape. "Glenn Miller?" I said.

"Mentioned to Rap once that I used to like him."

"But it's still in the wrapper. You've never played it."

"Too much bother, I guess. If you think you can get it to work, go ahead and stick it in. There's a hole where it goes, somewheres."

I found the hole, and soon the *Crociato* was filled with Swing.

"Now that's very nice." I said, sitting back.

"Yep."

"Did the Etruscans like music?"

"Yep. And dancing."

"Well. I guess that does beat fighting."

"Yep. Just listen to the music a minute. Okay?"

We listened all the way to Rapallo. I had expected Jim to make another stop someplace, because we weren't due to meet Ilene and Rap until the next day.

"We're a day early." I said as we drove along the seafront promenade.

"Nope. Might's well turn that music off."

I did.

"We got something to do here today. Remember? I told you there's somebody here that knows my old name. To convince you I'm really Jim Savorski."

"I'm convinced, Jim."

"But you gotta meet this person. I mean, I'd like you to. Not right here in Rapallo — I just said that to keep Rap off the track. We'll take another little boat ride."

At the far end of Rapallo there's a canal, and a place where we were able to park and muscle the boat down off the roof into the water. We buzzed out of the canal and into Rapallo's little bay. Little, but full of pleasure boats of every sort: speedboats, ferry boats, sailboats, and yachts criss-crossed around us. Jim seemed unperturbed and in control, so I refrained from crying out things like, "We'll be swamped!"

The yachts seemed to get bigger as we swung wide of Santa Margherita and approached Portofino. I had done some reading in my guide book that morning: Portofino has only got 800 inhabitants, but more yachts are registered there than in any other Italian port. Not little ones. Lots of them I could have sailed home to Chicago with.

God knows who they belong to; maybe one of them is His. Of course only a fraction of them are ever in port at one time, but it still looked like a rich man's D-Day. The town's buildings are tall and narrow and attached to one another, a defensive tactic that worked against the Saracens but is to no avail against this invasion. Rather than try to escape to the rear through the "pirate doors" that still exist, the inhabitants have shrugged, surrendered, and turned their little horseshoe port into some of the most expensive footage in the world.

But to my dismay, we buzzed right on by.

"Hey, Jim where we going?" I shouted into the spray.

"Not too far. Up around the promontory a piece."

Up around the promontory I could make out a few houses surrounding a big white church, but well before we got there, Jim cut the motor.

"Right about here," he said. We were about a half mile from the rocky shore.

150

"What's right about here?"

"Place where it happened. Place where I got to tell you a few things."

So Jim was going to tell me about how Rap's mother drowned in a storm. I looked around. At least the boat traffic was thinner here. I decided not to let on that I knew anything about it. "Okay, let's hear it. What happened here?"

I was facing him but he turned sideways, to talk towards the open sea. "I first came to Rapallo back in 1954, to look for a woman. Lorena Peruzzi. I killed her husband at Anzio. Course she didn't know that. I just wanted to find a way to do something for her and then leave."

"How did you kill her husband?"

"If we get to Anzio, that'll be the place to tell you that. Words is just words without the place. Here we'll talk about Lorena. I found her in a real bad way. Ten years, but I guess she had really loved that guy. Well, she wasn't very pretty for Italians, too tall and thin. She thought she'd lost her only chance for a family. That really got her, the fact that they hadn't had time to have children. She was in a bad way, Bob."

He didn't often call me by my name.

"So you...comforted her."

"Yep. We got pretty close. Real close. Closest I ever been. I guess you could say I...I..."

"You loved her." Jim nodded to the sky.

"Fact is, we got married. Not in a church, too much trouble, but married just the same."

"We're talking about Rap's mother, aren't we?"

"Yep. Kind of a shotgun wedding. She wasn't like Silvia, Agnese's mother. She hadda get married. And she hadda call the baby Renato. Her first husband's name.

151

'Course I told her I'd still be traveling a lot, I couldn't stop my work, but she accepted that, said it would be different even if I got myself killed with my mines, 'cause she'd have the baby, a kid of mine named Renato, to remind her of both her husbands. That's what she said. She always had funny ways of thinking."

"And you never told her how her first husband died."

"I'm gettin' round to that. I knew I had to, but I kept waitin' and waitin'. She was pretty when she smiled, and she was smiling all the time with little Rap. God, I didn't want to ruin that for her."

"And maybe you didn't want to ruin it for you."

"All right, I'll admit that. I was startin' to think there'd be nothing wrong if I settled down a bit, to take care of this woman, and, and...be allowed back in. But she would have to know. So one day I told her. All about Sgt. Jim Savorski. The whole thing, not just her husband. If she knew the whole thing and could still...accept me, well, I was set to take that as a Sign. Of being allowed back in."

"In where?"

Jim just shook his head.

"Well, how did she react when you told her?"

"Damnedest thing. She just got real quiet. I mean she didn't say nothing for days. So I decided to take her and Rap to San Fruttuoso. Right in front of us here, that little village with the big white abbey. I like it, it's real hard to get to by land, like Vernazza. Lorena liked it too, we'd been there a few times. I thought it would do her good, maybe bring her around. This here is as far as we got. In those days we had an old wooden boat with a round bottom, nothing like this. Well, right about here without a word she started rocking the boat. I mean hard, as hard as she could. I stopped the motor, but first thing you know, little Rap just tumbled right out. He wasn't even two, but

152

luckily he had on a little life preserver. I reached out to grab him as he went by, but Lorena, she just leaned as hard as she could in the same direction, and the boat flipped over. I'm telling you, I had one hell of a time. I was trying to save the boy, and Lorena kept trying to push us under! I had to stop her."

Jim turned and looked at me.

"I'd say so." I said. "Sure sounds like it. How did you do it?"

"In the jaw. You got no traction in the water, but I swung pretty hard. Then I drug her over and slung her across the hull of the boat. Rap was bobbing right side up, so he could wait till I could go get a hold of him. Then I just kept him in the water with me alongside the hull till somebody finally came and helped us."

"And what about Lorena? Jim, that punch in the jaw didn't — didn't kill her, did it?"

"No, but it didn't do her any good. She came around, but she still wouldn't say a word, and what's more she kept attacking Rap and me, but especially me. I had to have her committed."

"Is she still alive?"

"Yep. In a private clinic, up the coast just a little farther, near Camogli." Jim pointed to the left, towards the end of the shoreline. "You can't quite see it, but it's a big white building — looks like a plantation. With a big garden and a private beach."

"Sounds like you found a nice place for her."

"There are better ones. I tried one in Milan. She had a fit — turns out she wants to be where she can see the sea. This sea here, where it happened. Only place she'll stand for, 'cause from their beach you can see clear to here. Course I can never go see her, but they tell me she's peaceable enough. Stays in her room, mainly, and draws pictures. I guess that's where Rap gets it. But she ain't said a word in all these years."

"What kinds of pictures does she draw?"

"Oh, she just likes to copy things. She sees a face she likes in a magazine, she tries to copy it. They showed me a few last time; they ain't bad."

"Uh...Can Rap go and see her?" I knew the answer.

"Fact is, Rap thinks she's dead. Thinks we capsized in a storm out here, and she drowned. I paid a few people to back me up on it. Figured it was best. How would you like to know your mother's crazy and wants to kill you?"

"Not only that, but you don't want him to know why."

"He'll find out soon enough. It's written inside that Etruscan locket he wears around his neck. He'll open it when I die. Then Lorena will be up to him. Except for the expense. That's taken care of for as long as she lives."

"Is the whole thing about Anzio written there?"

"Yep. He's got a right, like Lorena had. Only I don't want...problems like I had with her, so that's why I put it all in that locket. Typed it, took me a week. God, that was tough going. And it didn't help me a bit. No way Rap can let me back in."

"Back into what?"

Jim paused and looked all around before looking at me. "Listen, will you do me a favor?" he asked, almost under his breath.

"If I can."

"I want to take you over to that clinic, and I want you to visit Lorena for me. See if she's to the point where she can stand to hear my real name."

"But...my Italian..."

"It's good enough for this. Hell, she don't talk, and all you gotta say is...is..."

"That you still love her."

"You know how to say that?"

"I know how to say that."

It was already noon, so we first had lunch in a *trattoria* in Camogli. Jim was sociable, by his standards: he asked me a few things about my teaching job and about life in the US today. But his idea was to avoid more conversation about his family. He had said all he intended to say. But he did hand me a letter he had prepared: a letter for the clinic, asking that I be allowed to visit his wife.

The letter worked fine, and that afternoon at three o'clock I found myself in my Aunt Lorena's private room. It was small but clean and furnished tastefully but impersonally. I don't know how many years she had been there, but she hadn't left her imprint anywhere I could see. She herself was sitting tightly at a small desk close to the window. She seemed to want to disturb her surroundings as little as possible.

She was drawing something on a piece of typing paper, but she kept the colored pencils she used in a little case on her lap, carefully putting each one back before fishing out a different one, as if not to create further disorder on the desk top, where there was already a magazine lying open but carefully folded to a photograph. She ignored my approach.

What I should say is that she was aware of my approach but wanted me to ignore her.

"Lorena?" I said softly. She was troubled, but didn't react. "*Zia* Lorena?" I continued, to see if calling her "Aunt" would get a reaction.

It did. She looked up. She stood up. She came to me and put her hands on the side of my face. Then she pulled me over by the face to the light of the window, to study me better. As Jim had said, she was thin and tall, able to look me in the eye. Her fingers were boney but her breath was not stale. As her gaze darted rapidly around my face I tried to read the madness behind it. I thought I caught a glimpse of hidden order.

"I am your nephew," I said slowly in Italian, "because Giacomo Savori is my mother's brother."

She nodded once. Her eyes and fingers agreed that there was something familiar in my face. They both dropped away. She again sat down at her desk. Now I could see the photograph in the magazine: it was the face of Tom Cruise. Her drawing was a copy about half done, and it looked fairly competent.

"That is very good," I said, pointing. I didn't know how to say "drawing" in Italian. She turned it over and closed the magazine. Then she turned her eyes to the window.

"Giacomo sent me here. He thinks he is going to die soon." No reaction.

"He wants me to tell you something." Almost imperceptibly she began shaking her head.

"He still loves you. Very much." Her head froze where it was, turned its furthest away from me.

"I think he wants to see you, Lorena. Before he dies." Her head took up shaking where it had left off.

"Or at least send him a sign. A sign that you forgive him." I stood there in silence for two minutes.

The head kept shaking, but I hoped she was also thinking. It also gave me time to put together a few more words of Italian:

"Lorena, he has lived his life in sadness because of Anzio. Let him die in peace." I paused, and then used his real name: "Let Jim Savorski die in peace."

The woman started to moan and sway, but her head

156

never stopped slowly shaking no. I decided to bring matters to a head:

"Good bye, Aunt Lorena. I wonder if you ever loved him." I turned and walked slowly to the door. As I put my hands on the knob I felt boney fingers on my shoulder, pulling me back. I hadn't heard her coming; even when walking she evidently tried to disturb the floor and the air as little as possible. She made a sign that I should wait there at the door; then she went back to her desk.

She got a key out of her pencil case and opened a drawer. She gave me a look of great reluctance and took out a thick manila folder. She placed it on the desk so that I couldn't see what was inside, but it was evidently a collection of her drawings. She quickly found the ones she wanted: two of them. She put them face down on the desk and carefully locked the folder back in its drawer.

Then she motioned me over and handed me one. It was a picture of Jim, from the waist up. Of Jim still young, not much different from the soldier in my photo, the one now on display in the *Crociato*. And like the photo, here also Jim was balancing a baby boy on his shoulder. Not me this time, but little Rap.

"So you did love him. You loved them both." She nodded quickly, once.

"And you still do." She again began shaking her head slowly. She continued as she handed me the second drawing. It showed a round-bottomed wooden boat. Capsized.

I handed it back to her.

"I don't like this one. They didn't die. I will take this other one to Giacomo." But she took the drawing of Jim and Rap away from me. Then she went to her desk, sat down, opened her pencil case and began working on the drawing. I started towards her, but she waved me back to the door. She didn't take long. Then she put away the drawing of the boat and gave me back the portrait of Jim and Rap. She had drawn small holes in their chests.

Bullet holes.

CHAPTER FOURTEEN
XIV

Sciacchetrà must be served at 16° Celsius in a smooth and transparent crystal chalice.

D o you think she understood who you were?"
"I think so, Jim. I think she saw a resemblance, the way Steno did."

"Damned if I can see it."

"You haven't got an artist's eye. She's pretty good, you know."

"And that's still all she does? Sits there and copies pictures out of magazines?"

"She seems happy enough, Jim."

"And she didn't react to none of those things you said. Not to my real name, not to nothing."

"Except that I could see it all meant something to her. Your name in particular."

"You convinced I'm Jim Savorski now?"

"Sure, Jim. I already was." Actually if I needed proof, it wasn't so much the woman's reaction to that name as it was the picture she had given me, of a young man I knew from a photo.

"Well, that's one good thing. Still, I thought she might've reacted to you."

"The impression I got is that it would cost her too much to react. She's found some sort of balance of her own. Maybe for her it's either that or nothing."

Jim sighed. "Well, I sure don't want to hurt her more. Dammit. I was hoping the Lord would give me some kind of idea through her, on how I been doin'"

"Still hoping to be 'let back in,' Jim?"

Jim looked at me hard, to see if there was any trace of mockery in my expression. Luckily there wasn't. I continued: "Exactly what do you mean about being let back in?"

"That's a thing I want you to try to get on your own, nephew. But Lorena, she's taken care of all right? Don't look like she needs anything?"

"She's fine, and it's very comfortable there. You've done well by her, Jim."

I had Lorena's drawing of Rap and Jim folded up in my wallet, but I couldn't bring myself to give it to him. On the other hand I couldn't pretend she had forgiven him, for fear that he would want to visit her. I don't like to hold back the truth from a man. Maybe I thought the moment might come to give him the drawing later.

That evening in Rapallo I called home to Beth. I'd been luckier than Jim. My wife was a good woman, we were helping each other live our lives. On the phone I told her I was drinking wine with my meals — here in Paris — and she asked me if they still crush the grapes with their feet in Europe. I really didn't know, but it was a chance for some fun:

"Sure they do, Beth. Up over their knees. It's a question of flavor. It'd be cheaper to use a crushing machine, but an expert can tell the difference in flavor."

"Oh, God in heaven."

"Beth, these are professional stompers."

"Does that mean they wash their feet?"

"It means they don't wash their feet. Not during the

stomping season. It's a question of..."

"I know, the flavor. Bob, how many dirty habits do you intend to bring home?"

That was a good question, and I wondered about it after I had hung up. How much had I changed in these past eight weeks? Beth doesn't really know me, she doesn't know what I'm capable of, but who says I know her and what she might be able to do? Back home I would find the way to tell her about Uncle Jim, and Rap and Ilene, and everything. After all, I had been faithful to her. Not heroically so, but I suppose it's the bottom line that counts here.

When I got back to the *Crociato*, Jim was already asleep. I quietly got in bed and went back to thinking about Beth. I owed it to her to try to fall back in love with her. Maybe I would return next summer and bring her along. We could stay at Egidio's, get our luggage stolen, both get jobs as Ghosts of the Forum...

The next day at 1 pm, Jim and I were sitting in Rosaria's restaurant waiting for Rap and Ilene to appear.

At 1:10 pm, Jim was ready to leave.

"Looks like they ain't gonna come."

"Jim, this is Italy. It's normal to be late."

"Not for Rap. I taught him better. Must mean they ain't coming. That girl of his turned him around somewheres, way she almost turned you around."

"She's a fine girl, Jim."

"Then what's she doing with a man like Rap?"

"What's that supposed to mean? Rap's a nice guy!"

"But he ain't someone a girl can get serious about. Wouldn't be no kind of a husband. He don't even believe in getting married."

"A lot of bachelors don't, until they meet a girl who changes their mind."

"Rap's a street artist. Serious girl can't marry no street artist."

"That's all *she* is, too. I suppose no serious boy should marry her."

"That's different. It's the man gotta put bread on the table. Every day. Gotta have a job."

"Jim, stick to mines. You're no marriage counselor."

"Hell, just making talk. First place, they ain't coming. Second place. Rap ain't about to get married."

And at that moment Rap and Ilene walked in, hand in hand. I stood up, Jim followed suit, albeit more slowly. After the first flurry of greetings, he looked hard at Rap and said, "You're late, boy."

"Not really, *Papà*. We got here before you did. We sat to wait for you in that bar across the street. We saw you walk in."

"Well then, why in hell ..?"

"My fault," said Ilene. "We got to talking about certain things. I wanted to clear them up before meeting with you...*Papà*."

"I'll be damned." said Jim, and he dropped back in his seat. He didn't say much else for a while. Rap and Ilene sat down and started talking about the wonderful trip they'd had together, about all the Madonnari at Grazia di Curtatone and the big hit Ilene had made with them, and about their decision to get married. I tried ordering some Guinness Stout in Ilene's honor, but I was glad there wasn't any, because it gave me a chance to order the *sciacchetrà* I knew and loved. And it seemed a better way to celebrate an engagement than with black beer. When it arrived and Ilene took a sip, she had to agree.

We let Rap order the food. For antipasto we had musciame, delicious on its bed of tomato slices, until I found out it was fillet of dolphin. I have this thing about dolphins. Father Tom, my Jesuit friend at school, thinks that maybe God created men to rule the land and dolphins to rule the sea. We fell from grace, but they didn't and still frolic in their paradise with no more need for civilization than Adam and Eve needed fig leaves. The theory might need a little work, but I'm not going to start eating creatures with bigger and maybe better brains than mine.

I kept these thoughts to myself. Actually Ilene didn't look too pleased either, when we found out it was dolphin. She let Rap finish hers. He loved it. Strange for an ecologist, a "Verde" — then again, Italians love horsemeat, too. They can be so sentimental but evidently not about what or who they eat. I kept this to myself, too, and anyway my enthusiasm for the rest of the meal was unreserved.

The first course was *trenette al pesto*, a Genoan pasta dish. Pesto is a sauce made of pine nuts, fresh basil, cheese, and garlic, and *trenette* are short, misshapen cords of pasta. Rap remarked that in Italy bearded professors have debated for centuries about why pasta changes its taste just by changing its shape. I had no insights to offer.

Ilene asked Jim for his opinion, and he spoke for the first time in a while: "Pasta is pasta to me. All I know is that it fills me right up. Listen, I think I'll be moving along, leave you kids to talk. Rap, why don't you order *cappun magru*, long as you're celebrating? It's on me."

"*Cappun magru*?" I asked.

"That's Ligurian dialect. You'll see, it's very special. Thank you, *Papà*."

"Ain't really doin' it for you. Doin' it for this pretty girl, here."

"You're a very sweet man," said Ilene. "I knew you had to be."

At that Jim jumped to his feet. "Well, be seeing you later," he said.

"When? Where?" I asked.

"I'll be in the van."

"Where are we heading next, Jim?"

"That's up to you, remember? I can put you on a plane out of Genoa tomorrow, if you want."

"You still have to show me how you use your minesweeper."

"I could do that this afternoon, on a piece of beach somewheres."

"All right, let's put it this way. There's much I don't know about you."

"Well, listen then. Your plane to Chicago leaves Paris on August 24th."

"That's right. At 8 pm. But I want to get to Paris at least a day or two before, to do some shopping."

"No problem. Stick with me till Sunday. I always have to be in Anzio on the first Sunday after Ferragosto — Ferragosto's today. August 15ᵗʰ."

"*Papà*, it's only Tuesday," said Rap. "Can we spend a day together? I mean, to celebrate? I'm getting married, *Papà*!"

"And I hope it works out for you. For both of you. But I got places to show Bob, and people to meet, and..."

"*Papà*," said Ilene, "I think that now I have a right to get to know you a bit."

"Can't we spare a day, Jim?" I said. He looked at me hard.

"All right, let's hear it. What you got in mind, Rap?" He was still standing up. In fact, he seemed more anxious than ever to get away.

"*Papà, c'è terra in piazza!*" exclaimed Rap. As far as I knew, it simply meant "there's dirt in the public square."

164

"Great God in Heaven, not that!"

"*Papà*, Ilene and Bob have never seen it..."

"Me neither, and I don't care to."

"But you're an *ocaiolo*; they have always wanted you to come, I can call..."

Jim had closed his eyes. He let his face lift towards the ceiling. The three of us waited in silence.

Then he lowered his face back down to us without opening his eyes and said quietly: "Well, this could be the Lord's doing. Just crazy enough. Rap, soon's it's over, we split." And with that he walked away.

"As soon as what's over?" I asked.

"The *Palio*, Bob!" cried Ilene. "We're going to see the *Palio*! Isn't that wonderful?"

"Sure is! What's the *Palio*?"

"In Siena, Bob," said Rap. "There are two *Palios*, one on July 2nd, and one tomorrow, August 16th."

I decided to put it in verse:

"Heidi, Heidi, Heidi, Ho,
What the hell's the *Palio*?"

The *sciacchetrà* had something to do with this, but I was a little peeved.

"You really don't know?"

"I'll tell you what the *Palio* in Siena is when you tell me what Bud Billiken's Day in Chicago is."

"Bud Billiken's Day?"

"Bud Billiken's Day?"

"Yes, Bud Billiken's Day! In Chicago in August! Bigger than twenty *Palios*! What exactly is a *Palio*?"

"The *Palio* is a Madonna."

"Oh, no..."

"Painted on silk, hanging down from a pole, like a standard."

"And hundreds of years old, I suppose."

"Hardly. The paint's probably still wet on it. They have to give it to the winner, you know."

"The winner of what?"

"The horse race, Bob, the horse race," said Rap. "Three times around the Piazza del Campo. It's the horse race that's hundreds of years old, not the *Palio* itself."

"And that's why you said there's dirt in the piazza. They spread it around for this race."

"Yes, *c'è terra in piazza*! The most exciting thing you can say to a Sienese."

"Big deal. In Chicago we have the Arlington Million. They race for a million bucks. That beats a wet-paint Madonna."

Ilene grimaced. "This must be American humor."

"Bob, the Sienese are very passionate about the *Palio*," said Rap. "You see, Siena is divided into 17 *contrade* — you might say boroughs, or something. Ten of these *contradas* compete in each *Palio*: the seven who didn't compete in the last one, plus three others chosen by lot. I think that's why they have two each summer — to make sure that every *contrada* competes at least once a year. And they...they have at it. They really have at it. As if the whole *contrada* was riding that horse..."

"Poor horse."

"Bob, I'm told it's thrilling!" said Ilene. "And we'll see it as outsiders rarely get to see it. Your uncle is an honorary *contradaiolo*!"

"A member of a *contrada*." Rap said with reverence.

"*La nobile contrada dell'Oca*, the noble contrada of the Goose. Jim is an *ocaiolo*. He did them a favor once."

"I can understand why he's not too excited about being an honorary goose."

"Bob, trust me, the *Palio* is an extraordinary thing. Wait until tomorrow. And now, tell me about your days

166

with *Papà*. I will order the *cappun magru*, we will have lots of time to talk."

"And let's get some more *sciacchetrà*," I said.

"Yes, let's," said Ilene.

Cappun magru turned out to be an incredible mixture of lobster, oysters, and God knows what else. I didn't want to know what it cost. But eating it took plenty of time, and the *sciacchetrà* loosened my tongue, so I gave my friends a vivid account of my travels with Uncle Jim, especially of the day with cousin Agnese, Rap's half-sister. He loved the story of the watermelons.

"Rap, when will you take me to meet Agnese?" asked Ilene. "She sounds delightful!"

"She's very nice, but I don't visit her often...I am not fond of her husband; I don't want to find him there."

"You won't find him there now," I said. "He's on a steamer to Buenos Aires. Why don't you like him?"

"Because of a thing he said once. He said he hates Italy. He prefers his foreign ports. A man who hates Italy, hates me."

"He was probably just saying that. Wait till you hear Ilene when she gets going on Ireland!"

"But I've never said I hate Ireland," Ilene protested. "Rap's right, that would be like hating myself."

"I think you should take Rap to Ireland and show him around. To let him get to know you better."

"But then I'd have to introduce him to my family!"

"And who would get the shock — Rap or your family?"

"Rap, definitely Rap — my family's been expecting me to come home with someone strange ever since I left Sligo."

"But I want to meet them!" said Rap. "Listen, you have met my family, what there is of it, and now I want to know yours! After my family, yours can't be so odd."

"Thanks a lot, cousin."

"Excuse me, Bob, I was thinking of *Papà*. By the way, did he talk to you about my mother?"

"Uh, yes. A bit. It didn't happen the way you think. He didn't let her drown in order to save you. You had a life jacket on."

"So *Papà* did try to save her."

"Yes he did. He did his best."

"So he doesn't have that on his conscience. I'm glad. And glad not to be a part of his anguish. But it makes him still harder for me to understand. I thought this explained at least why he cannot talk to me about *Mamma*."

"No. you're no part of his anguish, Rap. But I don't know much else about it, about his anguish, except that it's constant. I'm glad the two of you are with us, even if it's only for today and tomorrow. I need a few laughs."

"He knows that. He saw that you were anxious to spend a day with us. I think that's the real reason why he agreed to go to the *Palio*."

CHAPTER XV

*On Christmas Day 1944 the Germans crossed the
Serchio river and fell heavily on the 92nd Division.
Many of them were disguised as partisans.*

Rap must have been right, Jim really had decided to let me get a few laughs. Rap's Gilera was too big to strap onto the *Crociato*, so it looked like he and Ilene would be riding behind us to Siena, and I'd still be in the motor home with my Uncle Chuckles, but the next morning found Rap behind the wheel of the *Crociato* with Ilene and me at his side, and old Jim out in front on the motorcycle. He wouldn't have it any other way.

He even agreed to take the tollroad instead of the Roman road, to be sure to get to Siena early. There was some painting Rap absolutely wanted us to see before falling in with Jim's fellow "geese." Rap had called ahead, and they were waiting for us for lunch.

"It's probably just as well." Jim had said to resign himself to the tollroad. "Rap needs a straight road to get used to the *Crociato*, and for that matter, I ain't been on one of these damn bikes in years." But he roared out of Rapallo like Marlon Brando in *The Wild Ones*.

"Look at that old guy go!" I exclaimed.

"I'd say he's having fun!" said Ilene. "I'll bet that's why he insisted on riding the motorcycle."

"You'd lose your bet," I said.

"*Papà* never really has fun," said Rap. "But I know there is one thing he likes about riding the motorcycle. It leaves him alone with his thoughts."

"Well, he's got enough of them," I said.

169

"Forty-four, perhaps? What did he say when you told him about the belt with the nailheads that you gave me?"

"Why don't you wear it?"

"Oh, I first wanted to know what *Papà* thinks about it. But I have worn it all the time these past days."

"I don't care for it at all," said Ilene, "it hurts me sometimes. On the cycle. Riding behind."

"Not very far behind, if his belt could hurt you."

"Silly, you have to hold on tight, you know."

"But what did my father say about the belt?"

"Let's put it this way: I think you're wise not to wear it. He said he might get around to telling me about the forty-four nails, but his teeth were grinding the whole time."

"Well, there aren't forty-four nailheads..."

"Studs, Rap. Studs." said Ilene.

"Yes, the belt has many more studs than that."

"Don't wear it. He'd realize we just said forty-four to get a reaction. He wouldn't like that at all."

"Hmph! There is so much *Papà* doesn't like, so much darkness in his world! I don't really care, you know? My curiosity about him is very light, it passes quickly; I live easily without knowing all the mysteries of my father. I really don't want to get involved. I am glad you have come, Bob, and I don't envy you. I imagine you are holding back some things from me, some things you have already learned, but I don't mind. I long ago determined not to be affected by my father and his things. Nothing of his will change the kind of man I am."

"A man is not a man until his father dies," said Ilene. "Somebody said that."

"He need not have bothered," said Rap. "It's stupid."

"Not that stupid, I'm afraid," I said. "To a certain extent, for example, I'm just reacting against my father by

170

being here in Italy."

"So am I," said Ilene. "To a great extent."

"Not I," said Rap. "That old man out there has very little to do with me now, with what I have become. With what my life will be..."

"Methinks he doth protest a bit too much," said Ilene. "Somebody else said that."

This conversation made me feel better. In the restaurant the day before I had been uncomfortable about hiding what I knew regarding his mother and father from Rap, and it was good to know that he'd just as soon not be briefed on whatever I might discover. Unconsciously I glanced up at the old photo of Jim above the rear-view mirror, thinking of his wife's drawing of the same man ten years later. Really a good likeness. Ilene followed my eyes to the picture.

"Who are those people?"

"Can't you guess?" But Rap didn't give her a chance.

"My father!" he blurted out. And...and...that must be Aunt Agnes, your mother! With you!"

"Bob, you're bald as bald can be!" exclaimed Ilene.

The picture became just another source of levity, for which I was glad. As the miles rolled by in an endless alternation of tunnels and viaducts, it became clear that Rap and Ilene's relationship was not the sort of *egoisme a deux* that ends up making three a crowd; we were having fun together.

At one point I got out my trusty "Italy in Your Pocket" so that we could bone up on Siena.

"Did you know that for hundreds of years Siena and Florence fought for control of Tuscany?" I announced.

"Of course," said Rap, "and there is still bad blood between them."

"Sounds like Belfast and Dublin," said Ilene.

"No," said Rap, "because the trouble in Ireland is religious. Here it was political. Only power! The Italians are too intelligent to fight religious wars."

"The Italians aren't much at fighting wars, period," said Ilene.

"Wait a minute," I said. "There must have been religion involved between Siena and Florence; the pope was in it, you know, and..."

"That means nothing. The pope was not very religious in those days."

"Well, he excommunicated Siena. The whole city. That's a religious move, isn't it?"

"Something like that can be very political, Bob," said Ilene.

"As I recall, it was neither," said Rap. "It was economic. It ruined business for the Sienese merchants."

"Well anyway, Florence won in the end," I said, scanning my book. "The Medicis marched in and took Siena in 1559."

"But they took good care of it," said Rap. "The Medicis loved art and beauty. The city they conquered is still there, intact within its walls; little has changed."

"Tell us about this painting you want us to see!" said Ilene. "I'm afraid I never studied Duccio di Buoninsegna."

"Ah! A marvelous thing. It is called the Maestà. It is a Madonna in glory, in Paradise. When Duccio finished it, in 1311, it was carried in triumph by the entire city population from his workshop to the cathedral and wildly celebrated for three days. Art was something for the people then."

"Well, when they put Picasso's horsehead in front of the Civic Center in Chicago, the people got pretty wild."

"Somehow I do not imagine Chicago as a city for art," said Rap.

"Nor do I," said Ilene. "I think of New York."

"That's never a good idea. Bad for your digestion."

"Oh ho! Rivalry!" said Rap. "Like Florence and Siena!"

"But surely you must admit that New York is the most important city in America," said Ilene.

"New York isn't really in America, you know. It's an island. In the Atlantic."

So the talk swung easily from banter to discussion, from personal to abstract without ever letting up, and the time passed quickly. We only made one stop, when Jim eased the Gilera over into a rest area just after crossing a river called the Serchio.

"Are you tired, *Papà*? Does your back hurt? Let me ride the motorcycle now."

"Hell no, just wanted to stretch a second. And have a look around from here. S'pose you don't know where we are."

"That's the Serchio River, *Papà*. This is a beautiful area. *La romantica valle del Serchio*, they call it."

"Romantic. Ask the 92nd Division how romantic it was here back in '44. We're crossing the Gothic Line, boy! The Germans and Mussolini's Italians counter-attacked right here to celebrate Christmas. One hell of a mess. Damn good thing the Brits lent a hand with an Indian division..."

"*Papà*. You are ruining the view with these stories."

"Hold on," I said. "I'm interested in things like that."

"You are?" said Jim.

"Sure. War is the highest form of drama, as somebody said." I smiled at Ilene.

Rap shook his head before speaking: "War is the stupidest form of drama. I said that."

"Jim, how do you know about the battle here?" I decided to ask. "Were you involved?"

173

"Nope. I was...in the mountains. North of here."

"North of here? But if the Line was here, north of here was enemy territory."

"We'll get around to that. Reason I know about this area is I done a lotta sweeping here after the war. You learn a lot about a battle by cleaning up after it. That's how come I got involved with them damn geese in Siena. I got to sweeping on a hill called Montemaggio, up the valley a short ways, just got done digging out a mortar shell and was all set to fill in the hole when I noticed I could still get a signal from down in there. Well I dug some more and turned up an old piece of metal with a goose embossed on it. I showed it to one of the people I show these things to and he 'bout did a flip. It was a piece of a breastplate. Turns out Siena fought a battle here in 1145, and they won because of the bravery of the soldiers who came from the *Contrada* of the Goose. As they'll tell you about a million times, this battle gave them the right to call themselves the Noble *Contrada* of the Goose."

"And your breastplate backs up their story." I said. "Bet they coughed up a whole lot of lire to have it."

"I gave it to them. Belongs to them, don't it?"

"Wow. I can see why they made you a goose."

"*Papà*," said Ilene, "why do they call themselves geese in the first place? So many other animals are more..."

"Because of the racket geese make. In the old days they gave the first alarm when an enemy approached."

"Oh. Still, I wish you were a fox, or something. I rather like foxes."

"Ain't you got geese in Ireland?"

"Oh, yes, a great many, but..."

"Ain't never seen a mad goose? Don't never bet on no fox in a fight with a mad goose."

With that Jim got on the Gilera and roared off. Maybe

174

he wanted to prove he wasn't tired. Anyway, Rap had to step on it to catch him and stay with him; the old man never spared the horsepower all the way into Siena. Rap was happy to arrive early, but then it took a while to park the *Crociato*; in the end we got gas and gave the pump boy 5000 *lire* to let us put the motor home and the motorcycle behind his station — and another 5000 *lire* to keep an eye on them for us. By the time we were free, it was 11:30, but Rap was still determined to manage a visit to Duccio's Madonna before lunch. Jim wanted no part of it and said he'd meet us in the restaurant.

The painting was kind of a disappointment to me; not really the painting itself, which is a splendid thing, I suppose, but the way it's been treated. In the first place it's no longer in its rightful place over the main altar in the cathedral. It's in a museum next door. In the second place it's in pieces. It isn't a canvas. It's an enormous "*pala*." or wooden panel, painted on both sides, with dozens of smaller scenes surrounding both central scenes. Some jerk named Pandolfo Petrucci cut the whole thing up in 1505 — even separated the front from the back — and now there are parts of it all over the world.

Some are even missing. It disgusted me so much I walked away, leaving Rap to carry on with Ilene about how Duccio used eggs to mix his colors. I told them I just wanted to take a look upstairs.

I got the impression that nobody ever went upstairs in this museum; the big attraction was the Duccio thing. I wandered around alone up there till I came to a room where there was a little Madonna called the *Madonna dagli Occhi Grossi*, the Big-eyed Madonna, who looked very surprised to have a visitor. Her eyes were full of questions. I answered the easy ones, and then told her I had to be going, which was true, Rap and Ilene were already on the stairs coming up to get me.

"We must go now," said Rap, "or we'll be late."

"Come along," said Ilene, "I don't want to face mad geese after what your uncle said."

But once out on the street she couldn't resist taking a minute to buy a neckerchief. We kept seeing people wearing them loosely around the neck, in various patterns and colors. Rap explained that each of the seventeen *contradas* had its own. When she found a store that had some on display, she rushed in and bought a goose neckerchief, which turned out to be red, white and green and had a crowned goose in the middle. Rap helped her tie it on.

"Isn't it cute, Bob?"

"Very nice. Hope this restaurant isn't so far."

"We will be just a little late," said Rap, as we hurried off. "It is not a problem. We have a pretty girl with us. A pretty girl should always be a little late, to make a better entrance."

"What's the name of the place?"

"Da Bagoga. It's right in the middle of our...of the Goose *Contrada*. I think 'Bagoga' was a jockey who won a lot of the *Palio* races, and used the money to start the restaurant."

"The money?" I asked. "I thought they raced for a Madonna."

"Yes, she is the prize. But the jockeys are professionals, hired by the *contradas*. This race is — complicated. We will ask questions."

We turned a corner at full speed and almost ran into a group of six men all wearing neckerchiefs. These were dark red with a white-and-blue checkered border. One had his back turned, allowing us to get a glimpse of a little elephant carrying a tower in the middle of the dark red.

But then he wheeled around, and they all stared at Ilene. At her neckerchief, to be exact. They did not seem to find it cute at all. One of them, the biggest one, and he was very big, said — in Italian — something like:

"Nobody's allowed to wear that rag in our *Contrada*, my sweet little green-eyed goose."

Before Rap could react, or over-react, I said — in English:

"Hey. fellas, what's this all about? We're just tourists here for a good time." Play dumb. Ilene caught on right away:

"Oh, isn't that a pretty one! With a tower on an elephant! Is this the *Contrada* of the Elephant? Where can I buy one of your neckerchiefs?"

With an effort Rap smiled, and with an even greater effort he kept silent. None of the men facing us were smiling yet, but another stepped forward. He struggled to communicate:

"*La Torre*! The Tower. This is. *Contrada* of Tower. That," — he pointed to Ilene's neck — "is *Oca*." It evidently cost him a lot to pronounce this hated word, and he was holding us responsible. "The Tower hate the *Oca* — the Goose! The Tower *distrugge* — *schiaccia* — destroy the *Oca*. Not wear never that in this *Contrada*, is very bad."

"Oh, isn't this exciting?" said Ilene as she hurriedly removed her neckerchief.

"You want wear, go to *Oca*. That way." And they all pointed down the street with looks of disgust.

"Thanks ever so much," said Ilene with a wave.

"Have a nice day," I added, and off we went.

"A good performance," said Rap when we were out of range. "But then, you are both professional actors, Ghosts of the Forum."

"Stupid men!" said Ilene. I was surprised. She was really angry. "You noticed they were all men, didn't you? Women have more sense, thank God. And I thought the Italian men had more sense. I mean, they don't kill and maim each other at football matches the way the British fans do. I mean, it's nice to cheer for a horse or a team, but why do men have to get all hot and offensive towards their adversaries? In a sport! In a game!"

"Well, the *Palio* is something more than that, as you know," said Rap. "And not all the *contradas* are enemies to the Goose. Each *contrada* has a few friends and enemies, but for the most part they are neutral to each other, I think."

"Except when they race, I suppose," I said.

"We will ask about it," Rap said.

"I'm rapidly losing interest," Ilene said. And in fact, she never put her neckerchief on again, not even when the sight of other people with the goose's colors made it clear that we were in friendly territory.

CHAPTER XVI

On average, at least one horse dies each year in Siena during the Palio, either from heart failure or wounded and subsequently put to sleep.

Jim and two *ocaioli* were standing in front of the restaurant, waiting for us. We were only a few minutes late, but Jim was displeased. His two companions, Jacopo and Anacleto, made light of it and seemed glad to make our acquaintance.

Inside, the place seemed to be part museum — there were all sorts of objects hanging and lying about, clearly having to do with the *Palio*. I didn't understand a great deal of what was explained to us about the various helmets, bits, riding suits, and what-not — until we came to some stiff, tan-colored whips about a yard long. Jim wanted to know more about them and translated the parts I didn't catch. They were the whips, called *nervi*, that the jockeys used in the *Palio*. They were rough, almost rigid, and looked wicked. But when Jim said something about how they must sting, our guides laughed and showed us what the jockeys used until 1715: a thing called a *sovatto* that was a wooden handle for two long leather cords with lead balls at the ends. It was long enough for a jockey to be able to wrap it around an enemy jockey's arm and pull him off balance, even make him fall. Our guide said this with definite nostalgia. "But even today," he added to cheer us up — in Italian, but I'm translating — "a good jockey uses his *nervo* more on the other jockeys and horses than on his own."

"And that's legal?"

"It's more than legal. It is essential."

The four of us sat down to eat with our two hosts and to be patiently instructed in the true meaning of the *Palio*. Rap and Ilene sat together on one end of the table and somewhat out of the thick of the conversation, because Ilene had really been turned off by the excessive zeal of the men we had met. I think Rap would have liked to pay more attention, but to his credit he was a dutiful fiancé and tended to Ilene more than to us.

The food was very good, as far as I can recall. We had *capriolo*, which is really venison, but the deer in question is a small European deer whose meat is tender and tasty — at least in this restaurant it was. But I didn't pay much attention to the food — and I went easy on the *chianti* — because I was fascinated by the intensity of these two men as they talked about their *Palio*. This was not just the passion of young men, of "fans" of sports rivalry: these men were both over 50 and this was part of their lives, a big part of their idea of themselves. They wanted me to understand, so they spoke slowly and repeated often. They have a whole special vocabulary, a medieval Sienese vocabulary that they still use for all the elements of the *Palio*, and even Jim had to have lots of words explained. The horse isn't a *cavallo* but a *barbero*, the start of the race isn't the *partenza* but the *mossa*, and so on.

It became clear that we weren't only talking about a colorful pageant, but about something very fundamental: a battle against the adverse forces of the Universe. Each *contrada* stood pitted not only against the other sixteen, but also against the indifference and even hostility of the spirits, both pagan and Christian, who must be reckoned with at every *Palio*. And the greatest enemy, the one that required months of effort and millions of *lire* to placate, was the treachery in the heart of every man, both friend

180

and foe. But alas, treachery can only be countered by treachery. Thus it was that the jockey had to be richly paid, and tempted, and bought, and betrayed, and won back again. The horses, the *barberi*, had to be assigned by lot to the various *contradas* only three days before the race, and then guarded day and night. Even the *nervi*, those vicious whips, could only be distributed to the jockeys by a city official at the very last minute before the race, to prevent switching them for even deadlier versions. And there were the *partiti* — months of negotiations among the *contradas*, all trying to thwart the indifference of the Universe, to show that man, by his cunning and determination, can force the spirits to be propitious. Intricate alliances, counter-alliances, and oaths of iron are secretly made and still more secretly broken, more to be sure that an enemy *contrada* doesn't win than to guarantee one's own victory. Because victory in a *Palio* is the fickle product of so much chance and corruption — and even of ability and courage — that no single *contrada* can hope to control it all. I asked about the way things stood for the Noble Goose in that afternoon's *Palio*.

"We are not racing to win. Of course it could happen, but..."

"We have a nice horse, but the wrong jockey.'

"Wrong jockey! Why did you hire him?" asked Jim.

"To keep him from riding for the Tower. He's a very good jockey. In fact, they have drawn an excellent horse, a beautiful animal. He might have won for them."

"Why can't he win for you?"

"Because he takes money from the Snail. The Snail has an alliance with the Tower."

"So he won't ride your horse to win," I said.

"No, but we have promised him money to favor the

Turtle. The Turtle is an ally. If we can help them to victory, they will be in our debt for the future. And most of all the Tower will not win. The Tower must not win."

"But why do the Goose and the Tower hate each other?" This was one of Ilene's rare questions. I'm glad I didn't ask it. The two men looked at her as if she were a child who had just asked why dogs fight cats. Jacopo took it upon himself to answer:

"Because they have always hated each other." This reply and the condescension surrounding it did not help Ilene recover her interest in the *Palio*. Not at all. Jacopo turned back to Jim and me to continue: "We have promised money to four jockeys to make sure the Tower doesn't win."

"We will make an effort to win when we have the She-Wolf by our side," said Anacleto. "She isn't running today. We need her, she is a strong and faithful ally."

"The best thing is to run with the She-Wolf and the Turtle and find the Tower running alone, without allies. That is the golden opportunity."

"Wouldn't it be better still if the Tower were not competing?" I suggested carefully.

"Ah no, ah no. To be truly tasty, a victory must be seasoned with the salty tears of the Tower." This sounded better in Italian, I must admit.

"The *Torraioli* cannot be allowed to say that we won only because they were not running."

"Okay," I said, trying to sum things up, "but today we should look to see the Tower lose, and the Goose help the Turtle win. Is that it?"

"Well, yes. These are the *partiti chiari*, the open agreements. Not really open, but traditional. Everyone knows about them, or can assume that they exist."

"Then there are the *partiti segreti* — the secret

182

agreements. And they must remain secret, I'm afraid." A moment of disappointed silence. At least *I* was disappointed. We were at the end of the meal, waiting only for our coffee. I toyed with my spoon.

"...But Giacomo is an *Ocaiolo* now," said Jacopo, "a member of the *Contrada* in every respect. We must trust him."

"Yes," said Anacleto, "we must trust Giacomo, but..." And at this point he looked up and let his glance fall on Ilene. That did it.

"*Signori*," she said in Italian with a brogue, "I am only too happy to be left out of your silly *imbrogli*."

And she stood up. Of course, all the rest of us stood up, Jim last of all.

"I think we'll go for a little walk," said Rap. "Where can we meet?"

"In our chapel, for the blessing," said Anacleto. "In about an hour."

"I'll come with you," I said.

"Hell, there's no point in me staying here alone," said Jim in English. "You was the one that seemed interested in all this stuff."

"Well I am, but..."

Anacleto seemed to understand the problem and said to me: "You can stay. You are Giacomo's nephew, and you will not embarrass him by breaking our trust."

"What about Rap?" I said. "He's Giacomo's son!"

"He accompanies the girl." His tone of voice made it sound like whatever Ilene had, it was catching.

"That's right," said Rap, "stay and listen, Bob. You won't get another chance."

"We'll see you later, Bob," said Ilene. "We're just going to visit a church I wanted to see." So the two of them left, and the four of us sat back down.

"I am sorry she was offended," said Jacopo.

"No," I said, "I don't think these things matter much to her."

"She's a woman," observed Anacleto. "It would be dangerous to tell her certain things; she would treat them lightly."

"We don't even tell our women," said Jacopo.

"All right, what don't you tell them?" asked Jim, a little impatiently.

"For example, that we have a *partito segreto* with the Caterpillar. The Granny."

"The Granny?" I exclaimed.

"Shhhh!" they both said, looking around.

"Sorry," I whispered, "I thought this was Goose country."

"It is, but there are spies everywhere."

"Okay, so what's the Granny?" I asked softly.

"Now it's the Caterpillar. It's the Grandmother, the *contrada* that has lived the longest without a victory. A terrible thing. A sort of half-life, pitied by everyone except your enemy, who grows fat with gloating. The poor Caterpillar has not won a *Palio* in over 30 years. If they could only be made to win..." The speaker seemed to drift off into a beautiful dream. His friend continued for him:

"If the Caterpillar won, there would be a new Granny. And do you know who it would be?" His eyes lit up: there was only one possible answer.

"The Tower?"

"Yes!" they both said, "The Tower has not won since 1961! Their young men are virgins, joyless virgins!"

"In secret we have sewn together a Granny cap, a bonnet for the Tower. For the real Tower, the Mangia Tower, their symbol, with many white sheets. The day

184

the Caterpillar wins, a helicopter will drop the bonnet over the Mangia Tower."

"And there will be such rejoicing in this Noble *Contrada* as Siena has never seen!"

"But in order to help the Caterpillar," I said almost unwillingly, "you've got to double-cross your friends of the Turtle. Am I right?" Perhaps for a moment they felt embarrassment — but for me, not for themselves.

"What you say is not exact."

"These are hard things to understand, certainly."

"If the Caterpillar does not start well, we will still help the Turtle, of course."

"And if the Caterpillar should win with our help, we shall redouble our efforts for the Turtle at the next opportunity. They will understand."

"And if they don't, we will remind them of what happened in 1883."

"Yes, 1883. The Turtle's explanations have never convinced us. But for me, we do not need such justifications. You see, there is a transcendence here."

"Yes, a transcendence. To see the Tower wear the Granny's bonnet must transcend all other considerations."

"But how are you going to favor the Caterpillar?" I asked. Jim looked at me balefully. He was tiring of the intricacies of the *partiti*. Anacleto sighed, checked the room once more, and then leaned close:

"If the Panther can spring the Caterpillar off to a good start, look for the Dragon to run the Sea-Urchin into the wall on the second lap."

"Ooooh," I said.

"I'm afraid we can say no more."

"No problem, no problem," said Jim.

"Well, I hope...I hope it all works out for you," I said.

"It will work out as it must work out. And in the

end...*La Sorte*."

"The Quirk of Fate. *La Sorte*. She is no one's ally, she cannot be bought. Very often she decides the *Palio*. But we can try. We can try to impose order and sense on these things."

This last comment seemed to rekindle Jim's interest.

"Well," he said, "you can't be blamed for trying to do that, but there are ways and ways. I don't like the looks of those whips they use on the horses."

Jacopo ignored this, and took up where Anacleto had left off: "What men would we be to stand helplessly by and not take a hand in our destinies?"

I found myself agreeing. And I began to feel that what happened to the Goose and the Tower and the Giraffe and the rest of them was something of importance. It was the Middle Ages living on, its passions burning unchanged in generations of different Sienese keeping the same symbolic animals proudly alive and running: the Owl, the Snail, the Porcupine galloping wildly, banging into each other down through the centuries. In the end I was fervently drinking to the glory of the Noble Goose and the downfall of the Elephant's Tower.

When Jim was asked to propose a toast, he raised his glass of mineral water to the horses. This reminded our hosts that it was time to go to the chapel for the blessing, because it was the horse that would be blessed. Somehow this didn't surprise me at all. Everything possible had to be done to favor the cause of the Noble Goose, and it was only wise to bring to bear the ritual power of the Church.

The chapel was hard to distinguish from the other buildings attached to it along the populous old street. In fact it had originally been the workshop of a dyer named Jacopo Benincasa. That was in the 14th century. Jacopo's daughter Catherine worked in the shop, and now she's Saint Catherine, Patron of the Goose, of Siena and of all Italy. This was explained to me as we stood before the statue at the entrance to the chapel. Sure enough, she was wearing a Goose neckerchief.

"A great saint," Jacopo said. "A Doctor of the Church."

"Really?" I said. I would have something to say to Father Tom back at the Academy. "What was her doctrine?"

"The inner cell," he said, touching my chest. "Hard to find, but if you enter it, you find yourself." Jim and Anacleto had already gone in, and now we followed them into the chapel.

It was crowded with people, most of whom wore the colors of the *Contrada*. Ilene and Rap were nowhere to be seen. In the center there were the priest and the horse. Jacopo and Anacleto must have been Geese of some weight: a path was made for the four of us and we were allowed to stand close to the *barbero* that would carry our colors a few hours later. It was a beautiful animal. I can't say any more, because I don't know anything about horses, but this was a strong, proud creature with a brown coat and a long silken tail.

"Damn good-looking horse," whispered Jim.

"You know horses?"

"Poor fella. Bet he'd like to be someplace else."

"I think he's enjoying the attention."

The priest started his prayers and sprinklings. I'm not Catholic, but this has got to be the reason why this church just goes on and on. It knows how to be present in everything that reaches down inside people.

Ilene and Rap came in but didn't try to work their way to the middle where we were. We waved. I wondered if they brought horses inside the churches in

Ireland. Rap was nibbling Ilene's ear with explanations.

"Standing room only," I said to Anacleto, "and I was told that the Church is weak in Italy — that the Communist Party is very strong."

"Yes, the Party is strong in Siena. I'm Communist. But this is the *Palio*. The *Palio* without the Church would be a horse race. Look!" And he started clapping. Everybody started clapping. The horse was defecating. By that I mean he was crapping all over the floor of the chapel.

I saw Ilene turn her face away. The priest, without stopping his orations, made a motion with his hand and an acolyte hurried towards the sacristy.

"It's supposed to be a good sign," said my Communist friend. "The blessing is taking effect. In my opinion it is a good sign only because it means the animal has digested well and will be light on his hooves." The acolyte returned with a pail and shovel. He didn't seem at all displeased about his role in the ceremony.

"Damnedest thing I ever got into," said Jim.

"That can't be right," I answered. "You got into World War II."

"Then let's say it's the damnedest thing a horse ever got into. Beautiful horses like this one. Don't like the idea of these animals being cut with those thongs, whatever they call them."

"A *nervo*, I think it was." Jim was developing a negative attitude here, and I didn't know what to do about it. But I already knew enough about Jim to be a little worried.

CHAPTER XVII

According to the records, a jockey ran for the Torre in July and the opposing Oca in August of the same year. He raced with his body covered in soap to flee from the hands of the furious contradaioli at the end of the race. It was 1844.

After the ceremony the six of us headed towards Piazza del Campo, where the race would be held. It took us quite a while to get there, because those narrow medieval streets were really crowded now. A hundred thousand people were trying to get into the piazza and find a good vantage point. I was getting very psyched up, I must admit. I was ready to cheer for the Goose and the Turtle and even the Caterpillar like I hadn't cheered since that day in my junior year when Northwestern came within sixteen points of beating Ohio State. But the thicker the crowds got, the more Jim looked like he'd rather be back in World War II. Ilene was grinning and bearing the crush as best she could, but it was clear that this would be her last *Palio.*

I could see that Jacopo was concerned about her, and in fact before we entered the Piazza he called a little meeting.

"I have two places, two good places on a balcony, my aunt's apartment. I think Rap and the Signorina should use them. In the piazza itself, it can be hard."

"Assuming there's room in there," I said.

"Oh, our places are reserved," said Anacleto.

"Always. Right on St. Martin's Curve."

"It is not a place for the Signorina, Rap," said Jacopo. "And on the balcony you will see better."

Ilene didn't need a lot of convincing, and we agreed to meet directly back at the *Crociato* after the race. Jim wanted to get back on the road. So Rap was pointed at the right door of the right building and told what to say, and then the four of us forged ahead.

After all the small, shadowy, up-and-down streets and squares, we finally emerged into the enormous, sun-drenched Piazza del Campo, the main "square" of Siena that is anything but square. Its shape is hard to define: like an open fan, but concave, because the Piazza is really the valley in the middle of the three hills on which the city is built. It is completely surrounded and molded by beautiful old buildings, all the same style and height with the exception of the Public Palace, Siena's city hall, where the fingers would grasp the fan. The Palace is all arches, wide ones along the ground level, graceful triple ones at each of the many windows above, so we're talking about Gothic here, but the overall impression was one of strength and solidity because of the size and sober proportions of the building itself. Its only irregularity was the proud bell tower that rose alone into the blue sky from the extreme left front corner of the Palace. Anacleto saw me staring up at it.

"The Mangia Tower," he said. "It needs a bonnet."

"I thought 'Mangia' was a verb," I said in my broken Italian, which I am repairing and translating here — "a verb meaning 'eat.'"

"It was the nickname of the first bell ringer, a man in the 14th century named Giovanni di Duccio, but whom everybody called Mangiaguadagni — 'Profit-eater.' Or just 'Eater' for short."

"Had his hand in the till?"

"Something like that. But he was a good bell ringer, so the Tower still has his name — the Eater's Tower. I'm sure it sounds stupid to you. To an American."

"No, no, it's a great idea. Most of the buildings in Chicago could be named that way."

By this time we had got right up to a barrier, the outer edge of the track that had been marked out all around the Piazza — a one-lap distance of about 400 yards.

And sure enough, there was "dirt in the square," in accordance with the famous phrase Rap had used in Rapallo to announce the *Palio*. The "track" had in fact been covered with a layer of tuff sand, sand of volcanic origin, of which there's a lot around Siena. It's not so much to help the horses run, Jacopo informed us, as it is to soften the landings of the jockeys, who are often thrown off — because they ride bareback.

St. Martin's Curve, where we were standing, was the sharpest curve, about 75 degrees, before the horses dashed back down the "home stretch," the long straightaway in front of the Public Palace. Generations of ingenuity had found ways to jam people into every possible corner, every imaginable vantage point around the Piazza — besides the thousands packed into the "infield."

"Where are Rap and Ilene?" I asked.

"That balcony over there," answered Jacopo, pointing off to the right, "where the window shutters are blue."

"I can't make them out."

"They are probably inside, drinking wine with my aunt. My aunt is old and loves company."

"And she loves an excuse to drink," added Anacleto.

191

"Well, it looks like a wonderful place to watch the race," I said. "A good overview."

"Good for women and outsiders. The *contrada* people are down here, as close as we can get. And this is the curve where the race is won or lost. Every man you can see within fifteen yards is a *contradaiolo*, mostly geese because this is our sector, but even the others. All important *contradaioli*." Anacleto smiled at this moment of pride. "We're here to be sure that our agreements are respected, that our money is well-spent, that our friendship is well-placed. I warn you that after the race — even during the race — it is possible for fights to break out here. We must be careful. But the real *Palio* is here. If you just want to see the horses run, you can go to my house and watch it on television."

"*Col cavolo*," I said. "With cabbage" is the Italian way to say "not for the world." I looked at Jim. From his expression, he would have passed the whole thing up for a lot less. Even when the big pre-race parade started, Jim didn't cheer up. The only thing he seemed somewhat pleased about was the fact that I was clearly enjoying myself.

The parade took almost two hours. Our friends explained it all, they told us what rank this or that costumed figure held in medieval Siena, or what authority he still held in one or another of the seventeen *contradas* that solemnly paraded by, but now it's all a marvelous blur of color and drums and trumpets in my mind. A few things stand out: each *contrada* had two *alfieri* able to hurl the flags of the *contrada* back and forth to each other and high into the air — one of the Tower's *alfieri* dropped a flag, which was immediately welcomed by us as an excellent sign. At the end came the "Cart of Triumph" drawn by four white oxen and carrying trumpeters, medieval VIPs, and the *Palio* itself, hanging from a pole. I was sure Ilene could paint a nicer Madonna, but that wasn't the point. I had learned that much.

Ilene and Rap had since appeared at their balcony, together with all the old lady's other guests — she had no lack of company on *Palio* days. We had managed to wave to each other. Even Jim had raised his hand. This was the sum of his involvement with his surroundings, until the Cart of Triumph had passed.

Behind the Cart, almost as an afterthought, rode six armored, forlorn figures in unrecognizable costumes — by that I mean they didn't wear the colors of any of the seventeen *contradas*. And they did nothing, saluted no one, played no instruments, and hurled no flags — they just rode along in silence, visors down. Jim took some interest in them, enough to ask the question: "Who are these guys?"

"They are the knights of the six dead *contradas*," answered Jacopo. "Six *contradas* were suppressed in 1675. It is a reminder of them — and of the fact that all things can end, even the *Contrada*. Even the *Palio*."

I hadn't even seen one yet, and already this seemed a terrible thought to me.

The parade had ended. Now everyone's attention was focused far down the straightaway, where preparations were finally being made to start the race. All they had were two thick ropes strung across the track, and the idea seemed to be to get all the horses between the two ropes, drop the lead rope and that would be the start of the race. But they did this twice and called the horses back with a gunshot, because they were false starts. Our friends tried to explain that the *mossiere*, the guy that drops the rope, was following a complicated procedure, an order that

193

had to be respected, otherwise he would have angry *contradas* at his heels for months. In any case the *mossiere* never gets to see the race — he is always spirited away immediately after the start, because he can never satisfy everyone. Nine of the horses, skittish horses with conniving jockeys, have to line up in a certain way, and the tenth enters the roped area on the run — only then can the *mossiere* drop the rope. And there are some things jockeys can do to each other at the start, others they can't do until the race is underway. However it is, they finally did get the whole act together and off to a valid start on the third try.

And for the next few minutes this great and ancient Piazza was a single living thing, a thing that had resumed its life, the same unbroken, passionate life it had known twice a year for hundreds and hundreds of years. A high roar swept around her together with the careening horses, and she surged, literally surged and swayed behind them.

We got our first good look at them as they swung out of the back stretch and headed straight for us. It didn't look anything at all like the slick, streamlined races you see at regular racetracks. This was more like a stampede, or a cavalry charge. Into the valley of death rode the ten, bunching up and spreading out, cutting each other off and springing each other loose. And the *nervi*, the thongs Jim hated, kept flailing away, sometimes at the horses, sometimes at the jockeys. They charged right at us, swinging as wide as possible before having to veer sharply to the right, into St. Martin's curve. In three seconds they had pounded by, but in those three seconds the bricks shook beneath me, I smelled the heavy odor of powerful animals under great strain, I heard a tense babble of curses and commands, I saw one of those nervi

194

come within a foot of my nose.

"Did you see the way that son of a bitch was whipping that black horse?" cried Jim excitedly. "Did you see that? Nephew! Bob! You okay?"

I was staring rigidly and blankly down after the horses, breathing through clenched teeth. I was holding the barrier so hard my hands were white and sore.

"See? See?" Our friends had a moment to spare before the horses came back into view. "The...the...the positions are good!" They didn't want to tip their hand by shouting the wrong thing. "And the Tower is losing!"

"Can't lose enough to suit me," Jim said to me, "He's the one I mean, in dark red on the black horse. The one that was drawing blood with that damned thing. He better not come close to me again."

"Just watch the race, Jim!" I shouted in my excitement.

"There's some things I just don't like."

Now the great roar was approaching again, and I was determined not to be overwhelmed, to try to judge the positions and the chances of the horses we were interested in. This is about like standing in front of a speeding truck, trying to read the license plate. But Jim was unfazed. Mad as hell, but in control.

"That poor horse is in a frenzy," he said in a low, hard voice. "Look at the froth! Swing out over here again, you son of a bitch!"

I don't think that Jim really believed he could do what he then did. He probably just wanted to make the gesture, to show his anger, to leave nothing untried. He shot out his long left arm just as the black horse was thundering along our barrier, straining to make the turn. He caught the jockey's whip-thong in his big hand. As soon as he felt resistance, he let go, but it was too late. The whip was secured to the jockey's hand by a small loop around the wrist, and Jim's split-second pull was enough to unbalance the little man. He slid cleanly off the big horse's bare back. He landed on his own back, and skidded and rolled for about ten yards before crashing into the curving barrier. The horse just kept right on running.

The jockey slowly got to his feet. He was clearly not too sure about what had happened to him. Few people were, besides Jim and me and our two friends.

"Giacomo, *per l'amor di Dio*," hissed the Anacleto.

"Quiet, quiet!" whispered Jacopo. "Do nothing. Say nothing. Deny everything. Perhaps only our people noticed. It may have been well done. The Tower was moving up."

"No, not enough to win," answered Anacleto. "But it is an ignominious end for the Tower, very fitting. He was cruelly punishing that fine horse. *La Sorte*. Destiny. In this *Palio*, you are *La Sorte*, Giacomo."

The jockey was less confused now and, having tested his bones, was moving slowly back along the barrier asking angry questions.

"Here they come again!" I shouted in English, to fend off suspicion and distract everyone. And in fact the horses were coming for the third and last time. Rumbling madly towards us — and I had to laugh. The riderless black horse was out in front!

"Hah!" cried Jim. "You see? That horse is so happy he's running like the wind!"

The Tower's jockey, now only about five feet from us, let out a joyful whoop, as the horses ran by him, he used the whip still attached to his hand to selectively whack the legs of jockeys — particularly the Goose. I looked at Anacleto. Death was in his face.

"Wait a minute," I said. "A horse without a rider can't

win a race! Can it?" A cry of wild triumph went up from one particular sector of the crowd just beyond the finish line. The hated sector of the Tower. Our friends both plunged their faces into their hands and dug deep with their fingers.

And that's how Jim and I learned that in the *Palio* it's the horse that counts, and he can and sometimes does win without his rider. Not very often, but some horses, like the Tower's big black horse, evidently prefer running alone. So would I, for that matter. And in fact, that's what Jim and I started to do. Our Communist friend had begun remembering all our ideological differences and had started murmuring *cretini americani* over and over. Our other friend had simply moaned and said "Go as fast as you can."

So we took advantage of those first few moments of despair and abandon to slip and elbow away, amid scenes of agony that had probably inspired Dante for his Hell, if he ever saw a *Palio*.

CHAPTER XVIII

In Italy, anything older than 50 years found underground,
even in your own garden, is government property.

It happened right in front of you, didn't it?" Rap asked, when he and Ilene joined us an hour later back at the motor home.

"Yep. Sure did," answered Jim.

"Well, how did the jockey fall off? On TV he's saying he slid off on purpose, because he realized it was the kind of horse that didn't want a rider. But there's a videotape that seems to show an arm grabbing the jockey's whip."

"Awfully blurred, though," added Ilene.

"That's good," I said.

"What? You don't mean that...?" All three of us looked at Jim.

"You hadda see what he was doin' to that horse. Just no call for it. Didn't want to hurt the jockey none, and I sure didn't think it made much difference to the race, but a man can't just stand by."

"Wow!" exclaimed Ilene. "Quite a father-in-law I'm getting!"

"He should start calming down at his age," said Rap. "*Papà*, you had no right to interfere."

"It seemed right at the time. Listen, even if it was a mistake, the Lord must have wanted it to happen. So let's just leave it at that. We gotta get going."

"I believe it," said Rap. "You cannot show your face here again. Jacopo and Anacleto were mad, weren't they?"

"I wouldn't call on them for a few years, if I was you."

"Jacopo's aunt is such a dear," said Ilene. "She

certainly cheered for the Goose, but I'm sure she's no fanatic, like the men. She gave us a nice souvenir."

"She liked Ilene very much," said Rap.

"Well, Ilene's not all bad, you know," I said.

"Nephew, let's get on the road," said Jim.

Ilene pulled a piece of cloth out of her bag. "Take it with you. For good luck. She stitches them by hand. I think that's all she has to do all day."

And there it was, but only a foot wide and three feet long, a stitched version of the *Palio* that the Tower had just won. I still didn't like this Madonna. She looked too smug. Irene handed her over to Jim. He studied her in silence.

"Hope she brings you more luck than you did to the Geese, Jim," I said.

"We'll meet again, won't we, Bob?" asked Ilene. "I mean, before you leave Italy."

"Sure!" I said. "We can all get together again in Rome before I go. After Anzio, right Jim?"

"After Anzio, you run the show."

"I've got your phone number, Ilene. I'll call you when we arrive. How about going back to 'Da Leccarsi i Baffi'?"

"No, we'll have to do better than that," said Rap. "I will work on it. I will find a very nice place."

"So long, Rap," said Jim, taking his son's hand. "So long, young lady. This boy ain't bad, but he'll never be rich. You better think it over. Come on, Bob." And with that he jumped into the *Crociato* and started the engine.

That gave me time for one last laugh with Rap and Ilene, and then we were off.

"Back to the toll road, Jim, or is there a Roman road we can take?"

"The Via Cassia. Only about thirty miles, we'll be at Lake Bolsena, one of my favorite places. Nice and quiet.

A good place for the night, and a good place to talk. Good place to show you a few things. It's an important spot for me."

"Know something? I think that in the long run you did a great thing here. I mean *loong* run, years and years, but that's the way that race is measured. They spend all their time trying to screw it up — you heard about the deals and bribes — I mean that race exists to be fixed. That's what they talk about, and they'll still be talking about you a hundred years from now. You'll be a legend! They'll paint you on the backside of these *Palio* things here, see? They'll write 'The Madonna proposes and Giacomo disposes. '" I was examining Ilene's gift in the dim, remaining light. It was already past eight o'clock.

"Turn on a light if you want to see that thing better."

"So you shouldn't feel any deep regrets."

"Nephew, a man my age has got other things to regret besides spoiling somebody's fun. If you're hungry, go back and help yourself."

"That was a big meal we had with the Geese. I'll wait till we stop."

Lake Bolsena turned out to be a fair-sized lake, egg-shaped and maybe ten miles long, with a couple of small, wooded islands. Jim took a dirt road and parked right down at the edge, between a vineyard on the left and an olive grove on the right. Then he got out his little fold-up table and two chairs, some soft cheese and some crusty Tuscan bread that lasts for days and days, two big peaches, and a bottle of water, and we had a lakeside, moonlit supper. Around the lake we could see the lights of little towns and villages.

"There's fish in here still," said Jim. "Whitefish and pike. Might give it a try tomorrow morning early."

"I don't know where you get your energy, Jim. This

has been a long day, and I don't see how you can even think about getting up early."

"Don't like to sleep. Don't enjoy it. Hell, it rests me up just being out and away from all that racket and all those people."

"Well, you're in great shape. Tough as an old jeep. Good for thirty more years."

"God willing, nephew, God willing. But I don't think He is. I've run out of nails."

"The nails. Are you going to tell me about the nails now?"

"Don't like to just tell things. I like to show things. This is the place. I'll show you tomorrow."

We ate and drank in silence for a few minutes. I watched the "moonlight sleeping on a midnight lake," as it does in the Paul Simon song. The scene was giving rest and strength to Jim. What was the title of the song? 'Homeless.' That was me, out of place here. I was more at home back in Siena, conniving with the Geese. For example, the idea that Jim thought he was close to death was again making me wonder about what he was planning to leave me.

"Jim, I don't think you have a thing to worry about with Rap and Ilene, They know what they're doing. Great people, I love them both."

"A little responsibility might do Rap some good."

"And of course, you'll help them out."

"The Lord might give me the time to find them something nice for a wedding present. There's a few good spots I ain't never swept..."

"No. I mean setting them up..."

"Rap don't want that. Never has."

"I know, he told me, but..."

"A lotta money would ruin Rap. And in a different

way it would ruin Agnese. Wouldn't hurt you, though."

"I'm not so bad off, Jim. I've got a big house, a good job — you should at least get Agnese out from behind that fruit stand."

"Did she look unhappy to you?"

"No she didn't, but..."

"She loves that fruit stand. I think she's pretty rich, pretty prosperous in her own way."

"If she gets any more prosperous, she won't get through the door, for that matter. but..."

"Do you really think that she and her sailor husband would be better off home counting money? Or out buying junk?"

"Do you think that's what they'd do?"

"It happens a lot when simple folks fall into big money. I seen it, Bob. They don't know how to be rich. Way I see it, you gotta be brought up a certain way to use money right. Me, for example, I got no business trying to live rich, I'd make a damn fool of myself. Can you see me in a ballroom, or playing country-club golf?"

"Maybe not."

"And I can't see Agnese either. But I know that you play golf. You'd know what to do with money. George wrote and told me about your good education and good teaching job, and your wife and boy in a big house..."

"Who's George? That detective in Chicago?"

"Yep."

"In exchange for his services, do you help him find runaway husbands over here?"

"Hah! Ain't that low. Helped him find a kid once. No. I give George some old coins now and then. He collects them. He won't take regular pay from me. Says he owes it to me."

"Another favor? Who did you blow up for him?"

"Nobody. I kept him from getting blown up. He froze in a German minefield at Anzio. But the mine pattern was easy to read. Anyway I had his address, and I wrote to him a few years after the war, asked him to look into a few things for me. And later he helped me find a couple good buyers for my stuff. Figured I could trust him, and I was right. I see him every so often when he's over here for work. He's been a big help. Now he's retiring. This is his last year. But it's mine too, so I won't be needing him."

"Nonsense. We should talk about what I'll be leaving you, not what you'll be leaving me."

"Don't even let that cross your mind. Told you, I got more'n I know what to do with. Now you, you'll know what to do with what I leave you. Hell, there's all kinds of smart ways to spend money on the North Shore, where you live."

That called for a laugh, but I didn't. I have to admit I was excited. "Well, right now about the only smart thing that comes to my mind would be a good college for Bret. That's been a worry of mine."

"See? That's great."

"But what about Agnese's girl? What about putting her through college?"

"She wants to be a dental technician and marry a dentist. Don't need no degree for that."

"And if she changes her mind?"

"It don't cost hardly much at all to study in Italy, if you got the time, and she'd have plenty of that. She ain't in no necessity of earning her living."

"Well, in the States when you talk college, a good college, you're talking big bucks, Jim. I mean, like eighteen thousand a year."

"Listen, I want to show you something inside. We're done out here, aren't we? Should be getting to bed. Had a big day."

"That we have."

So we put away the table and chairs and got into the *Crociato*. "Now sit down there a minute, and turn on that light for yourself." I sat down on my bed. Jim opened a drawer, took out an envelope, and sat down on his, across from mine.

"Now some of the stuff I find, if I don't think that I can sell it easily, I just leave it in the ground where it was. The ground has taken care of it for all these years, it can stay there a few hundred more. The Lord'll let the right person find it. A fished-out lake is a sad and selfish thing." He opened the envelope and took out the sheet of paper inside. "Then there's a few things I keep, because I like them, or want to give them to somebody. But most of the stuff I sell. I've got buyers here and there. We're gonna meet one."

"You know," I said, "a friend of mine, the one who helped me sell that — what's it called — that *bulla* you sent me, he said...well, what it comes down to is that he said it's wrong for you to just dig this stuff up and sell it."

"Some of what I do is illegal, nephew, but that don't mean it's wrong. Now what your friend back there is worried about is knowledge, right? If I just throw these things around, the experts won't be able to study them and know what they mean and all that, right?"

"That's the idea, I guess."

"It ain't no real problem. I sell my stuff to the right people, people that write for magazines, people that hunt stuff up for museums and universities. I show them exactly where I found it. I even take pictures of important things before I pick them up, and pictures of the area. Most of my stuff is on display somewhere. Mostly foreigners. Italian museums ain't got no money, and if they did they wouldn't give it to me. Think everything belongs to them by right."

"Maybe it does. That's why you gave that piece of breastplate to your Geese friends, remember? You said it belonged to them."

"Sure did. It means a lot to them, and you should see how nice they got it all decked out. But hell, if the Italian government gets ahold of my stuff all they'll do is box it up and hide it away. Bob, there's enough stuff getting moldy in the basements of Italian museums to stock the world. There's more locked up than there is on display, and I ain't kidding. The Italians ain't got the money, the space, or the time to begin ordering and putting out what they got, let alone new stuff. I say, spread it around a bit. A man from Japan I deal with told me they're adding a new room to their museum there, whatever town it is, just for the things I been selling him. Here they have trouble keeping the museums open, for lack of money. They let beautiful old buildings and castles and what-not go all to hell, stuff that in other countries they'd restore with tweezers."

"I think maybe you're coming down too hard on the Italians. I think maybe you're rationalizing."

"I think maybe you got me wrong. And I hope you don't think you know the Italians better'n me."

"You can't expect them to all tiptoe around with tweezers and dust-cloths as if the whole country were a museum. They've got a present and a future, not just a past."

"I say, if there's people willing to come in and work, they should be encouraged somehow. Maybe with a percentage. I don't know. And they should be helped to do it right."

"How about the ring you gave to Agnese? And my

bulla? Was that done right? The museum people would love to know where it was found."

"I just wanted to do something nice for her. And for you. Lord, you should be a drill sergeant. You're the worst nit-pickin' stickler for detail I come across in a long time. We've all got enough to answer to God for, without making up stuff to answer to each other for. Unless maybe you're perfect. You perfect?"

"Not the last time I looked. I'm sorry, Jim. You've been in this business for years, and I don't know a thing about it."

"Teachers always think they gotta teach."

"That might be it."

"Well, I could teach you a few things about digging up old stuff, and cleaning it, and selling it. I've been cheated a few times, but now I pretty well know what a thing should fetch. Been doing all right, even after my...obligations. Take a look at this."

He handed me the sheet of paper he had been holding. It was a year-end statement from a Roman bank, for an account in Jim's name, James Savorski — and in mine. It was right there: Robert Svenson.

"That's the only place in the world where I still use my real name, otherwise on everything else it's Giacomo Savori. 'Cause it's James Savorski that's leaving you this money. And this here's a way to beat inheritance taxes. The bank just has orders to notify you if I ever let six months go by without contacting them. All you'll have to do is walk in, prove who you are, and collect. Now that you know about it, you could do it any time. Far as the bank's concerned, that money's as much yours as it is mine."

"As far as I'm concerned it's all yours, Jim."

"You can have some when you go home, and the rest

when I go belly up."

I smiled and read the bottom figure. I stopped smiling and started dividing by the current rate of exchange.

"I think it's 'bout enough to buy a nice house with," Jim said.

"Yes," I breathed, "one or two really nice ones."

CHAPTER XIX

*Scholars believe that Roman numerals originated
from the Etruscan way of counting years with
letters of their alphabet and...nails.*

The next morning with a supreme effort I rolled out of bed at seven o'clock, but of course Jim was already outside fishing. He was standing on a rock about fifteen feet from shore. His feet were bare, his pants were rolled up above the knees. He was casting in all directions.

"Any luck?" I called.

"Shnh! Whisper, dammit, or you'll scare them off! Had one strike but he spit it right out."

"What are you throwing?"

"Good ol' Silver Spoon with a little pork rind."

"Should I keep an eye out for the fish warden?"

"Hell no, I'm licensed for everything. Don't want no trouble. Listen nephew, long as you're out here, there's something I been meaning to ask you."

"Let's hear it."

"Was my sister Agnes happy with your father?" And with that he cast far off to the left.

"She might have done better, she could have done a lot worse," I answered. "He loved her, and he gave her security."

"That ain't hay."

"Not very exciting, either. She always spoke well of you, you know. She considered you an exciting person."

"She thought I was worth something. I knew that. I knew that. Even though I was a real son of a gun back then."

"So I've heard."

"What you heard?"

"Oh, the drinking, and the girls, and raising hell..."

Jim seemed to concentrate on his fishing for a minute before answering;

"Well, the drinking was easy to stop, 'cause that was only me. The girls wasn't so easy, 'cause sometimes it's them that wants it. And sometimes it's right, dammit. About the hell-raisin'..." he paused to cast, but then didn't continue.

"What about the hell-raising, Jim?"

"Still workin' on it. We're talking about a lotta hell. A lotta demons. Hah! Got him!"

Jim yanked on his pole and started to reel. The fish never jumped but was obviously pulling hard. It took Jim about five minutes to work it close enough to his rock so that he could squat down, reach into the water with his little hand net and lift it out. It was a pike, just like the northern pike I used to catch as a kid with my father on our annual fishing trip to Wisconsin.

The way it fought I expected it to be bigger, but it was only about 22 inches long.

"Good eating size," said Jim. So we had pike for breakfast that morning, cooked over an open fire. Great fish, if it weren't for all those little forked bones.

"You know," said Jim towards the end of our meal, "your mother was the only one who ever tried talking to me, back in Mattoon. Pa, he just whupped me. I think he whupped Ma, too, 'cause she never said much to anybody. But Agnes, she'd just come out and say what she thought. I was glad she cared, but I didn't pay no attention. So I been having to learn the hard way all my life. The Raséna been helping me. The Etruscans." He stood up. "No no, stay put and finish your pike. I'll make some coffee."

"Make it good and strong."

"It'll put lead in your pencil. Be right back. Got something to show you." He came back in a few seconds with a small pitcher of milk. "Here, take a look at this. It's Etruscan, one of the things I keep around. It means a lot to me, and that's why I got a right to keep it. See what you think of it. I'll be back with the coffee in a few minutes."

The pitcher was a beautifully shaped human head, a woman's head with her neck as the base and a simple cap, almost like a sailor's cap, as the opening. She had no handle, but was small enough to be easy to grasp. I picked her up carefully. She was made of black, shining ceramic that had been sparingly painted here and there with white and red to bring out her principal features: her finely-formed nose, her full, slightly parted lips, her large, knowing eyes...

"She's quite a gal, isn't she?" Jim was already back with the coffee. I wished he had taken longer.

"She's marvelous. Can't get over her."

"What do you like about her? Here's your coffee. Help yourself to the milk. Don't worry, I cleaned her up real good. I like thinking that I'm using something they used. Don't be scared, it won't break. They made things right. That's special Etruscan ceramic, experts call it *bucchero*. It's black and shiny all the way through, not just on the surface. And they still don't know how they did it."

I poured myself a little milk, but I didn't put the pitcher back down — I kept gazing into those big black eyes.

210

"Kind of gets you, don't it?" Jim said, sitting down.

"Sure does."

"But what is it that gets you?"

"I suppose her expression. Strong but serene. But there's something more. She's...She's..."

"She's trying to tell you something."

I gently put the pitcher back on the table. "That's it," I said quietly. "That's exactly it. You know, I saw a Madonna in Siena that struck me. The Big-eyed Madonna, it was called, but her eyes were all different. They were questioning eyes..."

"I told Rap once, for me the whole idea for Madonnas comes from the Raséna. I seen lots of them in the tombs. A mother sitting, talking to her boy. Teaching him something. A mouth like this one on the pitcher, with her lips open, ready to talk."

"What's she trying to say, Jim?"

"Wish to God I knew. She knows something about...about finding peace, you can see that. All the Raséna did. I got her out of a burial chamber I found near Cerveteri, a pretty good one. The gold and silver had all been stolen, but the rest was just lying there. Even a life-size bronze statue, that's what set my detector off. I told a Dutch magazine guy about the chamber — for some good money — and left everything as it was except for her, my pitcher here. She means more to me than...but I'll tell you, you can find that same expression of hers on other Etruscans — on statues, on the ones painted on walls, all over where they were, not just Cerveteri. And the funny thing is this: far as I can tell, they didn't have a whole lot to be happy and peaceful about. All kinds of troubles and dangers. They were good workmen, good traders, good sailors — but lousy soldiers."

"You told me that. And their secret weapon was

shoelaces. For running away."

"But later the Romans had 'em too. And they also had discipline, military discipline. The Raséna, hell, judging from their pictures they loved animals and fishing, and dancing and parties, and food and the ladies, not discipline. Whenever the Romans hit them, it was like German Panzers against the Poles."

"Well, with those fancy burial chambers of theirs, it probably means that they looked for happiness in the next world. Maybe that's what she's trying to say." I was staring at her again. That really didn't seem to be what she was saying.

"You'd think so, but then it don't make sense. There were thousands and thousands of demons in the Etruscan religion. I don't have any to show you because I don't like them. I sell them all, but I'm telling you that the next life for the Raséna looked like it had more dangers than this one. So how do you figure it?"

"Jim, it might just be a particular style of art."

He looked away, out over the morning lake.

"Jim, have you really gone into it? Have you read all about the Etruscans?"

Jim kept his head turned. "Ain't nothing much to read. Mostly I've talked to a few people. Nobody knows very much, because they don't know how to read Etruscan. I mean they can read the words, but they don't know what they mean, most of them. Damnedest thing. These people were just about wiped out. All their temples torn down, books destroyed, just about everything. Only the tombs — they was scared of wiping out the tombs."

"Who? Who was scared?"

"The Romans first. They wanted to wipe out the Etruscans because they liked to think they descended from Troy, you know, what's-his-name. Aeneas. But the

Romans were just dirt farmers at first. The Etruscans civilized them. The Etruscans really founded Rome for them. At least that's what this professor told me. So later the Romans tried to wipe out the evidence. Except for the tombs, which they were scared of touching. And then the Christians. They really did a job. The old Romans were good pagans; they had converted, so the Christians weren't so tough on their stuff, but the Raséna were bad pagans, the masters of black magic, and they had to be rubbed out.

"By the Middle Ages there wasn't nothing left. Except the tombs. They was scared of the tombs. There were grave robbers, but they just took some stuff, 'thout destroying the tombs. So there's still the pictures on the walls, and they tell you a lot."

"But not enough."

"Not enough for me. Know what I'd like to find? I know I never will, but I dream about it — the *Tyrrhenikà*. Know what that is?" Jim smiled a satisfied smile.

"Got me there."

"It's a book — really twenty books, a long thing, years of work, the complete story of the Etruscans. Written by a Roman emperor named Claudius. This Claudius was brought up by Etruscans, noble Raséna living in Rome. He was practically Etruscan, he married an Etruscan, he knew everything about them, he spoke the language, and he wanted to preserve all this, so he wrote this thing. But it was all destroyed after he died. The Romans didn't want any part of it. That was the end of it. Claudius was the last chance for the Etruscans. And they knew it right along. Knew they would be wiped out and knew when it would happen. At the end of their tenth age, their tenth century. They always knew it. 'The name of the Raséna' — this is what they said — 'The name of the Raséna will

213

stop being pronounced at the end of the tenth age.' Bingo. Corresponds right with the death of Claudius."

We finished our coffee. "This here lake," said Jim as he set his cup down, "this whole area here, was very important for the Etruscans. This was it, this was the center of the whole thing, the center of the League of the Twelve Cities. You know — Tarquinia, Fiesole, Volterra, Perugia, Arezzo..."

"And this was the center."

"Yep. Well, it's always been known that the center was around here somewhere, and that there was a kind of sanctuary where they worshipped two gods, Velthune and Nortia, who protected the League. Every year the Twelve Cities sent their representatives here. It was their biggest deal. They had games, they had a big market, they held their meeting and made their plans, they prayed and predicted the future — and at the end the High Priest hammered a nail in the wall in the temple of Nortia. Every year. This was a holy wall. The Etruscans knew that when they ran out of space for nails on this wall, that would be it. The end of Etruria. I've never got over that. They had this sense of being given only a certain amount of time by their gods, a definite time and a definite place in the world, then they would have to disappear."

"And that's what you mean when you say you've run out of nails."

"Yep."

"Go out and buy some more."

"Nope. I'm using theirs, and I can't find any more."

"Theirs? Whose? The Etruscans?"

"Who we been talking about? Now this is kind of a secret, nephew. I'm the only one who knows where that old sanctuary was. People been looking for it everywhere

214

from here to Orvieto, twelve miles away. It was completely destroyed by the Romans. I mean they obliterated it. It was the symbol of Etruscan unity, and they wanted people to forget where it was. Know what they did? I got it figured out. They carted off all the stones, plowed everything up and planted olive trees." I shot a glance into the olive grove on our right.

"That's right. Those might not be the same trees, but olive trees do live for hunnerds and hunnerds of years, and once an olive grove gets started it keeps going — you just replace the sick trees. In there is where it was, Bob. I got the suspicion when the professor told me about all the things, the market, the games — they'd want the lake for swimmin' races, but they'd need a big open area, and this is the best anywhere around the lake. You can see that in most places the banks are too steep, it's too hilly. This had to be the place."

"Who owns these olive trees?"

"Some old lady in Rome. A countess, or something. Talked to the caretaker once, gave him some silver coins. Course I stay away in November, in the picking season. Here, you sit still, I might's well show you my nails." So he got up and took the coffee cups and the milk pitcher back into the motor home. I didn't have the girl's face to look at anymore, so I looked at the olive trees. Many were thick and very old.

Jim came back and set an object on the table. He didn't say anything, he just let me examine it and finger it and turn it over and over. It was a piece of hardwood about two feet long, three inches wide and almost an inch thick. There were nails, tapered bronze nails about three inches long with thick heads an inch in diameter, driven into the wood, one right next to the other in a double file of twenty-two: forty-four nails. But between the nails and

215

the wood there was a long piece of paper — a yellowed newspaper clipping. The nail heads made it impossible to read anything but scattered bits of words — barely enough to see that it was in Italian.

"What's the piece of newspaper doing there?"

"One thing at a time. This here's the time to tell you about those nails."

"So these are Etruscan nails?"

"Yep. No doubt about that. You can ask if they were ever in the Holy Wall. I can't prove that, but I don't need to. I can feel it. I found them all in this grove here, over the years — the last one about seven years ago.

There's more, but I'm not meant to find them. There's hundreds more, but they're too far down — or they're right under the trees. I've covered the whole grove inch by inch with my sweeper. I dug holes all over, every time I got any sort of signal. But always real careful for the trees. I did 'em good, loosened the soil, they look better'n they did. Found forty-four, I swear to God. I guess I knew I would. And that's all I get. Forty-four years, counting from 1944, when everything started. And here we are in 1988. Ball game's over. No more nails."

"And you actually think you're supposed to die now. Jim, you can't be serious. Just because each nail meant a year to the Etruscans...I mean, if we're anything, we're Christians, aren't we?"

"Oh, as far as that goes. I think the Lord has had something to say to just about everybody, in all these different religions that there's been. And he said something real special to the Etruscans. I don't know exactly what it was, but the nails were important. And if I'm the one that found them, it's because they're important for me too. They mean there's an end to everything, and once the nails are finished God's done with you, so what's there to do but die? You know, the Raséna believed that a man shouldn't live more than 84 years — seven times twelve. Anybody that lived beyond that, he was just considered dead. Couldn't pray, couldn't work, couldn't say or do anything that meant anything. They were just ignored. I guess they died pretty quick."

"But that gives you about fifteen more years!"

"Nope. My limit's the nails. I was meant to find them. Forty-four of them! Now if that ain't a Sign...Listen, it'll make more sense when I get around to telling you the rest."

"You mean what's written under these nails."

"Yep. Pretty much. Well, we can get back on the road now."

"Listen, I'd like to take a little walk through the olive grove."

"Okay by me. Want me to come?"

"Yeah. And why don't you bring your sweeper?"

"'Cause I'll show you later today how I sweep. In the first place I already got my driving sneakers on, in the second place ain't nothin' left in there. When I sweep, I sweep right, and when you sweep right, you get it all. And ain't nobody sweeps righter than me."

"If I thought my life depended on it, I'd sweep and dig and sweep some more."

"See now? I think that's part of what the Etruscans knew. How to die with your dignity. I did my sweeping, and I ain't going to grovel. And I ain't that anxious. Nails is nails, nephew, they ain't rosebuds. I ain't lived them easy, the years they gave me. 'Bout ready to take my chances on dyin'." We were both looking deep into the olive grove. A slow and quiet place, where even the birds seemed calm.

"All right, forget your sweeper, but let's take a walk

217

anyway. Something to tell my grandkids."

So we walked among the trees with their gnarly trunks, silvery leaves, and hard little olives. Jim looked straight ahead. I couldn't help keeping my eyes on the ground.

"What're you looking for?" Jim said. "Ain't nothing stays up on top where you can see it for thousands of years. You ain't gonna find no nails."

I had to admit I wanted to. Finding exactly forty-four nails had the value of a Sign for Jim, although I still didn't know why, but if it meant he had to stop living, I wanted another nail to turn up to ruin things, to spring Jim loose from this superstition. As Jim himself had said, other nails were in here; he said he had looked carefully, but I didn't need a degree in psychology to figure he had an unconscious block against finding more than forty-four nails.

"What I like to do," said Jim, "is imagine this place when there wasn't no trees. Think of all the Raséna singing and dancing here. They were real musicians, you know, and—"

"They've got a mole problem over there. Look, all around that big tree. Must be a dozen mounds."

"Them moles are doing the tree good, loosening the soil. They's took up where I left off. Probably burrowed clear under. Look at that dark clay they brought up."

I looked at Jim, smiled without a word, and walked over to begin kicking the molehills apart. When I got to the third one Jim called over and said, "You know, if you find a nail, it's yours, not mine. Don't change nothing."

"Then get over here and start kicking."

"No way."

"Afraid to find another nail?"

"Wouldn't make no sense."

218

"Well, maybe the Lord wants to tell you that you've given the wrong sense to all this. Now if He went to all the trouble to get a mole to dig a nail out from under a tree and you wouldn't even step over here and kick a little dirt with your foot, He just might be displeased."

"Are you mocking me, nephew?"

"No, Jim, God, no. I'm just trying to say something in your terms. Something I believe very much, and in my terms it's this: it's never right to avoid the truth."

"I get it, with that talk about the Lord, you was talking down to me."

"No, Jim. I..."

"Well, maybe you was talking up to me, 'thout knowing it. Religion is one thing where goin' to college don't help much."

I walked back and put my hand on his shoulder, "Can't argue with you there. Let's head back."

"Wait a minute. You left a lotta those molehills. I'll get'em for you." And with a rare smile he walked over and started kicking the mounds, but not very meticulously.

I thought the smile entitled me to a little jab: "If that's the way you sweep for mines, you leave three for every one you find."

Wrong jab. He started kicking harder, and even stomping on the molehills, "Listen here, I ain't been to Northwestern, I didn't even finish high school, but there's a few things I know how to do, and the day I leave a mine—DAMNATION!" Up came Jim's foot and down went Jim. I thought I heard some old bones crack.

"You okay, Jim?"

"See what's in my foot first, then we'll see about the rest." He lifted his left sneaker, which I took and examined.

219

"So what's in there?" he asked painfully.

"You know damn well what's in there."

"Well, pull it out, for Chrissake." I pulled it out. It was black and rough, with blood on the point.

"Here's your forty-fifth nail." I handed it to him. For somebody who had just been given an extra year of life, he didn't look pleased.

"Shit," he said. "Help me stand up." I did, no broken bones. I helped him hobble back to the *Crociato*, where we medicated and bandaged the foot. The puncture wasn't deep, but I was worried about infection.

"Maybe you should get this looked at. Maybe there's something else we should put on it."

"Hell with it."

"Maybe you could get tetanus. I don't know, but—"

"Hell with it."

"Hell with it, hell with it. Sounds like you're determined to die regardless of what the Lord or anybody else says."

"What the Lord is saying ain't at all clear yet. 'Cept that only a damn fool goes stomping around outdoors in tennis shoes. Something I'd never have done alone. Now just stay out of my way a minute."

Jim limped around a bit, testing his foot, both inside and outside the motor home. "The foot'll be all right. Let's be on our way."

"Where are we going?"

"To Sant' Angelo. Listen, I'm gonna need you to be quiet a bit, 'cause I have to think about this. Gotta figure it out." He got into the driver's seat, and I took my place alongside him.

"That's what I get for letting you interfere," he muttered.

"Listen Jim, either it means that none of your nails

mean anything, which is my opinion, or it just means that you get another year of life, which isn't so bad. Maybe it's a...a reward, for faithful service or something." I guess I was saying these things to keep the dialogue open, until I could find out more.

"No. It means I ain't out of the minefield yet, and now I don't know the way. Reward! Ain't no rewards for what I done, nephew." And he started the engine.

"Don't start yet. Jim. Turn that thing off a minute." He looked at me hard, with something different in his deep-set eyes. Fear. He turned off the engine. "Listen," I said, "I admit I'm not a religious man, but I suppose I'm some kind of Christian. I don't know whether to hope there's an afterlife or to hope there isn't. If there is, I'm going to have to do some fast talking after I die. One thing I like about Christianity is that I think God will give me a chance to speak my piece, I mean He's a forgiving God. That's the whole thing about Jesus Christ, isn't it? Now, if you believe in Him, you've got to believe that nothing you've done goes beyond His mercy..."

"God can forgive me all He likes, but I got to live and die with myself. There ain't no fast talking when you die, there's just you and your demons, and if you ain't learned to control 'em in life...The Etruscans knew about the demons, nephew. When you die, you see what's left of you without them. And maybe..." He gripped the steering wheel hard and banged his head against it. "...and maybe there ain't enough left for God to forgive. And the damned Etruscans had some kind of a way. A way to live and die, to accept everything, even the demons, and not be taken over by them. But they ain't talking anymore. So I'm on my own, trying to keep my demons down. I figured I had forty-four. I figured I was given them nails and them years to bring them back under control. I thought I was on to it, I thought I had read the pattern, and now I don't know." He reached down to the ignition key. "Okay with you if we go now?" he whispered, looking straight ahead.

"Sure it is. Sure."

CHAPTER XX

Each minefield had to be detailed in a map as it was being laid.
The charting had to be completed before arming the minefield.

Jim drove absorbedly. I kept quiet and let him do his thinking. He really worked at it, shaking his head and banging his fist on his knee, swearing under his breath and from time to time letting out scraps of phrases, like:

"Can't be. No name."

"One more job to do."

"His demons are his business."

"They was forty-four!"

"Ain't right."

In the meantime I kept track of where we were on the road map. We had simply got back on the Via Cassia and were heading south, towards Rome. We went through the outskirts of Viterbo, and then by a little lake called Lago di Vico. Rome was only a half-hour away, but we were still in farmland. Big black-and-white magpies glided watchfully over the hayfields. Jim seemed to have calmed down, so I thought I'd take a chance:

"How're you doing?"

"Well, nephew, there's one thing it might mean. I sure as hell don't like it, so that's probably what it is. Still, it don't make much sense."

"What's that?"

"I s'pose you could say there was a 45th. And I don't

even know his name."

"A 45th what, Uncle Jim?"

"Dammit, I know what he owes me, but I didn't think I had any debt with him. He's not on the list. Guess I'll have to find out. And you'll be with me, so just sit tight, nephew."

So I sat tight, but only a few minutes later Jim made an effort to be sociable. "You know, anytime you need to take a leak you can just go back there and fire away."

"Thanks, maybe a little later. We're not heading into Rome, are we?"

"Hell, no. We'll pick up the G.R.A., the ring road, and swing around the city. It's just up ahead, near Veio."

"Veio's not on the map."

"Course not. Etruscan city. The first one the Romans took off the map. Just overgrown stones now. But I found Agnese's ring in there. See, there's the sign for the G.R.A. — the Grande Raccordo Anulare. On the other side of Rome we'll pick up Route Six to keep going south."

"Does it go all the way to Sant' Angelo?"

"Yep. Just about."

Of course I had never heard of Sant' Angelo, but with nothing better to do I thought I'd study the map until I found it. After twenty minutes I asked, "Do you mean Sant' Angelo d'Alife or Sant' Angelo dei Lombardi?"

"Neither. It's call Sant' Angelo in Theodice. You ain't gonna find it on that map."

"The Romans took it off, I suppose."

"Nope. We did. It's come back to life, but the population could just about ride with us in my van here. Wasn't always that way though. Back in the spring of '44 there were hundreds of thousands of men in and all around here. Seven different armies. Not me, mind you. I was holed up at Anzio with VI Corps. But we're gonna look up a man I know down here; he was in on it."

"Is he the 45th..?"

"Hell no, nephew, I'm trying to drop it for a while, and I want you to drop it for a while. No, this man is a... a business acquaintance. I want you to meet him. I seen you don't mind talking about the war. Now Rap, for instance, he can't stand it. I couldn't never get into it with him. Can't blame him. Wars are nothing to be proud of. Make people do awful, terrible things. Terrible things. But we ain't going there just to talk, I also want to show you how I work, how I sweep, and all around there is still pretty good. Back in '44, you couldn't even crap in that area without setting off a mine. You still find stuff — I've never missed. Here's our road, Route Six." We turned off the crowded G.R.A. onto a "provincial" road — which was almost as crowded.

"Is this another of those old Roman roads you like?"

"Sure is. Via Casilina. But I call it Route Six, because everybody talked about Route Six in those days, the war days. The best way to Rome from the south. The only way the Germans could escape north in one piece."

"Yeah. Egidio, he said something about it. How well do you know Egidio — besides helping him get his hotel?"

"I send him business now and then. George a few times, but mainly buyers for my stuff. Lots of times they like to avoid big flashy hotels, don't want to make waves. Egidio, he's some talker..."

"I'll vouch for that."

"Well, he talks to all his clients, and then I take him aside, get him drinking and he tells me all about them. Helps to know which buyers are liars."

"What did he tell you about me?"

"Oh, he likes you pretty much. Convinced you've got

a girl in Anzio for some reason. Listen, Rap told you just to leave him in the dark about us, didn't he?"

"He did. I backed up your story about offering me a job. Told him you wanted me to go around the US selling a new explosive for demolitions. Told him I turned you down."

"The man we're gonna look up in Sant' Angelo, that was his line once. Demolitions."

"Listen, about the girl in Anzio. Egidio thought the story about looking for my uncle was just a cover for a… a possible affair. A heavy date in Anzio."

"Well, now you got one. Anyway, what did he say about Route Six?"

"Well, he said Mark Clark was a fool not to take it and cut the Germans off."

"Mark Clark was no fool. A bastard, maybe, but no fool. And it takes bastards to win wars. You need lots of them. The side with the most bastards wins. Their country wins, but the bastards always lose. They got to live with what they did."

"Talk about being bastards. I see that Route Six is going to take us right by Montecassino."

"Yep."

"St. Benedict's abbey, the one we bombed."

"It was on Mount Cairo, nephew. And Mount Cairo was the heart of the Gustav Line. The Germans were dug in all around it. Right into the rock."

"But not in the abbey."

"Nope."

"And we bombed the abbey."

"You could say that. One thousand tons of bombs."

"But the abbey itself, Montecassino — it wasn't a part of the German defenses. was it? No Germans inside."

"Nary a one. Von Senger, their commander, was some

sort of a Benedictine himself! There was just monks and civilians hiding."

"All right, so whose fault was the bombing? Mark Clark's, I suppose."

"Hell, no. He was dead against it. Most of the Brass was against it."

"Okay, so who was for it?"

"The troops. The troops and the New Zealand general, a guy named Freyberg. He just kept insisting till he got his way. And the troops' way. They wanted that thing leveled."

"A 1400-year-old building. A landmark of civilization. Stupid bastards, not just bastards."

Jim thought about that one for a while. He checked his watch a couple of times, and then he said, "Nephew, I been sweeping all around Montecassino, and I want to tell you, it's really something. I want to show you what it looks like from a trench. Everything's different from a trench, nephew. Maybe you'll see. They built the abbey all up again, you know. After the war."

"That's about like my boy Bret. When he was eight he killed a robin with a slingshot. A fluke hit. It really shocked him. He didn't want me to bury it. He kept setting it back up in the tree. 'From far away he's still alive, isn't he, Dad?' That's what he said."

We stopped for lunch just after crossing a river, the Sacco River. Jim said. He turned off onto a dirt road and went about a hundred yards, far enough to put the *Crociato* between a vineyard and a stand of poplar trees. We got out the table and chairs, and Jim cooked up some spaghetti. We boiled the water over an open fire, just like the boy scouts.

"Ain't no point in getting the van all steamed up," Jim explained. "'Sides, I use gas as little as possible. You

227

know, them damn blue containers with propane gas inside. I just have one little one, real little, for when it's too cold or wet outside. It runs out quick but I refill it. Don't want big ones. They can leak, they can explode. And anyway, food don't never taste as good with gas."

"There can't be much difference with pasta."

"I think there's some. Water boils better."

Probably it was the power of suggestion, but that was good spaghetti. Or maybe it was the power of the condiment: when the pasta was on my plate he spooned on some boiling olive oil full of pieces of garlic, red pepper and onion.

"You've still got a pretty good stomach, eh, Jim?"

"Stomachs are like hands and feet," he answered with his mouth full. "You make them work, and they get callused and can take anything. After this I got some provolone someplace."

Jim was done with his spaghetti and provolone well before me. "Now you take your time and finish," he said. "I want to get squared around to give it a try here. Looks real good."

"How about your foot?"

"Hurts some, but no more'n I deserve. I ain't gonna pay no heed, 'cept to wear the right shoes this time."

Five minutes later he came back out of the motor home wearing his Timberlands and carrying a small spade and a dark wooden case, which he set on his chair. "You done yet?" he asked.

"Yes, just about," I answered with my mouth full. I wolfed down the rest of my food, then cleared the table so that Jim could open his case on it. When I came back from carrying in the dishes and changing my shoes, Jim was assembling what was obviously his mine detector.

"Here she is, the SCR 625, best damn broom they ever

made. Come over and take a look." The "broom" was in three pieces which Jim rapidly screwed together, making a "stick" almost six feet long. The middle piece was metal, and had an ampere-meter attached. The two end pieces were wooden. The round plate at the end of the stick was also made of wood, a little less than an inch thick and little over a foot in diameter. A cord came up out of the plate, and Jim attached it to a cord coming down out of the ampere-meter. Then he got a metal box out of the case. It was about 10" by 5" by 2" and had a canvas covering with a long strap. Jim unbuckled the canvas, opened the box and plugged two cords into it, one from the ampere-meter and the other from a small round receiver. The box contained the batteries, which Jim tested with a test button located on the ampere-meter. Then he laid the stick on the table to get the plate up into the air, and started to regulate the current and the magnetic field, using two knobs on the ampere-meter and one on the metal box. I heard crackling noises coming from the receiver.

"Take a look at the color of the soil around here," he said. "Lots of iron in it. But the 525 has a special setting that cuts out that kind of interference. Real good for false minefields, red herrings. There she is, that's just fine." He took the "broom," put it under his right arm and held the plate steady about seven inches from the ground, while with his left hand he did a little more fiddling with his knobs.

"Okay, now we're ready to go." He closed up the metal box, put its strap around his neck, and attached the receiver to the strap right next to his ear.

"Look around, Bob. Ain't this a nice place? You got the river back there, them nice hills beyond..."

"Yeah, it's nice enough."

"People been coming through here, and maybe saying these same things, for thousands of years. Walking, riding, with wagons and what-all. And armies, all kinds of armies have marched up and down here. If you were a general, where would you halt for a rest?"

"This would be fine, I suppose."

"Damn right. A wide space near a river. And people when they stop, they lose things. Now the last time I was through here this wasn't no vineyard. You can see, them vines are pretty new. It was pasture here. They've plowed it up. Done half my work for me. Get the spade, you can do the other half. Come on."

So we headed off into the field, walking slowly down between rows of young vines that were already reaching out horizontally along their sustaining wires, full of leaves but with grape clusters still few and far between.

Jim hobbled a bit with his wounded foot, even though he seemed determined to ignore it. He kept the plate seven inches from the ground and moved slowly forward, talking but listening carefully to the receiver, which now and then made strange noises. Whenever it did, he would stop and move his plate all around till he had an idea of the shape of whatever was underneath. Then he would say "piece of wire" or "tin can" or just "nope" and we would move on.

"Know how this thing works?" he asked.

"Magnetism."

"But it ain't as if my plate attracts the metals. No, sir. It's called mutual inductance. There's three inductance coils on the bottom here, and now they're balanced just right, but anything metal underneath the plate, or even a little outside it, will knock them out of balance and send a disturbance up here where I can see it on the meter and hear it in my ear. 'Tween the two I can pretty well guess what it is. I can read every sound, every flutter this baby makes. I've had her apart a hundred times over the years, had to replace lots of pieces. But she's still the same 625 I landed at Anzio with."

"How deep will it detect something?"

"Depends on how big it is. She's built to find an S-mine a foot down. But if you know how to use her, she'll do a lot better'n that. Hold it. This here's either a coin or a bottle cap. 'Bout five inches down. Right here." He indicated with the tip of his shoe where I should dig.

So dig I did, and without much effort I came up with a round flat black thing that Jim assured me was a coin, a very old coin.

"We'll clean it up back in the *Crociato*. How did you expect it to look? You ain't gonna look any better after a few years in the ground." We started walking again.

"What happens if the farmer comes along that owns this field?"

"I just tell him that I'm a crazy old soldier with a guilty conscience that's still sweeping for mines. Ain't far from the truth."

"No, I guess not. But do they buy it?"

"They usually do. That's another reason I've always got a few mines or shells in the van. Like I said, I shine 'em up and sell 'em, but they're also good for scaring landowners into letting me sweep for them. They don't want to hit something like that with a tractor. It happens, y'know. Anyway I give them a shined up shell for a souvenir, and that usually does the trick. Course with some landowners there's just no way, and I get chased off. Happens rarely. But that's one of the reasons I like sweeping the beaches now and then. The shoreline is public in Italy. Ain't nobody can own it, at least the last strip of it. I don't have to answer to nobody. I get the boat down, do a little fishing, do a little sweeping. Course it ain't serious sweeping, what you do on the beach. No mines or bombs any more, just little stuff, rifle shells, fragments."

"And no ancient coins?"

"Nope. No old stuff. Beaches are too unstable. But you can make a lot of money, yes, sir. Bracelets and rings and little gold chains and coin purses and you can't imagine all the stuff people lose on the beach. Found a set of platinum teeth once."

"And you cashed them in?"

"Yep. A jeweler melted them down. Good for a trained dog. Hold it. Try right there."

"A trained dog?"

"Just dig a minute. 'Bout nine inches."

A little spadework, and I turned up a key. Big, black, and barely recognizable, but definitely an old latch key. "Ugly thing, ain't it?" Jim commented. "I used to throw them away, then I found out they's worth two, even three hundred dollars. Old Roman keys. I guess some people like them."

"Are they good for a trained dog?"

"Hell, no. Let's head back. I just wanted to show you how this thing works." So we stooped under the vines to get into the next row, and starting working back towards the *Crociato*.

"Are you going to explain the trained dog business?" I insisted.

"I bought a seeing-eye dog once for a blind guy. Man, you can't imagine how expensive they are. But I liked doing that, 'cause I like animals."

I let my gaze float up to the bright, hot sky. That same sun was just barely coming up over Lake Michigan.

"Jim, who was this blind guy?"

"Oh, I owed him something. Like the others. He was the son of one of them. His house was bombed and he got his eyes scorched."

"How many people did you have a debt with?"

"That's why it's a sign. Forty-four. They was forty-four, just like the nails. So how do you like sweeping? No big deal, is it? Little different when you're after mines. Can't just waltz along like we're doing. Gotta be real careful. I'll show you when we get down to Sant' Angelo. Come on, let's get going. It ain't as good here as I hoped." So he slung the sweeper over his shoulder and limped quickly back towards the *Crociato*.

"One question."

"About what?"

"About the sweeping. If you can detect a coin while you're 'waltzing along' like that, why do you have to be so careful when you're after mines? They're a helluva lot bigger than coins!"

"Good question. The answer is that there's all kinds of mines and all kinds of ways to set them. That coin there don't take care if it's found, but a mine don't want to be found, no sir. So if it's big, a big 'ol anti-tank mine like a T-35, it's likely to be deep, and if it's small, an anti-personnel mine, well, it's in an unlikely place, or maybe it's mostly made of wood, like the Schu 42. Only thing my broom here can pick up is the metal parts, the detonator, mainly."

I found myself treading very lightly. "Kind of shakes you up," I said.

Jim laughed. It was the constipated laugh of someone who doesn't like to. "Hell, ain't no mines here. When the Germans came through here they was running as fast as they could. They'd only stop and fight when they thought a position was defendable. Look how open it is here.

233

Planes alone could drive you out. No mines here. They were hustling to get across the Sacco River and then blow up the bridge. Tell you something. Even in the old battle zones you don't find many mines. The Allies and the Italians got most of them out after the war. I just find the strays, 'cause I know where to look. Now what you do find is tank shells, grenades, bombs — stuff that was scattered all over and didn't explode. Ain't no systematic way to find it. Hell, up in Friuli you can still find stuff from World War I."

Back inside the motor home, Jim put the coin and the key into a jar and covered them with a yellow liquid. "This here's my own concoction. Olive oil, mostly. In a week they'll clean easy with a toothbrush."

He had carefully dismantled his "broom," and now I watched him secure the wooden case that contained it in its place of honor under his bed. Then we drove away.

For twenty minutes we rode along in silence again. I imagined Jim was back to thinking about his extra nail. I was thinking about his... forty-four debts. Finally I decided it'd do no harm for me to try once again to see how far I could get.

"You know, Jim, that's a fine thing you did for that blind guy."

"Tell you one thing: ain't nobody loves a dog like a blind person loves his. I like that. Like to see a good dog treated right."

"Why don't you get yourself a good dog?

"'Cause I couldn't treat him right."

"Bullshit." This sort of language was unusual for me, but in Jim's company it seemed to ring true.

In fact after a few minutes he simply said, "Could be. But it ain't never seemed right for me to have a dog."

"Maybe you owe something to yourself for a change,

234

Jim."

"Nope."

"Now you've got the forty-fifth nail. One more year to live. One more debt to pay."

"That must be it."

"Why couldn't it be to yourself?"

"Nephew, stick to French."

"Can I at least make a guess about those forty-four people you had a debt with?"

"Suppose I can't stop you."

"Their names are all printed in that newspaper article that you've covered with your forty-four nails."

Jim drove on a bit before he finally said, "And do you think you know what those names are doing in that article?"

"I could take a shot at it."

"Go ahead. Fire away."

"Well, they're forty-four people that died at Anzio. The ones I know about were Italian soldiers who fought for the Germans, so maybe I can assume that's what they all were. So they were your enemy, but somehow you feel responsible for their deaths. My guess is that you used some illegal mines on them, or they got out in the middle of one of your fields and wanted to surrender, but you didn't let them, you didn't show them how to get out. Wait a minute. Your wife's first husband was one of these forty-four, wasn't he?"

"Yep."

"And I know he was shot...." The reason I had this idea was the bullet holes Lorena had put in her drawing of Jim and Rap. Jim wheeled around and almost drove off the road.

"Did Lorena tell you that? Did she talk to you?"

"No, Jim. You know she doesn't talk. Didn't you tell

me you shot him?"

"Don't think so," he answered, settling down. "Thought I just said I killed him. Well, don't matter. You're off the track about how they died. Didn't think you'd get it. Almost wish you had. But you ain't been in a war; it'd be awful hard for you to imagine this sort of thing. Still, you ain't too far off. I'll tell you that much for now."

"But tell me this: did you ever lay any mines, or did you just sweep for them?"

"I laid 'em, I laid 'em, especially in the early days. Wasn't such a bad invasion at first. After ten days the Brits were thirteen miles up the Albano Road, almost to Campoleone, and we were half a mile from Cisterna on Route Seven. Then all hell broke loose. But I had time to plant a few fields for the Germans, to slow up their counter-attack. Good fields they were, too. Held up a Panzer division for twelve hours. I even got an official commendation. They should have given it to the mines, not to me. M4s, vicious little bastards. Only six pounds of TNT, but if you plant them thick enough, they do the job. On the base line of the fields I planted they were only two yards apart. No way for a tank to squeeze through, so they had to sweep them out. Poor devils. The M4 looks like a regular M1A1, same pressure ring and everything, but it has two extra detonators hidden on the side and underneath."

"Sounds like what you rigged up in that garage to end that protection racket."

"Yep. I got the idea from the M4. The Germans'd uncover them and reach down in there to lift them out...one good thing is that those poor devils never felt a thing. Six pounds of TNT will blow the treads off a tank, and they'll just about disintegrate a man. No wonder it

236

took them twelve hours to get through."

"And you were in charge of the mine-laying?"

"Yep. I was in charge of the whole platoon for a few days. About thirty-five men. I was only a sergeant, but our lieutenant stepped on a mustard pot, and it took a while to replace him."

"A mustard pot?"

"Sure, a German A-mine with a Buck detonator. Only about half a pound of picric acid inside, but that's terrible stuff. I'd rather work with TNT anytime."

"I think I'd rather teach French."

Jim pondered that one for a minute. "Nope," he said, "I'd rather work with TNT."

CHAPTER XXI

The crypt of Monte Cassino is carved into the stone of the mountain. Six monks hid there and survived. One returned after the bombing to wander among the ruins. German paratroopers thought he was a ghost.

We came up on Montecassino at about 5 pm. Coming from the north, it wasn't all that impressive. Italy is full of towers and castles on the sides and tops of mountains. This was a big building all right, but not intimidating.

"Jim, now I'm looking at it, and I still say it was a mistake to destroy it."

"You're looking at it, but it ain't looking at you. This is the friendly side. Just wait."

We drove on by the abbey and into the town of Cassino, an anonymous modern town that would look fine in Iowa. "I get it," I said, "rebuilt after the war."

"Yep. While they were at it, they moved it away from the foot of the mountain a bit and onto flat ground."

"There wasn't anything worth saving?"

"Well, old General Freyberg, his orders to the planes were to level the town so flat that a tank battalion could race over it. Not through it. Over it."

"What a fine guy he must have been!"

"Kind of guy that wins wars, nephew. Told you. Now I'll show you. I'll see if you can understand."

We crossed the river that borders the town on its

southern edge. Jim turned right onto a dirt road that ran along the bank. There was very little construction on that side of the river, just fields used for soccer, for motocross — and for dumping garbage. Jim drove along until we found a field that wasn't used for much of anything.

We stopped, got out, and walked along the bank that sloped sharply up from the fast-flowing river fifteen feet below.

"Here, this'll do fine. No new buildings in the way. Come on down here to the left, nephew. This here depression used to be a trench, an Allied trench. Okay, now flatten out on the side with me, like this." Jim turned toward the river we could no longer see though it was only ten yards away, and fell forward onto the side of the grassy depression so that his head barely stuck up above ground level. I did the same alongside him.

"That's good. Now take a look at the abbey. Look real good." I didn't have to look real good. On this side of Mount Cairo the huge white monastery loomed over everything like an avalanche ready to break loose.

"All right now, you keep looking while I'm talking. You been living in this trench, in the cold and wet, for over a month. By this time you thought you'd be in Rome, but the only way to get there is right under the monastery."

"Hold it! Remember the Frenchman in Pisa? They'll do that famous End Run...."

"Nobody knows that's possible yet! And you're just a G.I. You gotta go where they point you! And you gotta listen! Now the Germans say they ain't in that building up there, but since when did we start trusting Germans? They must at least be using it as an observation post — every time your outfit tries to cross the river the sides of that mountain light up with cannon fire and you damn near get your ass blown off. You're looking up at that thing and thinking it was the last thing a lot of your buddies ever saw on this earth. There it is. God damn it, the strongest point on the Gustav Line, and Axis Sally tells you every night that you might's well settle down 'cause Hitler has decided that this muddy hole here is as far as you go. You listening to me?"

"I'm listening."

"Don't look at me, keep looking up there. Now they tell you we gotta be real careful with our bombs and cannon, 'count of that's one hell of an old building up there, and the Pope says we can't touch it. Can't touch it, and it's hanging over every damn thing we do. Then you hear that there's a tough old general that says if they'd told him that in the European Theater you gotta trust the Krauts and take orders from the Pope of Rome, he'd have stayed in the Pacific to fight the Japs. And he says his boys are worth one helluva lot more than some old building. And he says that what we've got is air power and we ain't using it, so how dumb can you get? And now look a little higher, up over the building. 250 Flying Fortresses are rolling in, you can hardly hear me for the noise, and now they're blowing that sucker right off the mountain. Got the picture?"

"Got it."

"Okay, so now what do you think of General Freyberg?"

"Sorry Jim. He's still a bastard."

Jim sighed. "That's 'cause you're still a French teacher. Dammit, nephew, if you can't learn to think a bit like a soldier, you ain't never going to understand your Uncle Jim. Come on, let's go.

"Wait a minute. I'm taking this seriously, I'm trying to understand. Did we warn the monks and civilians inside that we were going to bomb?"

"Well, some leaflets were dropped. Didn't do much good. None of them fell inside the monastery."

"So the monastery wasn't evacuated in time."

"Nope,"

"I'll bet we're not very well liked around here."

"Italians are pretty understanding people. It wasn't easy for that plane with the leaflets to fly low over the monastery. The Germans weren't inside, but they had anti-aircraft guns within two hundred yards."

"If I were the pilot, I'm not sure I could live with a failure like that."

"You'd be surprised what you can live with. Let's get out of here."

"You still have to tell me the end."

"End of what?"

"The battle here. Did bombing the monastery help at all to break through the Gustav Line?"

"Hell, no. Made it worse. The Germans went up, dug into the rubble and beat us off for over three more months. Montecassino was finally taken as part of a coordinated action — with the French doing their End Run and us breaking out of Anzio. Then that French general, Alphonse Juin, had the brilliant idea of giving a bunch of his troops 50 hours of full freedom, and they spent 'em raping and killing civilians. But I still say you can't blame Freyberg."

"Let's get out of here, Jim."

We got into the *Crociato* and headed west out of Cassino, staying pretty close to the river. I saw a sign saying "Sant' Angelo in Theodice 7 km."

"Are you going to tell me about this town we're heading for?"

"Nope."

"Jim, you did a good job back in that trench. You're helping me understand. To understand is one thing, but you can't expect me to condone."

"Condoning ain't none of your business."

"Absolutely right. So what about Sant' Angelo?"

"I'll let Dieter tell you about it."

"Who's he?"

"Dieter Mauer, man I sell things to. In the war he was a non-com like me, but higher, some crazy word in German. Combat engineer, same as me. After the war he made a lot of money in Germany, in demolitions, like I said before. Lots of damaged buildings that had to be demolished and cleared away. But during the war he'd developed an interest in old Roman stuff, so with his money he came back down here and built a nice place — there it is — and became an ancient art dealer, a museum supplier — whatever you call them."

We pulled up in front of a beautiful modern villa. I could see that the river, the same river, ran close behind the house, but now we were on the other side. The German side. The acre of land surrounding the building was enclosed by a four-foot wall of old gray stones. The lawn inside was thick and green, in strong contrast with the dry and yellowy vegetation that struggled to survive outside. A muscular young man dressed only in khaki shorts was trimming around the trees. A big glossy gray Mercedes was parked in the driveway — even its tire treads looked clean. We sat looking for a moment before getting out.

"Lots of Germans that fought in Italy did that," said Jim. "Made money at home and came back to live here. Discovered they liked the place. Or it means something to them. Or they ain't so welcome at home. Or everything at home was destroyed. Anyway, there's lots of them around. Especially in Tuscany."

"And they're friends of yours."

"Some of them are. This one ain't. I hate his guts. But I gotta admire him. For two reasons. For one thing, he sure as hell knows his explosives. Come on, let's go see the old son of a bitch."

"Wait a second. What's the other thing you admire in him?"

"You'll find out. Listen, you ain't no relation of mine, you're just a friend. Don't want this bastard asking you questions about me and the family or anything. Ain't his business."

"But...does he know you're American?"

"Oh, yeah. Can't hide that for very long."

"Egidio doesn't know it."

"He's used to tourists. And he's used to doing the talking. Dieter's different: knows how to listen. Look, he's coming out toward us."

We got out of the *Crociato* and walked to the gate, which Dieter Mauer was now unlatching. He didn't look at all like Curt Jürgens, which was a big disappointment right off; he looked more like Henry Kissinger. His English pronunciation was better than Kissinger's, but his grammar was sometimes...deviant.

"Giacomo, my good friend, I am so glad for your coming! Quite very glad!"

"Hello, Dieter. This is Bob, Bob Svenson, a friend of mine. He teaches French in America. Here on vacation."

"*Ah oui? Mais c'est tres interessant! Moi, j'ai travaillé en France aussi, apres la guerre, mais malheureusement je ne connais pas l'Amérique. Et cette espéce d'américain, votre ami Giacomo, ne parle jamais de son pays!*"

"*Et moi, je ne connais pas l'Allemagne,*" I answered while shaking his smooth but vigorous hand.

243

"Well. I guess I'll be on my way," said Jim flatly.

"Don't be silly, my friend. We will speak your English. But I enjoy also French. I did demolitions also in France, after the war. And I was stationed there from 1940 to middle 1943. Then Italy. Hah, hah! Always I have been fortunate, Mr. Svenson. Quite fortunate. So many fought in the heat of the African desert, in the cold of the Russian winter, but Dieter Mauer, hah! France and Italy! Now come, come, into the house, it is hot today, better inside. Come!"

On the inside Dieter Mauer's house was very fine indeed, but it didn't really look lived in, just the way the lawn outside didn't look walked on and the Mercedes in the driveway didn't look driven. The reason soon became clear enough: he had a platoon of servants, all young and good-looking and hard-working. A fellow named Glauco was sent to the cellar for some white wine, a girl named Lisetta was told to inform the cook that there would be two guests for supper, and Jim was persuaded to bring the *Crociato* within range of a hose so that a man named Beppe could wash it!

Jim and I sat down in white leather armchairs in a large, shady living room. A ceiling fan with white wooden blades kept the air fresh. Our host sat down on the sofa across from us, but on the edge of it and leaning forward, as if to observe us more closely.

"Do you live here alone, Mr. Mauer?" I asked.

"Hah! So Giacomo has nothing told you about me! That is very normal of him. A man of little words, very little. I have no family. I never was married. But I am not so much alone, you can see." In fact Glauco came in with the wine — and with mineral water for Jim.

"German wine!" exulted Mauer. "*Gewürztraminer*! A white wine from red grapes, like the champagne comes!

Even Giacomo, who likes nothing, would like this wine. If he could be made to drink! It is *Qualitätswein mit Prädikat*! Try, Mr Svenson!"

It was a smooth, aromatic wine. I thought it was pretty good, but my "crash course" at Saverio's hadn't made me an expert, by any means.

"Well? What do you say?"

"Wonderful. I don't know much about wines, but—"

"Dieter, tell him about the war. Tell him how it was here. Tell him the things you did."

Mauer stopped smiling for the first time since we had arrived. For a moment he had a calm, dispassionate face, nothing really threatening, except the sense that something beneath was lying in wait. Something hard and cold. He took a long sip of his wine. Slowly his smile returned.

"Mr. Svenson, look at our friend Giacomo. The war, the war, always it's the war he thinks about. Me too, I like the thoughts of the war, but I think of what I have taken, have held, have become. Giacomo, always he thinks of what he has left behind, of what he was. Hah, hah! And I ask you, Mr. Svenson: which of us has won the war?"

I opened my mouth without the slightest idea of what to say, but luckily Jim broke in, "That ain't the point, Dieter. Point is, what the war forced us to do. Forced us to be. If you want to stay that way and call it winning, that's your business."

"No force, Giacomo, no force. I was a good soldier, good combat engineer. I observe, I see how the Americans attack. I plant perfect minefields, I destroy the attackers. I watch them do exactly what I expect, they run so full of their power, and they die. They die and I survive, never attacking. To attack is to expose everything, to give yourself away. To withdraw, to tempt,

245

to use the enemy's impetus against him — this is the true superiority. The Orientals understand this, it is the heart of their martial arts. Hitler, a political genius, but at last a fool — too much impetus. He should have stopped after Poland. It was enough. Then defend. Let the others spend energy, and in their heat, they make mistakes. Then today Germany would still be the world center." Mauer stopped for another long sip. "But Hitler and his Reich were not important for me. A man, a smart man can survive, he will be superior in any system, any country. He observes, he lays his plans, he waits. I was not forced, Giacomo. I am always like this. The best way."

"Ain't nobody knows what the best way was till it's all over and all the prizes been handed out."

"Yah, I forgot, you are a religious man. Are you a religious man also, Mr. Svenson?"

At this point I wished I was. I didn't want to come down on Dieter Mauer's side.

"There's morality even without religion, Mr. Mauer."

"Ah so? Perhaps — but then each can have his own."

"Go on, Dieter, tell him. Tell him about your morality. Thought you would enjoy the chance. Can't force you, but...."

"There is no question of that. I will talk. And then your friend will talk. I am curious about him. I have known very few Americans, real ones, not strange ones like you, Giacomo."

"Way you tell it, you killed most of us."

"Hah! Not most, but many! Now I will prattle, like an old woman — because I am curious about your reactions, Mr. Svenson. But it is nothing so tremendous. Giacomo is too sensitive. Like a priest."

"That wasn't my impression," I said. I was thinking of Jim's mines in the body shop.

"Well, we'll see. There is a river behind my house, Mr. Svenson."

"I know."

"It is called the Rapido. It is fast, and only ten feet deep, but deep enough. For four months it was the most important river in the world, Mr. Svenson. It was the first barrier of the Gustav Line. Kesselring and Von Senger with most of our 10th Army on this side, Alexander and your Mark Clark on the other with divisions of your 5th Army and the British 8th, and also the Poles, the French…a great confrontation, one of the greatest of the war. The Americans would try in every manner to cross the river, losing hundreds of men, and the survivors, those who touched this side, had to get through our minefields.

"Then they had no great problem — only 100,000 German soldiers in fortified positions. Hah, hah! You were thrown back again and again!" He slapped his knee.

"Tell about your part in it, Dieter."

"I was an *Oberfeldwebe* in the 1st Parachute Division under General Heidrich, an elite division, 16,000 of the best, we were. I planted mines all those months, thousands of mines all the length of the Rapido: in the water, on both banks, in the trees, the ground — everywhere, all kinds of mines, all kinds of fields. My property here was the most devastating field I ever planted — in fact, I planted it three times! Three times did they come through and were thrown back, I can say blown back, hah, hah! It bore such fruit, this field, it bore such fruit. I would watch them try, I would watch my field do its work, then I would have it back. And now I have it again. Hah! On this acre of ground I am the ultimate winner of the Battle for the Gustav Line!"

"Tell him about your shrapnel mines, Dieter."

247

"Very simple. Shrapnel mines are bounding mines."

"Bounding mines?"

"Lemme explain to him quick," said Jim. "They're planted shallow and they jump right out. Four seconds after you step on them or hit the trip wire they come bouncing up five feet — a cord keeps them from going higher — and then they explode. About a pound of Amatol, but that's plenty because this mine is full of pieces of metal that just riddle everything within twenty yards."

"Even farther, my friend."

"What's Amatol?"

"Lemme see, it's 80% TNT and 20%, uh..."

"Ammonium nitrate, my friend."

"What's that do?" I asked.

"Hah!" This time the laugh was Jim's. "Suppose you could say it makes it cleaner. Burns better, no poison gas produced by the explosion. But you dirtied it up good, didn't you. Dieter?"

The smiling German looked at me very hard. "Yes, very simple. I poisoned the shrapnel, the metal pieces. Was a war, you know."

If this old bastard thought I was going to wet my pants or something, he was mistaken. "Cool" is a Chicago word.

"What is your duty in war, Mr. Mauer?"

"To kill—"

"No, not really to kill. To put out of action, out of combat. You count casualties, not the dead, casualties include the wounded. If you disable an enemy, you've done your job. You don't have to kill him. In fact, a wounded man is a burden for his country. You were a fool to use poison, wounding was enough." "Fool" was the nicest word I could think of at the time. I looked at

248

Jim; he seemed pleased.

"Not always, Mr. Svenson. Some men wounded by shrapnel returned to kill Germans. Not with my shrapnel."

"Tell him about your dogs, Dieter."

"Ah, the dogs. The prime idea came from the Fuhrer — from Hitler. He wanted little robot tanks, remote controlled, that would roll into the enemy lines and be blown up. When the *Leichter Ladungsträger Goliath* were produced—"

"Dumb things were used at Anzio, we called 'em beetle tanks," continued Jim. "We caught on quick and just blew them up before they got close. Some got stuck in shell holes. Too slow and clumsy."

"But not my dogs," proceeded Mauer. "I convinced the Colonel to requisition thirty dogs, strong and fast German Shepherds that then I trained. Hah! It was easy and amusing. I taught them to look for their food, you know where? Under the tanks! We hung the meat under the belly of our Tiger tanks; after a few weeks they would run under any tank they saw. Even under moving tanks I taught them to go, eventually! Then we strapped four kilos on their backs for the last week, to have them accustomed to the weight..."

"Oh, God." This was me. Somehow this bothered me more than the poisoned shrapnel. Mauer was not displeased with my reaction.

"But Mr. Svenson, they were only animals! In a little time we shall go to the table and eat an animal, a pig or a cow or something! Should I have used pigs?"

"Mines. You should have stuck to your damn mines."

"Unfortunately German anti-tank mines, the Teller mines, had a little defect...."

"Cheer up, Dieter," said Jim. "I'm sure you'll have

better mines for the next war."

"I'm sure we shall."

"Okay," I said, "so what's wrong with German antitank mines?"

Jim answered. "Can't plant them close together. No closer than fourteen feet, otherwise if one explodes it sets off the others. No capacity for shock absorption, like ours."

"This means," continued Mauer, "that my most dense possible field was two mines per front meter — enough for the stopping of only half the tanks in transit. So you can understand, Mr. Svenson, that with my dogs I was making a valid addition to the efficacy of our defenses."

"Mr. Mauer, there's something very wrong in what you did. Basic humanity tells you that."

"Not to me. But I must admit that many people felt as how you feel, even in my regiment. I had to personally detonate my dogs — no one else would do it. And I received no commendation, even though my dogs were credited with six tanks. Six tanks! My best day was May 12th, I can never forget: I waited simply with my dogs in Sant' Angelo, our village here, or I should say in the rubble of Sant' Angelo. Hah, hah! You can hide anything in ruins, you know. The better the Allies got at the making of ruins, the better we got at the using of them. You know I booby-trapped every cellar..."

"Get back to the dogs, Dieter."

"Not the dogs, Giacomo, the tanks. It was the tanks that counted. On May 12th the Canadians finally got their tanks across the river, very heroic, and while that they rolled towards the village I sent my remaining dogs out to greet them. They hadn't eaten for two days! Hah, hah! Most were killed by the infantry, of course, but three were not. Three tanks that day, six all together: Well worth thirty dogs. Mr. Svenson, the Japanese used kamikaze pilots, human beings."

"What the human race wants to do to itself is one thing. Bringing innocent animals into it is another."

"Innocent! Interesting word."

"Dieter, now tell him about—"

"Enough, enough. Now I choose the topic. I have discovered a small bomb, Giacomo. In the woods. Just yesterday morning. I can only see a vane, but it's definitely an aerial bomb, not a shell — too flimsy. Probably an incendiary bomb. I covered it up again, to save it for you! We can look at it tomorrow."

"Can I ask a question here?" I said, looking at Mauer but thinking of Jim. "When you find these things — when people find bombs and mines and things, shouldn't they just notify the police and let them handle it? I mean, it's dangerous...."

"Most surely. People must notify the police. But then the police notify me. Here, anyway. Giacomo, in some other places. Am I correct, my friend?"

"Well, I know the *carabinieri* in lots of towns, in old battle areas. If I'm around, they ask my opinion on whether a shell can be moved, or what-not. Otherwise they just blow it up with dynamite."

"Such a big fuss they make! They block roads, they blow up the trees. Giacomo is so much more professional."

"But I don't take stupid chances, Dieter. If it looks bad, I call the *carabinieri* and let them blow it up."

"Still I think you like to defuse, if possible. Perhaps with just a shadow of risk."

"Right," I said with a weak smile. "Just to put things back in the Lord's hands now and then." Jim ignored me.

"Why didn't you defuse this one you found, Dieter?

251

You're as good as me."

"Thank you for this compliment. But the years lie more kindly upon you, my friend. I have only a few more than you, but my hands — look, my hands have begun to shake." He held up a hand that did shake a bit — the sort of shaking that could have been voluntary or involuntary.

"It is no longer wise to defuse with these hands."

"Which woods is it in?" Jim asked. "Across the road here?"

"A bit farther. Towards Pignataro. Not so far."

"Well, I was going to do some sweeping tomorrow morning anyway. I was thinking of the other side of Sant' Angelo, but we might's well try your spot. An incendiary bomb. In good shape?"

"It could be, my friend."

"Well, we'll have a look."

"Very good. And now Mr. Svenson, from where do you come in America?"

CHAPTER XXII

"Shrapnel" is named after the inventor of the
fragmenting shell. He was an English army officer.

The conversation never returned to World War II and
its explosives. Uncle Jim didn't seem to mind. He
hardly participated in what was said but seemed content
with his own reflections.

Mauer learned about Chicago and about American
high schools, I learned about post-war Germany and
about collectible Roman artifacts. This took us through
dinner, which was neither a pig nor a cow, for which I
was grateful on this occasion, but flounder.

"Cooked as we do near Hamburg, where I was born.
Breaded, and with little shrimps and chopped
mushrooms! A fine choice....I like to let Daniele choose,
and surprise me. I taught him this dish, and more. He is a
good cook, very devoted. All my servants are."

Jim was glad it was fish, which he always preferred
to meat, and ate a lot. He was brought into the
conversation once, when I mentioned the key and the
coin we had found in the cornfield.

"Are they good ones, Giacomo?"

"Can't tell. Ain't clean yet. Key looks pretty good. Got
a silver bowl of some sort I want to show you. And the
usual coins. Show you after dinner."

"That will be fine. You know, Mr. Svenson, Giacomo

brings me always interesting things. Roman things. His main interest is Etruscan, you must know, and he has other contacts for those things, as which is only proper. But his Roman things he brings to me."

"Some of them, Dieter."

"The best ones, I hope."

"I try to keep all my contacts happy."

"I think I pay you well, Giacomo."

"The important thing is whether I think so."

I instinctively broke in to smooth out this wrinkle. Then I wondered why I had bothered. Jlm could do worse than to break with Dieter Mauer, it seemed to me. Anyway what I said was:

"Is this a good area for Roman ruins?"

"Oh, it is so good as another. Except Rome, perhaps. Hah, hah! But yes, we have some places to see here, if you are pleased."

And so after dinner, in exchange for my thoughts on the AIDS epidemic in America, he told me about Ummidia, the Roman matron whose sepulchre near Cassino is still standing, transformed 800 years ago into a chapel. And about Marcus Terentius Varro, who hobnobbed with Pompey and Caesar and Octavian, and whose villa, in ruins, was right down the road. Varro wrote many books, some of which are preserved in their originals in the Montecassino monastery library.

"You mean the library wasn't destroyed by the bombs?" I asked.

"Of course it was. All was. But we took the books to a safe place well before. 100,000 irreplaceable volumes! We are not savages, you know."

Later a lot of cutting things came to mind that I could have said in response. All I actually said, after some hesitation, was, "That calls for a drink."

I felt free to say this because Glauco, now in a white jacket, was standing by the bar ready to bring us whatever we liked. Mauer and I had vodka tonics, Jim had Bloody Mary mix, without vodka.

Well after ten o'clock, Jim went out to the *Crociato* and got his silver bowl and his coins. The bowl was heavy and shiny, and looked more like a gravy dish than a bowl. That's what it was, Mauer said.

"Of course! Part of a table service, *vasa escaria*, not *vasa potoria*. Not to be drunk from, but for sauces. I have seen others."

"And you're sure it's Roman?" I asked.

"Yes, yes. Good quality silver, from the mines in Spain. Heavy, because the Romans liked to show their wealth at table. But not much decoration, just these simple spirals. Probably of the lst century AD. You see, the Emperor Tiberius made it to be illegal for private citizens to use gold in their table services — it was to be a royal prerogative. Thus wealthy citizens made great use of silver. Petronius tells us that some people had solid silver ovens for the roasting of fish. I quite wish you would find one for me, Giacomo. I would pay you very well."

"I expect you to pay me well for this here bowl, too. If you want it."

"Hmmm. Where did you find it?"

"Alongside the Via Flaminia, between Spoleto and Foligno — near the Springs of Clitumnus. I took pictures."

"Naturally." Mauer turned the dish around and around. "Near the Springs of Clitumnus. A beautiful area. A rich family, traveling north to escape the hot Roman summer, stopped its caravan there for having a picnic 1900 years ago — and a household slave left this behind. She probably for her carelessness paid dearly. Now let me

255

see the coins."

We looked at the coins. There were about thirty of them. The gravy dish was something to see, but to me the coins were just worn old coins. Mauer named the various emperors whose profiles were impressed on them and seemed very happy about a few of them, but I couldn't get excited. I guess I was tired. I said so.

"Very understandable. These things are of little interest to the profane. And unfortunately Giacomo and I must go on long. We must — what is the word — haggle. There is no need for you to undergo this. Your room has been prepared."

"That wasn't necessary. Very kind of you, but I can sleep in the motor home."

"Of course you can, but if you would rather, then there is something wrong with you. Please accept my hospitality." I looked at Jim.

"I always sleep in my van, but don't mind that," he said. "You're used to a regular room and bed, might's well use one. We gotta be here tomorrow anyway, for that fire bomb."

"Adele will show you to your room. *Glauco, fa venire Adele, per favore.*"

Adele was raven-haired and olive-skinned: a Mediterranean beauty. Someday she would balloon up big and round like Agnese, but right now her waist was kept tightly small by a big, black belt, and she only ballooned here and there.

"Adele is at your disposal, Mr. Svenson. Your complete disposal." The German didn't look up from the coins when he said this, but Jim did.

"Mauer! What kind of a man do you think Bob is?"

"Oh, I have no idea. I admit to the having of some curiosity. But I think he is man enough to know what he wants." Jim looked at me and I smiled vacantly. Then he looked back down at the coins with Mauer, and I went off with Adele.

On my way to the bedroom I quickly made the only reasonable decision. I decided to carefully consider the moral and social implications of this thing, sometime on the following day.

"*Bella*!" I started saying when Adele switched on the bedroom lights. I walked around, admiring the thick white rug: "*Bella*!" The big old painting — a Madonna, naturally — on the wall over the bed: "*Bella*!" The wide old Baroque mirror on the opposite wall, at the foot of the bed: "*Bella*!" And the bed itself, a large, modern double bed with rose-colored sheets: "*Bello*!" Then I looked at Adele, put my hands on her shoulders and said "*Bellissima*!" So far I figured Marcello Mastroianni couldn't have done it any better. I expected the girl to melt into my arms, the way they do with Marcello, but instead she slipped away.

Adele looked at herself in the mirror and said, in Southern Italian I had trouble understanding. "Everything you need is in the bathroom over there — the white door. Take a nice bath. I'll come back — later." Then she smiled briefly and left the room.

Now it was my turn to look at myself in the mirror. It was darkish glass, with fine lines to show its age. I was showing my age, too, and I did need a bath and a shave and a shampoo. Some lucky guys, like Harrison Ford, the grimier they are the sexier they get. Adele was not thrilled about getting the night shift with me, but now I was determined to teach her not to judge by appearances. In the mirror the Madonna on the wall behind had an expression of deep concern that seemed to be directed at me, because my reflection was covering the child in her

257

arms. Damned insensitive of Mauer to put a Madonna in a guest bordello. Or maybe it amused him. Anyway, it made me think of Ilene. She didn't have half the measurements of Adele, but I'd rather be doing this with her. Academically speaking. Stop thinking about Ilene that way — she deserves more respect. And doesn't Adele?

If I had kept this line of thought going I'd have blown the whole thing, so I cleaned out my mind and headed for the bathroom to clean my body. The bath was already drawn and bubbly. I enjoyed it thoroughly, working through a complicated sex fantasy which ended with an exhausted but ecstatic Adele begging me to carry her away from the cruel and impotent Dieter Mauer.

That's when it dawned on me that maybe he *was* impotent. No way to know, but it fit right in. Never married, gets his kicks in other ways — loves to watch. Loves to watch his mines explode, his dogs explode. Surrounds himself with young people, and watches them. Keeps them on at night. All that business about waiting in defense, using the impetus of others against them....

I got out of the tub, shaved with the electric razor that was there, used the expensive after-shave that was there, and put on the white silk pyjamas that were there. When I returned to the bedroom, Adele was sitting on the bed in a white robe — very likely with nothing under it. She looked at herself in the mirror again, and then at me. She was evidently unimpressed with the change, but she managed another smile and invited me to sit down beside her. I did. I put my hand on her knee. She picked it up and examined it.

"Manicure," she said, which is the same word in Italian and in English. "You need a manicure first. I am very good. Wait!" She went into the bathroom and came

258

back with a manicure kit and a chair. She sat down in front of me and grimly began trimming my nails. Every so often she would glance up to look in the mirror, smile at me, and then return to her work. She said nothing, and neither did I. I had begun to suspect I was being prepared to play a part in *someone else's* sex fantasy.

Adele was doing a good job with my hands, but taking her time with them — until the time that she looked up, looked in the mirror, and this huge change came over her. She brightened up, put down her tools, and threw herself over me. We rolled around on the bed for a minute or two, until I said "*Aspetta! Aspetta!* Stop!" Adele stopped.

"Striptease!" I said. This is another word that's the same in Italian and English. I got off the bed and went over to lean up against the wall right beside the mirror.

"Okay Adele, a nice striptease, right there on the bed."

She was uneasy again. I began to feel sorry for her. She was obviously new at this game and had a lot to learn. She half-heartedly began to slip her robe off one shoulder, then she said "No — you come and help me. Undress me."

"I give the orders, Adele. You are at my disposal, remember? I'm staying here."

She proceeded. Sadness is a real no-no for a striptease artist; she's supposed to make you think you're giving her as many kicks as she's giving you. But Adele was so...desirable, that I didn't care how she did it, or why she did it, I was way beyond control, except for one thing: I didn't want old Dieter Mauer drooling at the two of us from behind a false mirror. So, breathing heavily. I picked Adele's robe up from the floor when she had finished with it, and draped it carefully but quickly over the mirror. Then I spun around, my heart on fire. Adele burst into tears and ran out of the room.

I stood there watching the door for a few minutes, hoping Mauer would order her back. Then I half-heartedly examined the mirror for whatever signal had told Adele that Mauer was watching. I stopped when I became conscious of other eyes in the room. This time they were the Madonna's, not as reflected in the mirror but as burning into my back. I wished I had another robe to cover the painting.

Finally I locked the bedroom door and got into bed. It was very comfortable, but I wasn't sleepy. There was a phone on the night table. I decided to run up Mauer's phone bill a bit.

"Hello, Beth?"

"Bob! Are you all right?"

"I'm fine. I'm fine. How's Bret?"

"He wants a new computer. The one he's got doesn't have enough bite, or something."

"We'll talk about it when I get home. You know, I miss you, Beth."

"Bet you could use a decent meal."

"I could use more than that." Beth was silent for a few seconds.

"I miss you too, Bob."

"Listen, what can I get you for a souvenir?"

"Get me some blue jeans."

"French blue jeans?"

"Designer jeans. Dior, or somebody. How's your studying coming along? Speaking lots of French?"

"Oh, all the time. Everything's fine here."

"Be careful, Bob. Don't get sick."

"I'm real careful."

"Do you cover the toilet seats?"

"When they have them. Usually it's just a hole."
Another few seconds of silence.

"Well, you don't want to spend all your money on the phone. You need it for the Paris night life, I suppose."

"For tonight, I'm spending my night-life money to talk to my wife. Nothing wrong with that, is there?"

"You stay away from those women, Bob. Call me Instead, you hear?"

"That's what I'm doing, Beth."

"They've got all kinds of diseases over there, Bob."

"Don't worry about a thing. I've got a club, and I just keep beating them off."

"That's my good Bob. I'm glad you called, dear."

"Take care, Beth."

CHAPTER XXIII

*The 22,000 pound Grand Slam could penetrate 20 feet in
concrete and 130 feet in the ground before exploding.
It was known as an earthquake bomb.*

Jim, I...."

"Ain't my business what you did with that girl.
Least you didn't back off just to please me. Been worse."

"But let me tell you what happened. Mauer...."

"Shhh. Here he comes."

I hushed up. I was willing to tell Jim about Adele but
not in Mauer's presence. Any verbal attack I made, the
German would know how to turn against me.

Mauer turned out to be a bit reserved that morning
but determined to pretend that nothing had happened, as
I suspected he would be. When he discovered that I was
prepared to do the same, his usual smile returned in full.
He had one tight moment, when I asked Jim how the
haggling had gone.

"Did all right. Ol' Dieter here just pretty much give
me what I asked. We broke up pretty soon."

"Your things were good, and I was tired, simply,"
said Mauer quickly. "But now, a good breakfast and we
have a new day."

We ate fresh buffalo mozzarella from Caserta which,
as Jim put it, was to regular cow mozzarella what Betty
Grable was to Ma Kettle. I figured the only reason for Jim

to make an effort at humor like that was to see if the conversation would turn from Betty Grable to Adele, which it didn't. He may have decided she wasn't his business, but I sensed he was curious anyway. Or maybe he wanted to engage in some lighthearted man talk about women, just to put me at ease.

"That Betty Grable was some little lady, wasn't she?" he insisted. "'Course, Italian women are different, but—"

"There have been other nice ladies in the movies since Betty Grable," I said. The story of Adele would have to wait. "Farah Fawcett. Kim Basinger..."

"Last movie I seen was '30 Seconds over Tokyo.'"

"Hah!" said Mauer. "The war again. The explosives. Your real interest. What bombs were used over Tokyo?"

"Wouldn't know, Dieter. Bombing ain't really my line, except for defusing them." Here Jim smiled a bit. "Probably the same ones they dropped on Berlin."

"No, I don't think so, my friend. Probably they were 1,000-pound bombs only. Do you know at the end of the war you were on Germany dropping 22,000-pound bombs?"

That sounded like a lot. "22,000 pounds? A single bomb?"

"Yes, Mr. Svenson. It could destroy a building even without the exploding! I defused a few in Germany after the war. Nothing like that was used in Italy here."

"What about the one you're going to show us this morning?" I asked. "How much does it weigh?"

"Hell," said Jim, "incendiary bombs never weigh much at all. Don't have to. Come on, Dieter, let's go take a look at it."

"If you've finished your breakfast, gentlemen...."

And so all three of us got into the brightly-washed *Crociato,* and Dieter co-piloted us to a woods only a few miles from his house. When we started walking in among the trees I again had my trusty spade, but Jim was carrying some sort of tool kit. He would get out the 625 and do some sweeping later, he said. The bomb came first.

"Of course before we withdrew in May of 1944, we mined this woods," said Mauer. "Our squadron attached Stock mines to the trees. But all the mines were removed eventually. The ones that didn't do their job. The mine and trap removal was here quite easy, because after the war we surrendered our *Minenplan* for this area, with a *Sonderverteiler* — a detailed chart. I drew many such."

"I seen some," said Jim. "'Bout like ours. Sure makes things easier."

"But even with no mines now for finding, we were in easy range from you, and we had an important position just to the left there, so surely some stray shells, perhaps a good deal fell in here, so you might have good sweeping, Giacomo."

"Just want to give Bob an idea."

"I'd like that," I said, "but it isn't essential."

"Better let me be the judge of that," Jim replied.

"There it is!" cried Mauer. "That's the place, near those rocks. I discovered it quite while looking for mushrooms. Daniele used precisely those mushrooms on our flounder last night. I was probing among the leaves with a stick like this, and..."

The stick quickly removed the leaves from a metal fin of some sort that was sticking about two inches out of the dirt. With gloved fingers Jim uncovered enough of the bomb to be sure of its size and angle in the ground, then he took the spade from me and carefully started digging around it, never coming closer than six inches.

"Want me to spell you?" I asked after ten minutes.

"Nope. This ground's pretty soft. No problem. And you gotta be careful."

"You know, Mr. Svenson, with anyone else doing this I would stand behind a tree. At a good distance. But not with Giacomo. He can sense danger. Right, my friend?"

"No real danger, yet. Little fire bomb. Won't take me long." And in fact he soon had dug a semi-circular trench a foot wide and two feet deep halfway around the bomb. Then he got a wooden spoon out of his tool chest, got down flat on his stomach with his head over the trench and started scraping the remaining dirt away from it.

"So that's how it's done, is it?" I said shortly.

"Other people have their ways," answered Jim. "Dead, mostly. Take a look."

One side of the bomb was now exposed. It was about two feet long and six inches in diameter. On it you could read "A.L.N.12.35."

"British bomb," said Jim.

"Yes," said Mauer. "15 kilograms. Full of powdered magnesium, I believe. Or thermate. Arranged in twelve capsules that are blown out to start as many fires. Very effective."

"Looks like it's still intact," said Jim.

"Why didn't it explode?" I asked him.

"Maybe just a freak landing. Branch threw it off course and it didn't land on the percussor hard enough. Looks like it's in good shape. Dieter, let's lift it up out of here."

"No, I'll help you." I said — not to spare Mauer the work but to share the moment with Jim.

"Bob, when I need some French translated I'll call on you."

"Mr. Svenson," said the German with his usual smile. "This bomb was intended to kill me. Let's give it one chance more to perform its duty. You can stand over behind that tree. And watch." He smiled even wider on these last words, then he turned to the bomb, and I headed for the tree.

The two old men carefully freed the bomb from the soil that was still holding it, and then smoothly lifted it up and onto the flat ground. "What now?" I called over.

"Come have a look." The two men were getting down to examine the bomb's nose from all sides.

"See?" said Jim when I got there. "Sucker's in perfect shape. Give me the paint brush on the top shelf of my tool kit."

The brush had very soft bristles. Jim used it to gently clean the fuse.

"What do you think, Dieter?"

"For you, it is child's play."

"It's a simple powder fuse — no liquids or chemicals in here. Should be all right."

"But I shall get behind the tree with our friend. My hands — as I said, no good for fine work."

"There's lots of trees," I said. "No sense in doubling up." So we each got behind a tree while Jim did his thing. He studied the bomb a moment longer, then got a wrench and a screwdriver from his tool box and went to work. He knelt down with the bomb between his knees to keep it steady, and bent way over like an old monk doing penance. In ten minutes he had finished. He had removed the fuse, something looking vaguely like a six-inch spark plug.

"Okay," he said standing up, "now it's your turn to work, Bob. Pick her up and let's go back."

"Pick her up?"

"She's dead as a doornail. You could use her as a doorstop."

266

"But not as an ashtray, my friend," said Mauer.

"Nope. Don't drop any lit cigarettes down her nose."

"I don't smoke."

"Then you're the right man for this job. Pick her up."

So I slung the bomb over my shoulder, and we went back to the *Crociato*. Jim said we'd try a little sweeping — but first we'd take Mauer home.

"Why?" he asked. "Aren't you going to do the sweeping here?"

"Might come back. Looks pretty good. But I don't want to waste your time, Dieter."

"I have lunch today with the mayor of Sant' Angelo at 1:30 pm. But until then I am at liberty and would be happy to accompany you. My suggestions can be helpful. For example, I should start over there — the left edge, near our mortar emplacement, our *nebelwerfer*. Perhaps down in that depression."

And that's where we started. Jim got out his 625, changed the calibration, and started sweeping. But we found nothing. I didn't see any real difference in the way Jim was sweeping from the way he had swept for trinkets in the vineyard. I said so.

"Well. I'm looking for shells, ain't really afraid of stepping on a mine here. Dieter, you sure you didn't throw any strays around here that weren't on your charts?"

"Hah! *Minen in streueinsatz*! No, my friend, we had a lot of time here, we did everything with precision, German precision. No stray mines here."

"But this is how I'd do it if I was in a live field," said Jim, "might's well show you now. I start with a one-yard strip from here to that bush, quarter-circle sweeps like this, see — now once I get there, I'll take a step forward and come back."

267

"Looks like slow going," I said.

"That's the thing, nephew. It takes time to clear a whole minefield."

"And you've got to be very regular," I continued.

"Yep. If you're a beginner, you tie a guideline. Now if it was real rough terrain, I'd...hold it."

Jim had found something. He moved the plate up, down and all around in front of him. "Dieter, it's about the size of a Shrapnel mine. 'Bout four inches down."

"No. Not Shrapnel here. Not so efficacious in woods."

"Could just be a tin can. Let me have the spade, Bob."

So Jim started to dig, very carefully. After only a few light spadefuls, he got down and worked with his wooden spoon — and then with the paint brush.

"Take a look, Dieter." The German got down on his hands and knees.

"Yah. It's ours. That is the cap of a BZE fuse. Do you know what the blue color means, Giacomo?"

"Sure. A 4½-second delay. This is a hand grenade."

I got down close. The cap Jim had uncovered was like half of a blue metal ball, only about an inch in diameter.

"You unscrew it," he said, "and under there is the string you pull."

"Then you've got 4½ seconds," I said.

"Yep. If it was yellow, you'd have seven."

"And if it were red," said Mauer, "you'd only have one — but we used one-second fuses only on smoke bombs."

"So this one was never thrown," I said.

"No," said Mauer. "Simply it was lost. Left behind. Perhaps the owner was killed on this spot. Blown to pieces. And his grenade was blown here."

"And didn't explode? With the owner, I mean."

"They don't explode so easily. What soldier would

accept to carry them? Is it intact, Giacomo?"

"Seems so." Jim had gone on working with his wooden spoon. "Go on, get back aways. I'm gonna lift her out of here."

Mauer and I moved off about thirty feet. Jim put himself between us and the grenade, and gently picked it up. He examined it, then held it out so we could see it.

It was a fat oval, only about three inches long. I started forward, but Mauer stayed where he was.

"Giacomo!" he called out. "You had might as well pull and throw it! There's less risk in the throwing of it than in the defusing of it. The BZE is hard to remove. Throw it into that clearing, it will amuse your friend!"

I stopped about halfway between the two of them. Jim stared at Mauer, then at the grenade, then at Mauer again.

"I never threw one, Dieter," he finally said. "I might freeze. Why don't you do it? It's my turn to watch."

I couldn't buy that, and I'm sure Mauer couldn't either. Hell would freeze over before Jim froze with explosives in his hand. But Mauer just said, "That's all right. I shall take it to the *carabinieri*. For giving them some excitement. In fact, I shall give it to the mayor at lunch."

The two men walked toward each other. "You do that, Dieter. Tell him you tripped over it." And when they met, Jim dropped the grenade into the German's hands.

A half an hour later Jim and I were on the road again, heading away from Sant' Angelo and Dieter Mauer and toward the coast. We were driving in silence, which I didn't mind, because I was working out how I would tell the story of my night with Adele — I figured that's what Jim was waiting for. Wrong again.

"So what do you think of that dirty, slimy, smooth-talking son of a bitch?" he asked.

"Well, he's a strange one, all right, but...."

"Strange one! The old shithead tried to kill me. You too, for that matter: he didn't care."

"You mean with that grenade? I thought there was something funny there, with your excuse about freezing up. So it's dangerous to pull the string on one of those, huh?"

"It's dangerous enough to pull the string on any grenade that's forty years old, but it's damned lunacy to do it with a blue BZE. Mauer tried a shot in the dark for kicks, hoping I might not know it, but he shot at the wrong pigeon."

"Okay, so why is it lunacy?"

"The blue BZE has a 4½-second delay tube — it's just powder that takes that long to burn through. Even our guys knew about it. So the Germans started leaving them behind for us to find. And maybe to use."

"I get it. They took out the delay tube."

"You got it. Four guys at Anzio died that way. I don't know how many here."

"And you're sure Mauer knew about it?"

"Knew about it? It was probably his idea!"

"I admit it sounds a lot like him."

"Only thing that's hard to figure is why he'd do it."

"Well, he didn't actually do anything, did he? I mean, he just set you up and stood back to watch. That's what turns him on." And I told Jim the whole business with Adele. When I got to the end, where she jumped up and ran naked out of the bedroom, he almost lost control of the motor home, but it was not from laughter.

"So he really *was* behind your mirror! Listen, nephew, I had some other plans for that fire bomb we picked up, but if you want to, we can go back there and give the

270

Lord a real good shot at him."

"What? Oh, no, no harm was done. Let's just drop it — I mean...*not* drop it....Jim, you wouldn't really...."

"No harm was done? That man is worse than evil, he laughs at good and evil, Nothing means nothing to him. He's—"

"He's just an observer. He's never really lived." This sent Jim back into silence. I broke it after about five minutes by saying, "Now what I can't figure out is, how a man like that, with his past, and with the kind of help he has around the house, how someone like that could be accepted right here where there was so much destruction and suffering, and be very well accepted evidently, if he's going to have lunch with the mayor."

"Well, he didn't come down here empty-handed." Jim said.

"I get it. He's paid his way."

"Done a lot for Sant' Angelo, they say."

"Just goes to show you, nobody's all bad."

"Course not. Never said that."

"Is that the second thing you admire? His generosity?"

"Second thing I admire?"

"Just before I met him, you said you hate his guts but admire two things, and the first was his knowledge of explosives."

"Oh, yeah. I remember."

"Well?"

"Well, it was his way of not caring about what he done. That easy way he lives. Couldn't figure out how he did it. But it's what you said, he's just an observer, and that ain't livin'."

"Speaking of not living, aren't you afraid that the *carabinieri*, or whoever, will pull the string on that grenade? You can't count on Mauer telling them about the little trick."

"Their manual tells them just to blow them things up. Can't be trusted."

"Like Mauer."

"I'll tell you, he's worse than I thought. A bastard that just loves every minute of it. Now you just keep him in mind, nephew, when I show you what I got into at Anzio."

"Whatever it was, you're bound to look good in comparison to Dieter Mauer. Right, Jim?"

CHAPTER XXIV

"Chicory or steak, we live through the death of others."
Camillo Sbarbaro, Ligurian poet.

We didn't stop for anything until we got to the coast, when I asked Jim about lunch. He said he felt like "throwing some of Mauer's money away" in a restaurant, and he knew a few good ones in the town of Formia. We didn't sit down to eat till 2 pm, which isn't unusual in southern Italy, according to Jim. He ordered fish and I had lamb, which I had learned to appreciate in Rome, where it's a specialty. They do a good job with it in Formia, too.

Jim was pretty quiet, which was nothing new, but I was afraid he might be thinking up dire predicaments for Dieter Mauer, so I got him onto something else.

"Anything important about Formia for you?"

"Nope. It's on the Appian Way is all — my road to Naples and Salerno."

"Salerno. That's where you were last Christmas. You sent me that *bulla* from there."

"Yep. I was down picking up this here *Crociato*. Factory's in Salerno. Told you I had it custom-made inside, two big beds instead of lots of little ones. And where you sit up front, there's a bar in the regular model. It's a little factory, but they're easy to talk to and they do good work. Second *Crociato* I've had."

"And you rigged it with two beds because you were already thinking about taking this trip with me when you bought it."

"Well, there was more chance of that than of ever needing five beds."

"Why not just one? I'll bet in your first *Crociato* there was just one."

"Nope. Always had at least two. Got to give the Lord a chance, give Him a place to put somebody.

"Like Rap."

"Yep, sometimes."

"Like your wife, Lorena."

"Would have been real nice. I've always hoped the Lord would heal her, would send her with me. Never worked out. You talking to her — that was my last try."

"She still might come around someday, Jim." I didn't see how I could ever give him Lorena's drawing.

"She might. Hope so. I won't see it."

"You've got another nail, Jim. Another year."

"Hell, for that matter I'm into the forty-fifth year already. End could come anytime. But I guess I got to do something first. In Anzio. Then maybe I'll be left to live out the year, or even a bit more, like them Etruscans once they got over 84. Waiting to die when life's over."

"So before you found that 45th nail, you were in overtime. Waiting to die."

"That's about right. Figured the Lord might let me hang on enough to somehow see whether I'm back home after what I been doin' all these years. Ain't talkin' about no reward, I just want to see if I've read the mine pattern right. Been working hard to get through."

"I know. With your forty-four labors."

"That, and the sweeping. Always hadda be sweeping, to make up. But that's gotten to be easy for me, I almost

274

like it. It's the helping that's hard. You can't just give people money. I tried that, sometimes I screwed people up more'n I helped 'em. Then I had to help them again, till it came out right. And just finding people was no joke, no, sir, with only a name to go on. Course the Italian government started publishing lists of war dead, to help widows get their war pensions and all — that helped me find the towns they were from, then I had to find the right person to help. Wasn't always the widow, she might have remarried right off.

"Sometimes, especially in the beginning, it was the parents who needed help. Then brothers, sisters, or just friends if there was no family. Tried to figure who the man would've wanted me to help. I took my time choosing and deciding what to do. You seen a few things. I done forty-four. One for each. And it's taken me forty-four years. 'Course some years I did more'n one, first few years I couldn't do much of anything, but I got it all to average out to one a year. And it's a job to help right, nephew. I hadda get to know a lot of these people, even be friends with them in order to decide, and none of them know why. Hell, only a few even know I helped them — I learned it was better to keep it a secret. You oblige a person too much, you get tied down. 'Sides, I don't want no gratitude. Ain't got no right to gratitude. But maybe I got a right to be let back in."

I sipped my white wine. "How are you going to know, Jim? Who can let you back in?"

Jim drank his water and started looking out the restaurant window. "You know, I used to be down here a lot. I done a lot of sweeping in the mountains behind Salerno, and around the beaches just south. That's where the 5th Army landed from Sicily, you know. I found a lot around there. Found a whole ammo dump once, near

Santa Lucia, hidden in a cave. Back in '58. Funny thing, I was really looking for Etruscan stuff at the time...."

When Jim dropped a subject, he really dropped it. But if I could keep him talking, keep him relaxed, he might roll back to it, so I went along with the new topic: "Etruscan stuff? Did the Etruscans go that far south?"

"Sure did," he said with obvious relief. "This was way back when Rome was no problem, no barrier for them. Hell, in those days the kings of Rome were Etruscans! They pushed way down here, till they ran into the Greeks at Paestum and stopped. They were never looking for a fight, the Raséna. Nobody was scared of them. Know how they got the Greeks to be scared of them?"

"I can't imagine."

"By teaming up with the Carthaginians, that's how! Everybody was scared of the Carthaginians; they were real tough customers. 'Bout like what the Italians tried to do by teaming up with Germany."

"That didn't work out so well."

"Mussolini was no Etruscan. He didn't know what they knew about people and about life." Jim drank some more water, and I went on with my wine. "Anyway, even Formia here was Etruscan once," he continued. "Least that's what the experts say. I done a lot of looking around, and the only Etruscan stuff I found is stuff travelers might lose, nothing that would prove it was their town. Like if you lost an American nickel here, what would that prove 2,000 years from now? Just passing through. This has always been the coastal road, for travelers going south. Always. Know something? This fish isn't so good. Hope your lamb's better."

"This is great lamb. I never used to eat lamb. This is delicious."

"Well, if you want good fish, the only sure way is to

catch it yourself. Last time it was good here, but..." And
he let his fork drop unhappily onto his plate. "Tomorrow
morning let's get the boat down and do some fishing. Get
some decent fish."

"What about Fishing Rule One: go alone?"

"I'll break that one, if you'll obey all the other rules I
might make up out there on the water."

"You're the captain."

"Otherwise I'll remember Rule One and come back
alone."

I checked, and he was smiling, I think.

"Now for the rest of the day," he said as he peeled an
apple. "The museum director here is a good man, named
Bonazza, doesn't ask too many questions, I've got a few
things for him — the hilt and handle of a Roman sword, I
think. This became a big Roman town, you know. Guy
named Cicero lived here, got killed here — suppose you
know about him. I don't."

"I've heard of him. A politician."

"That would explain why he got killed."

"They say he was one of the better ones."

"Well, if you want to, you can see his tomb, and what-
not. While I'm with Bonazza."

"Oh, maybe I'll just walk around the town, or down
along the beach."

"I get it. Them girls with no tops."

"No, no… I thought I'd kick some sand around, try to
find some platinum teeth. Or maybe ask around if
anybody knows an old beachcomber named Giacomo.
Ask what they think of him."

"What do you think of him?" he asked casually. I was
pleased. With patience, I had got the talk to roll back to
Jim. But this question deserved a better answer than I
gave it.

"Well, every so often he says things that shake me up. Like this morning, when you said you've got plans for the incendiary bomb we're carrying around."

Jim sighed. "Yeah. I got an idea. Came to me right off when Mauer said he'd found it. More I think about it, more it looks like the Lord's doing."

"Oh, no."

"You know, nephew, I paid those forty-four debts of mine with the things the Lord lets me find in the ground. Some of it's Etruscan or Roman, and it's worth money, and I can use the money somehow, like with Egidio's hotel or with Nando's little train. But sometimes the stuff I find is German. Or English or American. War stuff. And I can use that too, like with Steno, or Agnese, or the Captain.

"Some of the people I helped had powerful enemies, nephew. Landowners who'd rather let the land go to hell than let farmers buy it for a decent price. I put 'em in a spot where they needed money fast. Politicians who was using hospital money to build villas on the coast. I had to blow one of them villas up twice. Then lately I run into drugs, people I want to help that has kids on drugs. One pusher, I give him a cigarette with a good dose of fulminate of mercury in it—"

"Stop! I don't want to hear any more."

"Anyway, what I got in mind for that fire bomb ain't gonna hurt anybody."

"I get it. You're going to use it in Anzio somehow, to pay your debt to this 45th man you mentioned."

"Nope. I got no idea what I can do for him. Told you. I gotta know a person, I gotta think about how to help. Don't even know what sort of debt I have with him. I only know what he owes me."

"All right, then what debt are you paying?"

"The only one of the forty-four that I never got right. Only one I screwed up so bad I never could set things straight again."

"Lorena. Your wife."

"Yep. But I done what I could, Lord can't ask more, and just to prove it I done...a few other things in her name. Extra things. Things that help everybody, since I can't help her. And there's a thing I been meaning to do down here, and I figure finding that bomb, and you being along to see, well, it looks like the Lord's hand to me."

"Jim, the Lord doesn't use fire bombs..."

"Who says He don't? Now you just wait and see. Wait till tomorrow afternoon."

"I'm sure I'll love it." I put just a touch too much sarcasm into this.

"Listen here, nephew, I'm sure you got some very fancy words to excuse what you were up to with Mauer's maid last night, but the fanciest words I can think of are that you was trying to take advantage of a young girl that wanted no part of you."

"Well, I don't know about that, but—"

"She was forced into it, and you didn't mind a bit."

"I minded, but—"

"And now the next day you're all set to tell me what I can't do with that little fire bomb! Now I wasn't gonna pass any judgments, I was even sort of glad to find out that you have your weaknesses, but it's no good if you refuse to admit them."

"I admit them, I admit them."

"Then be careful about passing judgement on me, nephew."

"I'm not about to pass judgement on you."

"That's better."

"But I have my own thoughts about the wisdom of

279

doing certain things. My own opinions."

"Keep 'em loose, nephew. Keep 'em loose."

We got to bed at sundown that evening, because Jim wanted to be on the water at sunup. But no matter how early you go to bed, getting up in the middle of the night is miserable. And lifting the boat off the *Crociato* roof and down to the water wasn't any more fun than the time before. But once we were out at sea, things got very pleasant. The Mediterranean is always beautiful, but in the light of dawn it makes you think there's never been any sin in the world.

"It's nice out here, Jim."

"Ought to be good fishing."

"What are we after?"

"*Sgombri*. Mackerel. Good time of year. In July and August they come in close to the shore to spawn. Otherwise they're way the hell out where only the big commercial boats can get them."

"Mackerel. That figures."

"Why should it? It's just a good eating fish."

"It's a good fish eater, too. Streamlined and deadly, same as the pike you also like."

The observation sent Jim into meditative silence, but only for about three minutes.

"Ain't nothing wrong with being a pike or a mackerel. That's good killing, it's natural, keeps everything in balance. Would you rather be an anchovy?"

"No, no, I'd rather be a mackerel. But way out there in the open sea, away from the likes of us."

"Where you're pointing ain't away from the likes of us. The island of Ponza's over that way, 'bout thirty miles. Might see it when the mist burns away. They run ferry boats from Formia."

"And you took one that time you went there looking

for Steno's wife."

"Nope. I took the one from Terracina. Further up the coast. We'll drive by tomorrow."

"Good man, Steno."

"Don't come much better."

"I wonder what we'd think of him if he could talk."

"Wouldn't improve him."

"Not many it does. Hey, where we going, anyway?"

"Well, Steno taught me two ways to fish for mackerel. One way is to get yourself a mess of little fish, crush them up in a net bag — most of them, you leave some alive — and drag the bag behind your boat, or just let it sit in the current. You can troll behind the bag, or just set here with a bobber; the fish'll eventually find the trail and come right to you."

"But we're not going to do that."

"Nope. Don't like it. Too messy. Ain't no real ability to it. I suppose if I needed to catch a lot of fish fast, but hell, we only need two or three. I don't catch fish I don't need. It's harder with artificial bait, but I like it more. Don't like using live bait. 'Course sometimes it's the only way."

"It's hard to think of you as being squeamish."

"Ain't being squeamish I'm talking about. Just don't like using living things that way 'less I have to. It makes me think of things like Dieter with his dogs. I can't help it. And the sheep. Makes me think of the sheep. Even though I know it ain't the same thing, still there's something about it..."

"The sheep?"

"Yeah, the sheep. Suppose I should tell you about the sheep. Sounds like something Dieter would dream up, but he told me the credit goes to somebody else. Anyway the fact is that if the Germans had to clear a minefield real quick it was no problem if they could find a herd of sheep or goats or something. They'd just stampede them right on through. Sheep are stupid as hell. I saw them do it near Anzio once and I know it was done in other places — I used to find wool and bones and what-not scattered in the field. Ain't kidding."

"Well, it's easier to take than Dieter's dogs. You know, if I had to clear a minefield real fast I suppose I could be talked into using sheep."

"You could? Well, what about horses?"

"Jesus. Let's stick to sheep. I don't think much of sheep."

"Look over there! That's what we're after— see all them seabirds way over there? We'll give them a try."

"That's Steno's other method?"

"Yep. There's probably a big school of sardines near the surface out there. The birds are working on them from above — and you can bet the mackerel or some other big fish are working on them from below."

We headed for the birds. There were maybe two hundred of them, circling smoothly over an acre of water, about fifty feet in the air. At any given moment five or six were plunging straight down into the sea, and coming up, half the time, with a small fish in their red bills.

They were beautiful birds, only a foot or so long but with a wide wingspread and a long forked tail. They were white, but tipped with black all around — on their heads, their wings and even their beaks.

"Those birds aren't gulls." I said.

"Can't argue with you there."

"But I don't know what they are."

"Those are terns. Working their way south for the winter. Better bird than a gull. Fly better, fish better, look better."

Jim stopped the motor about sixty yards from the

nearest bird. "Can you cast that far?" he asked.

"Maybe. Let's leave it in doubt. I'll use those oars and try to keep the boat lined up right — you go ahead and cast."

" 'Preciate that, nephew."

Jim pulled his pole out to its full length, put on a foot of steel leader ("Damn mackerel can bite right through nylon, nephew."), and chose a four-inch wooden lure, silvery but dark on top.

"Steno made this for me. You wheel her in fast, and she looks like a lame sardine."

"I'd go for it."

"So would I, but a mackerel is a smart fish, normally. Only ones we catch are the dumb ones."

Jim found a dumb one on his very first cast. The fish never jumped but ran all over the Mediterranean with Steno's bait in his mouth. Jim let him run, not trying to muscle the fish in, but letting him get good and tired. ("Otherwise there ain't no way to net him, nephew.") It was still no joke for me to get the net around the little torpedo that kept darting in all directions, until he finally darted the wrong way and I was able to lift him into the boat. He was fine to see, sleek and shining with rakish blue stripes.

"Maybe two pounds. Good eating size. Might be enough but I'll get one more. There's a little freezer in the *Crociato* — wouldn't mind having a little spare mackerel."

So he was soon back in the fray, casting Steno's lame sardine right where the terns were thickest. He didn't find a dumb mackerel so quickly this time, but he did find a dumb tern. The bird swooped down, grabbed Jim's lure and flew about ten feet before dropping it.

"How about that?" said Jim. "Don't happen very often. That bird ain't playing with a full deck."

283

Jim was enjoying himself. Even in his pleasure there was a certain tension, but the pleasure was as real as it was rare. I wanted to know more about this side of Jim.

"Have you got a full deck someplace in the motor home? Do you like playing cards?"

"Nope. Played Rummy in the army, that's about all. Don't miss it."

"Do you miss anything? From American life, I mean."

Jim was reeling in. He finished and then let loose with another cast before answering. Just before his lure hit the water he said "Yep!"

But that's when he got his second strike. "Hell, this here's just a little feller."

"Good eating size?"

"No, we'll throw him back if he ain't hooked too bad." Jim was reeling the fish in without much effort when all of a sudden the water roiled white at the end of his line: his pole bent sharply down and then snapped back free. Jim was sitting down, but lost his balance and flopped backwards against the inflated rubber side of the boat.

"You okay, Jim?"

"God-damned son of a bitch got my lure!"

"What was it?"

"Don't know, but he got Steno's lure, damn it."

"Something big took your mackerel, is that it?"

"And it don't happen very often either. Turning into a funny day. First time that's ever happened to me. It's happened to Steno, though. Damn! Hate to lose that lure."

"What could it have been?"

"A dogfish. Must have been one of those damn dogfish. Those little sharks they have around here."

"Sharks?"

"Some people eat them. *Palombo*, they call them. Hope this one chokes."

284

"Maybe he will. I mean, maybe he spit your bait right back out, and it's floating around here somewhere. Won't hurt to look."

"It ain't likely. If he spit it out with the mackerel it'll go to the bottom, 'cause mackerel don't float. But if he spit out just the bait, that'll come up. Pretty damned unlikely. I don't think sharks can spit."

"A quick look won't hurt." So I rowed towards where the line had been snapped, and we started searching for Steno's bait.

"Just before you had that strike you were going to tell me what it is that you miss, From the States."

"What? Oh yeah, well there is one thing. Baseball. The Cubs. Taking the morning train from Mattoon up to Chicago, to Wrigley Field to see the game, and then taking the evening train back home. Miss that."

"They've put lights in Wrigley Field, Jim. Night baseball. Starting this month." Jim silently scanned the sea, pondering this enormity.

"And I s'pose they put green plastic in place of the grass."

"No, no. Not yet, anyway. You know, they're not doing so bad this year, especially Andre Dawson, he's "

"Andre Dawson. You wanna talk to me about the Cubs, you gotta talk about Stan Hack and Peanuts Lowrey and Phil Cavarretta and Hank Sauer. After them I used to try to keep up a bit, with the radio and the papers, but for the names to mean something you have to see how they hit and run and field. You know something? I almost got myself caught back in '45 because of the Cubs. Helluva team, they won the pennant that year, you know. Almost won the World Series. They went down to the wire against the Detroit Tigers. Man, I wanted to hear that seventh game so bad I put on my uniform and sort of

285

fell in with a bunch of GIs in Florence — pretended I was on a three-day pass from Milan. I knew that at game time they'd head back to their Px radio. They did, all right, but I saw they were checking papers real careful at the entrance to the base, so I had to think up an excuse and keep on walking. I could feel them staring at my back."

"You almost got caught."

"Yep. A close one. Hell, I was missing in action. If I turn up alive, I'm a deserter!"

"But that isn't all, is it?"

"That's plenty, nephew. Deserting from a battle zone really gets their dander up."

"So why were you...missing when you weren't?"

"'Cause I was about to be charged with a war crime."

"So you're not the only one who thinks you're responsible for the deaths of those forty-four men, your forty-four nails. I mean, it's official."

"Yep. Official. And they'da had me dead to rights. Had their choice of books to throw at me. Heavy ones."

Jim and I weren't looking at each other. I was on one side of the boat, and he was on the other, and we were intently searching for a handmade wooden lure. He went on easily, aided perhaps by the illusion that he was addressing the fish: "It was tough avoiding the MPs back then, you know, while there was still the Allied Military Government in Italy. They were always on the lookout for strays. But Italians are real understanding people, I can tell you. They have natural sympathy for anybody who wants to quit being a soldier. Most unmilitary people in the world. And by that I don't mean chicken, no, sir. Great resistance fighters. I spent the winter of '44 with the Italian Resistance in the north, behind the Gothic line. We were all in somebody's black book. Fought like hell and ready to die. Ready and willing. A lot of us did

286

die. I didn't. And till the AMG packed up and went home, the Italians helped me lie low. And that's a debt I have with all of them, with the whole country. That was my first reason for sweeping after the war. To do something for this country that helped me hide."

"Did your Italian friends know about your war crime?"

"Nope. Don't think any of them ever knew. They just helped without asking. I wasn't on "Wanted" posters or anything. The Allies didn't want to do that kind of laundry in public. They couldn't hardly wait to declare me dead. We ain't gonna find that lure, dammit."

"Haven't you got another lure to use?"

"Wouldn't be as good. Besides, the school's broken up — the birds are scattering. Probably that damn dogfish started thrashing around in there. Maybe more than one. Head over where the school was a minute. I just hate to give up on that lure."

I started rowing slowly in that direction. "Next time you see Steno, ask him to make you another one."

"If I ever see him again, I will. There it is."

"There's what? The lure?"

"Nope. Look over there. The ferry boat to Ponza."

"Nice island, I bet."

"Sure is. Sure was. Probably all built over now."

"I don't suppose we have time for a quick trip."

"Nope."

"Wouldn't you be curious about how that guy is doing, what's-his-name, the guy that ran off with Steno's wife?"

"Dino. Nope."

"Just to see if he's still alive?"

And Jim looked at me in one of his stranger ways.

CHAPTER XXV

The Sicilian word "mafiusu" originally meant "bully",
it probably had Arabic origins.

The mackerel was delicious. Jim slapped it on his grill along with some onions and zucchini. Jim's basic approach to food was either to barbecue it or eat it as it was. Except for pasta of course, which he didn't have that often.

"But you make good pasta, Jim. That spaghetti we had on the way to Cassino was great."

"It's fussin', and I don't fuss much with food when I'm alone. Sometimes ain't no place to build a fire."

"That's right. You don't like to use kitchen gas."

"Hell, no, don't like them containers. It's like driving around with a bomb."

"Right. Wouldn't ever want to do that."

"I mean a live bomb, nephew. One that could go off. Stuff I carry you could take to bed."

"Sure."

"If it wasn't safe I'd be dead by now, wouldn't I? Anyway, let's go get rid of this fire bomb we're carrying, since it bothers you so much." And he gave me a pat on the back.

So off we went, following the coast from Formia, towards Gaeta. Jim's good mood put me at my ease. He wouldn't do anything really drastic with that bomb, not with me around. Or would he? Starting out with a little light conversation had proved to be the best way to find things out from Jim: "Hey. I'll bet you're going to give that bomb to some fisherman friend of yours to use as an anchor!"

"It'd make a terrible anchor. 'Sides, only fisherman I knew around here died of pneumonia last winter. Right up there in Gaeta."

"I've heard of Gaeta — what's it famous for?"

"You got me. II Corps took it real easy."

"I don't mean in the war. Something else."

He thought a minute. "Well, at one point that little mountain back there, Mount Orlando, is split right open, right down to the water. They say it happened when Christ died on the cross."

"Something else. Maybe I'll think of it."

"Check your guide book."

"I will. Later." I didn't want to take the conversation *that* far from the question of exactly where it was we were going with the bomb. And anyway Jim drove right past Gaeta. For my next approach I started with a road sign I noticed: "Hey, I thought you liked the old Roman roads. This isn't the Via Appia any more."

"Nope. The Appia cuts inland for a spell."

"Don't we need the Appia? To get to Anzio?"

"Oh, we pick her up again soon. In Terracina."

"I thought it was always a mistake to leave the Roman roads."

"It is. The Romans called this one here the Via Flacca. There's ruins of their villas all along here. Big resort area for those old Romans. And now it's all turning back into resorts and hotels. I s'pose that's all right. S'pose it's natural enough. But I want to show you something that I think is pretty unnatural. It's coming up here on the right."

The mountains, which were never more than a few miles away, here and there pushed right down to the sea, forcing our road to cut into the rocks and to jump across inlets or little valleys on viaducts. Just before driving out onto one of these viaducts, Jim pulled off the road into one of the many "panoramic parking" spaces that Italians put along their scenic roads.

"Now take a look down there, what we'll be going over. Ain't that awful?"

"What is it?"

"A *conceria*. A goddam tannery. You can't smell it now, 'cause they close in August, but otherwise we'd have to roll up the windows."

There was definitely a factory of some sort down in the valley, almost directly under the bridge we would soon be crossing. The building looked new.

"Why did they let them put something like that along here?"

"Look all around down there. Take a good look."

I did. No trees. Just a lot of shrub and black rock. "There's been a fire down there recently," I said.

"Forest fire. Now you're getting the picture. This spot was hands off — a nice woods, and there ain't too many left along here. The bastard who owns that tannery — guy named Pantano, Ciro Pantano — he got some flunky to start that fire, and after that you can buy the land and get the permits without any trouble. Especially if you got connections, and this guy is solid Mafia. It's shit, but it happens all the time."

"But why a tannery? Why not hotels and fancy homes?"

"They'll come, they'll come. That's the plan. First a factory. That entitles you to all kinds of state money, tax benefits; they'll build him a little port here, they'll improve the roads, the drainage, everything. Anybody willing to open a factory in southern Italy automatically gets a windfall. It comes out of the *Cassa del Mezzogiorno*, the southern development fund, government subsidies — mostly goes to the Mafia. Pantano is getting a giant helping. Then at just the right time, he'll declare bankruptcy and close the tannery. With government help. Then he'll present a 'reconversion plan' to take advantage of the port and the roads — a tourist village, or something. Bet that tannery was built so's to be converted to a gym or some damn thing overnight. More subsidies. He'll be rolling in it. He already is."

"How do you know all this?"

"Don't like tanneries. Smelled it last year and started asking around. Bonazza, the museum man back in Formia, he brought me up to date yesterday. Just what I thought. The time is ripe, and the Lord brings us here. You, me, and..." Jim rose from the driver's seat and moved back into the living area. He got out the fire bomb, brought it up front and put it in my lap.

"Jim, for the love of God..."

"Can't explode. Wait a minute." He went back and got the fuse. "Well. I've cleaned this up, and as far as I can see, everything's in working order inside the bomb, so God willing she'll explode."

"God willing, huh?"

"That's the whole point. If I'm wrong and He ain't willing, this thing'll be a dud just like it was 44 years ago."

"That's hogwash, Jim. You're old enough to know better."

"Hold still." And he started screwing the fuse into the bomb I held on my lap. I felt my skin trying to curl up away from it.

"Jim, you're liable to kill somebody. Some poor devil with a wife and six kids."

"Nope. Nobody's down there, 'cept maybe a guard there in the guardhouse, and he'll be all right. All closed up for summer holidays. They shut the country down in August."

"You might be doing your Mafia man a big favor. He might collect a fortune in insurance."

"Southern Italians hate insurance. Think it's bad luck. Anyway with no tannery they'd stop the new road down there and the new port. Pantano might take the hint and get out. I seen it happen, bombs make people nervous. Listen, nephew, I gotta do this thing, I feel it in my bones. One last thing for Lorena. Now hold still with that bomb." He had finished screwing in the fuse; now he started the *Crociato* and headed out onto the viaduct.

"Jim, this is crazy! In broad daylight! There's traffic on this road! We'll go to jail!"

"Southern Italians tend to mind their own business. Besides, I'll choose the right moment."

Actually there weren't many things I could do at this point. Any course of action had to start with getting a live 33-pound bomb off my lap. I realized that the only way to stop this madness would be for me not to let Jim have his bomb back — to hang on to it for dear life. But I didn't relish the idea of wrestling with a strong man over a fire bomb. I was also sure that a fight like that, even if we survived, would mean the end of my relationship with Jim. I swear I wasn't thinking about the money.

Or rather, it crossed my mind, but I didn't let it become a factor. What was a factor was my real desire to get to Anzio with Jim and find out what he had done there, and who he would meet there, and what meaning he would give to the 45th nail. It was at that moment, when Jim stopped the motor home over against the guard-rail in the middle of the bridge, that I understood how strongly I desired to discover these things.

"Gimme the bomb. Bob."

"What can I say or do that would make you give this up?"

"Nothin'."

"Don't you care what opinion I have of you?"

"Yep. That's one of the reasons I'm doing it. You gotta accept these things I been doing, if you're ever gonna accept what happened at Anzio. Otherwise ain't no sense to you letting me back in. Gimme that thing."

I didn't give it to him, but I let him take it. He got out of the *Crociato* but left the bomb on his seat.

First he walked around to the guard-rail, looked over the edge and picked the best spot — only about fifteen feet in front of us. Then he came back and stood by his door, waiting for a lull when no cars could be seen in either direction. Then he cradled the bomb in his arms like a sleeping child and walked swiftly back to his spot. He checked once more — the coast was still clear — and then dumped the child. Without waiting an instant he walked back to the motor home. The tannery was only about 150 feet beneath us, and we heard the bomb explode before Jim reached his door. In the distance a car could be seen coming in the other direction. Jim got in and drove off, quickly but not wildly. I looked at the car as it passed us. It was a family on vacation. They had heard the explosion or had seen something, because the whole family stared at us. Then they slowed down in the middle of the bridge, to look at the smoke that was already rising above them, but they didn't stop. We got a glimpse of the tannery once we got off the bridge, because the road curved sharply to the left before going around a cliff. The smoke was now billowing up more strongly from the building, and flames could be seen through the windows.

"Looks like I got her pretty good. Dropped that baby right through a sunlight."

"Great. And God didn't stick his hand out to stop it, but that's not your fault." Jim was silent, so I went on. "Is that what you're going to tell the judge? Better get your story polished, those people we passed will give the police a description of us."

"Their license plate was Naples. Ain't never any witnesses to anything in Naples. And if these people turn out to be different, well, that would be God's will, too."

"This God's will thing sounds like quite a high, Uncle Jim; if there were a way to inject it, it might beat cocaine."

"I don't like tanneries."

"Well, how about that? And I don't like banks. I think I'll blow up goddamn First National soon's I get back to Chicago."

Jim gave me a quick smile. "You're gonna need a good-sized bomb. This is kinda short notice, but I'll see what I can do."

"After Anzio."

"Whatever you say, nephew."

And so I had become an accomplice to an arsonist, but I decided I might as well put off further meditation on this point until after Anzio, along with the bomb for the First National. What was done, was done — and maybe we *had* ruined some *mafioso's* day.

"Tiberius was an emperor, wasn't he?" asked Jim a few minutes later.

"Yes, he was. When Christ died."

"We're going right by his house. Right through it, almost. See the sign? The town out there's called

Sperlonga. Mean anything to you?"

"No." And I wasn't going to check it out in "Italy in Your Pocket." I wasn't that relaxed yet. Jim was only from Mattoon, but on this occasion he was a lot cooler than I was.

"Me neither," he said like any tourist. "But it looks nice out there on that bluff."

"Suppose so. Listen!"

"Sirens," said Jim calmly. "Fire engines. There they are. Won't be easy to put out that fire, if it got to the pelts. Hope it did." Two fire engines raced by us, followed within seconds by two police cars.

"See, nephew? They saw us, but they aren't turning around. They don't have our description."

"Not yet."

Ten minutes further on, at the entrance to the town of Terracina, Jim turned off the main road, took some lefts and some rights and parked next to a wall of rock.

"Is this a good place to hide?" I asked.

"Nope."

"Is there another tannery here?"

"Nope. Just something I want to show you. Last time I was here I thought that if you ever came over I'd take you by here. Means something to me, anyway. You don't even have to get out. Just look at them markings going up the rock face there — see them? Every ten feet, on some you can still see the Roman numbers. XXX, LX, all the way up to CXX feet. Trajan's engineers, they just cut right through here. Trajan! Wasn't really an emperor, he was a soldier. A man I sell to in Arezzo has told me a lot about him. A real soldier. And soldiers make the best roads, let me tell you. They make 'em to take heavy loads, they make 'em not to wash away or get covered with rock slides — they think of the worst things that can happen, 'cause they always do. Soldiers know that. When the army builds a road, the generals are thinking about using it to advance, to bring up supplies. The foot soldiers who do the digging, they're thinking they might need it someday to get the hell out of there. And together they make damn good roads."

"You'd have stayed in the army if you could have, I bet. I mean, all things considered, you like soldiering."

Jim let his eyes fix upon the photo in the clip above his rear-view mirror — upon the tall young man in uniform.

"I thought about that many a time, nephew. Being a soldier is the right life for some kinds of men, and maybe it was for me. Man, you can say what you like about soldiers, but sometimes you need them. There wasn't no other way to get the Nazis out of here — somebody had to throw them out. And there's something about a head-on war, one army slugging it out with another; you got an enemy right there, and it's kill or be killed, and it's all strategy, and logistics, and guts, and you gotta admire some of the things you see. The things men can do. You never see it anywhere else."

"Jim, there won't be any more wars like that. It'll all be buttons and gas and sudden death. No more slugging it out head-on."

"Nope. I know that. Even then it was harder'n hell to keep it head-on, you and the enemy. All that power, it spills over against the wrong people, the wrong things."

"Even animals. Sheep and dogs."

"Even children, nephew. It's never clean. We took a little town called Ponte Rosso a week after we landed at Anzio. Held it for about five days. Anyway there was a friend of mine, a guy named Lou Minoli from Pittsburgh. Man, he hated the Germans so bad, he was all set to have

296

Kesselring for breakfast. So there we were in the piazza in Ponte Rosso and Lou thought he saw a gun flash in a second-story window and he opened up with his BAR and next thing you know, a little girl fell out of the window.

"Old Lou let out this scream and ran over there, but I didn't. I seen what a Browning can do to a man, I didn't need to see what it can do to a little girl. Poor Lou. We could never get him to say another word. He never came around; they had to ship him back. For all I know, he's still in a VA hospital somewhere. And that's just one little story, nephew. One little story."

"I can imagine."

"No you can't, and it's just as well. And there ain't no way to keep it clean, to keep it from spilling over. You try too hard to keep it clean, you lose."

"It's the bastards that win the wars for you."

"You're learning, nephew. Come on, I want to show you a nice place. A place where I like to come."

"Another place you've had in store for me?"

"Yep. Whole idea of this trip. Show you everything I can about me, about what I do, and what I like and don't like. Big things and little things, you gotta put it all together and decide."

"Decide what, Jim?"

"Whether I'm back in or not. Come on. I don't like this town, 'cept for these here markings."

That meant I wasn't to pursue the point. Anyway I thought I understood what Jim meant by getting "back in," even if my part in it still wasn't clear. I mentally shrugged, and decided to get back to my other little problem:

"I still think we should stay off the main road for a while, Jim. The police..."

297

"They's either looking for us or they ain't, and if they are, they'll find us anywhere we go."

"What's wrong with this town?"

"Hard to get in and out of. Always been. II Corps ran into some Panzer Grenadiers here and didn't get out for a while."

"That explains why so much of the town looks new."

"No, it don't. The Germans were here because they love rubble for defense. We'd bombed the hell out of Terracina on January 22nd, to cover the Anzio landing. To pull the Germans south."

"Did it do any good?"

"Nope."

"Okay, let's get out of here. Take me to that place you like."

And so we went through Terracina and started up the coast again, towards a tall promontory that stood out so sharply from the plain behind it that at a distance it seemed to be an island. I calmly asked Jim about it. I expected a police roadblock at any moment, but I wanted my uncle to remember which town the word "cool" came from.

"Yeah. That's where we're going. It's called the *Circeo*."

"Doesn't that mean 'circus'?"

"Nope. Circus is *circo*. *Circeo* has something to do with Ulysses. He stopped here for some reason. Some cock-and-bull story. I forget what."

"Circe! A sorceress who changed his crew into pigs!"

"Yeah, that's it. There's a cave there where it happened. Course it's all nonsense."

"It isn't nonsense, it's myth. It's legend. It's great literature!"

"It's still bullshit. Changing men into pigs."

298

"If it's bullshit, why do you like this place?"

"All I like is the view on the other side, where the Torre Paola is. This side of the *Circeo* is all ruined by construction — so many damn fences and signs you might as well be in Indiana for all you can see. But the other side..."

Jim was right. We crossed behind the *Circeo* by fighting our way through a long, congested resort area built up so thickly that we practically never saw the sea or the promontory that was supposed to be the main attraction. But on the other side the works and pomps of man all suddenly disappeared, as if by magic. The *Circeo* loomed up behind us and the sea stretched down and away to the north, a beautiful scene untrammeled by signs and fences and buildings. Except for the Torre Paola — Paul's Tower. A sign told us it had been built by Pope Paul III in the 16th century, to defend the Papal States against attacks from the sea. But it looked fine there, an example of times when men still had to work with nature, because they weren't yet strong enough to work against her. The promontory was naturally a defensive outpost of the land against the sea, and Paul III had only enhanced its role with his tower — although the sign said his real enemy never came from the sea, but from Germany...

"What do you think, nephew?"

"Great spot, uncle. How do they keep the resorts out?"

"This here was declared a national park by Mussolini, all along the coast, clear up practically to Nettuno and Anzio."

"He wasn't all bad, was he?"

"Nope. Nobody is. And he did a thing nobody before him had been able to do — he drained the Pontine Marshes, all this flatland off here to our right and clear up to the Alban Hills. Just about nobody lived there before. Mosquitoes and malaria. He drained it and brought 30,000 settlers in, farmers from the north. They were all settled by 1942. Just in time to catch World War II when it rolled right through here and blew everything back to hell."

"Looks nice now."

"Oh, they fixed it up again afterwards, and now this is a real productive area. You can't keep a good farmer down, you know." Jim bent down and picked a purple wildflower. He really liked the place, with the strength of the *Circeo* defending the vulnerable and fertile lowlands behind. We walked around for a while and then started driving down a wonderful road that ran cleanly atop the high dunes between the sea on the left and the Pontine Plain on the right.

"Bet this isn't a Roman road," I said after a bit.

"You lose. It's the Via Severiana. Course it had to be fixed up again. But it's a Roman road. The Romans loved this coast and took good care of it. The Pontine Marshes weren't half so bad then. The Romans knew how to make real good use of those lakes there, for drainage and what-not."

He meant a series of long, thin lakes, four in all, that ran alongside our elevated road and separated us four times from the lowland as if we were on a land bridge. A strange and delicate landscape, mercifully protected from man's heavy hand. Too beautiful to last, but it lasted unchanged for twenty miles. Halfway along the fourth lake Jim pulled the *Crociato* off the road.

"It's getting dark." he said. "No sense in driving into Anzio tonight. Might's well spend the night here. This here's Fogliano Lake. Biggest of the four."

"I can't imagine a nicer spot. There isn't even much

traffic."

"That's 'cause there's no bars, no pizzerias, no gas stations on this road. And there's faster ways of getting places. People do it once and then stay off it."

"What'll we eat?"

"You like eel?"

"No. Don't think so."

"Too bad. That lake's full of them. But maybe it's just as well, it's been a funny day for fishing."

"Not just for fishing..."

"Anyway, we gotta settle for beans, cheese, and onions."

"Sounds great."

I got the fire started this time, while Jim opened two cans of baked beans and sliced the cheese and onions. Then we heated the cans and grilled the onion slices, putting the cheese on them to melt just before taking them off. A fine supper, and it wasn't just because of the surroundings. Jim put mineral water in his Etruscan pitcher, which I turned so that the woman with the knowing eyes could look out to sea.

"I've stopped here other times," said Jim, his deep voice rising when necessary to stay above the sound of the waves. "This is an important spot, you know, but there ain't no sign telling about it, so I guess people will forget. Soon as us old soldiers all disappear. Right exactly here is where our boys pushing down from Anzio met up with II Corps pushing up from the south. On May 25th, that clinched it. That clinched the Breakout."

"I'd like you to tell me how it was at Anzio."

"I'll tell you a few things. Tomorrow when you can see. Tomorrow when we're there."

CHAPTER XXVI

*Over 12,000 American soldiers are buried
in Nettuno and Florence burial sites.*

And the next morning there we were, standing on
Anzio Beach. We'd have been there earlier, but I had
insisted on buying and carefully scanning the morning
papers. The tannery was a total loss, no one had been
injured, and police were waiting for the results of an
investigation into the causes of the fire. I was amazed at
our good luck. Jim seemed to have lost interest in the
whole affair. This was Anzio, and he was thinking back.
Way back.

It was nine o'clock, and the beach was filling up fast
with vacationers, at this hour mainly families with little
kids that just couldn't wait to get down to the beach and
start their long day of fun. Their shouts mixed perfectly
with the rustle of the waves that seemed to be urging the
children to come and play. Anzio itself rose up behind the
beach with its palms and pastel colors as if to defend the
children, and deny that anything amiss had ever taken
place here.

"You did a good job at Montecassino, Jim, but it isn't
going to be easy for you to set the mood here. This sure
isn't the Anzio you saw in 1944."

"That's partly because you ain't looking at Anzio right
now — this is Nettuno. Anzio starts a bit to the left there.

They've grown together now, but they was separate back then. We pretty much concentrated on Nettuno, and the Brits on Anzio."

"Who had the most trouble?"

"You mean when we landed? Nobody had trouble. Piece of cake. Perfect weather, complete success. We hit the beaches at 2 am, and Kesselring didn't know where we had landed until after eight. There was 50,000 of us, some 400 ships, and they didn't see us! They had no reconnaissance planes — we had bombed their airstrips."

"So the landing was no sweat."

"150 casualties, mainly mines."

"Didn't the Germans have anybody on guard here?"

"There was a battalion here, resting up."

"Just one battalion?"

"And a weak one at that."

"Then the Terracina bombing did work! They pulled men out of here..."

"Nope. Wasn't never any big garrisons here to pull out. Anyhow, the Germans in Italy never fell for too many diversionary tactics. They played their own game, made their own moves. They had Richard."

"Who was Richard?"

"Carlo." shouted a pretty woman from her beach towel, "*Vieni qui immediatamente! Metti giù quel pesce!*" Jim paused before answering me — maybe he felt the same way for a moment, that this bright, blue morning was much more suited to little Carlo playing with his fish and running to his mother than it was to an old man remembering Richard.

When Jim continued he was almost whispering: "Richard was the German code-name for what to do in case of a landing anywhere in Italy. All Kesselring did that morning was send out the message: Richard —

Anzio. Every Kraut in Italy knew exactly what he had to do. One sick battalion. Yep. And within a week we were up against Von Mackinsen and the 14th Army. In about two weeks we had about nine divisions — damn near 100,000 men. Wasn't for our air support, we'd have had to swim back to Naples."

I looked around at the smiling blue water filling up with kids and tried to imagine the dark terror of an army being thrown into the sea.

"Egidio was a kid in Rome, then. He says nobody there could figure out why you didn't just come straight up and liberate the city."

"The people in Rome wasn't the only ones that wondered about that. It sounded easy. Before the Krauts got organized, ol' General Lucas could have led a charge with 30,000 or so of us cowboys, right up the Alban road, just 38 miles, and we could have taken baths in the Trevi Fountain four days after the landing. Well, maybe not, it would've still been January, a little cold for a bath."

"So why didn't this General Lucas go for it?"

"Lucas wasn't the type, but Patton was — he'd have done it. And do you know what would have happened? Rome would have been our Stalingrad — the Germans would have locked us in and starved us out. We just didn't have the bulk at that point, nephew, and we didn't have it for months. We waited 'til we got up around 200,000."

"That doesn't sound very heroic on our part."

"You better be kidding, nephew."

"I suppose I am."

"'Cause if you ain't, we're back to square one."

"I was kidding."

"Heroes don't win wars."

"I know, I know. Bastards win wars. I was kidding."

304

"Come on, I'm gonna show you what happened to the heroes."

"I was kidding!" All to no avail. Jim marched up the beach with the determination of 44 years earlier, and we got back to the motor home and drove away.

Five minutes later we were in front of the American Military Cemetery. The huge iron gate was open, but Jim parked outside and we walked in.

"They'd let us drive around, but I'd rather walk, okay?"

"Okay by me."

"These guys deserve a little respect."

"More than a little, I'd say."

"Don't overdo it. A lot of them were just dumb. Stuck their heads out when they shouldn't have."

Now we were inside, walking among the perfect rows of white marble crosses, broken here and there by a Star of David. This was my first visit to a military cemetery, but of course I had seen pictures and knew what to expect. Still, when you're in the middle, you wish you weren't.

"My God, how many of them are there?"

"Only about 8,000, 'cause most of the bodies were shipped home. Look, there's one of your heroes." He pointed to a cross that had the usual information on the crossbeam: ANDREW POCHEK - SGT 15 INF 3 DIV - OHIO MAY 24 1944. But on the upright there was vertically inscribed: MEDAL OF HONOR.

"May 24th. Killed during the Breakout," Jim said. "Gung-ho. Lots of them in here, most without medals. Guys that forgot how it is you win wars."

"I get it. We're standing in the middle of a bunch of dumbos and hot dogs. Eight thousand of them. "

Jim looked away.

"Bullshit." I said.

"Yep," he said and walked on.

At the far end of the cemetery there was a large memorial, with a chapel. Jim walked straight in as if he'd been there many times. Like the cemetery, the chapel was just what you'd expect. It was dedicated to "Americans who gave their lives in the service of their country and sleep in unknown graves." All four walls were finely inscribed with names from top to bottom. And like the cemetery, there are lots of places where you feel better.

" 'Bout 3,000 in here," said Jim. "Guys they didn't find or didn't find enough of. Guys that caught bombs or sat on mines."

"No dumbos or hot dogs?"

"Shut up."

"You started it."

"Listen, nephew, if I want to be an asshole and bad-mouth these guys I can do it, because I was one of them. You ain't got no right at all, so just drop it."

"All right. Okay."

"I was one of them once."

"Hell, you still are." I was about to add "in spirit" when Jim said:

"Nope, I took myself out."

"You took yourself..."

"These are real MIAs, not fakes like me. I got no business with them."

Then he walked to the wall and pointed right to a spot about two feet from the ground. "But that's where I'd be. Right there, God damn it, Savorski James, between Sauklis John and Scarpinato Joseph."

I had to get down on my haunches to read the names in the chapel dimness. And there was a space between Sauklis John and Scarpinato Joseph!

"My name used to be there," said Jim from behind and above me. His low voice rumbled softly around the chapel like distant thunder. "These walls are Carrara marble. In Carrara the Captain helped me get some of the same marble paste the stone cutters use, and I just filled in where they etched my name."

I put my fingers on the space. Yes I could barely feel them, but the letters were there. Savorski James. And now I thought I could see them. But it might have been the power of suggestion.

"But...but haven't the caretakers noticed...?"

"Nope. Or if they do, they don't bother to ask about it. Who would care about a missing name?"

"Someone from the family..."

"And you're the first, nephew."

I looked at the space again, and at the name enclosing it. "Well, Jim. I'll bet that Sauklis John and Scarpinato Joseph would both like to fill in their names with paste, and stand there beside you."

"That's hard to say, nephew. There's a right time to die, the Etruscans knew that. I ain't a smart man. Ain't read five books all my life. Mine's been a tough life to make sense out of. Ain't sayin' a mistake was made, ain't sayin' I should have died, ain't sayin' that woulda been better..." Jim stopped to think. I waited patiently. "Trouble is," he went on, "I know what I ain't sayin' but I don't know what I am sayin'."

"Jim, I'm a teacher and I'd give you an 'A' for Effort even before reading your theme."

"Nope. You better read the whole thing first."

"Okay, lead on. Show me more."

"Just little stuff this morning. We meet the man this afternoon."

"You fought a war here. Tell me more."

"I'll show you what there is to see. Ain't much left. Anzio ain't Anzio anymore. And they're right, to hell with the war. But I'll show you one thing they did keep that I kinda like."

So we left the chapel, walked again through the field of crosses and stars, and drove back down to the beachfront. We parked just about exactly on the line between Anzio and Nettuno, and Jim showed me a concrete bunker, built by the Nazis to repel invaders, or maybe by the Fascists before them. It was one of many such that have all been destroyed, but this one remains because it has been transformed into a monument. With sheet metal the bunker has been made to seem the stern head of a Prussian soldier, with cold pupils in the gunslits that have become eyes, and with a massive helmet topped by a spearhead.

I didn't know what to make of it. I examined it up close, then walked out on the beach about thirty yards and stared back for a while at this grim Teuton rigidly and uselessly performing his duty.

"What's your reaction, Jim?"

"I think it's pretty funny."

"So do I, but I'm afraid that's not what we're supposed to think."

"That's 'cause you don't know the Italians well enough yet."

"Maybe. Maybe."

"Come on, let's leave the *Crociato* here and walk along the beachfront sidewalk. It's kinda nice."

It was, and it was long. Jim had time to tell me Anzio stories, like the story of Al Ricovero. During the Beachhead there were signs all over town, arrows that said "Al Ricovero." In Italian this means "to the shelter." but the GIs thought it meant some guy named Al. They followed the signs to the caves where the civilians hid whenever there was an air raid — and found that the caves were also wine cellars. Al Ricovero became everybody's favorite Italian, the toast of VI Corps.

In time we came upon another monument. A statue of a little girl playing with some sea gulls. Underneath was her name: Angelita di Anzio.

"Ever heard of her?" Jim asked. I said no. "Orphan girl, our troops adopted her, gave her that name. Look at her hands close." There were two small seashells in each hand. She was offering them to the birds.

"That's what she was holding when she died. Hit by a shell fragment."

"Sad story." I said.

"Lot more than that. You don't know the Italians well enough yet."

"So that's it. You've invented a new way to cut me short. 'Nephew, you don't know the Italians...'"

"Well, you don't. Took me years, and I still screw up. Come on, let's eat early, otherwise we won't get a table, today bein' Sunday. The place I go to is close by."

It was a tourist restaurant, one of those round panoramic places stuck on stilts out over the beach to give the best possible view. I thought it was a strange choice for an old hand like Jim, and it got even stranger when we went inside: it was a Spanish restaurant!

We were plenty early by southern Italian standards — it was only one o'clock, so we had our pick of tables, and we took one with a view of just about everything: the town, the beach, the sea, and everybody else that came into the restaurant. As soon as we sat down a big blond woman with long black eyelashes banged a bottle of Sangria down between us.

"Uncle Jim, what are we doing in this place?"

"This is where I always come."

"Okay, but why? Do you like Spanish food?"

"Not much. Don't pay much attention. It ain't bad. I come here because it's the last place in Anzio he would come to for a meal. I mean the Italian guy we'll see this afternoon. I'd hate to run into him in a restaurant. I don't think he'd recognize me any more, but maybe if he heard my voice...I dunno, something has always told me to steer clear of him. Something might happen."

"But today you are going to talk to him."

"I suppose. But not in a restaurant."

People were coming in. They were English. Then a group of Germans or Austrians. "I see what you mean." I said. "Don't get many Italians in here, it looks like."

"Nope, Italians are on to a pretty good thing with their own food. Foreign restaurants don't do well here. But in this place I think they do all right 'cause there's enough foreigners around. Even some Italians come in — young people, tourist types, families looking for fun."

"Not old Italians like the one we'll meet."

"Not likely. Tell you what. Let's order a *paella*. I can never order it 'cause there's gotta be two of you. I'll eat the fish parts and you eat the meat parts, how's that?"

The blond lady brought the *paella* in a big iron pan which she set in the middle of our table, and we dug in. It was great, and there was a lot of it, but since *paella* is mainly rice it's considered a first course in Italy, so the lady came back to take our orders for the main course.

"Jim, I'm pretty full already."

"Tell you what. Let's split an order of what I usually have in here. *Polipo alla Gallega*. Galician Octopus. Real spicy."

"You gotta be kidding." He wasn't. He ordered it.

"When did you start eating octopus?"

310

"With Steno. At the start I figured, 'Anything this dumb bastard can eat, I can eat.' And now I like it."

"Well, if you actually eat it. I guess I can figure the same thing."

Jim liked that. I didn't much like the octopus, although I'm ready to admit that it was largely a psychological problem — I kept imagining that those tentacles with their little suction cups would contract and latch onto my tongue.

"Look at those two old geezers in that English group," said Jim between bites. "'Bout my age. Bet you anything they were here with me 44 years ago. I'll bet you that a lot of them make the trip here sooner or later. The ones that can."

"Depends on what it meant to them. I'll bet this is the last place on earth that some of those guys want to see again."

Jim chewed meditatively on his octopus and stared at me. "That's your big trouble, nephew. Never in a war."

"How deprived can you get?"

Jim chewed some more, then said: "Well, you don't forget the people you knew then. Bill Bowen. Wish he was here. Don't even know if he's alive. You know, he could whistle just like Anzio Annie. That would be one way to see if those Brits did the Beachhead with me. He used to whistle like that for the hell of it and—"

"Anzio Annie? Another orphan girl like Angelita?"

"Yep. Little orphan girl. With a 280-millimeter mouth. Sitting all alone in a railroad tunnel 20 miles away. Her shells made this awful whistling sound, like no others. And you hit the deck fast. If Bill was here to do Annie's whistle, we'd find out quick who did the Beachhead. If you ain't gonna finish that octopus, I will."

He did, and we left. It was time to go and meet the

311

old Italian. We briskly walked the long way back to the *Crociato* — good for the digestion — and drove off, inland, breaking out of Anzio with ridiculous ease. But our breakout stopped a few miles into the country, on a road that eventually would have taken us to a town called Velletri. Instead Jim turned off to the right, onto a dirt lane that took us down among the haystacks.

"This is the first time I ever drove down in here — usually I walk it from the road. That's what he always does. But this time I'm ready to be seen. Okay, we can leave the van here." We were about 180 yards from the main road. We got out of the motor home and walked on another 20 yards to where the dirt lane turned abruptly right, back towards Anzio. The lane couldn't proceed because before us there was a grassy ravine about fifteen yards wide and maybe ten feet deep on the far side — less on our side where the terrain was lower. This ravine, the bed of some dead river, went off to the left, parallel to the main road, for about 150 yards before bearing to the right and out of sight. On our right it began veering away after only about ten yards.

"Okay, nephew, listen good."

CHAPTER XXVII

Many of the American officers guilty of war crimes in Italy claimed they were just following orders. Some were acquitted. Others were never court-martialed.

Back on May 23, 1944, on the day of the Breakout, this ravine was a German minefield. We didn't expect it. Our reconnaissance had reported that the Germans themselves used this ravine as a corridor for their own movements, their own patrols. But just before they pulled out, they planted hundreds of mines in through here, and all the way down to where the ravine bends right. Now we could send our tanks across the high flat ground over on the other side of the ravine. This here's a lousy place to come with tanks, anyway. But that high ground was a bad place to send the infantry, because the German machine guns up on that far ridge could just mow that flat ground as nice as you please. So the Brass said to shoot the infantry down through this ravine, in order to get by those machine gun emplacements and work around behind them. Man, our first guy got about ten feet — right down there — and stepped on a glass mine. So now I had a problem..."

"Wait, wait a minute. Wait for my problem. You said to listen good, and I'm trying. First question: why didn't the infantry use this hayfield we just came through? Or even the main road?"

"What we just came through was all thick woods then. Full of booby traps. And that road didn't exist."

"Second question: what's a glass mine?"

"Just what it says. Made of glass. Looks like a little casserole dish, six inches in diameter and four inches deep, enough TNT to blow your legs off. They're never buried deep, but they're harder'n hell to detect — only got a few small metal parts. Which was part of my problem — it takes time to sweep a minefield, I showed you that, and even more with glass mines."

"Which brings me to my last question: why was this whole thing your problem? Why were you in command? I mean, I remember that at the beginning of Anzio you were put in charge to lay a minefield because your officer had been killed, but that was in January and now we're talking about late May! Didn't you get a new officer by then?"

"Sure did. 'Bout the middle of February. A 90-day wonder, real gung-ho. So busy studying his books on mines that he forgot to take care of his feet. Lord, if there's one thing a foot soldier learns fast, it's how to take care of his feet. Most of the time nothing else matters. This guy, he got the worst case of trench-foot I ever seen. They hospitalized him a day before the Breakout, and that left me as chief sweeper for our Company. So I had a problem here. Can I go on, nephew?"

"Keep it simple, Jim. I'm only a French teacher."

"Okay. Now this was what we called a hasty field, which means they had just planted a whole lotta mines, different kinds, all over without any pattern, without being too careful about hiding them. Hell. I could spot a few from where we're standing now — dirt too fresh and things like that. So even though there were glass mines I figured me and my best men could clear a corridor all the way down in about four hours. Probably get there in pieces, but we'd get there. So I phoned the Captain and asked for four hours, but he said it would screw up the timetable for the Breakout in this sector. Our Company had to get around and knock out those machine guns within an hour, because Iron Mike O'Daniel was going to lead the whole damn 3rd Infantry across that high ground then, and if he was late, some other division, must have been the 34th, would have been exposed to a flank attack."

"Okay, so you had to clear the ravine in a hurry."

"Yep. And I couldn't use a Snake..."

"Hold it. What's a Snake?"

"A little stunt the 1st Armored Engineers came up with. It's a 300-foot steel tube packed with TNT. A tank can push it out over a minefield, then you just set it off and you got yourself a nice corridor right down through the field. But you can see that this ravine is too rough and rocky, the tube would never slide. But maybe a tank could just bull through, and we could follow in the treads. I thought, then one of my sweepers found a Land Pilz mine, and they wouldn't give me the tank. They're Dieter's favorite mines, because even though just a man's foot will set it off, it's so strong it'll cripple a tank, even set it on fire."

"So what did you do?"

Jim looked at me, then he looked all around — I mean he turned completely around — then he looked back at me and shook his head.

"You'd have had to be there. It's no good like this. This is nothing like it was. Look around, how it's all bright and peaceful and the birds are singing. Back then it was all sweat and smoke, and there was such an infernal racket from the planes strafing and the mortars and the

315

damn bazookas that a man could scream and die right behind you and you might not hear him. But I could hear the Captain on the Company phone, yes sir, I can still hear him: 'Savorski! If that ravine isn't clear in an hour I'll sweep it with your ass! No more crap about how to do it, just shut up and do it!' I can still hear that son of a bitch. He didn't know a goddam thing about mines."

Jim picked up a stone, discarded it, then picked up another and gave it to me. "Here. This weighs about the same as a hand grenade. Throw it as far as you can down the ravine from here." I did, and felt pain in my shoulder from the effort.

"Not bad. 'Course a younger man can do a little better. I tried that, too — my guys threw about fifty grenades, and we hit a few mines, maybe eight or nine. Not enough. And not far enough either — the ravine is more than twice as long as a man can throw a grenade. I knew it wouldn't do much good, but I needed a little time to think." He still did. He just stood staring at the ravine, as if he were still searching for the right way to clear it.

"Okay, so what did you come up with?"

"You're not going to like this."

Now it was my turn to pause. I watched a bird fly the length of the ravine. I even picked up another stone.

"Well. I already know that forty-four people died because of it. Forty-four Italians fighting with the Germans. Did you lure them down into the field or something? By pretending to surrender, or something?"

"Nope," Jim sighed. "They was already here with us. Italian POWs that had been captured that morning. They were in pretty bad shape. Our medics were still giving them some first aid before sending them to a compound. Lord, they'd been through it. A few were blind. When I think back, that had something to do with it. They were

316

half-dead anyway."

"Oh, God." I let the stone drop to the ground.

"Last time you said that was when you realized that ol' Dieter blew up his dogs to get our tanks. Well, I didn't have dogs, and I didn't have sheep or mules or anything else. All I had was this rag-tag, half-dead bunch of prisoners. Enemies, mind you. They had probably killed lots of our guys."

"I know you don't mean that as an excuse."

"I mean for you to understand what was going through my mind, I had to clear this field! And for some awful reason it just grabbed me that this was a way to do it. The only way. So I rounded them up..."

"Forty-four men." I said in a low voice.

"All told, there were forty-five, including the officer. A *tenente*, a lieutenant, with a little black beard. He understood English. I told him what they would have to do. I told him they would have to run, double file, down the middle of the ravine. I told him if they stayed in line some would get through. And then I'd have a corridor."

"Oh, God."

"I don't know where the hell He was, but he wasn't here in this ravine."

"Who?"

"God. This was a time and a place for demons. I seen it since, in the Etruscan paintings. Same fear, same colors, same eyes, like the eyes of that *tenente*. He thought I was crazy, thought I didn't mean it. I walked over to one of his men that was laying there with a mangled leg and counted to three. The *tenente* didn't give the order I wanted, so I shot the man in the chest."

"You shot him..."

"Point blank. That was Peruzzi. He was Lorena's man. My wife's first husband."

"Oh, God."

"God shouldn't give us guns and mines, and then go off and leave us. He wasn't here that day, nephew, but the demons were. Know how I know it was demons? 'Cause something in me enjoyed killing that poor devil, I swear to God. Anyway the point is, it worked, dammit! The *tenente* got his men up and into a double line. I don't know what he said to them, because I didn't understand Italian then. I told him to say I'd gun down any man who wouldn't run the ravine. About half of them started limping around, grabbing their legs in pain. The *tenente* told me that many of his men were injured and could hardly walk, let alone run. Well that was true of a few of them but not half of them. All I could do was insist that they would all have to go, whatever shape they were in. Only way to stop that nonsense. Italians are great actors, I can tell you."

"Listen Jim, what about your own men? I mean, how come our men let you get away with this? What you were doing was clearly against every rule of…of conduct."

"You say that real nice. Sure it was. A couple guys did speak up, I gotta hand it to them. Took guts. I was a real tough bastard in those days. I think most of my men were pretty relieved that I hadn't decided to run them down through the ravine. In fact that's what I said to the ones that objected: 'Either they do it or you do it, unless you got a better way.' Nobody had a better way.

"So they helped me. We pointed machine guns at them, and off they went, two by two, about six yards from pair to pair. Not really a safe distance, but I figured I couldn't drag the thing out forever — couldn't give them too much time to think. I was surprised that they obeyed as well as they did. You know, men get numb in a war. They'd been taking orders for years, these guys, and with

318

the Germans there must have been some pretty tough orders. This was just one more."

"The last."

"Yep, the last."

"And nobody got through."

"They'd stay in pairs and in the middle for a while, then they'd start dancing all over the ravine on their own — avoid the bodies of the dead ones, I guess. Stupid. That was the safest way to go. Right over the bodies."

"But they didn't turn around or stop. They kept going."

"Yep. Told you. It surprised me. A couple tried to get out of the ravine on the side over there, that's all."

"And you..."

"I had to stop them. Otherwise the others would all have followed them. Had to keep them in the ravine, keep them running. We fired a lot of rounds, but all into the air, except for the two guys that tried to get out."

"And nobody got through."

"One did. The *tenente*."

"The lieutenant? Didn't he lead his men? Didn't he get killed right off?"

"Nope. He was the last one through. And he used his head, went right over the bodies, got all the way to the end and kept right on going. I...I let him go. He must have re-joined the Germans."

"That's what I would have done. Even the SS would have looked good."

"Can't say you're wrong about that."

"But isn't it unusual for an officer to *follow* his men like that?"

"There's officers and officers. I've wondered about him. Today we might find out."

"Because he's the guy we're waiting to meet."

"Yep. I don't know his name, it wasn't in the article."

"The article under the nails?"

"Yep. It was published in a Roman newspaper a couple days later. *Atrocità Americana* was the title. Then a description of what happened, and the forty-four names of the guys who died. It must have been the *tenente*. He re-joined the Germans, told them about it, and gave them the names. They were happy to get things like that published in the Italian cities they still occupied. That's why I had to disappear. There was no way to cover up. The Captain, he would have hushed up the whole thing otherwise."

"I believe it. He was involved."

"I think maybe he was safe enough. He didn't order me to do it. But he gave me the article, and he warned me that the MPs were on their way. We shook hands, and he sent me on a quick 'mission,' so's he could declare me missing in action. Come right down to it, he was satisfied with the outcome, that was what mattered. He got his corridor. It was crooked, but it was good enough. I led him and the whole Company, single file, right down through this son of a bitch of a ravine. I could do it again today, even without the bodies."

Jim slowly headed down into the ravine. I followed right behind. We started straight down the middle, but then we began swerving, sometimes left, sometimes right.

"Why should that Italian lieutenant show up today?" I asked, following carefully in his footsteps. Of course there were no longer any mines in the ravine. But I stayed right behind Jim.

"Well, I'll tell you. I came back to Anzio for the first time in 1948, and it was the Sunday after *Ferragosto*, like it is today. I came here on a Sunday in order not to run into any farmers working in the fields. I suppose he comes on a Sunday for the same reason. In those first few years when I was still running scared and my Italian wasn't no good, *Ferragosto* for me was just a good time to move around, to pretend I was a tourist, but for him it must have really been his vacation. Still is. No, he must be retired. Anyway in 1948 I was standing back where we were before, and this guy with a beard came along and stood about twenty yards to one side of me, and we looked at each other. I recognized him, but he couldn't have recognized me — I had already grown my own beard. I was wearing sunglasses. I was still being real careful. It was a habit for a long time. I walked away. I pretended to leave. But I snuck back to see what he was up to. And he did just what we're doing — he retraced this corridor down through the ravine. The kind of thing a man is compelled to do. I had a hunch, and came back the next year on the same day, and sure enough, he turned up and did it again. I stayed hidden — he never saw me. He never has since. I've tried never to miss being here — he always comes, same day every year, and walks the corridor we made down through the ravine. I just hide and watch him. I didn't think I had any obligations to him — he made it through. He wasn't one of the 44."

"No," I said, "he was the 45th. And now there's a nail for him, too."

"Yep. Must be for him. I've lived 44 years for the other 44, and it must be that I'm supposed to do something for their *tenente*. It means I've got to talk to him. I ain't looking forward to it. I'm glad you're here, nephew."

"Turn left there." Someone had spoken behind us, in English. He hadn't shouted, but his voice had easily carried down the ravine to where we were, at about a third of its total length. Jim and I froze in our tracks.

CHAPTER XXVII

The phrase "Every man has his breaking point" was adopted by the U.S. Army in WWII to acknowledge the existence of "combat exhaustion" or PTSD.

"Turn left. Sergeant. It's safe. Finardi cleared it for us there. I stepped between his legs. There was lots of space between his legs."

We turned around and looked at the speaker, a thin, white-haired man dressed in white shoes and slacks, with a light-blue shirt covered by a white pullover in spite of the warmth of the afternoon.

"That's him," said Jim, and we started back towards him in a straight line, oblivious to the mines under our feet almost half a century before.

"Hello, Sergeant."

"Hello, *Tenente*. How did you recognize me?"

"Only two men in the world can walk that corridor, and I'm one of them. Who is your friend?"

"This is my nephew. Visiting me from America."

"Visiting you? You came to live here in Italy?"

"I never left, *Tenente*. I couldn't go home."

"Interesting. May I ask how you have lived?"

"Doing what I do best. Been sweeping all this time, *Tenente*. All over Italy. Found enough mines and bombs and shells to do Anzio all over again. I think I've saved a lot of lives. Italian lives."

"More than you took, Sergeant?"

"Yep. More than I took. I took 44."

"No, you took 45. You took mine, too. But tell me, how does one make money sweeping for old explosives?"

"By finding other things. Coins and old things that people are willing to pay money for."

The lieutenant smiled. He had perfect teeth that couldn't have been his own. "I see. Of course. Doing what you do best. Very good. I, too, have kept on doing what I do best. Translating and interpreting, German and English, for Siemens, in Milan. But you know, I have come down here every year during my holidays. I am retired now, but I have continued—"

"Yep. I know that."

"You know!" The two old men looked each other in the eye for the first time. They looked hard and long and exchanged things I can only guess at. Then they again lowered their gaze — or rather, looked down and away into the ravine.

"Been kinda tough, huh, *Tenente*?"

"Did you understand why I didn't lead my men into the minefield?"

"I didn't care who went first. You sure as hell ain't obliged to explain."

"I'm definitely obliged. But not to you, Sergeant. I have no obligations to you. You're the only man to whom I have no obligations. The only man before whom I do not tremble inside. And because you alone have no right to know, I shall tell you." Then he looked at me. I started to move away.

"No, no, you needn't leave," he said. "We are just two old men. These things no longer have importance, for you or anyone. Please stay. For me you are the world I wanted to talk to, that would not have listened and now no longer cares, I am sure. Listen. I saw it in your eyes, Sergeant. I had seen it before. You were going to do it. You were going to kill every one of us, just like poor Peruzzi, if we didn't go. Am I right?"

"Damn right. I'd have mowed you all down. Personally. That was an awful thing that was going on inside of me."

The Italian sighed deeply. "I knew it. And I knew my men. If I had led them, of course I would have been quickly killed. And then, Sergeant, you would have had to mow them down, because with their officer dead they would have lost all heart, all hope, and they would take no orders from you. I stayed behind to push them, to keep them in line, to encourage them — I believed you, Sergeant. You said that some would get through. I stayed behind, so that at least some would survive. Not to save my life. Not for that."

All three of us were staring into the ravine. I saw grass, and wildflowers, and rocks, and a flock of sparrows. I was grateful not to see what the other two were seeing again.

"Some would have made it, *Tenente*. If you had only kept them in the middle. Straight down the middle."

"Straight down the middle! Like a Sherman tank! These were men, Sergeant, men of flesh and blood."

"I know that."

"Men with wives and children, Sergeant. Did you know that?"

"Didn't think about it then. Later I did."

"I could never get married, Sergeant. I always thought of the wives and children of the men I drove before me like sheep to the slaughter."

"You had to do it, *Tenente*."

"Ah yes, I had to do it. Do you really believe that,

324

Sergeant? And did you really have to clear the minefield in that way? And if you had to, why are you here? This is no place for innocent men."

"I ain't no innocent man."

"No, you are not. But I am a part of your sin."

"What you did wasn't much. You still don't know all of what I did," Jim said.

"He doesn't? We don't?" This was me. The conversation was not the kind you would normally butt into, but I really thought I had finally heard the whole story, and I was surprised when Jim said there was more. The Italian wasn't so surprised.

"Yes," he said. "Perhaps it's the thing I have been wondering about all these years."

"So what've you been wondering about?"

"Not all of the men I stepped over were dead, Sergeant. Mines don't always kill. Some were maimed but still alive. Some called out to me as I went by. What happened to them?"

"They all...died. Right where they were. That's what I wanted to say. There weren't that many. Six. Six that maybe could have been saved, I don't know; they were all pretty bad. They were suffering, *Tenente*."

"Were you the one who...ended their pain, Sergeant?"

"Yep. I did it clean. And I didn't want nobody else to have to answer for anything. I did it."

"Why?" I asked. "Just because they were suffering? Did they want to die?"

Jim went into one of his long pauses. Then he looked up and away as far as he could, and said: "No, they sure as hell didn't want to die. But I didn't want to leave people who would talk about this."

Another pause. The Italian closed his eyes before speaking. "Then you should have shot me, too. You had a chance."

"Wasn't thinking, I guess."

"I was afraid you'd say something noble, like, 'I don't shoot men in the back'."

"Nope. Nothing noble. Fact is, I did take aim at you. But you was pretty far off; I'da missed you anyway."

"No, you wouldn't have. You let yourself be stopped by some absurd sense of fair play. 'He's earned his right to live,' you thought, or some such nonsense."

"It wasn't absurd," I said quietly. Jim had said that this man was in his debt, now I knew why. "It wasn't nonsense," I continued.

"Young man, in the context of what your uncle had just done to 44 men, it was... only stupid. And useless. You didn't save my life, Sergeant, you great, stupid American fool! It would have been so much better if you had shot me. The life I have lived! My life ended here, in this ravine. Only here do I feel alive, about to go through it again. About to lead my men. To lead them this time. Now I could lead them safely through!"

"The hell you could."

The Italian and I both looked at Jim in surprise.

"But I know the way! I learned it well. Sergeant. You know, I have lost my health, and soon I will die, but I am sure that as my mind turns itself off, its last glimmer, the last image to fade away will be this ravine. And if it is true that restless spirits haunt the earth, mine will be forever here, retracing your precious corridor."

"That ain't my corridor, and it ain't yours. It belongs to your men. They opened it. And I say you ain't got the guts to lead the way, to find your own corridor. You didn't have the guts then, and you ain't got them now."

"Jim, what the devil are you driving at? What right have you got to..."

326

"Your uncle has absolutely no rights at all, which is why nothing he says can offend me, or humiliate me, or shame me. And I can tell him that he is a cold-blooded murderer whose every breath is an insult to those 44 men, and to all the men in the world except to me, because I am a part of his guilt. I know him, and I know that he would do it again. He is a bastard and a killer, no matter how many mines he has defused."

"A lot of them, *Tenente*. A lot of them. And I kept some. Only takes a short time to put the fuses back in."

"Oh, no!" I said. "Oh, no, this is where we stop. No more mines and bombs; they don't solve anybody's problems. Sorry, but this is as far as we go. Do you hear me? The war's over, men. All over. What's done is done!"

I might as well have been talking to the sparrows. The sergeant and the lieutenant were staring at each other again, communicating things for which the words will never be found — or have been lost, like the Etruscan words. But then the Italian slowly turned to me:

"Yes, what's done is done, young man. And your uncle and I are simply thinking of the most logical conclusion. No, it isn't a question of logic, it's…it's…"

"It's a debt that has to be paid," said Jim.

"Now wait a minute," I said, "just who owes what to whom here…?"

"Your nephew is right, Sergeant. 'Debt' is perhaps a misleading word. Look at it this way, young man. Look at it my way. Down in this ravine somewhere I lost…myself. And your uncle is right. I cannot find myself by walking through the corridor that others have made. I must make my own. Your uncle is right. And if he can mine this field again for me, he is a Godsend."

"I'll mine it for you, *Tenente*. Damnedest thing. For the other 44 I spent my time diggin'em up. For the 45th I have to plant 'em. But it all makes sense, Bob."

"The day this makes sense I'll have myself committed."

"This is something between the sergeant and me," said the Italian. "Please stay out of it."

"I'm not going to stand by and let you or anyone else be killed! I'd be an accomplice. For God's sake, think a minute! When you're dead, you're dead! It isn't a liberation, it's just...nothing. The end."

"My goodness! Christianity is very dead in America, isn't it? Young man, if it's really the end as you say, then it isn't the end of anything worth worrying about. But I want to think longer on this. Yes, it mustn't be done as a whim. How long will it take you to prepare your mines, Sergeant?"

"I've only got five, *Tenente*."

"What sort of chance will I have?"

"Well, the way I plant 'em, you won't spot 'em. And we'll limit the field a bit — you'll have about a 50-50 chance."

"That sounds right somehow. As it should be. Don't you think so, Sergeant?"

"If you can walk through my mines, you'll sure as hell shut me up, for what it's worth."

"Have you two ever heard of Alzheimer's disease?" I said in disgust.

"I have to walk through a minefield to shut your uncle up — what must I do to shut you up, young man?"

"Listen, *Tenente*, it'll take me about forty minutes to re-arm those mines and plant them."

"That's plenty of time. If I decide against it, I hope you won't be too disappointed."

"The last time I forced you. This time you get to decide." Then Jim turned and headed for the *Crociato*.

After about four steps he turned his head and said, "You coming, nephew?"

"Yes," said the Italian. "By all means, he's coming. Leave me alone. Please."

A bank full of dollars might buy a chunk of my conscience, but not all of it.

When I realized this, I was relieved. This time, I had several alternatives. I could bolt for the nearest phone and call the police. How far was the nearest phone? How well could I explain all this in Italian? Or I could sock my uncle in the jaw, before he started re-arming his mines, and drive off with him. He was strong, but he was almost seventy, for Christ's sake, and I should be able to handle him. Or I could try to talk him out of it. To do that, I'd have to find a brilliant line of argument before we entered the motor home. I didn't. As we climbed inside, I decided to take advantage of the first clean shot I had at his jaw.

"Now just cool down, nephew," he said without turning around. "I ain't gonna kill that ol' bastard. I couldn't even if I wanted to. Take a look here." And he got out his mines, five of them, cans about five inches tall and four inches in diameter. He threw one to me. It weighed maybe ten pounds.

"These are S-44 mines — a type of shrapnel mine. About a pound of Amatol in there, but harmless as a baby."

"I know. No fuse. I can see the hole. I'm catching on."

"Not only that. No percussion cap. These suckers have to explode twice. We talked about shrapnel mines at Dieter's. The fuse gets the mine five feet into the air, and then the percussion cap explodes the Amatol that scatters the shrapnel. Look, I saved the original caps. They're still good, because they used lead azide — real stable stuff." He got out an old cigar box and opened it. In a nest of

329

wood shavings there were five aluminum capsules, each about 2½ inches long. He took one out.

"Number 8 ordnance. Now unscrew that little round thing on the top of your mine. That's what protected the cap all these years — now see the hole there? This cap fits right in..." It looked like Jim was going to insert his capsule into my mine, and I instinctively stepped back.

"I'll take your word for it. Anyway, that's your plan — you're not going to put the caps back in, right?"

"Wrong. Don't make no difference if I put 'em back in or not. Caps don't work without that first little explosion that kicks the mine up into the air, like I told you. And to kick the mine up I need a fuse, just like with any kinda mine. And I ain't got the fuses for these mines! Not one! The ones they had when I found them were all shot to hell, especially the firing pins, all eaten up. So unless you got some new Z.44 fuses…'course I could rig something up, but I don't want to kill anybody, I just want to help that old geezer prove he's got guts, prove that he was ready to die for his men."

"And that he still is."

"Yep."

"And you think that's all he needs?"

"It's the best I can do. I'm supposed to help this bastard, and I'm doing my best. That's why I sorta provoked him into it. Now are you gonna help me?"

"What can I do?"

"Take one of these percussion caps out and show it to him. Tell him I got lots of them, tell him I really mean business. He's gotta believe he's going through a live field. Otherwise this whole thing will just be a real bad joke, and he wouldn't laugh."

"No. You're right about that."

"So convince him I'm serious, and that you couldn't

talk me out of it, and you can even try to talk *him* out of it if he'll let you, but give him the idea that you ain't gonna stop him if it comes right down to it. You know, he might be counting on you deep down; he might figure you'll step in."

"I was going to."

"I figured that. But now you gotta kick that out from under him. Put the ol' bastard through hell, Bob — that's what he needs. The worse it is, the better he'll feel at the other end of the field."

"What if he chickens out?"

"Well, he'll learn something he's been dying to know. That's better than the doubt, maybe. Chance we'll have to take. But I think I've got him sized up pretty well. He's gonna do it. Now go on and show him that cap — I don't expect he knows anything in particular about these mines. You're a smart feller, you can find out. Pick up a stone — if he don't know beans, drop it when I come out. If he does know something, put it in your pocket, and I won't let him have a good look at them."

"Okay," I said, but didn't move.

"Well, nephew?"

"What are you going to do in the meantime?"

"Sit here another fifteen minutes, so he'll think I'm arming these mines. I'll be screwing in the other caps, in case he comes barging in. They can't do no harm without the fuse, I told you that. Now git!"

I stood my ground, looking him square in the eye. He squared me back, "Nephew, just how crazy do you think I am?"

I looked at him for a full five seconds more, then turned to go. "You're crazy enough, but I don't think you're dumb enough," I said as I closed the door.

331

CHAPTER XXVIII

Over sixty thousand UXOs, unexploded ordinance,
are found in Italy each year.

The lieutenant was now standing about twenty-five yards down into the "minefield." He was turned sideways to me, and I wasn't sure he was aware of my approach until he said, in his fine, professional English: "This was where Zangrilli finally came to rest. Zangrilli, you see, was zealous in everything. He fathered eight children, won three medals for valor, and even died doing more than the others. Here he stepped squarely onto a mine that blew him high and forward, only to land on another mine that blew most of him back here again. He did your uncle a double service. I suppose one could almost laugh about the way Zangrilli died."

"Did anyone laugh? Did my uncle laugh?"

"No, he did not."

"I can't excuse what he did, but—"

"No, you cannot."

"...calling him a cold-blooded murderer, when there was nothing cold..."

"Ah well. I suppose no words can define us, either him or me. I admit I was touched by his story about sweeping for mines all these years. So very American. Like rebuilding Montecassino. A fine gesture but ultimately futile. Nothing can atone for such things. If you were a Christian, you would understand. That's the whole point of hell. It lasts forever. Such sins are never erased."

"But you think you can atone for what you did by walking through a minefield."

"Ah, no, ah, no. But perhaps I shall find out what it is that I did. I don't know what I am! I lost myself here. I can even envy your uncle for the certainty of his guilt. I saw it in his eyes."

"And did you also see that he's not the kind who plays around? He's really arming those mines, you know."

"Yes. Your uncle is a serious man."

"Look here. Know what this is?" I showed him the percussion cap.

"No, I don't. Part of a mine. I imagine. Is it the fuse?"

"It…it's what activates the mine. He has a lot of them — I took one to show you he isn't kidding."

"It wasn't necessary. You know, I don't think your uncle will be displeased if I step on one of his mines."

I put the percussion cap back in my pocket and picked up a stone that I began toying with. "Well," I said, "there's one thing I want you to know. I've decided not to interfere."

"For which I thank you."

"I mean, I believe in euthanasia, the right to die, and this may be a bit bizarre, but that's what it comes down to…"

"*Bravo*! Euthanasia is Godless nonsense, but if it will keep you at a safe distance, then I heartily agree."

Jim stepped out of the *Crociato* with a canvas bag around his neck, like a sower of years ago ready to sow his seed. I dropped the stone and we started towards him. He silently took one of the mines out of his bag and began turning it slowly in his hands. The percussion cap was in its place, but protruding, to be more visible and menacing. I could see that there was only a hole where the fuse should go.

"Anybody you want us to notify in case you tromp on one of these, *Tenente?*"

"You didn't give that opportunity to the other forty-four, Sergeant. And in any case, I have no one. I assure you I shall not be missed."

Jim got his little spade from the compartment under the motor home, when he straightened back up, he said "Are you real sure you want to do this?"

"Are you toying with me, Sergeant?"

"No. Hell, no. All right, then lemme give you some idea. These are shrapnel mines, and I can set them for trip wires or for direct pressure..."

"Spare me the details. Set your mines as you would for an enemy. I am your enemy, Sergeant. And I'm sure you never provided your enemies with details and instructions."

The two men looked at each other in the eye again. I looked away.

"Okay, *Tenente*. All I need is about twenty minutes. Get somewhere...I suggest you get somewhere that you can't see me."

"Of course. Behind your motor-home?"

"That'll be fine. Stay with him, Bob."

"Why?"

The Italian answered. "Because your presence will prevent me from...peeking. I want the sergeant to have no doubts. His opinion has become important to me. That's strange, isn't it? Come now, let's leave your uncle to the things he knows so well."

Jim started towards the ravine, and we slipped

behind the *Crociato*. Then the Italian reached into his pocket and pulled out — a rosary!

"Young man, I hope you won't be offended if I say that I would rather not spend what may be the last twenty minutes of my life chatting with you."

"Oh, absolutely not. Belief in God—"

"—is irrelevant. What matters is whether God believes in us. Now be silent, please."

And I was. There were questions I could have asked, but with my watery theology I certainly couldn't have evoked anything more than a wry smile from this intense, complex old man. Better to leave him to whatever sort of comfort he could find in the imaginary company of a simple Jewish girl.

I spent the time staring blankly at the road in the distance, where cars of vacationers hurried by, surfboards strapped on top, stereos blaring through the open windows. The present day. But I was standing in World War II, with two soldiers for whom peace had never come. I was out of place, no more than an observer. Well, I had taken Rap's place in order to "officially" observe the life Jim's been leading, and now, after observing this last labor, this 45th nail for his 45th demon, I would tell him that yes, for God's sake, yes, he had earned his right to be let back into the community of men. His demons were still in him, he knew that. But he controlled them, he used their energy. Isn't that what we all try to do? Jim had forty-five demons, but he had not lost himself to them, he had conquered them one by one. He could be James Savorski again. Hopefully, with his long battle won, he would rest, and find some enjoyment in life. And as to how many years of rest he would have, he should put that in the Lord's hands the way he did everything else.

I would find good words to tell him these things, and

then my job would be done. I could return to the present day, to my own place in life. Not among the relics of a dead war. Or among the ruins of Rome and the Raséna. Or among the fans of the Goose in Siena. Or among the Madonnari. I'd be seeing Rap and Ilene in Rome soon. To say good-bye. I was a little tired of being an observer. I'd had enough of Roman roads, all leading me to other people's destinations. I chuckled to myself. My roads are the Indian trails on the North Shore — Green Bay Road, Ridge Road, Sheridan Road. The Indians chose their trails pretty well. Those are still good roads. They can lead me to fight against my own demons.

The Italian had his eyes closed. Only a few beads of his rosary were visible, wrapped around his clenched fingers. He was swaying slowly back and forth. It looked like nothing or no one could break through to him, but his eyes popped open when we heard that deep voice:

"Whenever you're ready, *Tenente*." Jim was calling from the other side of the motor home. Then we heard him open the door, and saw the *Crociato* wobble as he climbed inside.

"That isn't the way you said it 44 years ago, Sergeant!" the Italian called back. "Do you remember how you said it then?"

"Nope. Can't recall," came the response through the open window of the home.

"Oh, come now, Sergeant. I'm sure you can."

This time the response came after a pause, but it came loud and strong: "Either you and your goddam Wops run down that field right now, or I'll run this bayonet right up your ass!"

"Ah!" said the Italian as we started around the home. "Perfect! The tone has lowered somewhat, but I note the same intensity, the same power in your voice. You

336

haven't changed much, Sergeant. The years have been good to you."

Jim came out of the *Crociato* — with his souvenir from Siena, his *Palio* with the smug Madonna that Ilene had been given and that she had given to him. For luck.

"Is this to be my prize if I reach the other end?" asked the lieutenant. It was hard to say how much sarcasm he intended.

"Nope. We're gonna change things a bit, *Tenente* — if you don't mind."

"In what way, Sergeant?"

"Well, what bothers you is that instead of leading your men, you followed them."

"Let's say that I think I had a good reason, but I doubt that any reason was good enough."

"Right. So I'm gonna give you a chance to do the leading this time. You can lead me."

There was silence for a moment. Jim was a sly old devil, and although I couldn't see the point of this, I decided to back him up — which in this case meant opposing him, as if there were real danger in the minefield.

"Jim, for God's sake, not you, too! Why should you have to die? What's that going to prove?"

"I...I thank you, Sergeant, but it won't be necessary."

"It was something you said, *Tenente*. You said you're a part of my sin. And I'm a part of yours. Ain't no sense in one of us doing this. God has got to have a crack at us both."

"I...well, I suppose your desire deserves...respect, Sergeant. But how can it be done? You planted the mines, you already know..." Jim folded the *Palio* lengthwise several times and held it up to his eyes.

"Ah! And I shall lead you like a seeing-eye dog!"

"More like the blind leading the blind," I said. I understood now. Jim wanted this man's respect, so that they could part friends. Or at least without hatred. I would play my little part as best I could. "If you two die, how am I going to explain this? Who's going to believe this?"

"Don't do any explaining." said Jim. "If we blow up, just git. Clear out of here."

"But there is one problem, Sergeant. If we die, there will still be four live mines left in the field."

Jim paused for a moment. "You got a point, *Tenente*."

"Your nephew will have to call the police anonymously and have the field swept."

"That sounds all right," said Jim.

"Not to me," I said. "My Italian isn't good enough. If you two fools want to get yourselves killed, at least let me decide what to do afterwards. Show me where the mines are, Jim, I've been with you long enough. I know how to deactivate a shrapnel mine. No trick to it, you just unscrew the...percussion cap, right?"

"Uh...right," said Jim. I wanted one more look at those mines. Something was still bothering me.

"*Tenente*," I said, "would you mind stepping back behind the home for a moment while my uncle points out the mines to me? It'll only take a moment."

"Are you sure I won't peek, Sergeant?"

"You were ready to go. I don't think you'll start cheating now."

"You're proud of your ability to judge people, aren't you? You know what to expect of them. So do I. Of everyone except myself." And he turned and walked behind the *Crociato*.

"What's all this about?" whispered Jim.

"I'm just playing along, making it all sound real.

Come on, where are those mines? Afterwards he'll expect me to know."

So Jim sighed and we walked about fifty yards down the side of the ravine. "With only five mines, I shortened and narrowed the field. The last one's right to the left of that rock."

"Can you show it to me?"

"So that's it! Can't be too careful, can you, nephew?" He slapped me on the back, walked over to the place he had indicated, took hold of the tall grass and carefully lifted a chunk of sod out of the ground. Under it was a mine, with the percussion cap screwed in half way — and clearly with no fuse.

"See? I left the cap like that so it kinda looks like a firing pin, a fuse of some sort in case he gets nosey afterwards. But he can jump on it and it won't do a thing. They're all five just set in the ground like this, I didn't use no trip wires anywhere. He'll waltz right through here and think he was lucky and brave as hell."

He put the chunk of sod back in place, stood up and stomped on it hard. I think my heart stopped. "See? Dead without a fuse. Want to see the others? Want to be sure about the fuses?"

"No need for that. You know, Jim, I don't want you to think..."

"...that you don't trust me, but you don't. That's okay, nephew, I guess I am a strange ol' buck. Come on, I'll show you where the others are."

So Jim pointed out the four other spots where he had put the mines, and I took my bearings as best I could, to be able to help recover them. I wouldn't mind walking fearlessly around afterwards with a couple of mines.

"Okay, *Tenente*, we're all set!"

I resumed my role. "This is crazy, absolutely crazy!

339

You've got a real good chance of dying down in there, I hope you realize that."

"I do indeed. Your uncle is a thorough man. I'm quite sure it won't be easy."

"Damn right it won't," said Jim. "Now, the field's limited, when we get by that horse-chestnut tree up there, we're out of it — we're safe. And I only planted the right half of the ravine, so the field's only about twenty feet wide. Stay in the field, but use your head, *Tenente*."

"Sergeant, I used my head the first time, you must admit."

"Yep, I must admit."

"I assure you I shall not panic."

"Glad to hear it. Nephew, tie this on me real good. Rap's girl said it would bring me luck."

He handed me the *Palio*. As I folded it up. I caught a glimpse of the Madonna's face again, she seemed to have lost her smugness. I left her eyes on the outside, so that at least she could see where she was going.

"Come along then, Sergeant," said the Italian. He tried to give strength to his voice, but it rang hollow. "Here, take hold of my belt in the back. Let's go now. What does Tennyson say? 'Into the valley of death...'"

"Get back, Bob! Get behind a tree!" shouted Jim as they started down.

"I remember. Shrapnel can kill at 100 yards."

"Glad I got to know you, nephew!"

"Me too, Jim!" I was almost enjoying this now. I got behind a tree. The two old men made it past the first mine, and then stopped. The Italian turned around, and I was just able to hear what they said,

"If we make it through, Sergeant, I hope you won't mind if I ask you for a demonstration of the...power of your mines."

"Won't mind a bit. You gotta be sure. I understand that."

"Then let's proceed." And on they went, while I tried to figure out how Jim would get one of his mines to explode afterwards to keep his lieutenant happy. That crafty old shark must have something planned, some trick of his — and if anybody could do it, he could. He knew more about those mines than the long-dead Germans who had invented them. I smiled and watched the strange procession — they got past the second mine. But the Italian was not walking the way I would in a minefield, he was zig-zagging in a way that seemed intended to cover more territory. The more I watched, the more I was convinced — the old fool was actually hoping to step on a mine! Hah! Damn good thing they had no fuses...

The two old soldiers had passed way wide of the third mine when a thought hit me. Jim had somehow armed one of those mines. Just one, to have it ready if the Italian demanded a demonstration...and to give God a crack at them, a real crack at them both! What a fool I was! Jim had said it straight out, and it made perfect sense, knowing him. I had no doubts, which mine? Hopefully the first, second or third, which they had already passed. Certainly not the fifth, which I had already seen. The only danger was from the—

I heard two distinct sounds. The first was no more than a muffled thud, and I saw the mine leap out of the ground behind the two men. Simultaneously Jim began diving for the ground. The mine stopped short for an instant, held by a cord at a height of five feet, and then with a sharp "*brang!*" it exploded. I whirled back behind my tree and heard things swishing through the air. One crashed through a side window of the Crociato. I didn't hear any cries of pain. Had the mine killed them both instantly?

I stayed there for a moment, up against the tree, staring out towards the road where cars continued to hurry by. No one had stopped, no one seemed to have noticed. And now I had to look. I turned back sharply towards the field.

The two men were lying face down and still, about five yards apart. They were covered with blood. I started towards them, slowly at first, then faster and faster till I reached them. The shrapnel had done an awful job on the Italian, who had made no effort to duck, perhaps because he hadn't understood the meaning of that first muffled sound. The metal pieces had slammed flush into him, and through him, from behind. He was very, very dead.

"Bob."

It was Jim, calling me softly. I moved to his side. Because of his dive he had taken most of his metal pieces in the lower body, which I will not describe, but how he could still be alive was incredible to me. I got down close to his face. The Madonna looked at me almost mockingly. I slipped the *Palio* off his head, and he slowly opened his eyes.

"Jim, for Christ's sake."

"Don't worry, it ain't so bad. Can't feel hardly nothin'. Colder'n hell. Almost gone, just another minute. *Tenente?*"

"Gone. Way gone."

"Know how many pieces of shrapnel I got in me, I'll bet anything?"

"I can imagine."

"Yep. Just like the nails. Got a piece to take along for each demon. But that wasn't my intention, Bob. Not directly. I had to arm one of those mines for the *tenente...*"

"I know. To demonstrate."

342

"Know how I did it?"

"Doesn't matter."

"Yes it does. I used that goddam 45th nail. Rigged it up as a firing pin. That bastard had to step right square onto it, and he did. Now you can't say that ain't the hand of God."

"No. Can't say it." I resisted the urge to scream.

"He got me to step on that nail the first time, and the *tenente* the second time."

"Yes. Take it easy, Jim."

"I did every damn thing I could do to find the sense of all this, Bob. Did my best to read the pattern."

"You sure did."

"God. I hope I got it right."

And with that he died.

CHAPTER XXIX

According to Cicero, the Etruscan religion was revealed to the Raséna by a supernatural being which appeared from a furrow in a plowed field. He had the appearance of a child and the wisdom of an old man..

I suppose this was the most critical time of my life, which isn't saying much. The point being that my very uncritical existence hadn't prepared me for situations like this. There were so many things I could have done, or should have done. I felt like three different people: the first one who was physically moving and talking, the second one who was observing and wondering at the actions of the first one, and a strange third one who now and then would voicelessly and incoherently scream.

Anyway, these were the things the first one of me actually did: I got Jim's keys out of his pocket, picked up the *Palio* and walked back to the *Crociato*. I went inside and got out the Etruscan pitcher, the one with the face of the woman with the knowing eyes, and stared at her. Then I shouted "Well, did he get it right?" I was about to smash her to the floor when the third one of me screamed something, and the second one smiled and shook his head, so the first one put the pitcher down, and for some reason stuffed the *Palio* inside it.

Now I looked for the piece of shrapnel that had crashed through the window. I was terrified that it might be the 45th nail. It was not, but the third one of me screamed something anyway. It was sharp and jagged, but I wrapped it in a handkerchief and put it into my pocket.

I took Jim's bag, slung it over my shoulder. Went back into the field and unerringly picked up the other four mines. I got back into the motor home and dumped the bag on the floor. The second one of me seemed to approve of this. There was no telling what the third one wanted. I drove to the American Military Cemetery. I drove around back to the Memorial Chapel, where I stared for a long time at the space between Sauklis, John, and Scarpinato, Joseph. When no one was around I used the sharpest point on the piece of shrapnel to carefully remove the marble paste from the letters of Jim's name. Then, in the shadows of the Chapel, I stood and saluted. The second one of me laughed. The third one yelled something.

Then I drove to the train station and caught the first train to Rome. I took James Savorski's bank correspondence with me. Nothing else in the world bore that name, according to Jim. I also took the pitcher and the piece of wood with the old newspaper clipping, nailed on with 44 nails in double file. Just before going down the *Crociato's* steps for the last time, I pulled the old picture from its clip above the rearview mirror.

I checked into a fine hotel and asked them to book me on a plane to Paris the next afternoon. I had a light supper in the hotel restaurant, then went upstairs and wrote a letter. I went to bed. The first one of me slept well enough, except for being woken up three times by the screams of the third. The second just lay there musing.

The next morning I went to Jim's bank with a new suitcase. They checked my passport carefully and even

345

made a photocopy of it, but then they let me withdraw all those *lire*, which I put into the suitcase. I walked out and down the street into another bank, where I opened a numbered savings account using the name "Roberto Sensoni."

The second one of me thought this Italianizing of my name was just plain silly. I walked out of the bank with only enough money to get home comfortably.

I called Ilene at noon from my hotel room. The second one of me was really curious about what I might say. The third one screamed something just as Ilene picked up the phone.

"*Pronto?*" she said. "*Pronto? Chi é?*"

"Hello...Ilene?"

"Bob! Is that you?"

"Yep."

"Well, where are you?"

"Uh...Paris. You know I always phone from Paris."

"Oh come on now! You're kidding, I hope! Aren't you?"

"Yep. I'm here in Rome."

"Wonderful! Is Jim there with you?"

"Uh...Nope."

"'Yep.' 'Nope.' You sound just like him. What's happened to you, Bob?"

"Nothing, compared to what's happened to Jim."

"Oh, no! What's happened to him?"

At this point the third one of me screamed so loud that even the imperturbable second one seemed alarmed.

"Bob? Bob? What's happened to Jim?"

"I...I wish I knew. Listen, there's a girl here with all the answers."

"A girl? What sort of girl? How old is she?"

I looked at the Etruscan pitcher sitting on the dresser.

"Oh, God only knows. But I'm…having a little trouble understanding her. You and Rap had better come over."

"You can't understand her? Does she speak a dialect?"

"And it's a tough one. Can you both come this afternoon?"

"Of course! Rap's here with me, we'll be over right away. Where are you?"

"The Hotel Imperiale. Ask for me at the desk."

"Just a minute, Rap wants to talk to you."

"But…"

"Bob, what has happened to my father?"

"Hello, Rap. I think you'd better just come."

"Nothing bad, I hope."

"I'm not sure." There was a pause here.

"You sound strange. Bob. Maybe because of what Shakespeare says: The nature of bad news affects the teller."

I quoted back at him, with the first lines that came to mind: "'We are such stuff as dreams are made on. And our little life is rounded with a sleep.'"

Then I hung up. They would be here soon, but I was ready to go. Once more I read the letter I had written, because the second one of me asked me to, having already forgotten most of it:

Dear Friends,

Rap, your father is dead. He finally managed to die in World War II, at Anzio. I have already held funeral services for him. You can open up your medallion now. In it Jim tells you about himself. I'm sure I can add nothing, except what I have put inside this Etruscan pitcher that he loved so much.

You will find the keys to the *Crociato*, which is parked in the long-term lot beside the train station in

Anzio. And you will find a jagged piece of metal, of shrapnel, from the mine that killed him. And Ilene, you will find the *Palio* you gave him for luck, it's dirty and speckled with blood because he had it with him when he died. Perhaps it brought him the luck he wanted. No, he didn't commit suicide. He died in combat, in the line of duty.

The old picture of your father, your aunt, and me is yours to keep now. And Rap, you will find another picture, one that your mother drew of you and Jim. Yes, she is alive, living in her own world. You and your father are dead to her, and in your medallion he explains why. But the news of Jim's real death, the sight of you and Ilene — your ability to communicate with pictures might bring her back.

But the first thing you will see is the piece of wood resting on top of the pitcher, with the 44 nails you'd heard about. Those are Etruscan nails, and as I'm sure Jim explains in your medallion, they represent the 44 names in the article they cover.

But they meant much more than that to him. Look carefully at the pitcher, at the girl's expression. She knows.

There was a 45th nail. It's in a minefield now, with the man it represented. He died there, twice. Or maybe it represented Jim. Or maybe it even represented me. Maybe I was Jim's last labor.

Anyway the nail's gone, Jim's gone, and now I must go. Rap, you gave me your father all whole, and now I have to leave you with these pieces — you can put together as much of your father as you need. But as I remember that isn't very much. Too bad I couldn't take your place with Jim as well as you took mine with Ilene. I wish you two all the best — you've got a beautiful thing going. I have to get home and try to get something going of my own. I'm not saying I'll never be back, I'm not saying I shouldn't have come. I'm not saying that would've been better. Trouble is, I know what I'm not saying, but I don't know what I am saying.

Roberto Sensoni

The second one of me insisted on knowing just how far I was going to carry this "Roberto Sensoni" business, so much so that the first one said out loud, "Oh, don't worry. But if I can't use it with them, then who can I use it with?"

This answer amused the second one of me enough to keep him quiet, and I was able to slip the letter under the pitcher and leave the room. At the hotel desk I paid, and explained to the concierge that I had left some things in my room for two people who would be here very soon. And when they asked for me would he please allow them to go up and get them? Then I headed for the airport.

The few days I spent in Paris before flying home didn't do me much good. I made a nuisance of myself on a tour bus — whenever the poor girl pointed out something on the left, I asked about something on the right, and vice versa. I know by experience this is the way to drive a guide batty. And in the French restaurants I kept ordering Italian wines they didn't have, then sending back the French ones they did. I think I acted this way because that third voice, the incoherent one, was getting me down and seemed to have no intention of fading away. There was anguish and urgency in whatever it was that it would shout from time to time. Even the second one of me seemed more and more concerned about it.

349

I thought that at least once I should really call my wife Beth from Paris. So on the last evening I did. "Beth. I've got some bad news."

"It's not a disease, is it?"

"No, it's that a thief got into my room this afternoon and stole most of the stuff I bought here. Most of my books, the souvenirs I had bought for you and Bret..."

"Oh, that's terrible!"

"...and some money, too. But I'm really mad about the books. It took me weeks to find them all."

"Well, I suppose we had to expect something like this, with all those foreigners over there..."

"But they didn't get my ticket or my passport, and I've still got some money, so I'll be home on schedule tomorrow."

"That's the important thing, darling. Did you take lots of nice pictures? I promised the girls at the bridge club..."

"Uh, I took lots of them, but I didn't have them developed, and the rolls were all stolen, Beth, they were...in a bag with some of my books. I'm very sorry. I'll get some postcards at the airport tomorrow. And I'll try to get some new souvenirs."

"Don't worry, dear. Just get home in one piece."

Easier said than done. I went home in three pieces. The first one, the one who still does all the walking and talking, doesn't seem to be quite the same Bob Svenson that everyone once knew and loved, even though he insists that all is well and France was great. In confidence he told my father and Father Tom Perini at school that yes, he did make a trip down into Italy to look for his uncle, but now he knows less about where James Savorski might be than when he started. He said he'll just have to wait for old Jim to make another move — maybe send another Etruscan trinket.

The second one of me knows that sooner or later the first one will have to come to terms with...everything, in order to get something going. He is sure that the first one must be just marking time — and he wonders what on earth I'm going to do with all that money in a bank in Rome.

The third one is the real problem. He's grown too intense, he frightens the first two. And he speaks a language we don't understand.

THE END

ABOUT THE AUTHORS

Michael Lahey was born in 1942, in Cleveland, Ohio. He visited Italy in the 1960s and fell in love with it, so he moved there to teach English and learn Italian. In the 80's he toured the country and collected interviews and information about the events which had taken place during the war. He brought his wife and children along on the trip.

He lives in northern Italy with his wife, Rosalba, and is regularly visited by his many Italian friends.

His father was a U.S. Marine. This book is dedicated to him.

Ian Lahey was born in Milan, Italy, to an American father and an Italian mother. In the 80's his dad took him and his brother on a long tour around Italy, he still has a green "Contrada dell'Oca" banner from Siena to remember that tour. He teaches English Literature and Aviation English in Udine and leads a quiet and ordinary life with his wife, his two children and his invisible cat, Laurelin.

Connect with the authors at 45thNail.com
Or follow them on facebook.com/45thnail

CPSIA information can be obtained at www.ICGtesting.com
Printed in the USA
BVOW05s1612050616

450827BV00027B/240/P